BY PAMELA TERRY

Through an Open Window

When the Moon Turns Blue

The Sweet Taste of Muscadines

Through an Open Window

Through an Open Window

A NOVEL

Pamela Terry

BALLANTINE BOOKS
NEW YORK

Ballantine Books
An imprint of Random House
A division of Penguin Random House LLC
1745 Broadway, New York, NY 10019
randomhousebooks.com
penguinrandomhouse.com

A Ballantine Books Trade Paperback Original

Copyright © 2025 by Pamela Terry

Penguin Random House values and supports copyright. Copyright fuels creativity, encourages diverse voices, promotes free speech, and creates a vibrant culture. Thank you for buying an authorized edition of this book and for complying with copyright laws by not reproducing, scanning, or distributing any part of it in any form without permission. You are supporting writers and allowing Penguin Random House to continue to publish books for every reader. Please note that no part of this book may be used or reproduced in any manner for the purpose of training artificial intelligence technologies or systems.

BALLANTINE BOOKS & colophon are registered trademarks of Penguin Random House LLC.

ISBN 978-0-593-72463-7
Ebook ISBN 978-0-593-72462-0

Printed in the United States of America on acid-free paper

2 4 6 8 9 7 5 3 1

BOOK TEAM: Production editor: Cindy Berman • Managing editor: Pamela Alders • Production manager: Richard Elman • Copy editor: Susan Brown • Proofreader: Judy Kiviat

Book design by Caroline Cunningham
Title page and part opener image: Springfield Gallery/Adobe Stock

The authorized representative in the EU for product safety and compliance is Penguin Random House Ireland, Morrison Chambers, 32 Nassau Street, Dublin D02 YH68, Ireland. https://eu-contact.penguin.ie.

For Aunt Susie

But in through the open window,

Which I had forgot to close,

There had burst a gush of sunshine

And a summer scent of rose.
>   —Edward Rowland Sill

Cruel blows of fate call for extreme kindness in the family circle.
>   —Dodie Smith

Through an Open Window

OCTOBER 1956

BENTONIA, MISSISSIPPI

Fall came late to Mississippi that year. Long after the rest of the country had pulled out the sweaters and unplugged the fans, black gnats still swarmed in the humid air and heat lightning split the night sky. Down at the end of Pepper Creek Road, tempers flared, and hope was thin on the ground.

Sheriff Dilbeck had been called to the house before. Today as he drove through the packed, rutted dirt, he didn't push his cruiser over thirty. No churning cloud of red dust followed behind him, looking for cracks in the windows. He was in no danger of hitting those tire-busting potholes at speed. There was no need to hurry; Hutch Dilbeck knew what to expect. Later that night, he would remember how he sang along to the radio on the way. "The Tennessee Waltz." His wife's favorite. He would never sing that song again.

The house squatted back off the road in wire grass, like a tick on a long-haired dog. The porch had collapsed on one end, as though God himself had just balled up his fist and punched it, and Hutch had never seen a blade of green grass in the yard.

He stopped the car, rolled down the window, and listened. The air was as still as held breath. He should have known then, but he didn't. Of course, he didn't.

Until the day that he died, forty years later, Sheriff Hutch Dilbeck couldn't remember walking up to the door. All that remained was the baby girl he grabbed off the blood-spattered floor, the one who sat so still and quiet on his lap in the cruiser while the two of them waited for the ambulance to come screaming back down the road.

Everybody had gone by the time the lightning bugs began sprinkling the pine trees with yellow. Nobody saw the little boy when he toddled out of the woods and stood by the ruined porch, looking this way and that way for the family that was now gone for good.

Hutch told Martine they'd have to call the midwife. She was the person who'd know what to do. But Martine said one night wouldn't hurt anybody. "You're the sheriff. Nobody will care." And Hutch let his wife have her way. She looked so right holding that baby.

So, they kept the little girl in their room that night. Hutch took a drawer from out of the old dresser, removed his clean undershirts, and laid them neatly on top of the cedar chest like a stack of little white books. Then he lined the empty drawer with the plaid blanket from their bed.

Martine held the tiny hand till the blue lids closed tight. Hutch said she slept as sound as that beagle puppy had done the night after he'd found him out behind the Blue Front Cafe. "Remember?" he said. She did. Both creatures had had a rough start, Hutch thought, as he turned out the light. With luck, neither one would remember.

He phoned up Carrie Whitlock at ten the next morning and she knocked on their front door at noon. Said, yes, she remembered the birth. Nearly a year ago now. She didn't know much else about them. No more than he did, anyway. They weren't from around here, she said. "They came for me late. The smell of drink on that man. The girl so thin and so young, I could hardly believe she was pregnant." It hadn't been easy, and in the end, Carrie had to take the girl to the hospital in Jackson. Thirty-eight miles away. Couldn't get her to quit bleeding, she said.

Carrie had filled in the names the girl had recited. Was pretty sure the certificate had been filed with the county. Relatives could most likely be traced. Yes, she'd let them both know if no one was found. "You've gone above and beyond," she told them.

They handed the baby over to Carrie, Martine holding on to the edge of the blanket a second too long. And they stood on the porch holding hands till the midwife's old car was barely a speck on the road, both knowing they'd never again lay eyes on that little girl.

Hutch spent the rest of that day wishing the phone on the wall in the kitchen would ring. Wishing that it wasn't a Sunday. He sat in the porch swing most all afternoon, one toe pushing the thing up and back, till the sky began bruising up over the pines.

He had to go back; he knew it. Just to look, to make sure. To fix it all in his mind. Then, if he could help it, never again. He'd bury it all with those things he'd seen in the war. Without telling Martine, he got up and walked out to the driveway, jangling the car keys in his pants pocket. He'd be back before she called him to supper.

Pepper Creek Road looked different to him now. Fire ants in the red dirt. Copperheads in the grass. Hutch slowed as he came close to the house, gravel grinding like cornmeal under his tires. He turned off the car, rolled down the windows to let in a breeze. The wind wiped the sweat from his face. The engine crackled, cooling. Hutch stared at the beaten-down house.

He could tell that it wouldn't be long before kudzu crawled out of the woods to eat what was left of the porch. Time would rip more boards from the roof every season. But he couldn't know the house would blow off completely the day of the Luckney tornado. He and his family would be long gone by then.

Hutch was never sure why he got out of the car. Why he went back inside. Martine said God crooked his finger. And who knows? Maybe he did.

He steeled himself before going in, didn't look at the dark stains on the floor. It felt wrong for him to be here. Like walking on top of a newly dug grave.

As if holding a map in his hands, he went straight to the room at the back of the house and stopped still. No glass in the windows, no paint on the walls, the tiny boy asleep on a bed with no sheets, his small hands balled up into fists. Mosquito bites were spattered all over his legs, his legs as thin as white straws. Hutch picked him up without thinking. Carried him out of the room still asleep.

The day's dying light fell through the darkness of those rooms like a straight yellow road leading out the front door. Hutch put one foot ahead of the other until he was back outside in clean air.

He tiptoed through the dead grass. He settled the still-sleeping boy beside him in the car, took a towel from the backseat and put it under the boy's head. Then Hutch turned the cruiser around and drove home.

From a half mile away, he could see her. Standing alone on the porch, one palm held above her eyes to shield out the last of the sun. Watching the road, waiting. She'd always say that she knew they were coming.

They told everyone the boy was her sister's child. The one who'd had cancer and died. Martine didn't feel guilt for the lie. She didn't have a sister, but nobody in Bentonia, Mississippi, knew that.

Two months later, when the job offer came in, Hutch Dilbeck applied without even asking his wife, knowing she'd want to go just as much as he did. A new start for them all, a cloud blown away from over their heads. Someplace where he could give the boy his name outright, without explanations or questions.

And besides, who wouldn't want to live on the coast?

OCTOBER 1956

WESLEYAN, GEORGIA

It had been the longest summer Ida Mae Hines could ever remember, and she'd lived here in Wesleyan since before the Great War. She'd never been able to take the humidity like Edith could. It pressed against the windows of the old farmhouse like the devil's hot hand, trapping her inside. So many long afternoons spent fanning herself with one of those hard paper fans from the funeral home, the ones with the flat wooden handles. The heat paid no heed to the calendar. It was the first week of October and the roses still bloomed. Edith was still picking tomatoes.

But something was different this morning. Ida Mae knew it the minute she woke. Through an open window, she heard the leaves on the pecan trees singing in a wind that, though still warm, was finally crisp on the edges. She lifted her head from the pillow and felt the first breath of fall touch her cheek. She smiled. Just when she'd thought nothing was changing, something came in the night to surprise her. Life was like that, she thought. And Ida Mae was an optimist. She believed in fresh starts.

The quiet house told her that Edith was already out. Opening the back door, walking onto the porch, Ida Mae could see her down in the grove, her pink dress moving through the shade like a light. She was playing catch with the little Elliot boy again. Seeing Ida Mae, Edith threw both arms up over her head and waved back and forth like she was signaling a boat to the shore. And Ida Mae felt like she always did seeing Edith for the first time each morning. Like a flowering vine was growing inside her, straight up from her toes to her heart.

They opened the mail over breakfast, never expecting more than the usual fare. The light bill, *Reader's Digest*, *McCall's*. Sometimes a letter from one of their friends from Bessie Tift College, though those were much fewer these days. When Edith picked up the official-looking white envelope postmarked Mississippi, they stared across the table at each other, and Ida Mae felt an unsettling tingle of fear. She sat her coffee cup back in its saucer, flinching when it made a small clatter. She folded her hands in her lap.

Edith hadn't heard from her brother, Maynard, in over nineteen years. One postcard written in pencil, postmarked Mississippi, to tell her that he'd had a son. Ten years after that, there'd been a telegram from a doctor somewhere out in Texas, letting them know Maynard had died. Texas, somewhere they'd never been.

In the photograph that sat by Edith's bed, Maynard Lowry remained as he once was, forever handsome and young. She never talked about the man who'd arrived here so changed after that war, the one who'd chased Ida Mae out of the house not long after, shouting words that cut to the bone. Ida Mae had fallen down the front stairs that night—her limp now so slight but always a reminder—and Edith had sent Maynard away. Edith's choice had been made. She would never see her brother again. It was a wound that would never quite heal.

Using her father's old letter opener, the brass one with the owl's head, Edith opened the envelope with one brisk slash and pulled out a sheet of paper so thin it was almost transparent. Ida Mae watched Edith's eyes move back and forth, then fill to the lashes with tears. "He's a merciful God," Edith said.

The baby girl arrived on their doorstep three short days later. A gift, an atonement, a new start for them all. Someone the two women would love and protect for the rest of their days.

And she'd never know all the hurt she had come from. Not if Edith Lowry could help it, that is.

PART ONE

OCTOBER 2019
WESLEYAN, GEORGIA

1

Aunt Edith

Lawrence Elliot's urn was still in the box the first night Aunt Edith appeared. A hint of spring had been threading the early March air and Lawrence's widow, Margaret, had gone to bed with the windows wide open like always, knowing sleep was nothing more than a wish. The fragrance of tea olive was drifting into the room—heavy and sweet as buttercream frosting—and just as Margaret's eyes were becoming used to the darkness, there she was, standing regal and tall at the end of the bed. Great-Aunt Edith. In her blue shirtwaist dress and that string of discolored pearls, the old lady was as unambiguous as the Lincoln Memorial, despite being fashioned of shadow. Margaret had sat straight up like she'd been poked in the back with a stick.

But Aunt Edith was dead as a doornail and had been for over four decades. Margaret Elliot was sure about that. Her aunt was lying beneath a red maple tree out in Crestwood Cemetery; you could see her marble headstone from the street. When she'd been eighteen years old, Margaret had watched the silver coffin disappear into that deep red hole in the ground while Myrtle Phipps sang "The Strife Is O'er," a little off-key. The coffin had reminded her of Aunt Edith's old Buick. Same color, same chrome.

Even so, Aunt Edith had shown up at the foot of Margaret's bed again last night; it was the third time she'd seen her this week. Once again, the old lady had stood in a slice of white moonlight, holding a long yellow envelope out to Margaret, and looking for all the world like she was just about to say something important but disappearing before she could manage to formulate words. She left behind a familiar fragrance that lingered in the air until morning. Arpège and Ivory soap. Margaret hadn't yet been able to call Aunt Edith a ghost, but really, with her shimmering shape more cobweb than concrete, what else could she possibly be? This, of course, was something Margaret Elliot had been keeping to herself. Seeing ghosts was never a good sign of anything.

She'd personally never known anyone in Wesleyan who'd fallen off the balance beam of sanity except for old Miss Little, who, after her mother died, started climbing in the fountain on the square and hollering at the top of her lungs. Margaret had witnessed this spectacle for herself one sweltering afternoon when she'd taken the kids out for ice cream. She'd had to grab Lawrie's hand to keep him from pointing. Miss Little's cousins had finally sent her to Brawner's, way up near Atlanta, where they were used to dealing with that sort of thing. But far as Margaret knew, not even on one of her bad days had Miss Little seen ghosts in her bedroom.

At first, she'd put these sightings down to Lawrence's death. After all, she'd known women to behave in extraordinary ways after the shock of losing their husbands. Joining the ranks of the Wesleyan widows was something nobody wanted to do, and some took extravagant steps to avoid. Unforeseen marriages were known to happen. For instance, despite Betsy Waldron's open aversion to the barrel-chested, pocket-size Puddin' Mabry, one the woman had nurtured since their days at Wesleyan High, she'd nevertheless walked up the aisle as his bride a scant three months after her thirty-five-year marriage to her six-foot-four husband, Chance, had ended with his death. Then there was the case of Jessie Pelham, the part-time librarian that nobody seemed to know as well as they should have. Less than six weeks after her husband, Brodie, fell over with an aneurysm in Bloomin' Nursery, looking for all the world like he'd just decided to take his afternoon nap on a fat sack of peat moss, Jessie had up and disappeared. A whole summer went by before they all found out she'd moved to Orlando and was working as a chipmunk at Disney's Wilderness Lodge. Either Chip or Dale, nobody quite knew for sure.

Margaret had felt better prepared than most of the newly bereaved. Lawrence, bless him, had inherited his father's bad heart, his first attack coming before he was thirty. The one that finally claimed him had been his fourth, and she'd been sure he was going to die every time. She'd presumed she was ready for this change in her life and on the whole, thought she was handling it well, these ghostly visits from Aunt Edith notwithstanding, of course.

Her aunt never stayed long, just a few moments or so, but after she'd gone it was impossible for Margaret to simply turn over, fluff up her pillows, and fall asleep as though nothing had happened. Instead, she'd often lie awake until just before sunrise, when the night is the blackest it gets. Then and only then would exhaustion pull her down into dreams of such color and clarity they were like the sorts of time travels children invent.

These felt more like visions than dreams. In them, Aunt Edith's old house on the edge of the pecan grove still stood, as warm and welcoming as outstretched arms. Margaret could climb the wide front stairs and walk right inside. The screen door would slap hard behind her as she entered the hallway, and she could feel how cool the house had always been, even when a wet Southern sun dripped down hot in July. All those open windows, all that dark wood. The breeze would come in the front door and wash out the back, taking the heat and humidity with it. Margaret could feel that breeze on her face in these dreams.

She could stand in this house of her childhood, smell a pound cake baking, and hear Ida Mae's laughter bubbling down the hall from the living room as she sang those old Baptist hymns while Aunt Edith played the piano. "Onward, Christian Soldiers." "Love Lifted Me." The lyrics would come back to Margaret verbatim. She sang along in these dreams.

As silent as Socrates, the fat gray cat who watched from the landing, Margaret could wander freely up the stairs and into Aunt Edith's blue bedroom, where the old lady's four-poster still sat, its starched sheets stretched tight and tucked in. Oh, how she'd loved this beautiful room. Once again, she could see herself running down the long hallway and climbing into this bed with her aunt on those hot summer nights when the skies cracked open, and thunder hit the red earth, rattling the windows and shaking the walls as though they were made out of paper. She could see Aunt Edith's massive old dollhouse, the one her brother, Maynard, had made, sitting proudly in its spot by the window, its many porches and turrets still forbidden to Margaret even in dreams, yet as tempting as unopened candy. She could smell the freshly picked hyacinths in the cut glass vase on the night table, watch the clear drops of dew hit the wood.

Some nights she saw Lawrence's family, the details of their faces no longer obscured by the mists of impotent memory, but as clear as the first day she met them. His father, whose own heart had seized and stopped at forty-two. His grief-stricken mother, who'd followed soon after. Forrest, his quick, funny brother, the one who'd died of AIDS up in Atlanta before anyone in Wesleyan even knew what it was. And his sister, brilliant, beautiful Prudie, the family favorite, who'd drifted into Alzheimer's while still in her fifties, finally slipping away with her magnificent mind as threadbare as moth-eaten silk, just like poor Ida Mae had. Unimpeded by illness or age, they all walked through these dreams with smiles on their faces, leaving Margaret with a feeling of inexplicable peace that some days evaporated only after the sun was high in the sky.

Anticipation being more acute than reality, the worst nights were the ones when nothing happened at all. No visits from Aunt Edith. No sleep. No dreams. On these nights, anxious and fidgety, Margaret would meander through the house, opening doors, straightening pictures, gazing out windows. Chasing sleep, she'd make herself a cup of hot chocolate or pour a thimbleful of Lawrence's bourbon into a juice glass but be unable to drink either one. Sometimes she'd start one of his Agatha Christies—he'd owned every volume—only to put it down after reading the same sentence six times. She'd turn on the television, find the programs on offer too silly or loud, and immediately switch it back off. One early spring night, she'd gone outside in the dark and pruned all the Limelight hydrangeas, getting mud on the hem of her nightgown. Those stains would never come out.

It had been on one of these nights when, back in June, desperate for soporific distractions, Margaret had turned on her computer and found the little house by the ocean. She couldn't remember what trail she'd followed to lead her to the real estate site, and she'd since wondered if Aunt Edith, who, after three months, still hadn't communicated her reasons for visiting, might have had a hand in the discovery. There had to be some purpose for her appearances. After all, she'd been quiet for over four decades. She must be trying to tell me *something*, thought Margaret. Maybe Aunt Edith thought she should leave this house full of memories now that Lawrence was gone. Maybe she was trying to show Margaret just where she needed to go.

It appeared to be hardly more than a cottage. Far smaller than this big blue house on Albemarle Way where Margaret and Lawrence had lived for the past forty-two years, raising three kids and an assortment of pets. But from that first night when the house appeared on her screen, it had stayed lodged in Margaret's imagination like a good idea. Belted with a deep porch and topped with a scarlet tin roof, the little house was ringed on three sides by tall palms, each one bending over the last like crossed fingers of the hopeful. A bow-shaped beach hemmed the tiny back porch to the sea, and she could easily imagine standing on that porch and seeing nothing but salt water and stars.

That night, Margaret had printed out a picture of the house and left it lying on her desk in the den. But the next morning when she'd walked into the kitchen, there it was, hanging at eye level on her refrigerator door, secured with a magnet from Silver Springs, Florida. Ida Mae and Aunt Edith had loved those glass-bottom boats.

Margaret had put gin in her coffee that morning. She'd sat at her kitchen table as the clock on the den mantelpiece ticked louder and louder, watching the sun take small steps across the checkerboard floor—each inch a few minutes, each foot a half hour—until, propelled by a fevered confusion, she'd jumped to her feet and grabbed the picture off the refrigerator. She'd thrown the magnet back into the junk drawer, where it had sat in the dark for decades, stuck the printed picture tight inside the latest issue of *Southern Living*, and stuffed the magazine in the laundry room behind a roll of Brawny paper towels.

But the little house was back the next morning, its picture hanging at eye level just like before, the Silver Springs magnet square in the center. This happened three nights in a row. Margaret wouldn't move the thing again.

The picture of the cottage had hung on the refrigerator for over four months now; it was the first thing Margaret saw when she came into the kitchen each morning. Its edges were now curling inward, but the image of the little house remained as clear as the night she'd printed it out. She'd gone back online several times to read more about it, but for the very life of her, she couldn't find the place again.

"What? Do you want me to *leave*? Is *that* what you're trying to tell me?" Margaret had asked this question again tonight, a bit louder than she usually did. But Aunt Edith had just evaporated at the foot of the bed like always, yellow envelope held out in her hand, unspoken words still on the tip of her tongue. All she'd left behind was an echoing silence that pressed against Margaret's temples like fists. That, and the smell of Arpège.

2

Margaret

Ray Kuckleburg was the type of mailman who always had treats for the neighborhood dogs. They'd come to expect them, often lying in their front yards with their eyes trained up Albemarle Way like Milk-Bone-shaped lasers. After twenty-nine years on the same daily route, Ray knew all the dogs and most of the people by name and was known to hand-deliver the mail right to the front door whenever somebody was sick or, as in the case with Mr. Rigby around the corner, just perpetually down in the dumps. As Margaret descended the stairs this morning, one hand rubbing her aching temple, she saw the mailman pacing in front of her living room windows like a duck in a shooting gallery, his arms laden with boxes too big to fit in the mailbox.

"Oh, good," said Ray, when Margaret opened the door. "You're up. I couldn't figure out where to put these and I didn't want to knock in case you were still asleep." He handed over the boxes, a small stack of envelopes balancing on top. "I know it ain't Christmas, Margaret, so it must be your birthday. Am I right?" He grinned down at her like he'd figured out a secret nobody else knew.

"You're absolutely right, Ray. Hard to believe it's come around again so soon."

"Yeah, well..." He grinned at her over his shoulder as he hurried back down the front steps. "Turning forty ain't easy for any of us. You have a good 'un, Margaret."

She laughed and went back inside, closing the door with her foot. Forty, indeed. She'd seen the backside of forty over twenty years ago. Her arms full, she sat the boxes and cards on the hall table. She'd look at them later. Right now, she needed coffee more than anything else.

The dawn light pouring in through the open window was a light seen only in October. Shadowless and clear, it rode into the kitchen on a cool breeze that filled the room with the fragrance unique to a Wesleyan fall—part red clay, part salt marsh, with top notes of Winesap and pine. Margaret switched on the coffeemaker, put a tray of frozen biscuits in the oven, and leaned against the counter, comforted by the familiar surroundings.

This was her favorite room in the house. Large and lit by the sun, no matter the weather, it was always the perfect temperature, the old checkerboard floor cool on bare feet in summer, the honey-colored walls cozy and warm on the most frigid February day. Family photos covered one wall and Po'boy's bed was still pushed into the corner, though the basset hound had been gone for over a year. Margaret missed having a dog to talk to, especially now that she had so much to say.

When the coffee was ready, she poured herself some and sat down in her usual spot at the long wooden table, her fingers laced around the hot mug. It wasn't long before she could feel the caffeine slowly diluting the headache that had crouched like a bullfrog behind her eyes since the moment she'd opened them. If Lawrence had still been here, they would've had to make two pots, Margaret thought, smiling weakly to herself. He could never stand his coffee as strong as she'd made it this morning.

Margaret had always known that everyone in Wesleyan saw her as an extension of her husband. Lawrence had been the face of the family. There were now enough books with his name on the spine to fill up a shelf of their own at Epiphanies Bookshop. He was the first person that came to mind when anyone thought of the Elliot family. Margaret had never minded this. She'd liked the anonymity. She'd hidden behind Lawrence just as she'd hidden behind her elementary school principal, that formidable woman who just happened to be her great-aunt. It had always felt so safe looking out at the world from behind those two pairs of squared shoulders. Margaret knew some people thought she'd been spoiled by them both—you could always tell the ones who did—and maybe they were right. But she'd had such a happy life, and she could never manage to feel guilty about that.

Lawrence Elliot had published his first book at twenty-four, a biography of Brendan Bracken that had taken critics by surprise and enthralled readers of British history on both sides of the pond. Through the years, he'd added many hefty tomes to his credit, works that nearly always hit the high trifecta of being seminal, esteemed, *and* bestselling. A creature whose brain was overoccupied with the events of the past and how they echoed—increasingly loudly, according to him—through the present, Lawrence, with his sea-blue eyes and tousled hair, was frequently recognized on the streets of his hometown as that fellow who appeared on the news whenever an international crisis arose. As he connected the dots for the public, his delivery was always so reasonable, his demeanor so calm, that he never once managed to court controversy, thus fostering pride in the citizens of Wesleyan, no matter on which side of the political sword they happened to dance.

Margaret stirred some more sugar into her coffee. She knew most people would've been surprised to learn that, while he could cogently parse the battle strategies of the Lancasters and the Yorks in the War of the Roses or discuss, at length, the intricacies of Napoleon's narcissistic psychology and how they led to the little general's ultimate downfall and disgrace, Lawrence could not, on threat of death, tell you when the property taxes were due, or when to renew the car tags. He hadn't paid a bill since they married, and the look that came across his face when asked how much money they had in the bank was so vacant it was practically comical. The minutiae of their daily lives had always been Margaret's purview, so the loss of his everyday presence, though pronounced on an emotional level, was not particularly devastating on a practical one, and for this, she supposed she was grateful. Still, as she sat here slowly sipping her coffee, something told Margaret that Aunt Edith would never have made an appearance if Lawrence Elliot had still been alive.

She'd heard the Elliots before she ever met them, their voices flying through those pecan trees straight at her each day, as though there was a target on her bedroom window. Loud laughter that could change in an instant to argument before coming full circle to laughter again. And Aunt Edith's house was so quiet. It wasn't long before Margaret was going out into the backyard and standing there, listening. Soon she was venturing farther and farther into the grove, until one day she pressed right up against that old chain-link fence, her fingers closed tight around its diamond-shaped wires. Soon she was like the Elliots' baby sister.

Margaret took another sip of coffee, smiling. Even now, so many years later, it was easy to remember lying in bed on those still autumn nights in her bedroom at Aunt Edith's old house, listening to the pecans falling every now and then, hitting the ground as if somebody were casually plucking violin strings. She could close her eyes now and see the light from Lawrence's bedroom window, drifting through those trees like smoke, brighter than the lightning bugs, but soft as candlelight in the corners of her room. And she'd wait for his light to go out before she turned hers off. She couldn't even remember the first time she realized she loved him. They'd been best friends for so long.

The ping of the oven sounded like the first five notes of the rock opera *Tommy*. Da, da, da, da, da. In an act both habitual and unconscious, Margaret hummed the second line of the song as she rose to take out the tray of hot biscuits, her eyes squinting against the sudden blast of heat that flew into her face when she opened the oven door. She grabbed a jar of grape jelly off the counter, then went back to her place at the table, avoiding her watery reflection as she passed by the window. She knew there were bags under her eyes. She didn't need a visual reminder, today of all days.

Margaret didn't *feel* crazy. Who knows, she thought, sticking her knife down deep in the jelly jar and swirling it around, maybe the veil just gets thinner as you grow older. Maybe people see ghosts all the time and just choose to keep it to themselves. From where she now sat, that certainly seemed like a reasonable response. But Margaret secretly feared this was all coming from a part of her brain she neither recognized nor relied on, because nobody who'd known her great-aunt would expect the woman to ever come back as a ghost. It was something like heresy to even consider the thought.

Wesleyan, Georgia, had never known a soul more guaranteed to serenely stroll the streets of gold for eternity than Edith Jane Lowry. She'd been the principal of Tillman Elementary School for over forty years, and she'd sat beside Ida Mae in the third row of the right side of Second Baptist Church every Sunday morning for longer than that, in the same pew where both of her parents had sat before her, and their parents before them. Almost everyone remembered her name with the sort of reverence reserved for statesmen and saints, and if word were to get out that Principal Lowry, of all people, wasn't resting as comfortably as a good Christian woman should rightly expect to be, well, lesser mortals might well wonder what awaited *them* when they turned up their toes.

Great-Aunt Edith had been the only family Margaret ever knew. She'd been well settled into her sixties when Margaret came to live in her big white house on the edge of the pecan grove out on Boundary Road, barely two weeks after Margaret's parents had slammed a borrowed motorcycle into a pine tree outside Bentonia, Mississippi. Aunt Edith had told her the story. Helms and Lorena Lowry were still in their teens when it happened; Margaret was scarcely a dozen months old. Her first steps were taken in Aunt Edith's kitchen.

She must have been around seven the day Aunt Edith pulled out her birth certificate, the one that came with her when she'd arrived that first day. Margaret had held the piece of paper in her hands. Typed black letters on a sheet of white paper. Two-dimensional, thin. She'd read her parents' names, Helms and Lorena. And her own name, Mary Margaret.

She was told that her grandfather, Aunt Edith's only brother, Maynard, had left Wesleyan not long after returning from that war that was supposed to end all the others. There were two photographs of him in the house. One sat by Aunt Edith's bed in a Black Forest frame; Margaret knew it well. It showed Maynard Lowry in uniform; his wide hat and high collar looked almost comical, worn as they were by someone with such a young face. The second, Aunt Edith kept in a hatbox under her bed. She showed it to Margaret that day. A candid shot of Maynard sitting alone on the front porch, his shoulders hunched, the ash from his cigarette like a long finger pointing down to the floor. "He left in the night not a month after that photo was taken," Aunt Edith told her. "He had a bad war. He was just nineteen years old."

She said that a postcard had come, the week Maynard's son, Helms—Margaret's father—was born, but Aunt Edith said that was the last she ever heard from her brother. Then one day, Margaret showed up at her door, too little to have any memories of her own.

Any other questions Margaret had had about her parents during the ensuing years had been answered by Aunt Edith almost absent-mindedly, the subject changed so deftly Margaret hardly noticed. She'd accepted this mysterious gap in her history, her parents had been faceless all her life, most of the time it hardly seemed to matter. But now these visits from Aunt Edith had awakened some of those buried questions, and Margaret just wanted them to stop. The answers had been lost long ago.

Lawrence always said history was a series of stories made up by a God with too much time on his hands. Margaret certainly understood this; her own life had been such a story. She'd grown up identifying with Anne Shirley and Mary Lennox, little heroines in her favorite books, who, like herself, had been tragically orphaned yet plucked from calamity and gingerly placed into situations that seemed to practically guarantee happy lives. Aunt Edith always said God brought Margaret to her door, and who knows? Maybe he had. But privately, Margaret sometimes wondered whether, like most of life seemed to be, it was merely another cosmic coin toss that had landed in her favor. Was it luck, or God's will? Luck was what Margaret would choose.

To protect her aunt's reputation, she hadn't told a soul about these visitations. She'd just kept on behaving as though everything was perfectly fine, and that wasn't as hard as it sounds, secrets being easy to keep in the South. Southern women are used to pretending things are better than they actually are, Margaret thought as she sat chewing her biscuit. Trained by the examples of those gone before them, they knew how to smile through boredom, laugh through sadness, and swallow anger as though it were cake. Hadn't she watched Aunt Edith and Ida Mae walk through life as everyone's idea of best friends, their pretense so convincing even Margaret herself hadn't guessed they'd been so much more. She didn't find out the truth until Lawrence told her, and even then, she hadn't quite believed him. She and Aunt Edith had never mentioned the relationship once.

But if she were being honest, Margaret thought, as she licked jelly off the tip of her forefinger, she was getting weary of keeping this secret. So far, Aunt Edith had appeared only in her bedroom, but that hadn't stopped Margaret from starting to look for her all over the place. A few weeks ago, she could have sworn she'd seen her aunt in line at the post office with that long yellow envelope in her white-gloved hands. Margaret had turned right around and left without getting her stamps. Trying to figure out what Aunt Edith wanted was, frankly, losing its charm.

She topped up her coffee. Maybe if she told somebody, she thought, the visits would stop. Ever since they'd been children, whenever she was worried about one thing or another, telling Lawrence had seemed to cut those worries in half. But who could she tell now that Lawrence was gone? Not the kids, surely. Margaret shook her head. There were some things her children did not need to know. For instance, while it was true that most of their father's ashes were buried out in Crestwood Cemetery, a few shady rows down from Ida Mae and Aunt Edith, it was also true that she'd scattered some in the green waters of Bobbin Lake. Some she kept in a little rosewood pencil box in the back of her night table drawer, and some were in a Walker's shortbread tin in the glove compartment of her car. Lawrence had loved those cookies—he ate three of the things every night—and Margaret liked to talk to him while she drove. She'd never tell the kids any of that. Besides, she thought, frowning slightly, she couldn't remember ever talking about anything really personal with her children. And as far as she could tell, they never talked about personal things with one another. It was something they just didn't do.

She remembered those first several nights after they'd brought Mouse home. She and Lawrence were so young, that baby such an unplanned surprise. Margaret had sat beside her daughter's crib, almost afraid to look over the railing, her amazement occasionally scraping against intimidation whenever she saw the tiny pink face. She'd never been around babies. The baby had always been her. And Mouse was so perfectly put together, a creature only the wildest imagination could conjure, each eyelash an impossibility, each fingernail a wonder. Margaret had been terrified she'd make a mistake. No wonder she'd waited a decade to have Lawrie and Tom. Of course, they'd been surprises as well.

And had she made mistakes? Well, how could she not have? Had those mistakes affected her children? Probably so, though truthfully, Margaret couldn't say *what* made people the way they were. She herself had been born with a sunny nature and found it difficult to understand people who weren't. She glanced down at the little finger on her right hand. It had always stuck out to the side like that, like a comma at the end of a sentence. Mouse had the same little finger on her right hand. Had they inherited it from some ancient ancestor? Or was it just theirs alone? Margaret had no idea how much of who she'd become was because of her life with Aunt Edith or the parents that she'd never known. And all three of her children were so very different. Was it because of how she'd raised them, or in spite of it?

She knew the answers to these questions could never be found in the history books lining the walls of Lawrence's office upstairs. Nor could she find them in Aunt Edith's Bible. No passage, chapter, or verse could ever reveal why there was an invisible curtain that hung between her and Mouse. Or why Lawrie's bow was strung so loosely while Tom's was forever on the verge of snapping in two. Those boys were twins, for God's sake, raised in the same house by the same parents. You'd think that would've meant something.

Margaret could picture her children right now, lined up on the other side of the table in order of their birth: Mouse first, Lawrie in the middle, and beside him, Tom, only a half hour younger than his brother, but as different as water from sand, despite their identical faces. Which one should she tell about Aunt Edith's visits? Mouse was the eldest, so it should, no doubt, be her, but the thought of telling her stoic, inscrutable daughter that she'd been seeing a ghost made Margaret inwardly wince. It was Lawrence to whom Mouse had been close. He was the one who'd helped with her homework and made her Halloween costumes. It was Lawrence she'd wanted by her bed anytime she was sick. Margaret had never minded this. It wasn't a competition, after all. But Lawrence's death had shown Margaret just how little she knew her own daughter. She'd hardly seen Mouse in a month, even though she lived only three streets away.

Mouse had handled the funeral better than any of them. While Lawrie wept openly, and Tom's violent clenching and unclenching of his jaw showed how hard he was trying not to be seen doing the same, Mouse had sat quietly in her seat, her reserved serenity a testament to the private relationship she'd had with her father. It was obvious Mouse wasn't going to share her grief with a soul.

Margaret turned to look at the wall of photographs behind her and found the one of Mouse at eleven, standing right here in this kitchen, wearing the toque Lawrence had bought her when she cooked her first Christmas dinner all by herself. He'd told her how elegant she looked. That unabashed pride on Mouse's young face still made Margaret smile. Noticing the picture was hanging a bit crooked again this morning, she leaned over to straighten it.

Early on, they'd mistaken their daughter's resolute nature for shyness, her quiet reserve earning her the nickname she still carried to this day. Mouse had always known what she wanted in life: to cook professionally as soon as she could, to fall in love only once, just like her parents had done, and then to have two children, a boy and a girl. She'd ticked every box by the time she turned twenty-three. The catering business she'd started soon after graduation had become so successful she'd moved it out of her kitchen and into the old Stieglitz Icehouse out past the high school over a decade ago. She'd fallen head over heels for the young doctor Nick Moretti while still in culinary school and, even now, they seemed to Margaret like teenagers in love. And as for the two kids, well, barely a year separated Carly and Ben. Irish twins, Lawrence had called them. Ben had followed his sister to Davidson College just two months ago, and Mouse, only forty-two, still had a whole life to live. Margaret paused, chewing her biscuit. If she herself lived as long as Aunt Edith, she'd see... what... twenty-one more summers? That still seemed like quite a long time. Time enough for both her and Mouse.

With Mouse's picture now hanging level, Margaret's eyes drifted over to a photograph of the twins, so alike in appearance it seemed like a trick. Consistently optimistic and cheerful, Lawrie was the child most like her: he didn't worry about much. Woke up pretty happy each morning. He'd always been the easiest of her children, and like Mouse, he'd known what he wanted to do since childhood. He'd never once wavered from the path he'd chosen, and now there was the animal clinic on Lullwater Road with his name on the door. He'd been with the same girl for years, and Margaret loved Emlynn like one of her own. She couldn't help but be proud of Lawrie. Mouse called her Mother, but Lawrie still called her Mama. And was he her favorite? Probably so, but since that thought was as forbidden to a mother as murder, Margaret never let it loose in her mind. Imagining the worried look on Lawrie's face if she told *him* about these visitations from Aunt Edith was enough to stop her from even considering the idea.

And Lord knows she couldn't tell Tom. Tom called her Margaret.

She turned from the photos and sighed. Tom was a mystery no mother could solve. She still remembered the day he'd sat at this very table and asked her, "Why didn't you name *me* after Daddy? Why did Lawrie get his name and not *me*? What was wrong with *me*?" "Good Lord, Tom," she'd told him, losing patience. "It wasn't a slight. Y'all were *twins*! We had to paint a blue dot on your foot to tell you apart. It could just as easily have been you who was named after your father instead of Lawrie, and I'll tell you what, if it upsets you so much then the two of you can switch names anytime you want. Won't bother me, or your dad, one iota." Tom had paused for a moment and then said, "Why was *my* foot the one you painted blue?"

Margaret pulled apart another biscuit, shaking her head. Tommy had always seemed to feel like he was the third monkey on the ramp to the ark. Who knew why? It couldn't have just been that they'd named Lawrie after his father instead of Tommy, could it? Margaret sighed heavily. Any attempt she'd ever made to reassure or encourage Tom was inevitably read by him as a patronizing gesture that only further revealed just how inadequate she actually thought he was. No, she wouldn't tell Tom about Aunt Edith.

She had now eaten two biscuits, one more than she usually did. Stacking up her dishes, Margaret took them to the sink and turned on the water, pausing to look past her reflection and out into the leafy backyard. The chartreuse blooms of the Limelight hydrangeas had begun to change over to pink on the edges. She'd need to cut some for the house pretty soon. They'd turn brown as cardboard at the first frost.

Standing on her tiptoes, Margaret could just see the Hollifields' place, facing the street far behind her. "Nobody's given in yet, I see," she said. The big oak limb still lay across the Hollifields' roof, its green leaves now desiccated and gray, evidence of the ongoing, and increasingly acrimonious, dispute between the Hollifields and their next-door neighbors. The massive tree that sat squarely on the property line had dropped its large, heavy limb onto the Hollifields' garage over three weeks ago, but the onus still hovered between the two houses like a noxious cloud.

A breath of wind floated into the kitchen, crisp and cool as a just-fallen leaf. Margaret stuck her hands into Lawrence's old tartan robe, releasing the aroma of pencils and peppermints that had been as unique to the man as his signature. She reached for this robe every morning, no matter how warm it happened to be outside. Today it perfectly matched the weather. The wind through the window ruffled her hair, erasing the last of her headache.

This was the first day it had really felt like fall, a gift Margaret intended to claim for her own. Something about the quality of the light, she thought, gazing out at the serrated shadows lying beneath the tall poplars. She was glad now she'd suggested Micheline's when her neighbor Harriet invited Margaret to meet her for lunch today. Harriet Spalding always treated Margaret to lunch on her birthday. It was a tradition they'd started way back when the Elliot children were small, and Harriet, already a grandmother's age, was their regular babysitter. All week, Margaret had been looking forward to sitting with Harriet at one of those little, red-draped tables under the trees on the square.

Smiling, she picked up her lukewarm coffee and walked down the hall to the living room, switching on lamps as she went. It would be afternoon before the sun made it around to this part of the house. She passed by Aunt Edith's old upright piano, the fallboard pulled out and covering the long-yellowed keys, and settled herself in her favorite chair by the window, looking around with sincere satisfaction.

It was Lawrence who'd named this the Red Room, years ago, when Margaret was sprucing everything up for Mouse's wedding reception and had brought home those two matching red lampshades that still sat on either side of the green camelback sofa. Through the years, inspired by the warm glow those lampshades provided, she'd continued picking up little touches of red wherever and whenever she found them, the room growing in eccentricity like an aging woman whose lifelong love of fanciful jewelry keeps her from knowing when enough is enough. She'd glued red floral wallpaper to the back walls of the bookcases and needlepointed roses for cushions and chairs. There was always a row of dark ruby candles lined up on the mantelpiece, a Moroccan red rug on the old hardwood floor. The Christmas tree looked magical in here.

The very thought of moving away, even to a place as lovely as that little beachside cottage, suddenly made her catch her breath, almost as though she'd been hit in the stomach. *Surely*, this wasn't what Aunt Edith was trying to tell her. Margaret loved this house. It was home. She paused for a quiet moment, then shook her head and rose to go upstairs and fix her face. She had to meet Harriet at noon.

3

Mouse

Mouse Moretti was sitting on a gold Philippe Starck stool, her elbows resting on the highest-grade soapstone money could buy, gazing around with a critical eye. The Goldsmiths' kitchen gleamed like new money, which was, she knew, exactly what had been used to buy it. Mouse could always tell when a kitchen belonged to a real cook and when it was just for show. Looking out the tall windows, she easily found Kitty Goldsmith, standing in the middle of her immaculately tended garden in an Hervé Léger dress that looked two sizes too small, proudly playing her role as mother of the bride at the first of many such parties on tap for her daughter, Paris. Mouse would've bet anything if you put a gun to the woman's head, she couldn't tell you how to hard-boil an egg.

Unable to resist, she glanced over again at the long La Cornue stove, as shiny as the day it was made, and thought what a waste all this was. At least it had landed the Goldsmiths a four-page spread in *Veranda* magazine, so it had probably served its purpose, she thought, realizing she'd already broken her resolution to be less bitchy more times than she could count, and it wasn't even noon yet.

She felt ashamed about this, but try as she might, Mouse couldn't really remember Kitty Goldsmith. She'd been Kitty Zimmerman back then, forever seated in the last desk of the alphabetically arranged classrooms at Tillman Elementary, too far removed both physically and socially from Mouse's circle of friends to ever make an impression. Kitty had moved away before everyone shifted over to Wesleyan High and Mouse couldn't recall a single conversation they'd ever had. But Kitty certainly remembered her. Claiming a friendship they'd never owned, since hiring Mouse to cater her daughter's wedding activities Kitty had crossed Mouse's carefully drawn boundaries between client and friend every chance she got. Mouse couldn't wait till this wedding was past her, in spite of these lucrative parties.

She glanced back through the windows at Kitty, inwardly pleased to see her red stilettos sinking into the grass. Well, what was the woman expecting? Wearing those hooker shoes to a garden party two days after a rain? Instantly ruing the viperish thought, Mouse turned from the window and closed her eyes. What was *wrong* with her?

It seemed to be getting harder for Mouse to exercise her basic observational skills—a necessary activity for a caterer—without drifting off into a cynicism that was getting worse every day. On a business level as well as a personal one, it was important that she maintain a neutrality about her clients while at the same time understanding them well enough to efficiently tailor her work to their personalities. This, of course, required a certain amount of collation. For instance, here on the west side of Wesleyan, most of the money was new. In neighborhoods like this, where each house was larger than the last, posing imperiously behind gates of royal proportions on treeless lots hardly big enough to comfortably accommodate a double-wide trailer, the events Mouse catered were generally hosted by those reveling in recently acquired wealth. She'd never considered it judgmental to notice that much like their houses, these people sometimes appeared simultaneously anxious and smug.

It was that anxiety she had most to regard. While Mouse knew she was seen as a servant of sorts on these occasions, she could often catch a certain look in a client's eye, one that told her they feared she knew much more than they did. For people who generally came from disparate backgrounds where money was a thing other people possessed, to suddenly find so much of it themselves was often a discombobulating experience. If they were difficult and demanding, even sometimes bordering on rude, then it was her job to make them feel comfortable, and Mouse knew she did her job well. She liked to make her clients happy, even if they were jerks. To her, this had always been the most satisfying thing about having her own catering company, and with that as her aim, she excelled at hiding her true feelings. Or at least that used to be true.

Lately there'd been this unpleasant commentary going on in her head, one that was less than magnanimous, one that seemed only to be getting louder, and one Mouse feared was beginning to breach the confines of thought and slide into unacceptable action. With a grimace, she remembered last Tuesday when she'd pulled into the drive-thru at Chick-fil-A to get a Diet Coke with extra ice. When the poor teenage boy had said "My pleasure" after she thanked him, she'd rolled her eyes in his face. "Yeah, right," she'd said, before driving off. Embarrassment and regret had slapped her in the face before she'd gone a mile down the road. Sure, "My pleasure" was the anodyne response the employees were required to give, but what the hell? It was better than a stick in the eye. And then, just this morning as she'd been on her way here to the Goldsmiths', she'd pulled up to the stop sign by Second Baptist Church and noticed the uneven wreaths on the double front doors. Season in, season out, for as long as she could remember, those wreaths had hung cockeyed, and today had been no exception. Full of fake leaves in fall colors, the one on the right hung a good quarter inch higher than its twin on the left. Normally the sight made her laugh, but Mouse couldn't summon a chuckle this morning. Instead, she'd pulled her car onto the sidewalk, strode right up to those wide doors, and yanked down that higher wreath. Then wiggling the nail back and forth till it loosened, she'd pulled it out, moved it down a fraction, and banged it back in with her shoe. The wreath now hung at the appropriate height. Really, what was *wrong* with her?

Sitting here now, though, Mouse thought it couldn't possibly be considered ugly to notice the Goldsmiths' house was the type she liked least. Sharp-edged, clean-lined, and bright white, she felt it would be of better use as the lobby in the sort of discreetly impersonal hotel frequented by movie stars hungry to enjoy their celebrity status anonymously, checking in under floppy hats and aliases. It was a house so erased of individuality it told you nothing about the owners beyond their desire for acceptance in an increasingly homogeneous world. And that, she thought, shaking her head, wasn't judgmental. It was simply a fact.

Mouse had grown up in a house very different from this one; its memory was implanted in her heart. She'd not lived there in years but hand her a pencil and she could draw every detail of that place on Albemarle Way—every quirky nook, every cozy cranny. Much more eccentric than grand, it was painted the palest of blues, with odd little upstairs porches that could be reached only from bedroom windows, and a widow's walk on the roof, where she and her little brothers had lain on their backs on hot summer nights, searching the skies for shooting stars. The high-ceilinged rooms always smelled like the seasons—honeysuckle in springtime, cut grass in summer, woodsmoke and dried leaves in the fall—because her mother loved open windows and closed them only on the coldest of days. Unique among the houses of Wesleyan, it had always reminded Mouse of the pirate ship in *Peter Pan*. The USS *Elliot*, her brother Lawrie had called it, and their father had gotten a little brass plate engraved with that name to hang by the yellow front door. It had been a wonderful place to grow up. Mouse could still feel her dad in those rooms.

In the midst of her reverie, the glass double doors opened, and Marcy Weller came into the kitchen, bearing three satisfactorily empty trays. "These cheese thingies you made are a hit and a half. I hope we've got plenty." She grinned broadly as she sat the trays down beside Mouse and looked around for more.

"Happy to hear it. Here are some clean trays, and there are more 'cheese thingies' over behind the glasses. There, just there." Mouse pointed to the stack of pink-lidded boxes lined up by the triple-doored Hestan refrigerator, each one emblazoned with the name Elegant Agatha's across the top in green cursive print.

Marcy began to arrange the palmiers on shiny silver platters. "I'm telling you, Mrs. Moretti," she said, "these are a long way from what we had at my sister's bridal shower last spring. Sausage balls, cheese straws, and pink lemonade. 'Course, Mama made it all herself, and don't get me wrong, it was delicious. But I guess you gotta up your game when you're catering for people like this, huh?"

Mouse smiled. It was rare to hear an accent like Marcy's anymore. As thick and sugary as sorghum syrup, with a graciousness that smoothed the edges soft, it was the accent of the elderly women Mouse remembered from childhood, one she'd thought gone forever. Georgia had become such a melting pot of cultures; those who still thought of it as drenched in the dialects of an imagined Old South would be surprised to find this impression was no longer accurate. But then, over from Thomasville comes Marcy Weller, a twenty-one-year-old blonde fresh out of Valdosta State with a newly minted degree in early education, a voice like Melanie Wilkes's, and all her weekends free. Mouse had hired Marcy the first hour she met her, and every time the girl opened her mouth, Mouse couldn't help but smile.

"So, I've been wondering," said Marcy. "Who exactly is *Agatha*?"

"It's me," Mouse said, a little taken aback. "I thought you knew."

"You? You mean Mouse isn't your real name?"

"It's hardly the name I was christened with."

"Well, shoot, you never know. Back in Thomasville, I went all the way through school with two girls named Sunbeam and Cricket, and I swear to God, both those names were on *their* birth certificates. Nobody even questioned it. And my sister? The one who just got married? She swears she's gonna name her first baby La La, even though I told her that was one of the Teletubbies. By those measures, Mouse is not all that unusual."

"I guess not," Mouse said, laughing in spite of her mood. Marcy always had this effect on her.

"So, your real name is Agatha?"

"Yep. I choose who I let call me Mouse. But Agatha is indeed my real name. I was named after my dad's favorite writer."

This time it was Marcy who laughed. "Lord, I can't imagine my daddy having a favorite writer. Maybe the fellow who writes the sports page in *The Thomasville Times*. But I'm glad he didn't name me after *him*. Man's got a face like a baby possum."

Marcy opened the double doors with her hip and glided across the Goldsmiths' green carpet of lawn, silver tray held aloft, smiling all the way. Not for the first time, Mouse felt grateful she'd found her.

Running this catering business was all she'd ever wanted to do. Mouse had known she'd be a cook since that long-ago afternoon when she'd grilled her father a cheese sandwich for lunch and he'd made such a fuss over how perfect it was. She couldn't have been more than six, but the thrill of making something that gave him such pleasure was overwhelming; it gave her the fillip she needed. After that lunch, Mouse became fascinated with creating dishes, then meals, and before long she was in charge of Thanksgiving. Gathering all the ingredients, mixing them together, and ending up with something that made everybody so happy? It felt like magic.

Before she reached her teens, Mouse had learned to trust her own taste, spending hours in the cozy old kitchen on Albemarle Way, altering recipes, sometimes writing her own, or even more exciting, ignoring them altogether. Single-minded, she'd gone straight to Hyde Park after high school, spending two blissful years at the Culinary Institute, then interning in top restaurants just long enough to learn that she wanted to be her own boss. When she started Elegant Agatha's, her kids were both still in diapers, a decision she'd never make today, and wouldn't have been able to make then had Lawrence not loaned her the money, making her promise not to tell her mother he'd done it. But that decision had soon proved to be profitable, and when she'd tried to pay her father back, he wouldn't let her. Now that he was gone, Mouse wondered if Lawrence had ever known how he'd practically picked her up and placed her on the path she would walk, just by his praise of that first grilled cheese sandwich.

Mouse felt a rogue wave of tears rising inside her, but even as she reached into the pocket of her linen apron for a tissue to catch them before anybody could see, they'd ebbed away into nothing. Just as they always did. Lord, why wasn't she able to cry? Replacing the tissue, she walked around the counter and poured some pink champagne into her empty coffee cup. Downing it in one go, she placed both the cup and her palms down on the cool soapstone and took a deep, shuddering breath.

Lawrence Elliot had been gone for seven long months, but it still felt like last week to his daughter. His obituary had filled the front page of the *Wesleyan Journal*; the funeral had brought news reporters down from Atlanta. Mouse could never get used to strangers knowing who her father was. He'd been her hero for the whole of her life. She still felt his presence, sometimes so strongly she'd turn around, halfway expecting to see him. This wasn't a comfort, just another reminder that Lawrence was no longer here, something Mouse still wasn't able to really believe. She'd told no one how she was feeling. Even Nick didn't know.

Thinking of Nick made Mouse feel like her stomach was falling into her shoes again, so she began to pour champagne into the tall crystal flutes that sat empty and clean on the counter beside her. She'd promised herself she wouldn't let her thoughts come close to the thing that had been ruining her sleep, her appetite, and—she hated to admit it—her confidence for weeks now, and if there was one part of her psyche for which she was grateful, it was her ability to compartmentalize her worries when she had to. For example, she hadn't once thought about the birthday dinner she and her brothers were giving tonight for her mother. She dreaded going, dreaded sitting in a dress at Jessamine

Country Club and pretending everything was just fine, but until she gave her family the okay, they might as well not even exist. So now, she stuffed Nick behind the same dark door in the back of her mind and slammed the sucker shut.

The tray of champagne finally full, Mouse lifted it up and pushed through the glass doors to the garden outside. Bright fall sunshine tempered the nip in the air, and the three large ginkgo trees by the stone terrace, full of lemon-yellow leaves, cast a nearly numinous glow over the guests. The Goldsmiths couldn't have ordered a more perfect day even if they did have the money to pay for it.

Mouse wandered through the crowd, as faceless as any server. She never put on makeup for events like this, always made sure her dark hair was pulled back. It was important both she and her crew be invisible. What people needed to remember was the delicious food, the beautiful décor, and an atmosphere of nonchalant serenity. Mouse didn't care if the client got the credit, which only endeared her more to everyone who hired her, which in turn made Elegant Agatha's even more popular.

As if on cue, Kitty Goldsmith appeared at Mouse's elbow and said, "This is all so perfect, Agatha. Y'all are just brilliant."

Startled, Mouse turned and said, "Well, thank you, Mrs. Goldsmith. We aim to please. And Paris looks happy today, which is everyone's goal, I know."

"Oh, come *on*! How many times do I have to tell you? Call me *Kitty*. It's not like we don't *know* each other. I realize we weren't best friends way back then, but we *did* go to elementary school together. And you were always so nice to me. It might've been thirty years ago, but don't you think I've forgotten." Kitty scanned the crowd for her daughter, finding her laughing in the center of a circle of similarly short-skirted, long-legged girls who were making kissy faces at the camera she was holding aloft. Kitty's eyes narrowed, and Mouse noticed the lines around them for the first time. They were worry lines, not laugh ones. Mouse's mirror knew the difference.

"Do you think anybody can tell?" Kitty whispered, clasping Mouse's arm as her eyes stayed trained on her daughter.

"Tell what?" asked Mouse.

"Then that's a *no*, thank God! If somebody as detail oriented as you are can't tell Paris is two months pregnant, then nobody else here can. If we can just keep her looking like that till she walks down the aisle in two weeks, I'll be able to breathe a bit easier. At least for six months or so. Don't know what I'm gonna tell people then."

A surge of compassion washed over Mouse, surprising her. In an instant she knew money couldn't buy what Kitty Goldsmith craved. The longing for acceptance is a harsh mistress, and Kitty had probably served her for years, no doubt pinning hopes onto her beautiful daughter, who was unaware of their weight, even now. A baby in Paris's freshman year at college was not what Kitty had planned; Mouse knew this without being told.

Instinctively, she sat the tray of champagne on the table behind her and placed her hand on Kitty's shoulder. "Trust me," she said in a low voice, "every woman here is totally preoccupied with their *own* kids, not to mention their own *husbands*. By the time Paris has this baby, not a single one of them will remember when she got married."

Kitty turned to Mouse, her eyes bright. "Oh, thank you, Agatha. That's so sweet of you to say. Like I said, you were always nice." She took Mouse's hand and led her over to a pair of wrought-iron chairs in the shade. The two of them sat down.

"You know, if she hadn't gotten sick, we would've been home

free," Kitty said, tugging at the hemline of her close-fitting dress. "Paris was doing fine at school. Her grades were even better than I'd hoped for—a whole lot better than mine ever were—and she was dating this really nice boy. And then"—she snapped her fingers—"she up and got chicken pox and had to come home. Sadder than a lost hound dog. Still hasn't stopped blamin' me for not gettin' her vaccinated, but hell, I didn't even know chicken pox was still a thing. I couldn't tell you what happened to that boy she was datin' at school. She had Donnie, this new one, before she stopped itchin'." Kitty crossed her long legs, pulling at her dress again. "I knew she was pregnant a week before she told me," she said. "It's a gift I have. Women go all squidgy around the eyes in the early stages. I can always spot it.

"Of course, my mother-in-law'll blame me for this baby the minute she finds out Paris is pregnant," Kitty continued, tapping her long pink nails on the arm of her chair. "I've been like gum on that woman's shoe ever since I talked Vincent into leaving Atlanta and moving back down here so I could keep a closer eye on my mama. You'd think ol' Florence Ann Goldsmith woulda been happy when her boy sold those apps he came up with and we got all this ..." Kitty waved her hand in front of her. "But no. The woman never did think a place like Wesleyan was good enough for her little boy, even though she herself hails from a pea-size town downwind from a paper mill in north Louisiana. That place stinks to high heaven. But she thinks her little Vinnie oughta live in New York or L.A., someplace where he'd fit in better with the A-listers, you know. Wesleyan was a big ol' step backwards, according to her."

Mouse's eyes were round. She wasn't used to somebody spilling their secrets so liberally. Most women in Wesleyan held their cards very close to their vests. She glanced toward the upper floor of the house, where she knew Vincent Goldsmith was hiding from this party of overdressed women. He'd been the one to open the back door for her and Marcy this morning, and Mouse's initial impression of the man was that he was far too short for his high-ceilinged kitchen, another time she'd broken her self-imposed rule about bitchy thoughts. But as she'd watched him standing at the side of the room, observing their work with a condescending eye, she could see that in addition to his diminutive size, Vincent was one of those men who seemed constantly on the lookout for the unspoken insult, the disrespecting slight. She recognized the quality. Through the years, she'd watched it take root in her brother Tom, as his personality bent beneath the tyranny of a resentment whose source was as unknown to her as it probably was to him.

As the two women sat there in silence, each one lost in her own thoughts, a clutch of golden ginkgo leaves drifted slowly to the ground, covering Kitty's red Jimmy Choos and Mouse's black loafers. Mouse picked a couple of the leaves from her shirt, holding them gently in her hand and wondering if she should press them in a book like her father used to do. There were old photos and leaves in most of his books; you never knew what might fall out when you opened one.

"Oh, look," Kitty said. "They're startin' to go. I never can get used to these trees droppin' all their leaves at once. Ginkgoes do that, did you know? Here one day, gone tomorrow. I'm glad they stayed for the party."

Mouse glanced around at the assemblage of women now planted in groups of four or five all around the Goldsmiths' backyard. An elderly woman in a navy-blue dress stood smiling at her from a spot in the shade. She was standing alone, and Mouse held her gaze for longer than she normally would've done with someone she didn't know. But there was something about this old lady that seemed familiar to her. "Kitty," she said, "I don't think I remember your mother. Is that her?" She nodded to the old woman standing under the trees.

Leaning to the right and looking across the lawn, Kitty shook her head. "I can't see who you're talkin' about, but it doesn't matter, I can tell you my mama's not here, thank the Lord. She was gonna come, till she heard there weren't gonna be any men here. Always on the lookout for stepdad number five. Or is it six? I swear to you, I can never remember. I think she was on her third one back when you and me were in school together. It was number four who moved us down to Ocala." She leaned toward Mouse like a good friend. "God, I had so many dads. You know, she told me the real one ran off and joined the circus, but I found out after he died, he'd just been living in Tuscaloosa with a woman who owned a couple of alpacas. Mama thinks this baby is a *fabulous* idea, by the way." Kitty's laugh came out like a yodel.

The breeze that was casually drifting through the sunlit yard suddenly picked up speed as if to remind everyone that it was really October, not May. Out on the green lawn, a couple of women rubbed their bare arms vigorously in the chill. Mouse's eyes went back to the spot where the old lady had stood and found her right where she'd been, still smiling over at Mouse. Returning her smile, Mouse suddenly shivered as the wind wrapped back around to where she and Kitty were sitting. Unrolling the sleeves of her black shirt, she buttoned them tight at her wrists. When she looked back up, the old woman was gone, and Mouse suddenly felt colder than ever. Then, without plan or preamble, she said, "I'm scared my husband's going to have an affair if I don't get my act together."

Mouse spoke so softly, almost in a whisper, but Kitty heard

her words like a shout. She didn't laugh this time. She just stared at Mouse for a long moment before turning back to look at her guests, her eyes sweeping the lawn till she found Paris standing by a border of monkey grass with her left hand outstretched, showing off her ring.

"Well, shit, Agatha honey," Kitty whispered, slowly shaking her head as she gazed at her daughter. "In my book, one cheatin' husband equals one pregnant bride any day. Seeing as how we're old friends, you and me need to have lunch." She reached over and patted Mouse's arm. Mouse felt tears sting her eyes.

"Call me Mouse," she said, and Kitty Goldsmith laughed loudly again.

4

Margaret

No matter how much time had passed, Po'boy the basset hound remained a pungent presence in Margaret's old Volvo. Today, his long-buried smells were reactivated by a noon sun that shone straight down on the top of the car; they greeted her as soon as she opened the door. "Poor old Po'boy," she said, her words carving a path in the fuggy air. With his droopy ears and despondent expression, this had been how she'd always addressed the basset hound, even in his puppyhood, and as she pulled on her seatbelt and backed out into Albemarle Way, Margaret told herself, once again, that she really should get another dog.

The row of crepe myrtles that marched down the median of the street was now ankle-deep in faded pink blossoms that swirled into the air as the Volvo rolled past. Margaret could remember the year everyone on the street had contributed money to have these trees planted, an effort indicative of the neighborhood's spirit. Margaret had loved living here since those long-ago days when she and Lawrence had been the youngest couple on the block.

Albemarle Way was part of a cluster of streets that had been threaded through this forest of Southern hardwoods long before neighborhoods had associations to ensure uniformity of architecture and conduct as most did today. When people moved in, they didn't have to sign any sort of form guaranteeing never to fill their front yard with plastic flamingos. The Searcys had fifteen in theirs. There had never been a ban on flags or garage sales, nor was there a limit on the number of cats one could own, which was a comforting point for Corinda LeCraw, who was up to eight at last count. The houses had sprung up organically, as had their inhabitants, each one unrelated to the others in personality, structure, or style, and this left the door wide open for a potpourri of individuals, none of whom had ever been inclined to formulate opinions on the tastes or proclivities of their neighbors. Even ghosts were obviously welcome in here.

Turning up Dornoch Lane, Margaret couldn't help but grin when she spied the window boxes full of plastic flowers outside Harriet's neat little white house. Harriet, who was circumspect about her age—though she had to be knocking on eighty by now—was unmarried and childless and had, at one time or another, babysat nearly every kid in the neighborhood, some of whom were now so settled into adulthood they should probably be called middle-aged. She'd always had too much shade to grow anything colorful, and since discovering the unfading reliability of plastic, had completely given up trying. If you discounted the fact that the flowers weren't real, Harriet's window boxes were some of the prettiest in Wesleyan.

Waiting her chance to pull into Meridian Street, Margaret turned the radio up and put the car window down. Reaching behind her, she pulled her hair from the clip that was holding it back, and the wind lifted it up off her neck. She stretched her arm out on the edge of the open window. No longer thick with summer, the light bounced off every surface with a buoyancy Margaret couldn't help but catch. She breathed in the cool autumn air, her sleepless night forgotten. If today had to be her birthday, she couldn't have asked for a prettier one.

Cars poured out from the various streets surrounding Griffin Park, and soon Margaret was part of a slow-moving line clearly bound for Wesleyan Square. Even if she hadn't known what day it was, the traffic would have told her it was Saturday. It wasn't that there was more of it than on any other day of the week but that it seemed less hurried, more relaxed. People leaned against parked cars in conversation, kids jumped around in backseats. Cherry-tongued dogs hung their heads out car windows, pretending they could fly. Couples ambled along the sidewalks, licking ice cream cones, holding hands. This was the day for long, gossipy lunches and leisurely shopping, the kind of day at which small towns in the South generally excel, especially in the month of October.

The Wesleyan Wasps had obviously won their homecoming game the night before, as several players were out strutting the sun-dappled sidewalks in their neon-yellow jerseys, followed by entourages of adoring classmates and admiring alumni for whom a homecoming win still retained the power to inordinately cheer the soul. Sitting at the red light on the corner, Margaret tooted her horn and waved at Buster Yozzo, her city councilman's son—sixteen years old and already as big as a Maytag refrigerator—and received a two-armed, fist-pumping wave back from the grinning defensive tackle, along with an ursine roar of residual triumph unique to the high schooler who's just won his first homecoming game. "Buster, you'll remember this weekend for the rest of your life," said Margaret out loud to the empty car as Buster lumbered off toward Mama's Way Cafe, trailed by a covey of fawning young females who'd no doubt pay for the large piece of pie he was about to order.

Margaret didn't mind change. We'd all stagnate without it, she thought. Still, it gave her a warm feeling to see those kids going inside Mama's Way. She'd eaten chicken salad plates there with Aunt Edith and Ida Mae on countless summer afternoons, the three of them sitting on those same leatherette stools at the counter, back when Margaret's black-and-white saddle shoes still dangled high above the linoleum floor. So many of the old places were gone now, it made the ones that remained seem precious somehow.

Inching between red lights, she stopped in front of the spot on the corner where Ryman Dewberry's paint store had once been, replaced five years ago by Emlynn's popular, pretty shop. From the get-go, everybody agreed that had been an improvement. With no son to pass the place on to, Ryman had grown grumpy as he aged. He'd stopped stirring the paint properly a good three years before he finally sold up. Most of the cans had gone rusty.

Spying the red brake lights on a silver Honda parked just to her right made Margaret stop short and flip her turn signal on. This spot wasn't necessarily convenient—she'd have to cross the street, then walk several blocks to Micheline's—but you couldn't be choosy on a Saturday afternoon. Feeling lucky, she whipped in the minute the Honda pulled out.

Taking her place in the flow of pedestrian traffic on the sidewalk, Margaret crossed at the light and passed through the gates of the square, its brick pathways shaded by ancient live oaks. Up ahead in the sunlight, the waters of the large marble fountain swayed and swirled in the wind, landing on her as mist as she neared them. She stopped briefly, lifting her face, enjoying the sensation of coolness on her skin.

Wesleyan had always been her home. She loved it here. How could Aunt Edith want her to leave? And why now? Margaret thought about the photo of the little cottage hanging on her refrigerator door, sighed, and hitched her purse higher up on her shoulder, continuing on till she reached the other side of the square, crossed the street, and turned right.

The noonday sun soaked through the awnings of Micheline's Restaurant, painting long ruby-red rectangles beneath the tall trees. From twenty feet away, Margaret spied a free table and quickened her pace. She reached it just as a couple of teenagers were about to sit down, but on seeing Margaret, they looked at each other and offered the table to her. This was something she would normally have refused on principle, but it *was* her birthday, so she just gave them a grateful smile and sat down, pretending not to notice the disappointment clearly written on each of their faces. She ordered a bottle of prosecco and positioned her chair to better see when Harriet arrived.

Despite her years, Harriet Spalding was still a tall woman—Margaret always felt a bit skimpy beside her, as she did around those people with whom she had to stand on her tiptoes to look in the eye. Harriet's height only added to the authority she wore as casually as people wear shoes. A card-carrying member of that dwindling class of old Southern women who'd possessed the witchy sort of wisdom that told them the things nobody else knew, Harriet Spalding could spot four-leaf clovers from ten feet away. She knew her phone was going to ring a good seven seconds before it did. Thirty-one years ago, she'd told Margaret she was having twins long before the doctor was certain himself, and last March, Harriet had shown up at the house five minutes after

Margaret found Lawrence slumped at his desk, snatched away by that very last heart attack. "I just had a feeling," she'd said.

Harriet was the person to whom Margaret turned whenever she felt overwhelmed, and she was inordinately happy today as she caught sight of the old woman's head bobbing along above the crowd on the sidewalk, her Chihuahua, Gatsby, leading the way on a short leash. The dog went everywhere Harriet went. Margaret let out a deep sigh, smiled, and pushed a chair out with her foot.

"Heigh-ho, the birthday girl," said Harriet, bending down to kiss Margaret soundly on the top of her head as Gatsby let out a series of effusive barks. "You don't look a day over whatever age you want to be."

"I have no idea what age I'd pick," said Margaret, reaching down to pat the Chihuahua and earning a small warning growl for her trouble. "Do you?"

Harriet put her large handbag under her chair and Gatsby immediately jumped right inside it, settling down with his fist-size head on the handle. She flipped her napkin out onto her lap. "Me? Well, let's see. I wouldn't be a kid again if you paid me. As pudgy and soft as pluff mud back then, before I grew into myself. And mean as hell when I went through the change. You remember. Honestly, you may not believe me, but I'd say I'm fine with the age I am right now. There's a lot to be said for getting old, if you can keep a good hold on your health, that is. And you don't have a whole lot of beauty to lose." She grinned.

"You're fishing for compliments, aren't you?"

The old woman laughed. "No, ma'am. I just cheerfully accept facts." Harriet's face bore the irrefutable evidence of a lifelong disregard for either the injurious power of a Southern sun or the remedial power of potions and creams. It was as brown and wrinkled as a wadded-up paper bag. She placed her right hand over her heart. "Darlin', I am well aware of my assets. I can be downright charming when I want to be. I can enjoy a tipple or three in the evening and still walk a straight line to bed. I can sing harmony. I can do the *Times* crossword in under ten minutes, and in ink. But beauty? Beauty is something I never had and never wanted. Just look at the women who had it. They're the ones so upset about getting old." She raised her glass high in the air and winked. "You never miss what you didn't have," she said. "Write that one down."

Margaret laughed again. "First chance I get," she said. "But I still say you're fishing."

They both ordered Prosciutto di Parma with melon, then Harriet reached under the table and held up a green-and-white shopping bag. "Sorry I was a little bit late. Book club ran long. Cora Lynn was there again today, and you know how that woman loves to argue. Then I hotfooted it over to Emlynn's and, I swear, I think I bought out her entire stock of honeysuckle bubble bath. Could not resist. That stuff is inspired. Here . . . Happy Birthday!" She rooted around in the bag, came up with a pretty glass jar tied with white silk ribbons, and slid it across the table to Margaret. "Of course I got some for me, too," she said, and grinned.

"Oh, Harriet," said Margaret, pulling the beribboned jar toward her. "What a treat! Thank you." She opened it up and took a deep breath. "That smells divine," she said. "I'll use it tonight."

"You have big plans?" asked Harriet, settling back in her chair.

"Just dinner with the kids. At Jessamine. I considered cooking for half a minute, but when Tommy suggested the country club, well, I just thought, why not? They gave Lawrence full privileges years and years ago, and we never used them nearly as much as I'm sure they expected us to. But now, of course, as luck would have it, Nick's on call at the hospital and Tom's wife, Meghan, is up in Virginia visiting her parents. So, it'll be a small group. Which is fine. It'll be good just to have all my kids around the same table. You know, I don't think those three hardly ever see one another. We haven't all been together since the funeral."

"Well, I'll be seeing one of them Monday morning. Gatsby's due for his monthly nail trim, and he won't let anyone touch his paws but Lawrie."

Margaret looked under the table where the little Chihuahua was asleep in Harriet's handbag. "I want another dog," she sighed.

"You need one," said Harriet, firmly. "When you have a dog, it becomes conversation when you talk to yourself." Margaret laughed.

A soft breeze floated down through the oak trees, the gray moss swaying like clothes on a line. Harriet crossed her legs and closed her eyes. "What a day for your birthday," she said. "Sublime weather. The only thing that could make it better would be the sound of the sea. I swear, for as long as I can remember, I've threatened to leave this town when the weather turns malarial in the summer, but then fall comes, and I forget all about it. Better enjoy it while we can, though. I heard it's supposed to start pouring down rain tomorrow."

They sat in stippled sunlight sipping their wine for a good minute or so, both enjoying the companionable silence. Finally, Margaret said, "You wouldn't ever do it, though? Ever leave here?"

"Oh, no," said Harriet, eyes still closed. "I'm just like you. This is the only place I've ever lived. How could I possibly leave?" The waiter sat a basket of hot bread on the table and Harriet reached for a slice. "No, I imagine I'll kick the bucket right here in Wesleyan," she said, putting her knife in the butter. "There are worse places."

"Hmmm," said Margaret, running her finger around the rim of her wineglass. "I guess. But sometimes, oh, I don't know. With Lawrence gone, you know . . . sometimes I wonder if . . ."

Harriet lifted her eyes and stared straight at Margaret. "What? Don't tell me *you're* thinking about moving, Margaret Elliot. You've lived here all your life. It'd be easier to uproot one of these oak trees. Besides, where on earth would you go?"

"No . . . I'm not really . . . I'm just talking," said Margaret, turning to watch the people passing by on the sidewalk. She could sense Harriet's stare like a sharp ray of light. "Oh, *I* don't know," she said, sighing heavily. "Maybe it's just this birthday. One more year till Medicare, Harriet! Who knows how much longer I've got to make a big change." She turned up her glass, finishing the wine in one gulp. "Don't listen to me," she said. "Like I said, it's probably just my birthday. Making me think all sorts of unacceptable things. And I haven't been sleeping all that well lately."

"Hmmm," said Harriet, eyes narrowed. "I can tell." Margaret looked over at her, frowning. "And between you and me," Harriet continued, undaunted, "it's beginning to show. You're got some dark circles under your eyes, dear, and people notice that on someone as fair as you are. Don't you glare at me. It's only been seven months since Lawrence died. That can't have been easy. Is there anything you want to talk to me about? You know, something *specific*?"

The waiter brought over their lunches and Margaret stared down at her plate, seeing only Aunt Edith's face. She would never have told any of her other friends; she knew them all too well. Kendra Mitchell would look at her the same way she'd done back in first grade when Margaret told her the truth about Santa Claus. Josie Peterson would laugh so hard she'd wet her pants, and Connie Washburn, who'd never managed to keep a secret for more than five minutes, would stand up in Wednesday night prayer meeting at Solid Rock Church of God and request that everyone *"please pray for Margaret."* But sitting here in the sunlight with Harriet Spalding, somebody who'd always been older and wiser than her, telling her secret just seemed like the right thing to do.

"Listen," Margaret said, bending over the table, her hands laced under her chin, "if you tell anybody what I'm about to tell you, I'll deny it and tell them you drink. Plus, I'll never speak to you again as long as I live, which I'll admit might seem a blessing after you hear me out. See . . ." Margaret looked around the table and lowered her voice. "I've been . . . well, I *think* I've been . . . seeing my aunt Edith at night. I mean, I know I have. Right at the foot of my bed. I'll fall asleep, then wake up around three, and there she'll be, in her navy-blue dress and her pearls, just standing there looking at me with this long yellow envelope in her hands. She'll hold the thing out like she wants me to take it, but when I reach for it, she just disappears."

Harriet's jaw had gone slack, a forkful of prosciutto wriggling like bait in midair. But now that she'd started, Margaret didn't seem to be able to stop.

"It's beginning to get to me, Harriet. I mean, it's not like I'm scared or anything. I could never be scared of Aunt *Edith*. It's only later, after the sun comes up, that I get all nervy about it. At first, I thought she was just, you know, just looking out for me or something. Checking in to see that I was all right now that Lawrence was gone, you know? I mean, I've heard of that happening, haven't you? You know, like guardian angels? And she doesn't come every night, stays for only a minute or two when she does. But on the nights when she doesn't show up, I've started . . . well, I swear it's almost worse. See, I've been having all these crystal-clear dreams. Or maybe visions? I don't know. Scenes from the past, things I didn't even know I remembered. And they're as real as if I were living them all over again. I don't know what's weirder, Aunt Edith's visits, or these dreams. But I mean, like I said, I don't see her every night, just a couple of times a week or so, and . . ."

Harriet swallowed hard and let out a snort. "Your dead aunt's just been dropping by 'a couple of times a week,' has she?"

Margaret waved at the air as though swatting a fly. "Just listen. See . . . I've been trying to figure out why this is happening and, I don't know . . . lately I've been thinking that she might be trying to tell me something. Or remind me? And then I walk around all day long feeling like I've forgotten something important. You know that feeling? Like there's something just out of your reach, that for the life of you, you just can't seem to remember. And then one night"—Margaret poured more prosecco into her glass—"one night, about four months ago, she found me this house, sitting on a beach someplace, all white sand and palm trees. Anyway, I *say* Aunt Edith found it because I sure wasn't looking for it, but I opened up the computer this one night and just seemed to go straight to it. And I printed out a picture of the place and it . . . well . . ." Margaret paused, deciding to omit the part about the picture showing up on her refrigerator for three nights in a row without her putting it there. "And anyway . . . now, I can't get that house out of my mind. I can't find it anymore, so I guess it sold. Hell, maybe it never existed. But I think about it every day. I swear, Harriet, it's started to feel like homesickness. And I've begun to wonder if maybe Aunt Edith is trying to, maybe, you know, shoo me away or something? Get me to move? I mean, Lawrence is everywhere in my house. Maybe Aunt Edith is just afraid I'm going to dry up and blow away if I stay there all by myself with those memories. Maybe she wants me to make a move while I still can. What do you think?"

Harriet swallowed hard, blinking at Margaret, silent.

Margaret met her gaze, then let out a weak laugh and ran her hands through her hair. "I know. I *know*! I sound crazy. But I swear to you, Harriet, I see her as clearly as I see you right now." She stared over at the fountain across the street in the square, sunlight glittering on the silver water. She could feel Harriet looking at her. "Nobody I know remembers Aunt Edith," she said, softly. "I never had a brother or sister, you know. I guess Lawrence filled that role for me growing up. We were like family from the first moment we met. We were lucky we fell in love. But now... Well, it would be nice to have someone who remembers your past. Like a puzzle piece that completes you. When you're the last one with memories, it's like trying to hold on to hot sand. My kids have no idea how lucky they are to have one another. And it's something they take completely for granted. You could understand it with Mouse, I suppose, being ten years older than the boys. But Lawrie and Tom act like strangers most of the time. As far as I know, they hardly ever talk to each other unless something comes up that they can't avoid. Like this dinner tonight. My first birthday since Lawrence died. I know they think they have to do something special."

Harriet sat quietly for a moment, then whispered, "I don't suppose you've told *them* about any of this."

"The *kids*?" said Margaret, turning. "Lord, no. Can you imagine? I'd be better off telling them I'd seen Elvis in the Piggly Wiggly." She rubbed her forehead with the palm of her hand. "Kids don't like it when you veer off into unknown territory. You remember Mona Faye Hitchcock, don't you? Remember that summer after her husband died, and she took the grandkids up to Splash Country? Slipped out of her inner tube on Big Bear Plunge? Sank to the bottom like a rock, and when they fished her out, she was speaking in tongues. Lifelong Lutheran, and she came out of there babbling like a Pentecostal. Drove straight home, joined the Apostolic Church the very next Sunday—you remember, that low-slung cinder-block building that used to be out on the highway near Simeon—started wearing those long sack dresses, and didn't cut her hair again. Total transformation. Everybody was shocked, but especially her two daughters. That woman died six years ago, and you know as well as I do, Harriet, neither one of those girls even acts like they remember her name. As for my three, what do you think they'd do if I up and told them I'd been seeing the ghost of Aunt Edith? I'll tell you what they'd do. They'd slap me in Delmar Gardens before you could blink a blue eye. Laugh all you want to, but there are some things you just don't tell your kids."

Harriet, who'd begun to snicker at the mental image of Mona Faye Hitchcock in her inner tube, was now laughing out loud.

"I'm glad somebody finds this funny," said Margaret, wryly. "Believe you me, when it's the middle of the night and you're sitting up in bed asking your long-dead great-aunt what she wants to tell you, it doesn't exactly feel like the most comical thing in the world."

Slowly, Harriet's laughter lost steam. Picking up a corner of her napkin, she blotted her watering eyes, then studied Margaret for a long moment, frowning.

When she finally spoke, her voice didn't rise above a whisper. "Let me tell you something," she said, pushing her plate away and folding her hands on the table. She glanced down at Gatsby, who'd begun to snore, then back up at Margaret. "Before she died, my mother told me something similar that happened to my daddy back when his father died." Harriet paused, dropped her voice, and Margaret leaned in a bit closer. "This was before I was born, back when they still lived in Savannah. Well, the two men never had a good relationship, and they'd had a big row, as usual. Last thing Daddy said to his father was something smart and then the old man dropped dead in his kitchen the very next day. And Daddy couldn't get past it. Mama said he started getting angry at the littlest things. Couldn't sleep, wouldn't eat. And that wasn't like him." Harriet reached for her water glass and took a sip, her eyes still fastened on Margaret. "Then one night... Mama never forgot it... Daddy shook her awake around three in the morning. It was December. She said the Christmas lights were on at the house next door, a whole bunch of colors coming in through the window and shining all over Daddy's face. He told her he'd woken up and seen his father, sitting in the chair across their bedroom. Daddy said he sat up, and the old man just smiled at him and said, *It's all right, Son.* That's all, just *It's all right, Son.* And then, Daddy said, his father just sort of melted away. Mother said Daddy started to cry like a baby. I mean, well, you would, wouldn't you?" Harriet paused again, eyebrows raised. "But she said Daddy was different after that. Said he just seemed to stop worrying so much about things. And he stayed like that from then on, like he had his eyes on something level. He was one of the most contented men I ever knew." Harriet sat up straighter and smiled. "So, don't you go thinking Aunt Edith's not real."

When she'd been little, Margaret had liked to stand in the doorway of her bedroom, pressing her arms against the wooden frame as hard as she could. If she stayed like that for about five minutes, then suddenly stepped out into the hall, her arms would fly up into the air without her control, as weightless as a bird's wings. As she listened to Harriet talk about what her own father had seen, Margaret remembered that feeling of uncontrolled lightness. She felt it inside of her now. The two women sat quietly looking at each other until the waiter came to take their plates away.

"You always make me feel better," said Margaret. She shook her head slowly. "You know, there was this quote Lawrence always loved... What was it? 'There are more things in heaven and earth than you can shake a stick at?' Something like that, I think. Anyway, I guess he was right."

Harriet closed her eyes tight, holding up a forefinger. "There are more things in heaven and earth, Horatio, than are dreamt of in your philosophy." I had to memorize that in school. Way back when. *Hamlet*. Funny thing is, he was also talking about ghosts."

5

Emlynn

Verbena Apothecary always closed a few hours early on the first Saturday in October. This was a special day for Emlynn, the day she created the Halloween display in the big bay window that faced the sidewalk on Wesleyan Square. She looked forward to it all year.

She'd said goodbye to the last customer twenty minutes ago and shooed her two employees out the back door not long after that. Now she dimmed the lights, put the teakettle on the hot plate, turned up the music, and lit another of the coffee-scented candles that were her signature fragrance for fall. She hated the more ubiquitous smell of pumpkin spice. Here at Verbena Apothecary, it was always jasmine for spring, gardenia for summer, Fraser fir for the Christmas season, and the smell of warm espresso as soon as the leaves started to turn.

Emlynn had been eleven when she saw *Practical Magic* for the first time, just on the cusp of that age when girls are so often prone to transformative phases, their imaginations ensnared by one or another of society's cultural pied pipers: some old, some new, some eternal. Madonna, Britney Spears, Jane Eyre. But for eleven-year-old Emily Lynn Cates, nothing was more impressive than that sunny movie of 1998, with its beautiful witches in their grand old Victorian house by the sea. She'd wanted to look like the Owens sisters, dress like them, *be* them.

While realistic enough to know she could never jump from the roof of her house with nothing more than an opened umbrella to guarantee a soft landing—as the witches in the movie had so impressively done—Emlynn longed to get as close as she could to their magical fictional lives while keeping her feet on the ground. And then, "They're not really witches you know," her mother had called out over the hiss and sputter of the steam iron one day while Emlynn was rewatching the movie for the umpteenth time. "Those girls there in those black dresses. They're just actors, Emmy. Actors get to be different people all the time." And it didn't take long for Emlynn to completely alter her goals.

She left her parents in New Orleans and moved to Atlanta after high school. With its tempting tax breaks designed to lure the film industry out of its usual locations, this historic Southern city was well on its way to earning its eventual nickname of Y'allywood, and work was plentiful for a leggy brunette with a not-too-beautiful face.

Emlynn had been happy to do the more menial jobs. Getting coffee, mopping sets, and once, babysitting a recalcitrant llama who'd been hired as comic relief on a dystopian drama that mercifully never made it to air. As a thank-you for maintaining her good humor throughout that long day, the director had given her a small speaking part, which caught the eyes of those best poised to pull strings, and before she knew it, she had a regular role on a popular detective show that earned her enough money to save up for what she'd since decided she really wanted to do: open a shop just like the one in *Practical Magic*.

Emlynn poured herself a cup of peppermint tea and had just placed one arm through the handle of the wicker basket full of cleaning supplies when she heard the clock on the courthouse begin to chime four o'clock. She'd nearly forgotten! Hurriedly, she went back through the shop and straight to the door. Opening it, she stuck her head out and looked down the sidewalk toward Epiphanies Bookshop. Five minutes from now, the impromptu parade would begin, just as it did every week. Sipping her tea, Emlynn leaned against the doorframe and waited.

Story hour started at three every Saturday. At two minutes past four, the door to Epiphanies would open and the line of toddlers would emerge, swaying and weaving like a cooked noodle, and bookended by mothers leading the way toward Rocky's Road Ice Cream Shop on the corner. Sometimes they stopped as a group to look at the dollhouse in Emlynn's front window and she'd step outside to say hello to them all. She knew most of these kids by first name. And she longed to be one of these mothers.

As she stood in the doorway greeting today's happy procession, Emlynn saw her own child in her head as clearly as she saw little Sergio Harper in his bright blue sweater, one hand holding a picture book close to his chest, the other held tight by his mother, Enid, who smiled broadly at Emlynn as she went past. Her own little boy would be tall, Emlynn thought, like her. But he'd have Lawrie's blue eyes and that handsome cleft in his chin. As the line of toddlers made their way down the sidewalk, it occurred to Emlynn that Lawrie might possibly be right. Maybe it was time they got married.

She'd met Lawrie Elliot one blistering Sunday morning in Atlanta when, convinced by heat and humidity to abandon her regular run, she'd stopped into Revolution Doughnuts for an iced latte and whatever decadent treat she considered most tempting. Comprised of sweaty customers clad in ensembles clearly chosen for comfort rather than style, the line to the counter was long and appeared to be unmoving. It took Emlynn a short second to see what the holdup was.

A young man stood at the counter, two Kung Fu Panda backpacks slung over his shoulder, one eye on a table outside where a couple of tired-looking kids sat, clearly up to their eyes in an argument. A large stuffed panda bear was equidistant between them, looking damp and forlorn in the blistering heat. "I'm sorry," said Lawrie, his hands deep in his pockets. "I can't find my wallet." He patted his shirt pocket and frowned, clearly flustered. "It's my nephew's tenth birthday tomorrow and we've ... we've been to the zoo. I ... I know I had it when I bought these stupid things." He let the backpacks fall to the floor, where they landed with a soft thud. "Mouse warned me not to do all this in one day," he said, his color rising. "She told me they'd get too tired, and then they'd get cranky. Mouse. That's my sister. I guess none of us expected it to be so damn hot today." Lawrie let out a self-conscious laugh that was pointedly returned by no one, then, twisting around, finally managed to locate his wallet in his back pocket. He tossed it onto the counter with more force than was necessary, and the thing sailed past its target to land at the feet of the poker-faced teenager who'd stood mutely staring all this time, waiting to be paid.

"Shit," Lawrie had said, louder than he should have, and Emlynn, spurred into action by his plight, had moved quickly and quietly to the front of the line, picking up the backpacks, taking the sackful of donuts off the counter, and motioning for Lawrie to follow her. They'd both paused at the door, looking out at the arguing kids.

"Obviously, I should've bought two of those stuffed bears," he'd said, smiling down at Emlynn weakly. "They're gonna fight over that thing all the way home, aren't they?"

His eyes were the color of sea glass and right then, at that moment, she'd known, as sure as she was of the sunrise, that this man was her future. This was the man for her. It had been months before she told Lawrie, of course, but by then he was equally certain himself. They'd been together for over eight years.

Having always longed for roots that ran deep, Emlynn understood Lawrie's desire to return to his hometown after he finished school. She was happy to relocate to Wesleyan. She'd loved the town at first sight. She and Lawrie settled into their two-bedroom Tudor in a leafy old neighborhood known as The Glade, where she set about creating the garden she'd always wanted, one full of sunflowers, moonflowers, and thyme. The house was cozy, which suited them both, and most important to Emlynn, it had a small sunny bedroom upstairs overlooking the garden, with sloped ceilings and two dormer windows. The moment she stepped inside, Emlynn had known, when the time was right, this would be the perfect room for a nursery.

She still did a few plays and commercials up in Atlanta, but five years ago, when the old paint store on the square went out of business, Emlynn finally found the perfect place to realize her childhood dream. She'd christened the shop Verbena Apothecary, just like the one in the movie, and with its glass-fronted cabinets full of colorful bottles of imported bath salts, hand creams, lotions, and balms, its counters decorated with clear antique cloches, and its many vases of white paper flowers, anyone would be hard-pressed to see any difference.

Everyone in Wesleyan loved the windows of Verbena Apothecary, and Emlynn had Margaret to thank. Before opening, she'd given Lawrie's parents a tour of the place, telling them both all about the movie that had inspired its purchase, and Margaret had cocked her head to one side, then looked over at Lawrence, grinning. "I might have just the thing," she'd said.

Lawrence hadn't liked the idea, Emlynn remembered now. He'd said he was certain the dollhouse would never fit in the window, and when Margaret assured him it would, then he'd said it might fall apart in their hands. Though he'd tried his dead level best to dissuade her, Margaret had remained adamant. "It'll be the perfect place for it," she'd said. "Sitting there in that window, on display for everyone in town to admire but not touch. Just what Aunt Edith would want."

Emlynn and Lawrie had followed his parents back to the big blue house on Albemarle Way and sat with Margaret at the long kitchen table, listening to Lawrence's footfalls in the attic above them. It had taken him ages to bring the thing down. "He's right, it is old," Margaret had said, a hint of a smile on her lips. "Like I said, Aunt Edith never let me touch it. Her brother made it for her when he was a teenager, and I have to say, it's a real work of art. I would have been fine letting the kids play with it, but Lawrence wouldn't ever hear of it. 'A family heirloom,' he said. It sat upstairs in his office for years, just gathering dust. I finally talked him into moving it to the attic when we put in more bookcases, and it's been sitting up there ever since. Seems a shame not to let people enjoy it."

The old Gothic dollhouse was so large Lawrence had to bend his head around it to see where he was going when he brought it into the kitchen. It wasn't open on the back but solid, like a real house, and with its tall, square turret; its gables, scrollwork, and wraparound porch, it was the house from *Practical Magic* in miniature. Emlynn had squealed like a girl and thrown her arms around Margaret in delight.

The dollhouse filled the window of Verbena Apothecary as though custom-made for the spot, and every three months Emlynn decorated it for the appropriate season: daffodils and a miniature maypole in springtime, tiny Christmas lights and cotton-ball snowmen in winter. For summer, she filled thimbles with moss and hung them along the front porch like Lilliputian baskets of ferns. But the October window was special. Baby Boo pumpkins lined the front stairs and a little black cauldron full of silver-wrapped chocolate Kisses sat on the porch. She always kept the shop open late on Halloween night, serving hot cider to shoppers and cookies to their children, thus making Verbena Apothecary one of the most popular places in town.

Turning back inside, Emlynn locked the door and set her tea on the counter. Amy Winehouse's well-seasoned voice swirled around the dimly lit shop as she climbed into the front window, pulling the white curtains shut. She didn't want anyone to see her work until it was done.

Squatting down, she removed all the accoutrements of the past summer and placed them off to one side. Then she began to clean last season's dust off the dollhouse, using a fluffy beige artist's brush, humming while she worked, and sneezing when tiny feathers of dust tickled her nose. She had just made her way around the square turret when she noticed the front stairs appeared loose. *I'll need to glue those*, she thought, but when she touched the little stairs, they pulled away from the house, just enough to reveal a small opening under the porch. Emlynn rocked back on her heels, staring.

Bending her head down and peering inside, she could just see the edge of a yellowed piece of old paper that looked like it had been folded over a good many times. Instinctively, she took hold of the paper and gently rocked it back and forth until, coaxed from its hiding place, it slipped out of the gap and fell to the floor of the window. Emlynn turned her head and sneezed again.

What she'd thought was just paper she now saw was a long yellow envelope that had been folded over four times. Freed from the restriction of its hiding place, it began to slowly open by itself, just like the wings of a bird. Gingerly, Emlynn picked the envelope up, holding it lightly in her hands. She could see it was sealed, and on the front, in looping, old-fashioned script, was written: *For Margaret.*

With her curiosity flaming, Emlynn's first instinct was to rip the thing open, but her hand was stalled at the sight of Lawrie's mother's name. She'd need to take this to Margaret, she knew, and she could hardly do so if it had been so obviously opened. Emlynn loved Margaret Elliot; Margaret was, for all practical purposes, her mother-in-law, and not only that, she considered Margaret a friend. Invading her privacy was out of the question.

She turned the envelope over and over and held it up to the light. But the yellow paper was too thick to reveal any secrets. Frustrated, Emlynn wriggled out of the window and took the envelope into the back room, where she carefully placed it inside her large canvas tote bag. She'd give it to Margaret at dinner tonight. A little surprise for her birthday.

The sound Emlynn heard next was high-pitched and thin. It might have been laughter, or it might have just been the wind, whistling around the eaves of Verbena Apothecary, on its way down the street.

6

Margaret

Tall and thickly planted, an old holly hedge pushes against the pristine white fencing that separates Jessamine Country Club from the plebeian traffic that travels Highway 4 every day. Cars pass by so quickly, most drivers never even notice the modest bronze sign that swings in the wind by the gap in that hedge, and even if they do, the narrow driveway that opens up at that point curves immediately out of sight, almost as if by design. Hidden away from the public, the long drive bends up and over the greenest of hills, past sunny tennis courts and shady stables, under oak trees and pines, till it reaches an ivy-covered brick mansion known to most people in Wesleyan by reputation alone.

Nobody asks to join Jessamine, no matter how badly they crave admittance. A person must wait to be invited, and for decades, the criteria for those invitations were hardly a mystery to anyone with a few brains and a conscience. Aunt Edith had called it the Blue Vein Club when Margaret was little—meaning that no one got onto the rolls unless their skin was so white you could see the blood in their veins—and the red-hot glare of media attention that had finally managed to change things in the late seventies was still resented by more than a few. When Louis Goldberg was voted in as president in 2002, the membership dropped by fifteen.

The club had always bestowed honorary privileges on those it deemed worthy, however. They had to admit at least two a year on merit alone; it was written down in the bylaws. Wesleyan's mayors were included for life, as were a few prominent judges, a couple of noncontroversial clergymen, and Lawrence Elliot himself. His invitation had been hand-delivered one cold December morning a month after his third book was published, two days after his first interview on the national news, and just a week before Christmas. The timing of the invitation had been almost comical. The year was nearly over, and a quota, obviously, had to be filled.

Tonight, Margaret had been seated in the Yamacraw Room, the club restaurant, named, unironically, she assumed, for the original owners of the land on which Jessamine Country Club sat. Six Venetian chandeliers floated celestially above tables draped in starched white linen, and portraits of past club presidents lined the peach-colored walls, their subjects suited, stern, and exclusively male, for some barriers had yet to be broken. At the Steinway in the corner, a florid-faced man in a Masters-green blazer sat softly playing Ray Charles's "Born to Lose" at such a slow tempo it was doubtful anyone in the room recognized how incongruous the song was for the setting.

Unlike the more modern restaurants in Wesleyan, whose hard surfaces, metal chairs, and naked windows bounced even the quietest conversations from table to table at deafening decibels, causing everyone to speak louder and louder just to be heard, here the double-lined curtains and plush patterned carpets devoured all spoken sound. The place was as hushed as a funeral home. People whispered. You could hear the tinkling of ice in the glasses. It had been years since Margaret had been in this place, and she wished like the dickens she hadn't been seated right in the center of the room.

She was always early, and her kids were always a few minutes late. Never enough to be rude, but never exactly on time. Margaret took a sip of cold water and felt its iciness fall through her body. The sleeves of her red silk blouse were cold; she shivered whenever they touched her bare skin, and she thought longingly of her old wool cardigan hanging on its peg in the hallway back home.

With a sixth sense she'd always possessed when it came to her family, Margaret knew Mouse and Lawrie had entered the restaurant seconds before she saw them. That old familiar quickening in the air, a recognition of blood to blood, which to Margaret, was louder than Gabriel's trumpet. Certain now of who she would see, Margaret turned her head and smiled at the two of them as they wove their way through the tables toward her.

"Look at you," said Lawrie, bending down to give Margaret a one-armed hug and a kiss on the cheek. "Don't you look pretty in red!" He'd worn a suit, which for some inexplicable reason, made Margaret feel proud. "It's my fault we're late," he said. Mouse, makeup-free in a black sleeveless dress, had sat down on the other side of the table. "Today was our monthly staff meeting," Lawrie continued, "and time just got away from me." He smiled at the two of them apologetically.

Mouse shook her head. "It's just hard to believe *my* baby brother is somebody's boss."

"Hey," said Lawrie, feigning shock. "I'll have you know, I'm the boss of quite a lot these days. And I run a very tight ship. Just ask Rosie."

"I like Rosie," said Mouse, unfolding her large damask napkin. "She's sweet. And somehow, I think she just might be the one at the helm of that ship you're running."

"Everybody likes Rosie. She's a gem." Lawrie turned to Margaret and grinned. "Happy Birthday, Mama." He pulled a small wrapped present from his suit pocket and placed it on the table beside her plate. "I guess you can tell by the size of this box that Emlynn talked me out of what I really wanted to give you."

"What was that?" asked Margaret, picking up the little box and shaking it.

"A dog, of course," said Lawrie. "You need another one, Mama. You know you do."

Mouse snorted and looked to her mother for a similar reaction, only to be surprised not to find it.

"I *do* need another dog," Margaret said, her shoulders dropping. "Harriet told me the very same thing at lunch not six hours ago." She sighed. "I just don't think I could ever go to the shelter and get one. Your dad always did that for us. I'd never have been able to come home with just one. I would've adopted them all. I still would."

"Well, heck," said Lawrie. "I can do that for you if that's all it is. I'll pick out a good one. After all, don't forget, I'm an expert." He nudged the package closer to Margaret's water glass. "Emlynn picked this out for you when she was on that buying trip to Paris in June. I think you'll like it. Wait till she gets here to open it, though." He looked down at his watch. "Should be any minute. She had to stay late and do the shop window."

"I love her Halloween window," said Mouse, reaching into her large black handbag and retrieving a present of her own. "I guess I love everything about that shop of hers." She pushed the lavishly wrapped gift toward Margaret, and Margaret recognized

Emlynn's shop logo on the ribbon's tag. "And Happy Birthday from us, too, Mother. Nick's sorry he couldn't be here. He had to take Bogey Crawford's calls this weekend. His daughter's in a cheerleading competition in Charlotte and Ellen swore up and down she'd hang him out to dry if he missed another one."

"Well, I hate it he's not with us, but I'm tickled to see you two," said Margaret. "I told Harriet today, I can't remember the last time I had all my kids around the same table."

"Where *is* our Tommy Boy, anyway?" asked Lawrie, eyes circling the room with poorly disguised amusement. "This place has his fingerprints all over it. I'd'a thought he'd be the first one here."

"*Please* don't start off by teasing Tom," said Mouse, and Margaret heard a weary tone in her voice.

"Oh, come on, Mouse," said Lawrie, dropping his voice to a playful whisper. "You think Mama would've chosen this place? Give me a break." He looked over at Margaret and raised his eyebrows theatrically. "Tell the truth now," he said, a mischievous look on his face. "This was all Tommy's idea. Am I right?"

"Well, he was just trying to do something nice for my birthday," said Margaret, trying to stifle a grin. "There's nothing wrong with that."

"Oh, please," said Lawrie, both validated and amused. "He wants to act the big shot, just like always. And what better place?" He raised his arms, palms up. "I'll bet you a plug nickel he tries to pick up the check."

"And I will be happy to let him," said Mouse, her menu open, perusing the specials. "But, Lawrie, I'm serious . . . don't needle him. Please. You know he can't take it. And frankly, tonight, neither can I."

Margaret was about to underline her daughter's instruction

when, as though someone tapped her on the shoulder, she turned and saw Tom, pushing past the teenage hostess and heading toward their table, the expression on his face antithetical to a festive occasion. Margaret could see her reflection in his mirrored Ray-Bans as he bent down to kiss the air two inches away from her cheek.

"Hello all," he said, without smiling, and pulled out the chair next to Mouse. "I can't believe I actually thought I could drive down here and back in one day. Traffic around Macon just gets worse all the time. You'd think they could work on those damn roads at night, at the very least. Not right in the middle of the day when everybody's trying to get somewhere."

"And a Happy Birthday to you, too," said Lawrie, raising his glass to Tom. "Ow!" He reached down to rub his shin and glared over at Mouse, who serenely kept her eyes on her menu.

"I told you, honey," said Margaret. "You should just stay over tonight. Your room is always ready. You could drive back tomorrow after breakfast."

"And I told *you*, I can't," said Tom. "I've got tons of work to do this weekend, and I so rarely get the house to myself. Need to take advantage of Meghan being away. I'll be fine. A good dinner's all I need." He opened his menu, oblivious to the three pairs of eyes that watched him, two with disapproval, one with concern. The man at the piano, who'd obviously come prepared with a Ray Charles songbook, began to play "Busted."

Lawrie was about to say something provoking to Tom—Margaret could feel it—but as she watched, his eyes softened, crinkling up at the corners, and she followed his gaze across the room, where, just as she'd hoped, Emlynn was coming toward them, a fast-moving blur of color and warmth.

"I'm *so* sorry I'm late," she said, throwing her arms around

Margaret and squeezing her tight. "Oh, you have to drive by tomorrow and see the window, Margaret. It's spectacular, if I do say so myself. Little white fairy lights everywhere, and I found these orange ones, really tiny, so I put them all along the porch of the dollhouse this year. Took me forever, I had to use a toothpick to help thread them through all that gingerbread stuff... Hi, honey," she said as she sat down beside Lawrie—who still wore the smile that had taken over his face at the first sight of her—and put her large canvas tote under the table. "But it was totally worth it. And do you know? When I finished and pulled back the curtains, there were at least a dozen people waiting on the sidewalk to see. I couldn't believe it. Have y'all ordered yet?"

Emlynn's guileless effusiveness had silenced the table. Grinning, she looked from each of the Elliots to the next, expecting an answer. "No, we haven't," said Mouse. "Here, take my menu."

Emlynn was another creature who defied explanation. Despite what Margaret knew of her peripatetic childhood, being blown around the country like dandelion fluff by parents who could never seem to find enough peace or stability to share with their only child, Emlynn appeared to be one of the most well-adjusted women Margaret had ever met, bright, funny, and caring. If Margaret had been given the power to choose a partner for Lawrie, Emlynn would have been it.

"Oooh, I haven't had risotto in *ages!*" she exclaimed, handing the menu back across the table to Mouse. Swiveling around in her chair to take in the décor, she looked straight back at Tom. "You must have suggested this place, Tom. I guess I've been passing by for years and didn't even know it was here."

Lawrie laughed, and Mouse kicked him under the table again.

Wine was poured—sparkling water for Tom—and dinners were ordered. Starting perfunctorily with work and the weather, the conversation lurched along, often so guarded that Margaret thought it was probably bad for digestion. Emlynn and Mouse frequently guided it past topics most poised for contention, as women are wont to do, and all the while, Margaret watched her three kids like a hawk. Mouse had lost weight. She looked paler than usual, and there were dark circles under her eyes. Tommy seemed prickly and peevish as usual. Only Lawrie, reliably, seemed truly happy to be here.

"By the way," said Tom, spearing his T-bone with focus and nodding his head in Margaret's direction. "I see somebody's finally decided to sell all that land out where you grew up. On the way here, I tried to bypass some traffic and took the shortcut onto Boundary Road. Big, fancy For Sale sign out there. Possible subdivision, it says. Gotta be worth a fortune. There's some pretty high-end stuff being built on some of those old farms out near Seabrook."

Margaret's muscles reacted with a mind of their own, and she gripped the stem of her wineglass. She never took that shortcut to the highway. Protective of her memories, she hadn't driven past Aunt Edith's house in years. Now, the prospect of a gray web of streets crisscrossing the ground where the pecan grove had once stood, the land scraped bare to make room for new houses, no matter how fancy, made her feel slightly sick. If that happened, she'd never travel Boundary Road again. The sight would stick in her brain like a sandspur.

"Daddy grew up there, too, Tommy," said Mouse, tersely. "On the other side of that old pecan orchard."

"I *know* that, Mouse," said Tom, irritated by the diminutive version of his name, which nobody except his family used. "But he's not here right *now*, so I was addressing Margaret."

"Well, I don't know about you, but I can't think of that place without thinking about Daddy," said Mouse, turning to her mother. "Y'all got married under those trees in the grove, right where you first met. He used to tell me all about that, how you'd been best friends since you were both little. He said he remembered you standing at the fence that separated his house from yours, watching him play with his brother and sister. I loved those stories so much."

Margaret smiled at Mouse. "It was your aunt Prudie who first saw me standing there under the trees," she said. "I was barely out of diapers, but I thought she was the most beautiful girl in the world, and I guess I still do, present company excepted, of course." She raised her wineglass to Emlynn and Mouse.

Margaret paused; the rest of the table was silent before her. "Her hair was as dark as the wings of a crow, Prudie," she continued, softly. "Like yours, Mouse. And it stayed that way till the day she died. I remember I went all shy the first time I saw her looking at me. Hid behind a tree trunk. But Prudie just waved and called out to me, and before I knew what was happening, the three of them had come down to the fence. They put an old chair over on my side so I could step up, and Lawrence helped me climb over." She shook her head slowly, lost in the memory. "I was basically the Elliots' little sister from then on. Pretty soon, I could climb that back fence by myself. I'd run through all those pecan trees to their house the minute I finished my breakfast, wouldn't come home until dark. Lawrence's daddy managed the farm, you know. They were all so protective of me. The Elliots were like family all through my childhood, long before your father and I up and made it official."

"Didn't your aunt Edith worry about you, gone all day?" asked Emlynn, gazing at Margaret, chin on her hand, her risotto growing cold.

"Aunt Edith?" Margaret laughed. "No, she didn't worry about me. It wasn't like it is now. Kids went out to play in the morning and didn't come home until dark. I'm pretty sure she was just happy I had some friends my own age to play with. She was pretty far up in her sixties by the time I came to live with her, you know. Still said words like 'fiddlesticks.' Wore white gloves in the daytime and called her earrings 'earbobs.'"

"I'd've liked an aunt Edith," said Emlynn, her voice wistful.

The prisms that hung from the large chandeliers caught the sharp dying rays of a sun sliding rapidly down the tall windows, splitting the light into lines of bright color that danced atop the white tablecloths. The room seemed to get quieter as the light dimmed. And suddenly, there was Aunt Edith again. Margaret saw her first as one sees a shadow, in a corner, across the quiet room. Her navy-blue dress. That string of old pearls, the color of ivory. The same thing she'd worn just last night.

"You know," Margaret said, almost as though to herself, "you can usually see the child in an older person. I notice this more and more these days. Something in the way they laugh, or how they look when they think no one is watching. It's easy to see who they once were. I used to catch Lawrence reading outside on the porch. The way he turned the pages, it was the same way he'd done it when he was little—always picking the right one up from the bottom instead of the top, then purposefully laying it down on the left side of the book. Like he was worried the wind might take it. One of the wonderful things about marrying someone you knew as a child—I could always see the boy in him, still there like the first day we met. But it was never that way with Aunt Edith. To me, she was just always old." Margaret closed her eyes briefly, to banish her aunt, but when she opened them, she found the hint of Aunt Edith still there, a tiny half smile on her face, her head cocked, almost as though she were listening. Margaret held her chimerical gaze, unafraid, memories like movies bright in her mind.

"She read to me every night, let me sleep in her bed when it stormed," she said softly, remembering. "And she always wore dresses. I don't think the woman owned a pair of pants. She cut the grass in a dress. Baked a pound cake every Friday night in case people dropped by on the weekend. That's where Mouse gets it, I suppose." Margaret looked at her daughter and smiled. "Her best friend, Ida Mae, lived with us, you know, and the two of them always seemed to be in the kitchen. All those men who used to come harvest the pecans every fall? Ida Mae and Aunt Edith fed everyone. I remember that long dining room table just loaded with food. The polished silver, the tall vases of sunflowers and mums lined up down the center. I think Aunt Edith always longed for a big family. She only had the one brother, Maynard, but he disappeared soon after the war. He made the dollhouse, Emlynn. Remember? Anyway, Aunt Edith would've loved all of you. She . . . she gave me a wonderful childhood." Margaret heard the catch in her voice and coughed a bit to disguise it.

The melancholy notes of "Georgia on My Mind" filled the restaurant, and at the table nearest the door a group of men on the cusp of inebriation began singing along, effectively shattering Margaret's reflection, as well as the decorous calm of the room. Withering stares from the tables around them soon silenced the singers, and Margaret looked back to see all three of her children staring at her, discomfort written all over their faces. Her eyes darted to the other side of the room, but Aunt Edith was no longer there.

Blinking, Emlynn said, "Oh! I'm such an *idiot*. I completely forgot." She reached under the table and pulled her tote bag up onto her lap. "I found something in that dollhouse today. An old envelope. I thought it might be the building plans or something. Now where did I put it?"

As Emlynn dug through her bag, muttering to herself, Mouse cleared her throat and said, "Well, I think it'll be a crime if they tear that big old house down. And all those beautiful trees."

"And what are the current owners supposed to do with it all?" asked Tom. Margaret could tell by the tone of his voice he was grateful to be back on the firm ground of a topic he knew. "Just let the place sit there empty till it falls down? That's valuable land. And people have the right to develop it as they see fit, make as much money as they can. Besides, Mouse, our parents were the first ones to sell."

"We *had* to sell," Margaret interjected. "Aunt Edith had died, and we needed to pay for Dad's college. Your father's parents had already passed; his brother, Forrest, had no intention of ever moving back to Wesleyan; and Prudie was married and living up in Chattanooga. What were we all supposed to do? The people who bought it offered us what seemed like a fortune. That money kept our heads above water for years."

"You can't possibly blame Mama for what might happen to the place now, Tom," said Lawrie. "It's been sold so many times over the years. The people who own it now are the ones courting *developers*."

"You say that word like it's profanity," said Tom. "Did you forget that's how I make my money?"

"Oh, noooo," said Lawrie. "Nobody ever forgets about your money, Tommy. You won't let us."

"That's not what I meant, and you know it. I'm just saying, when people get ready to sell their houses and move, it's up to them and them alone. It's nobody else's business what they do."

Clearly unused to this tone in Lawrie's voice, Emlynn had frozen with her hand in her bag, and Margaret, anxious to circumvent the argument that was rapidly getting out of control, spoke up. "It's funny you should say that, Tom," she said. "Because I recently found this place online. One night when ... well ... when I couldn't sleep. This lovely house on the beach. It reminded me of that summer we all went to Fripp Island. You remember? Sometimes I wonder what it might be like to move somewhere like that myself. You know, the house here really *is* big. Maybe too big for one person? And sometimes I get a bit tired of ..."

"Tired?" Tom pounced before she'd even begun to explain what she meant by the word. "Who isn't *tired*? I just drove all the way down here from Atlanta, and I'm turning right around to drive back. *I'm* tired." His laugh was out of place and came perilously close to a sneer. "I'm sure you miss Dad, but running away won't change that, Margaret."

Emlynn had located what she'd been looking for in her tote and was holding something out toward Margaret, but Margaret ignored her, still facing Tom. "You didn't let me finish, *Son*," she said, sharply stressing that last word. "*If* I ever decided to move, I certainly wouldn't be *running away*, as you put it. I'd just be starting something new. Now that your father is gone."

"Here, I've found it," began Emlynn, clearly hoping to steer the subject into friendlier waters, but Mouse, who'd been glaring at Tom, quickly turned back to her mother. "We all miss Daddy," she said, her voice wavering so slightly nobody noticed but Margaret. "Of course we do. And if the house is too much for you, well, we could get somebody in. You know, to clean, and do the ironing. Maybe even cook a few nights a week."

It was due to the soft lighting that Mouse failed to notice how Margaret's spine had suddenly stiffened, and she continued moving toward the edge of her mother's patience without pause. "I don't think it would be a good idea to *move*, Mother. Certainly not to someplace like Fripp. You're too . . . I mean . . . you're not . . . well, that far away? All by yourself? I don't think that would be *safe*. Not . . . not now, anyway."

Out of the corner of her eye Margaret saw Emlynn shake her head slowly as she looked at Mouse with wide eyes.

"First off," Margaret said, now feeling compelled to argue for something she knew she didn't even really want. "I do not need a maid, or a cook. For God's sake, Mouse. If you're trying to say that I'm too *old* to move, let me remind you that I'm only sixty-four, and barely that. You can ask Sam Peters whatever you want to ask him concerning my health. I had a checkup with him less than two months ago, and he'll tell you I'm in as good a shape as any of you. And if you remember, you couldn't even get onto Fripp Island without a pass. I'm sure it is every bit as safe as Wesleyan."

"Then I can't believe you'd even consider someplace like that," Tom said, then snorted. "It just sounds like one of those gated communities you all hate so much."

"You mean like yours?" Lawrie stared at Tom, instantly indignant on his mother's behalf. Emlynn put her hand on his arm.

"If *you* ever manage to get married to this girlfriend of yours, maybe one day you might even have children, and if you do, you just see if places like mine don't become more attractive to you," snapped Tom. "Life's not like it was when we were kids, Lawrie. Even in a bite-size little town like this one. You don't just let kids play outside all day by themselves like Margaret used to do. Like *we* used to do, for that matter. Not anymore. They'll end up on the six o'clock news. Kidnapped, shot, or worse. Mouse is right. You'll see. You just might want to live someplace safe one day, too."

Emlynn slipped what she'd been holding atop Margaret's small stack of presents, then wrapped her arms around her big purse and held it tight to her chest.

"My *girlfriend* has a name, you know," said Lawrie, his voice rising. Margaret saw Emlynn wince, a bright blush creeping up her neck and settling onto her cheeks. "And you don't even *have* any kids. See, that's your problem, Tommy. You watch too much so-called news. It's destroying your pleasant personality. Gotta keep everyone *safe*. Just what are you so scared of, huh? From what I can tell, you spend way too much time checking your bank account and not enough time considering that one day you just might trip and fall into that new saltwater swimming pool you paid so much money for. Just how safe are you, really?"

"Lawrie!" Margaret and Mouse erupted in unison, and Emlynn looked down at her hands.

"Oh, let him talk," said Tom, pouring more San Pellegrino into his half-empty glass. "He'd think it was a great idea if Margaret wanted to move to the moon. Anything she wanted to do would be just *fine* with him."

"Excuse me," said Emlynn, quietly. "Powder room." Pushing her chair back, she rose and slipped out of the room. Only Margaret and Mouse watched her go.

"She's your mother, too, Tom, even if you never call her by that name. And at least I manage to see her more than once a year. I'm surprised you even remember how to get to Wesleyan anymore now that you're in that big house that's ... oh, remind me ... where is it again? *Just a half mile from the governor's mansion?*"

"Oops, now my brother's jealousy is showing," said Tom, acidly. "Guess spending your days separating hound dogs from their balls ain't as lucrative as you thought it might be when you were toiling away in vet school, huh? Sad. Well, at least it's fulfilling."

"Oh, for God's *sake*, Tommy," hissed Mouse. "Keep your voice down. When did you get to be such an unmitigated jackass?"

"Now, you listen to me . . ." Tom pointed his finger at his sister, clearly geared up for a fight.

"Don't you dare start on Mouse," warned Lawrie, leaning across the table toward his brother.

"*Stop* it!" All of you. Stop it *right now!*" Margaret had spoken so loudly it surprised even her. The patriciate of the Yamacraw Room turned to stare at her family just as a dark-suited waiter came through the door to the sound of "Hit the Road, Jack," his smile illuminated by the tiny candles rising out of a three-tiered cake on which *Happy Birthday, Mother,* was written in icing as red as Margaret Elliot's face.

She didn't acknowledge the waiter but kept her eyes on the table. And that's when she saw it. The envelope Emlynn had pulled from her tote bag. The yellow envelope. Aunt Edith's yellow envelope. It was lying there on top of her birthday presents; Margaret recognized it at once. Her own name was written on the deeply creased paper, the handwriting faded, but profoundly familiar. And it felt like someone had reached into her chest and taken hold of her heart.

Without another word to her children, Margaret grabbed the envelope and stood up. As the three of them sat there, speechless and staring, she pushed past the waiter and headed hard for the door, the room spinning around her like leaves in the wind.

7

Margaret

The first time Lawrence proposed to her, they'd both been eleven years old. It hadn't been a real proposal, of course. More like an abiding assumption spoken out loud. They'd been leaning against the hood of his brother's new tomato-red Thunderbird, waiting for Forrest to come out of the house and give them the ride that he'd promised. Bobby Darin was singing "Beyond the Sea" on the little transistor radio in Margaret's hand when Lawrence had said, "When we grow up and get married, we'll get us a convertible, too."

"When we get *married*?" She'd giggled, pushing him hard on the shoulder. Lawrence had blushed, and that told her more than his words had just done. "Well, yeah," he'd said. "I mean, sure."

The letters had started coming not long after that. Lawrence would write them at night. Margaret could lie in bed and see the warm glow from his lamp seeping through the pecan trees on its way to her window. If that light stayed on till past midnight, she knew there'd be a letter waiting for her in the crook of the oak tree that sat in the side yard, the one nearest the house, the one draped with curtains of moss. She'd head straight there in the morning.

These weren't love letters at first—those would come later—just the knots of life he was trying, even then, to work loose by turning them all into a story. Things got clearer when he wrote them on paper, he told her. And she was always a safe place for his thoughts. That strange war starting up in those faraway jungles, the murder of the new president, and finally, his own father's death... everything he couldn't understand pushed Lawrence down into all he could know about why.

She'd kept these letters, stuck them in books, drawers, and boxes, and through the years they would laugh at his boyish wonderings whenever they came across the earliest ones, full as they were of those nascent thoughts and opinions that he'd not yet lived long enough to succinctly refine but that would, over time, coalesce into something like wisdom.

When Emlynn laid the yellow envelope on the table beside Margaret at dinner, she'd done so as though it were an ordinary thing, never realizing that it had been sent straight to her by Aunt Edith. Margaret was sure about this. Hadn't she seen it often enough in the old lady's hands as Aunt Edith had stood by her bed in the dark? But it had been the handwriting on the front of that envelope that had seemed to audibly speak Margaret's name. It was that same looping script of those early letters. Lawrence's hand as a teenager. She would have recognized it anywhere, anytime.

Still unopened, the envelope now lay on Margaret's bed. She could see it from where she stood on her little balcony, her arms wrapped around her shoulders in a solitary hug as she waited for her heart to slow down. She'd been standing out here for a good fifteen minutes, wanting to know what the envelope contained but afraid to find out all the same. Just touching it had felt like reaching into icy water.

The wind had risen since she returned home. It traveled from far out in the marshes, salted and chill, a portent of colder nights to come. Margaret could hear the wind chimes singing from the porches downstairs; their euphonic tones seemed to drift farther and farther away until they joined the susurrus of fern-shaped leaves on the pecan trees at Aunt Edith's old house. She could no longer tell the difference between them. With leaden feet, Margaret left the balcony and went back into the bedroom.

Her heart pounding loud enough to hear, she sat down on the side of her bed and picked up the long yellow envelope. Hesitating briefly, she took a deep breath and opened it, cutting her index finger on the paper's edge, a dotted line of red blood appearing instantly. Sticking her finger into her mouth for a second, Margaret thought, even hoped, the envelope was empty. Then she opened it wider, turned it upside down, and shook it like a saltshaker. An old piece of newsprint floated and fell in slow motion, followed in the next breath by a small black-and-white photo, both landing faceup on the bed.

The newspaper was brittle, it crackled as she carefully spread it open. It was from page twenty-two of *The Clarion-Ledger*, from Jackson, Mississippi, dated October 7, 1956. Only a few lines that had lacked the importance to warrant a more prominent placement.

LOCAL MAN AND WOMAN DEAD IN APPARENT MURDER SUICIDE

A couple was found dead in their home on Pepper Creek Road outside Bentonia in what appears to be a murder suicide. The woman was found in the kitchen, dead from a gunshot wound, the man found hanged in the front room. Sheriff Hutch Dilbeck says the baby girl found at the scene will be taken in by family. No further details are available.

For a long moment, Margaret sat frozen, hardly breathing. Then with a shaking hand, she picked up the small photograph. It had obviously been taken decades ago, before people felt obliged to obey the commandment to smile. The four black-and-white figures were ghostly with age. A man, and a woman. The woman was wearing a coat with a patchy fur collar, holding a baby girl in her arms. The man was clad in overalls, just like the small boy who was standing beside him. The only person whose features were halfway clear was the woman, and with a hand to her mouth, Margaret recognized the eyes. They looked like her own.

Moon shadows were roaming the bedroom as the trees bent and swayed outside in a wind blowing hard from the west. The weather was changing, a metallic smell of rain filled the air.

Slowly, Margaret rose from the bed and walked back out onto the balcony, drinking in the cool air like it was the water of Lethe even as she knew down deep in her bones this was no dream that would crumble into shards of color and evaporate with the dawn. This was what Aunt Edith had been coming to tell her.

Then from somewhere downstairs, Margaret heard a piano, the skill of the player exceeding the reach of an instrument whose keys were deadened and dulled by age and disuse. Adrenaline mixing with fear, she stared out into the dark, her heart naming the song her head had forgotten. "Love Lifted Me," Aunt Edith's favorite old hymn.

8

Margaret

When she was six, Margaret asked her Sunday School teacher how all those people in the jungles of Africa were going to make it to heaven if nobody ever told them the way. The teacher had hemmed and hawed for a few minutes, before awkwardly saying, "Well, that's why we take up money for the missionaries twice a year." Margaret's follow-up questions had been summarily dismissed, and she'd gone away feeling like she knew less than she had coming in. Little bug-eyed Brother Ponder, who wore snap-buttoned shirts and had food in his teeth more often than not, was the only missionary Margaret had ever seen in the flesh. She'd resolved to drop a few more nickels in the plate next time he came to church for a fundraiser, because in her mind, he hardly seemed up to the task.

It had taken several years of disappointing answers to questions like this before Margaret concluded that you were probably missing the point if you came to church looking for facts. She could tell this wasn't a popular position to take at Second Baptist Church, yet she kept attending long past the point when she could have refused to do so, out of respect for her aunt, who'd sat in the same spot—third pew, right side—for longer than Margaret could remember. She stopped going the week after Aunt Edith died.

She sometimes wondered if it had been the memories of Aunt Edith that caused her to drift over here to St. Cyprian's Episcopal not long after Mouse had been born. Doubts seemed a little more welcome in these pews and as strange as it seemed to her then, Margaret had found she occasionally missed the familiar Sunday ritual she'd known as a child, that mysterious connection to something outside of herself. Looking around her now, she wondered if it might simply have been the beauty of this place that had lured her here all those years ago. The tall Gothic spires that seemed to have hope built right into their architecture, always reaching up to God in the faithful assumption that he was still there. The colorful stained-glass windows, which, even on a day like this one, cast prisms of light over everything, radiating a holy presence that Margaret practically felt on her skin. Of course, her attendance was anything but regular. Mostly, she came here when Sunday morning coincided with a weight too heavy for her to carry alone. She sat in the back pew today.

Rain beat against the stained-glass windows with such ferocity it made the saints and apostles inside them look as though they were weeping. Dean Vaught simply couldn't compete with the sound. His voice wasn't particularly strong on an ordinary day; it barely carried past the altar on this one. Margaret twisted her rain hat around in her hands. She could tell the people sitting near her had stopped trying to hear what the Reverend was saying at least several paragraphs back. She knew she certainly had.

Unable to stop herself, Margaret searched the shadows of St. Cyprian's for Aunt Edith, but of course, she was nowhere to be seen. If the contents of that yellow envelope were indeed what her aunt had been trying to give her, then surely, the old lady must know, they came with many more questions than answers. Aunt Edith couldn't simply disappear and leave it here. Didn't Margaret deserve the whole story? As Dean Vaught droned on, she sifted through her memories of Aunt Edith's last years, looking and listening for any hint of a secret, any piece of a lie.

Edith Lowry had faded away slowly. Ida Mae had died two years before, asleep in the bedroom next door, where the walls were covered in rose-patterned wallpaper, and the window looked out on the trees. Her death extinguished a certain light from Aunt Edith's eyes that most people attributed to her intelligence but which Margaret now knew had much more to do with the relationship both women had worked for so many years to conceal. She'd wondered how Aunt Edith would make it without Ida Mae beside her. It didn't take long to find out.

Less than a year after Ida Mae's death, with a green bean casserole still warm in her hands, Aunt Edith had fallen up the brick stairs upon arriving at Colleen Hardeman's Christmas party. Green beans and fried onions had flown from their dish, defying the laws of gravity for exactly two seconds before painting a culinary Jackson Pollock on the Hardemans' front porch, and Aunt Edith had fractured six bones: two in her right leg, one in her left, a big toe, a rib, and a finger. Advanced osteoporosis had been the diagnosis. "She's as fragile as a chicken egg," old Dr. Wilmer had said to Margaret in the hallway of Elberta County General. "And there's probably other things going on, too, but Miss Lowry says I'm not to go looking for them. Quite firm about that." Margaret had peered into the room where Aunt Edith lay just out of earshot, eating red Jell-O, her long gray hair spread across a foam pillow like seaweed on a rock.

Her aunt's ramrod-straight posture had always seemed more of a byproduct of her will than anything related to physical health, but Margaret had watched helplessly as both dwindled—the fixity of nature, the reliability of bone—the two of them turning to sand. Soon, Aunt Edith's spine was no longer capable of staying erect, and the old lady took to her bed. Margaret read to her every night. The Brontës, then Austen. Welty and Wharton. By the time they got round to the Bible, Aunt Edith only wanted to hear the red words, her lips silently moving in memory with Margaret's as she read the familiar verses out loud. The comfort those words gave Aunt Edith was apparent, and she drifted away for good one night right after whispering, "Walk while ye have the light."

But sitting here in the back pew of St. Cyprian's this morning, Margaret remembered another afternoon when she'd been about ten, long before Ida Mae's mind began to slide away from her grasp. Aunt Edith had had a meeting with the school superintendent, so Margaret had been given a ride home by Kathy Ledbetter's mother. On the way, they'd passed by Sister Yvonne's, that white clapboard cottage with the baize-green shutters that once stood on the corner of Tenth Street and Pine. Sister Yvonne read palms. This wasn't a secret—a neon sign glowed in her window. She kept the thing on till past midnight.

From Aunt Edith's reaction whenever they passed by, Margaret knew Sister Yvonne's was a place forbidden to people of faith, or to anybody with even a spoonful of sense. But something had caught Margaret's eye that afternoon as she looked out the back window of the Ledbetters' car. A flash of bright yellow that made her turn around in her seat as they passed. It had been Ida Mae, in her favorite dotted-swiss dress, going up the stairs at Sister Yvonne's with her purse on her arm. Right in front of God and everybody.

All through supper that night, Margaret had watched Ida Mae for any sign that she knew what she'd done had been wrong. But there'd been no evident guilt or shame. Ida Mae had bowed her head and closed her eyes for the blessing like always. Margaret had kept her own open just to make sure. It was three days before she gathered up enough nerve to ask Ida Mae about it.

"Oh, you saw me, did you?" Ida Mae had said, as she stirred some fried corn for Sunday afternoon lunch, one eye looking out through the window to where Aunt Edith was picking hyacinths to bring in for the table.

"Yes, ma'am, I did," said Margaret, slicing cucumbers, her chin slightly raised.

"Well, I'm not ashamed of it, if that's what you're waiting for." Ida Mae looked amused. She was still wearing the dress that she'd worn to church.

"But Aunt Edith says . . ."

"Your aunt Edith and I don't see eye to eye on everything, you know."

"But you believe in God, don't you?" whispered Margaret, fear nibbling at the edges of her voice.

"Well, a course I do. Goodness, what a question. But what if all I believe doesn't turn out to be the whole story? Sometimes religion doesn't explain everything well enough for my liking. Plus, it's fun to see what Sister Yvonne thinks might happen. You know, she told me once, years ago, that one day I'd have a little girl. And I laughed and laughed. Because I knew this time, she was dead wrong. But then, years later, who shows up on our porch?" She tickled Margaret's side, and Margaret giggled in spite of herself. "Life's such a mystery, darlin'," Ida Mae said, continuing to stir the corn. "But crazy as it sounds, I find some comfort in that. To me, truth is like a garden full of birdsong. I never listen for the loudest voice. I listen to the chorus instead. I guess I just like to keep an open mind, is all. And an open mind is like an open window, you can't hear the birdsong if you keep it shut."

The screen door had slammed at that moment, and Aunt Edith had entered the kitchen, the hem of her dress speckled with hyacinth petals. "Just make sure your mind's not so open your brains fall out," she'd said as she passed them. And Ida Mae had laughed and thrown Margaret a wink, the look on her face communicating amusement and serenity in one.

Margaret shifted in her seat, the roar of the rain in her ears. Last night's discovery was proving too persistent to ignore. Every time she remembered, a cold nausea washed over her, and suddenly, she thought of Wendell Gillespie.

Wendell had found out he was adopted when he was twelve. A cousin of his let it slip during a family reunion on Tybee Island, and Wendell, after looking around the crowded picnic table at the people who, up until that very moment, he'd thought were his relatives, took off on foot right in the middle of the watermelon cutting, hitchhiking all the way back to Wesleyan and sending his parents into paroxysms of fear and regret for not having told him the truth at an earlier age. State troopers found him sitting on the front steps of Tillman Elementary two days later. By that time Wendell had come to the humiliating conclusion that he'd been the last person in town to know the most seminal fact of his own existence, though due to him being the only redhead in an entire family of people who claimed to have Cherokee heritage, most folks had assumed he would have figured it out long ago.

The story of Wendell's life had changed in an instant, and Margaret had never once wondered how that made him feel. I guess he felt just like I'm feeling now, she thought, leaning over to pass the collection plate to the young man seated a few spots down in her pew. But was she getting ahead of herself? That old newspaper clipping hadn't mentioned her parents by name. But that accompanying photo . . . that woman's face, so like her own. And that little boy. What if he was her brother?

She remembered those days when family was the be-all and end-all here in the South. "Where are your people from?" was the ubiquitous question, and growing up, Margaret had watched some people wither beneath its weight, while others almost visibly grew with pride, eager to provide the questioner with the correct, most impressive credentials to prove they belonged where they stood. As the grandniece of the formidable Principal Lowry, Margaret had never faced that inquisition herself. Aunt Edith, whose own people had lived in that big white house in the pecan grove for longer than anyone could remember, and who trailed loyalty and respect like that scent of Arpège still lingering in Margaret's own bedroom, had been immune from any need to prove who she was, which meant, of course, that Margaret was, too. No one would've ever believed Edith Lowry had any secrets, or that Margaret might possibly be one of them. If Aunt Edith told people her grandniece's parents had died in a motorcycle accident, then everyone, certainly Margaret herself, would've believed it.

The congregation stood to recite the Nicene Creed, and Margaret rose with everyone else, unconsciously mouthing the words that didn't answer the questions roaming around in her head. Did secrets become secrets only when they were told? Unacknowledged, were they something else entirely, unspoken truths that cut so close to the bone they required—perhaps, deserved—protection? For example, surely everyone in Wesleyan had known the truth about Ida Mae and Aunt Edith. But nobody ever admitted that fact. Margaret had never told her own children the truth about the two women. And why not?

But Lawrence, she thought, sitting back down. How had Lawrence found out? And why hadn't *he* ever told her? They'd had no secrets from each other, not since the first day they met. Or at least, she'd never thought they had.

Whenever someone spoke of life as a journey, they seemed to imply a straight line. A pathway, a runway, a road. But Margaret had always seen her life as a circle, the last years looping back toward the beginning before closing as neatly as two clasped hands at the end. Whether vision or wish, it was an image that had given her comfort whenever she brought it to mind. She was nearly at the top arc of that circle, and she could see now that it had always contained a chasm, one she'd jumped neatly over as though it didn't even exist. And she suddenly knew it couldn't successfully close unless it was repaired.

Margaret couldn't turn away from this. This was what Aunt Edith had been coming to tell her, and the old lady had waited until Lawrence died to do it, somehow knowing Lawrence hadn't wanted Margaret to know. But for God's sake, she thought, as Reverend Whipple announced Hymn 34 from the pulpit and everyone around her stood up again, what was she supposed to do with this knowledge now? And what did that house on the beach have to do with anything? Why couldn't she get that place out of her mind?

Margaret joined everyone else standing, but she didn't turn to Hymn 34. Instead, she picked up her purse, pulled on her rain hat, and slipped out the back of the church.

PART TWO

9

Tom

The offices of Warren Creek Development looked down on a wide bend in the Chattahoochee River. Army green and deliberately lazy, the river flowed south toward Atlanta, as opaque as the back of a mirror, oblivious to the pelting rain that was currently covering the whole state of Georgia.

From his window on the twenty-fifth floor, the Chattahoochee appeared as inconsequential to Tom Elliot as a backyard creek, though it could, when drunk on hurricane rain, climb its muddy, root-rutted banks as swiftly as a scalded cat and spread out in all directions, gulping down roadways and houses, and leaving behind an unholy stench when it finally slunk back to where it belonged. Tom remembered the last time this had happened. Hurricane Ivan had hovered over the city on a mid-September day, dumping a sea of water in a matter of hours, and transforming the river into a ravenous beast nobody recognized. He'd helped rescue some of his friends from their houses in a rented canoe.

At least that sort of disaster wasn't expected today. In the feeble light of a hesitant sun only now starting to pull itself up from below the horizon, the river looked as it always did, easygoing and slow, despite the rain bouncing white all over its surface. Tom laid his forehead on the glass of his wide office window, grateful for the cool sensation on his skin. He felt like he had a fever. Was this possible? Could worry do that to a person?

The offices on this early Monday morning were predictably quiet. Tom was the only person here. He liked the way the dark building felt without anyone else in it, just like Tillman Elementary had felt that night the janitor let him back inside to retrieve the history book he'd left behind at his third-grade desk. He'd never forgotten how strangely calm the halls had seemed as he walked to his classroom alone. Like an entirely different place. Silent and shadowy, the school had held no terror for him then, no teachers to tell him he'd gotten something wrong, no one to try and impress with the charm or intellectual prowess he feared he didn't have. No one to compare him to his brother, his twin.

If he closed his eyes, Tom could still see himself at the country club in Wesleyan two nights ago. That arrogant lift of his chin, that self-satisfied smile, the memory of both made him cringe. Why did he behave that way whenever he was around his family? They'd never cared about the things he brought to the table, the evidence he felt compelled to provide that proved how little he needed them, how well he was doing without them. The money, the house, the beautiful wife. He wore them all like medals. But none had impressed his family the way that he wanted, so he acted as though their opinions meant nothing to him, even as he continued to search for some tangible thing that would prove his worth to them all. A shudder of recrimination crawled up his spine, and he curled his hands into fists, like a wailing infant in its first photo.

Had he been asked, Tom wouldn't have been able to articulate the origins of that old animosity, that burning bit of coal in the hollow of his stomach that felt so much like fear. It had been with him for so long now, at the back of his every thought, in the blood that swam through his veins, in the voices he heard just before sleep; he'd long ago given up trying to elucidate the unknowable. He'd just always been able to tell that people preferred his brother to him, even though no one could tell them apart.

His parents hadn't dressed them alike. Nor had they been given rhyming names like poor Tracy and Stacy Scoggins, the twins who had grown up around the corner on Albemarle Way and who still lived together in a condo in Clearwater, Florida. No, as far back as Tom could remember, both he and his brother had been treated as complete and separate individuals, a gift Lawrie had seized like a golden ticket, venturing off into his own curiosities and passions with the sort of confidence explorers must possess. There was something about that vigorous spirit that just drew people to Lawrie, and away from Tom. It was a competition Tom felt destined to lose from the moment he realized its existence.

Lawrie had decided to become a vet the day Tinker, the family's wirehaired dachshund, got hit by a car. While both Tom and Mouse had stood wailing in the driveway, Margaret's arms around their shoulders, Lawrie had helped Lawrence get the dog into the family's old station wagon, never flinching once. With the stoicism of an army surgeon, he'd held the bleeding Tinker in his lap all the way to Dr. Banks's clinic. The vet even broke his own rule and let eight-year-old Lawrie spend the night with the dog, sleeping on a pile of towels next to Tinker's crate. Whereas once that dachshund had belonged to them all, when Tinker came home from his medical adventure, hale and hearty again, he was exclusively Lawrie Elliot's dog and would be until eleven years later, when he died of old age.

From then on, when asked what he wanted to be when he grew up, Lawrie never wavered. "A veterinarian," he'd say, fixing his inquisitor with a serious stare that invariably gave them pause. That sort of rapier focus was rare in a child. He volunteered at animal shelters all through high school, sweeping up and mucking out, and shadowing Dr. Banks at the clinic whenever he could, finding both experience and encouragement at the veterinarian's side. Lawrie shot through high school and got his bachelor of science degree at Clemson with the sort of grade-point average necessary to achieve a full scholarship to the UC Davis School of Veterinary Medicine, finally emerging from the halls of education at twenty-seven and returning to Wesleyan to open his own clinic not six miles away from where he grew up.

And then there was Mouse, quietly determined, always singing along to the radio in the kitchen, cooking dinners for them all, gifted not only with natural ability but with her eye on that same northern star as her brother, as certain of her path through the world as a bloodhound with a sure scent. That old brick icehouse back in Wesleyan that was home to Elegant Agatha's was a place Tom knew his sister had envisioned for nearly the whole of her life.

"If you want to know who you are, look at what you love." He'd seen those words scrawled on the wall of an underpass a couple of months ago and they'd brought tears to his eyes. Tom had no idea who he was. More than anything his siblings could buy or achieve, it was their surety he envied, and the lack of his own that plagued him. He knew both Lawrie and Mouse were living the lives they'd always wanted, certain of their place in the world. Tom couldn't even imagine the feeling.

After high school, he'd migrated up to the University of Georgia along with most of his class, those who, like him, figured they'd stumble on a clear direction after a few business classes and glasses of beer. But Tom never did figure it out. He drifted through college without a fixed target till he hit the brick wall of graduation with prospects as dull and dry as the paper on which his business degree was printed. His choice of career had been random. He'd wandered into property development because it had seemed lucrative, and it had turned out to be just that, but it had never been his passion. Maybe things wouldn't have turned out like this if it had been.

Making money had seemed almost laughably easy, too, like a grown-up game of Monopoly, all that moving it from one place to another to finance a life constructed so far above his means the air was practically thin. But a few missed payments, a few lost accounts, and Tom was finding it harder and harder to breathe.

He'd been living with the continual headache of financial fear for so long, afraid to open the mail or answer the phone, that when the group of investors out of South Carolina approached him about their intentions to develop a tract of desirable land inside Atlanta's perimeter, Tom had thought this might be the answer to all those prayers he'd meant to pray. He could still see himself ensconced in a red leather chair at that corner table at Bones with a steak as big as his head on the plate in front of him while he listened to the polo-shirted group take turns telling him about the land they planned to acquire. A good thirty acres covered in old-growth trees, it ran alongside the neighborhood of

Pinckney Green, one of the oldest in the city, its leafy streets full of families who'd lived there for generations.

"The people there will put up a fight," said Tom, holding a rudimentary rendering of the multistory condominiums proposed for the site. "I'm sure of it."

"Hell, son," one of the men said, "by the time they get wind of this, it'll be a done deal." And they'd all laughed loudly, like it was funny.

But it hadn't been funny to Tom. He knew someone who lived in Pinckney Green. She'd lived there for most of her life. She'd shown him pictures of her garden in springtime, brought him homegrown tomatoes in summer. He knew those ancient oak trees behind her house were full of bobwhites and brown thrashers. Her grandchildren played in those woods.

Tom's eyes had traveled slowly around the table, taking in the smug faces one at a time, and that's when it had happened: a rage bubbled up inside him from a source as deep and black as an untapped oil well. None of the men saw it coming, and by the time Tom had finished telling them what he thought, every one of them was as red in the face as a uakari monkey.

If he'd thought about it, no doubt he wouldn't have done it, but Tom didn't think. Instead, when the valet at Bones brought him his car, he climbed in and called every reporter and conservation group he knew of before he got back to his office. It had taken less than a week for everything to blow up and hit the local news. Petitions were signed, protests were organized, and the investors from South Carolina soon retreated to where they had come from, vowing to tarnish the reputation of Warren Creek Development at every conceivable opportunity. Tom had been taken off all his accounts, and his position at the company was quietly "being reevaluated." He expected to be fired any day.

He hadn't bothered to look at his phone this morning. He knew Meghan hadn't called. He knew she wasn't going to. Eight days of silence had confirmed what he should have known before he even opened his mouth to tell her what happened. So much for those archaic vows she'd parroted back to old Reverend Lamb in that little chapel at Callaway Gardens ten years ago. "For better or worse, richer or poorer," she'd said. His forehead still pressed against the cool window, Tom would have laughed right out loud if his head hadn't been throbbing as hard as it was.

She'd been such a catch, the ultimate prize to show off to his family and anyone else who'd ever counted him out. Tom could still see himself standing straight as an arrow at the end of that flagstone aisle as Meghan floated down it on the arm of her father, her blond head swiveling this way and that to take in the admiring glances, the June sun streaming in through all that abstract stained glass, splashing her white dress with triangles of color. Her constant frivolity had been an escape for him once, the mile-wide difference in their personalities a ceaseless source of fun. He could scarcely believe how she deferred to him, treated him like the boss he'd always wanted to be. And he'd liked the way she laughed things off, even though he truly believed she'd become more serious after they married, that her indifference to the more sobering realities of life was merely a symptom of her youth. He'd thought change was what people did, when they got older. It was what he'd planned to do.

Reluctantly, Tom turned from the view of the rain and the river and went to sit down at his large, cluttered desk. He'd requested this modern version of a workspace—in reality, nothing more than a long acrylic box—when the offices were being redecorated last year. As sleek and clear as a chunk of ice, of all the desks in the catalog Chuck Warren had handed him, this one had seemed to Tom to be the least complicated, the cleanest. That had appealed to him then, and still did. But of course, it had taken only a week before that bare, see-through surface was totally obscured by the sort of detritus normally shoved into the drawers that it lacked, and now it might as well have been made of something as heavy and dark as bronze.

Pushing away a teetering pile of industry magazines, Tom pulled a stack of fat red files closer and laid his head on top of them, shutting his eyes. His head was thumping harder than ever now. Was he sick? He felt like he might be, but then, he'd not slept well in so long, maybe that was just all it was. He needed rest—he knew that—a good, long rest, but he couldn't even fathom getting that anytime soon, if ever again. He swallowed hard. His throat was really burning now.

The main door opened in reception, and Tom heard the familiar sound of the cleaning cart trundling up the hall in his direction. A moment later a plump, smiling face appeared in his doorway.

"Only light on in the place. Should've known it was you. What you doing in here this early, Mr. Elliot? What's so important it could pull you out of a warm bed on a wet day like this one, huh?"

"Oh, you know me, Gloria. Early bird, and all that." Tom's throat felt raw when he spoke.

The woman took a bottle of Windex and a roll of paper towels out of her cart with one hand and pointed at him with the other. "I'll tell you what, Mr. Elliot," she said, refusing for the millionth time to call him by his Christian name, "it's been days since I was able to get that funny-looking desk of yours as clean as I'd like to.

I don't never like to move anybody's stuff around without them present. But seeing as you're here right in front of me, and you don't look too awfully busy, how's about helping me move all those things, and let's get that glass table of yours looking like it's supposed to."

Tom had known Gloria Hogan since the day he started at Warren Creek, straight out of college. As round as a Disney fairy and just as consistently cheerful, she'd been with the company since the nineties, when Chuck had first opened the doors of the old house on Juniper Street, and was a welcome fixture at every Christmas and birthday party, often baking the cakes for each occasion herself. As the company grew, she'd followed along to higher and higher offices until landing in this skyscraper alongside the river. Tom had watched Gloria's close-cropped hair change color over the years, from owl brown to dove white, with a couple of unfortunate stop-offs at pink, but he couldn't begin to guess how old she was and knew that he'd never ask.

The nature of their relationship made him do as he was told. Standing up, Tom began stacking files on top of one another and sliding them down to the end of his desk, scooping up paper clips and pens as he did so. Arms full, and aware of how hapless and disorganized he must look, he let the lot fall into a black leather chair sitting vacant in the corner, then stood quietly beside it, unsure of what to do or say next.

Squirting the desk with glass cleaner, Gloria looked over at him and cocked her head. "You okay, Mr. Elliot? You look a little peaked to me. Family all good? How's that handsome brother of yours? Still the spittin' image of Paul Newman?"

She always referred to Lawrie this way despite having met him only once, and though Tom got the flattering joke, it still irritated him more than he would've liked to admit. "Oh yeah . . . he's . . . Everybody's well, I guess. I mean, my mother's . . . Well, yeah, we're all good."

Gloria turned to look at him, forehead furrowed. "Your mother's what? She's all right, isn't she?"

"Yeah, yeah. She's all right. I was just down there Saturday night for her birthday." Tom walked over to the window and leaned against the sill, his back to the rain that continued to fall.

"Well, tell her Happy Birthday from me," said Gloria. "I like Margaret, always have done. She sends me a box of homemade sugar cookies every Christmas, and I'm looking forward to those again this year, I can tell you. Been saving up the calories."

"She does?" asked Tom. "I mean, she has? Since when?"

Gloria wiped the sides of the desk, squinting to see if any streaks of glass cleaner remained. "Oh, Lord . . . let's see. Since way back when you first started here, I reckon. I met her the day she visited, when you showed your family around. You didn't know?"

"No." Tom sighed, theatrically. "But there's probably a lot I don't know." He turned back around to face the window, catching his sullen reflection in the rain-spattered glass. He definitely looked ill. "For example," he continued, "Margaret told us just the other night she's seen someplace at the beach, on the internet, you know, and she's actually thought about moving there. Can you imagine? At her age. Didn't even ask us about it or anything. Dad's only been dead seven months." Tom pictured a For Sale sign sticking out of the ground in front of the big blue house. He felt his fingers curl again.

Gloria stood up straight and fixed Tom with a stare that he saw in the window's reflection. He turned around, slowly, as she said, "Well, what's wrong with that? You're a grown man, aren't you?

Got your own life to look after, right? You let your mama do what she wants for as long as she can. She knows better than you what she needs. And as far as *age* is concerned, she's a lot younger than me, so you just watch your tongue."

Sensing a crosscurrent of meanings in this outburst, Tom chose to remain silent, knowing Gloria would continue without any encouragement from him.

Sure enough, she grabbed a feather duster and began wielding the thing like a saber, punctuating the air. "I swear to goodness, I wish somebody could tell me what happens to kids when they're grown. You wipe their noses and their fannies when they're little. Feed 'em and clothe 'em, send them to school and on out to the world, hopin' they'll find families and kids of their own. And they usually do. Then, just when you least expect it, here they come back again, knowing more than you do. Acting like you don't know nothing. Telling you what you should do. When it ain't one teaspoon's full of their business."

Tom let silence drift slowly down on the room before tentatively asking, "Is this about your kids wanting you to move again?"

"Don't you just know it is," said Gloria. "You want *your* mama to stay where she is, they want *me* to get out. They're convinced it's just a matter of time before something happens to the old neighborhood, and they want me to sell before it does. They've heard rumors, apparently. Say I'll get a lot more if I get out right now. Want me to move to a condo. A condo? Can you picture me in one of them things? Strangers right there on the other side of your living room walls and no room for a garden?" She walked over to the corner chair, picked up the armload of files, and slammed them down on the sparkling clean desk. "Listen here," she said, turning back to face Tom, "I don't care what your mama wants to do, Mr. Elliot. Unless she's up and lost her marbles since your daddy died, which I seriously doubt she has, then she's more than able to decide for herself where and how she wants to live."

Tom swallowed hard and winced. "I'm sorry, Gloria," he said. "I didn't mean to upset you." He turned back toward the window and noticed it was now raining harder than ever. "Shit. I didn't mean to upset anybody."

"Leave the swearing to the stupid, son," said Gloria.

"I'm sorry," muttered Tom.

"Quit saying you're sorry. I'm not upset. Not at you, anyway."

Tom nodded at Gloria's reflection in the window before him. After hesitating a second, he said, "Listen, you can tell your family nothing's going to happen to your neighborhood. I've heard those rumors about Pinckney Green. If that's what they're worried about, well . . . they shouldn't be."

Gloria grabbed the handle of the cleaning trolley and backed out into the hallway. "Well, I ain't movin', even if I'm the last one on the whole block. You can take that to the bank." Pulling the trolley behind her, she turned back around to face him. "And if you'll take some advice from an old lady, I suggest you leave here right now and go straight back home. You're really not looking all that good, Mr. Elliot." She gave him a wink that seemed more fuss than favor and left the room. Tom heard the cleaning cart trundle off up the hall.

He now felt sicker than ever. When he suddenly heard Gloria's footsteps returning, the sound flooded him with embarrassing relief. Tom walked over to the door and opened it. "What'd you forget to tell me?" he said, sticking his head out into the hall.

An old woman in a navy-blue dress passed by right in front of him, trailing a sweet-smelling fragrance. Surprised, Tom took a step back, swallowed hard, winced, and then sneezed, his eyes closing with the effort. When he opened them again, the old woman was standing in the shadows at the end of the hallway, looking back at him. Blinking, his eyes watering, Tom stared as she gave him a tiny half smile. Then Gloria stuck her head out of the office two doors up. "What'd you say?" she called out.

"That . . . that woman," whispered Tom, turning toward Gloria and pointing back over his shoulder. "Who is she?"

"What woman?"

Turning back, Tom saw a now empty hallway. "That old woman that just came past here," he said. "Was she with you?" He pointed again to the end of the hall, and both of them stared.

"There's nobody else in this whole place, son," said Gloria, frowning. "Like I told you, you're not looking so good. You need to go home."

And the feeling came over him like a punch to the jaw. A shiver rose up through his body, clutching his heart in its fist, and suddenly, surprisingly, all Tom Elliot wanted to do was just what Gloria said. He wanted to go home. But not to his own house with the three-car garage and the saltwater pool. Tom wanted to go back home to Wesleyan.

10

Lawrie

The ceaseless red chain of brake lights that stretched out before Lawrie was broken only by the recurrent flash of blue that reflected off the rain-slicked streets, letting everyone know this was no ordinary Monday morning traffic jam. He couldn't see the wreck from where he sat but could tell by the unmoving line of cars that he was going to be here for a while, so, grateful to have stopped for coffee before he hit this part of Meridian Street, Lawrie reached for the tall paper cup. He popped his Ford Bronco into neutral, leaned back in the seat, and turned on some music, sipping his coffee and gazing around, unbothered by the delay. This was one of the perks of being the boss. His first patient wasn't scheduled till ten.

"Rockin' Robin" sang out from the speakers just as a woman walked by on the leaf-pasted sidewalk, her Jack Russell on a short leash. Both dog and owner were fitted up against the weather, the woman in a large down jacket that transformed her already rotund shape into something akin to a Jersey Giant chicken, the Jack Russell covered from ears to tail in a red plaid raincoat that, though more than adequate for protection against the downpour, did absolutely nothing to disguise the dog's delight in splashing through every puddle it encountered. To add entertainment value to the already amusing scene, both were walking in perfect time to the song:

He rocks in the tree tops all day long
Hoppin' and a-boppin' and a-singing his song
All the little birds on Jaybird Street
Love to hear the robin go tweet, tweet, tweet

Lawrie laughed out loud.

He had a fondness for Jack Russells, despite having been bitten by a few through the years, those who, understandably, he thought, found his method of taking their temperatures highly intrusive. Perpetually optimistic about their chances of achieving whatever they put their minds to—activities usually forbidden, or at least ill-advised—the breed had a constant enthusiasm for life that always made Lawrie smile. In his experience, a Jack Russell was up for anything, even, or maybe especially, if it was something guaranteed to muddy its paws. This one was clearly having the time of its life, despite, or maybe because of, the rain. If he were a dog, Lawrie thought, he'd be a Jack Russell.

His eyes followed the pair as they took a right turn into an empty neighborhood side street where most of the houses looked dark, their curtains still drawn against the inclement weather. About three houses down on the right, a group of young women held a circle of umbrellas over a clutch of waist-high children, everyone waiting on the school bus to arrive. Lawrie looked in his rearview mirror and found the bright yellow conveyance about fifty yards back, rising out of a row of stock-still cars. Glancing back to the miserable band huddled on the wet sidewalk, the wind pushing them this way and that, he considered taking a photo to show Emlynn at an opportune moment.

"See this?" he imagined himself saying, as the two of them lay, legs entwined, on the sofa later this evening, a movie on television, a half-full bottle of wine between them, and their three large dogs sprawled out on the floor. "This, right here," he'd say, pointing to the picture and waggling his phone for emphasis, "this is what having kids is like. Standing out in the pouring rain at eight A.M. on a cold Monday morning, waiting on a school bus that's going to be at least a half hour late. It's not all little sailor suits and velvet dresses, you know."

But he didn't reach for his phone. He didn't take the photo. He already knew how Emlynn would respond. She'd just give him that Cheshire cat grin of hers, the grin that told him she knew much more than he did, no matter the quantity or quality of evidence he produced to persuade her otherwise. Lawrie loved that grin.

And it wasn't that he didn't *want* children. Whenever he'd been around Mouse's kids, they'd always seemed pretty great. Also, as Emlynn frequently told him, it was even better when the kids were your own. Apparently, you were guaranteed to be besotted. It was just that—as difficult as it was for him to admit to himself that he was this prosaic, this traditional—Lawrie thought they should be married before they had kids. They'd been together for eight years. It was past time.

He'd heard all her arguments against it. According to Emlynn, compared to the foundational love they had for each other, a wedding was an outdated, superfluous ritual purely designed for show, the marriage certificate merely a government document akin to the deed to a house. And he could see her point: he'd been to more extravagant weddings than he could count, lavish, lily-scented affairs that seemed to prioritize the spectacle far above the sacrament. Mentally sifting through the outcomes of those debt-inducing ceremonies, he found it hard to think of an enviable pair still around. The divorce rate was high, and the few couples who'd managed to stay together now appeared to be more like businesses than marriages. Emlynn never failed to point this out.

But, and Lawrie thought this was a pertinent fact, Emlynn's parents' marriage had been an unusually acrimonious one, her erratic childhood mottled by their seething anger and explosive fights. Bradley and Carmel Cates had tried to make it work in nearly every state in the Union, thinking each time that a change of scenery might change the people they were, but it never did. Although they finally divorced when Emlynn was twelve, she continued to be pulled apart by their mutual loathing, which only increased year after year until their hatred finally bore lethal fruit and they died early, in the same New Orleans hospital, within six months of each other. As their only child, Emlynn had stood at both grave sites the year she turned twenty, relieved to no longer be expected to serve as intermediary for two such incendiary forces and determined never to be joined in matrimony herself. It was the only superstition he'd ever known her to have.

By contrast, Lawrie's parents had had a happy marriage; he'd seen it from the inside and knew this to be true. The only disagreements he'd ever witnessed between Lawrence and Margaret had been embroidered with the same thread of humor that ran through all their interactions, the result, he supposed, of their close childhood friendship—they all knew this story by heart—one that had turned early on into love. He knew this was rare, he didn't have to be told, but the marks of a happy childhood can be carved into the psyche just as deeply as those of an unhappy one, and Lawrie remained convinced of the possibility of lifelong loves.

Of course, Emlynn was mad at him at the moment, had been since Saturday night. A spasm of regret made Lawrie beat his palm on the steering wheel. His brother had humiliated Emlynn at that dinner, and even provoked the normally temperate Mouse into a pugnacity he'd rarely seen her display. But Emlynn had told Lawrie *he* was the one who'd acted like a big jerk, the one who'd embarrassed her so much that she'd left the table.

Thinking of Tom made Lawrie's jaw tighten. He'd envisioned knocking the shit out of his brother several times this morning alone, but strangely, this only made him feel worse. They'd never had an out-and-out fight. Maybe it would've been better if they had. Maybe keeping feelings on simmer like they'd always done was far worse in the long run than letting them boil right on over. Lawrie took another sip of hot coffee and laid his head back on the seat, the blue lights from the police cars up ahead flashing inside of his car.

Most of the time Tommy was easy to ignore, living all the way up in Atlanta—and married to a woman whose indifference toward her husband's family was as obvious as an odor. If it wasn't for those obligatory occasions at which everyone's presence was an unspoken agreement—those weddings, graduations, and deaths—Lawrie would hardly have to see his brother at all. This lack of proximity allowed him to pretend their relationship was normal. Or at least it usually did.

As the rain hammered the roof of his car, Lawrie thought about some of the other brothers he'd known growing up. There'd been the Hulseys, Harvey and Sam, who'd lived in the house around the corner, one of them nearly always sporting a black eye or busted lip courtesy of the other. And the Wingos, DeWitt and Denny, who'd stolen each other's girlfriends all through high school, resulting in a long-running minor-league soap opera, the details of which dominated the lunch tables of Wesleyan High for the whole four years of their tenure. Despite those cantankerous childhood relationships, both pairs of brothers were best friends today. Lawrie had seen them together often enough to know this as fact.

Was his dislike of his brother (and let's face it, Lawrie thought, surely that's what it was, on *both* sides) made worse because they were twins? Weren't those special couples meant to be closer than normal the whole of their lives? Hell, twins could supposedly tell what each other was thinking and feeling despite being oceans apart. He'd seen a documentary once. Being the exception that proved the rule lacked any comfort for Lawrie.

His taste in music was eclectic, and "Rockin' Robin" had now been replaced by Duke Ellington. In between sips of sugary coffee, Lawrie drummed out the beat to "Take the A Train" on the steering wheel as the traffic began to creep forward a foot at a time until it crawled past the wreck that had so scrambled the schedules of Wesleyan's morning commuters. The two responsible vehicles had been moved to the side of the road. The broken taillights of a Mercedes glowered at the crumpled front end of an old Chevy as their clearly depressed owners stood, shoulders sagging identically, by a police car in the rain. Feeling that universal mixture of empathy and relief, Lawrie inched past, trying not to stare, then, his way clear, he hit the gas, heading for the animal clinic that bore his name on the door.

⁕

Though it hadn't been spared the migrations of modern society, Wesleyan still boasted a generous number of genuine natives, those who not only were born here but had chosen to stay for the whole of their lives. This stalwart chunk of the population, while often voicing support for growth and diversity in general, tended to be utterly appalled when the general became specific, as it had in recent years on the west side of town. The area's close proximity to the highway, along with its tempting swaths of virgin land, had lured developers from all over the region, those whose flagrant confidence in both the necessity and the aesthetic appeal of their mixed-use office complexes and multifamily housing units, not to mention their tacit threats of lawsuits should they be denied their requests, generally overwhelmed the ability of Wesleyan's City Council to deny any zoning changes they asked for. One by one, most of the old houses in this part of town had been torn down, replaced with structures whose designs were more in keeping with what was expected in 2019.

As the sole remaining cottage on the once entirely residential Lullwater Road, the Elliot Animal Clinic stood out, its location attracting new clients who'd recently moved to the area, its historic charm comforting those old ones so reluctant to see anything change. With its tall sash windows still in place and its four aged sweet gum trees standing sentry, one at each corner, it nestled in the middle of the street's new sleek, interchangeable buildings like a gilt-edged fairy tale in a row of contemporary novels. Despite the hand-painted sign in the yard, the only real clue that the sweet old house was, in fact, a veterinary clinic came when you pulled into the parking lot out back, where the addition of a surgery wing was both surprising and impressive. It gave Lawrie a thrill every time he came up the brick driveway.

The rain had only increased by the time he saw the crowded parking lot, and he was grateful for the one space that remained empty and reserved just for him. It was always this way on Monday morning. A sore paw, an upset stomach. Niggling little issues that seemed easy to ignore on a Friday afternoon invariably became worrisome as the weekend wore on. But Lawrie loved the chaos, loved meeting people who loved their pets, loved being able to help a sick animal who couldn't verbally tell him where it hurt.

Pulling into his spot, he switched off the car and swiveled around in his seat to grab his umbrella off the back floorboard. This effort proved to be pointless the moment he opened the door. A gust of wind blew the umbrella inside out and threw a bucket of rain right into his face. Pulling his raincoat up over his head, Lawrie tucked the useless umbrella under his arm and ran for the clinic's side door. As an exhalation of wind blew him inside, he heard something that was both unpleasant and rare: the raised voice of his normally placid receptionist, Rosie.

Barely five foot two and blond as a child, with bovine eyes that tended to widen dramatically whenever she was making a point, Rosie Long ran the front desk with a calmness a scout leader would envy. Lawrie had watched her cry with grief-stricken families as they said goodbye to their pets as well as seen her silence an aggressive dog or combative client by narrowing those big eyes down to slits and settling her voice into a steely register unexpected from someone so small. It was that voice he heard now as he shook out his inverted umbrella and jammed it hastily into a corner.

"I appreciate your problem, ma'am. But as I've told you three times already, we are *not* an animal shelter. You need to take . . .

What's his name again? Jubal? Yes, well, you need to take Jubal here to a rescue facility. There are two of them, right there on that sheet of paper I gave you, the one you are holding in your hand."

The voice that answered Rosie's was older, and icy. Condescension dripped off every drawling syllable with an acidic sweetness unique to a certain type of privileged Southern female.

"My *dear*," said the woman, "you don't seem to be *capable* of grasping my predicament. As I told you, I am on my way back home and have neither the time nor the inclination to cart this creature all over town when *you* can so easily take him off my hands. My mother-in-law's neighbor, Mrs. Bentley Green? A valued client of yours, I believe... You see her Pomeranian? Well, she will be so disappointed when I tell her you *flatly refused* to help me out."

Listening outside the door, Lawrie heard the scrape of a chair and knew Rosie had stood up. Hitching a smile onto his face, he entered the waiting room, where the assembled clients, both human and animal, sat staring, all clearly enjoying the show. Even Gatsby, Harriet Spalding's Chihuahua, who tended to yap without ceasing whenever he found himself in this room, was apparently rendered mute by the palpable tension that filled the air every bit as much as the heavy scent of fake rose perfume emanating from the woman with the leash in her hand.

"Can I help out here?" Lawrie asked, meeting Rosie's narrowed eyes with what he hoped was a calming look.

"Yes, Doctor," she began, "I was just trying to—"

"You most certainly *can* help," interrupted the woman standing in front of the counter in a cinch-belted, red patent leather raincoat. She took a step closer to Lawrie, deliberately turning her back to Rosie. "As I was telling your... your... *adjutant*... here... my mother-in-law passed away last week. Her funeral was yesterday—and thank God the weather wasn't like it is today—but she had this *dog* here..." She pointed toward the floor with a finger whose nail exactly matched the color of her raincoat. "Lord *knows*, we can't take him with us all the way back up to Lynchburg. Mercer, that's my husband, he's allergic. He's out there in the car right now, sneezing his fool head off. We're heading back home today and I'm sure *you* can appreciate the fact that I don't have time to drive all over Elberta County to some *rescue facility* when you all are more than able to take him here." Turning slightly, she somehow managed to glare at Rosie and smile sweetly at Lawrie at the same time.

While she was speaking, Lawrie's eyes had gone to the floor, where a wetly despondent Clumber spaniel sat in a puddle of rainwater, obviously attempting to maintain his innate dignity despite his unfortunate state. His four paws were caked with red mud. Instinctively, Lawrie bent down and scratched the dog behind the ears, eliciting a grateful wag of the tail. When he stood back up and glanced at Rosie, he saw she was refusing to look at the dog. She gave him a mutinous stare, eyes widening to nearly twice their normal size, and said, "As I *tried* to tell her, the nearest shelter is only five minutes from here and they are better equipped to..."

"Listen here, Gidget," said the woman, dropping all pretense and bending toward Rosie, "it says 'animal clinic' right out there on your sign and I'm—"

"Yes! It says *clinic*, not *shelter*! There's a diff—"

"Whoa, whoa!" said Lawrie, holding up one hand. Unlike Rosie, he'd looked the spaniel in the eyes and knew what he was going to do. Reaching over, he took the dog's leash from the woman's hands. "You just be on your way, ma'am. We'll take care of Jubal here."

"Well. Now. Thank *you* very much," she said, rubbing her hands down the front of her coat as if to erase any undesirable trace of wet dog. Needlessly tightening her red belt with a jerk, she turned to go, but unable to resist throwing one last defiant look at Rosie, she added, "Just see how *easy* that was, my dear?" The woman opened the door, and a wet wind rushed into the room, circled around the assembled clients, and pushed the door shut behind her with an emphatic bang. No one, particularly Jubal, seemed sorry to see her go.

"What a *bitch*!" Harriet Spalding said, loudly. Gatsby underscored his owner's assessment with a yipping rant at full volume, and everyone in the waiting room paused for a half second, then burst out in full-throated laughter, signaling their collective agreement before looking back down at their phones.

Lawrie cocked his head toward Rosie, and the two of them moved out into the hallway and down to Lawrie's office, Jubal padding along in silence behind, his fortunes having apparently changed. Closing the door, Lawrie turned quickly to Rosie and held up his hands.

"Before you start, what'd you expect me to do? Just look at this guy." Both gazed down at the dog, who gave them a hesitant stare. Rosie exhaled hard and closed her eyes.

"Yes, all right. But that woman was so . . . so . . ."

"I know. Miss Spalding pretty much nailed it. Which is the main reason I couldn't let her walk out of here, in the pouring rain, with this sweet guy." Lawrie sat down at his desk, patted his knees enthusiastically, and Jubal went to him immediately, placing his large head in Lawrie's lap and staring up at his savior in complete adoration. "See there? He's saying thank you."

Rosie sank down in the chair by the bookcase, pushing a large dog bed aside with her foot. "Okay," she sighed. "But what do *you* plan to do with him? I doubt Emlynn wants another dog. You've got three."

Lawrie thought of Eric, Ginger, and Jack, all oversize, and all acquired in similar fashion, and slowly shook his head. "We'd have to get a bigger bed," he said.

"Exactly," said Rosie.

The two of them stared at Jubal, whose unruly white fur, jowly face, and sober expression called to mind a sapient old Southern lawyer. "I gotta say," said Rosie, "he's one of the cutest dogs I think I've ever seen. He sure doesn't look like a mutt."

"This guy?" said Lawrie, placing his hands on either side of Jubal's face. "This fellow is no mutt. This is a Clumber spaniel, and the only breeder of these that I know of anywhere around here is way up in Virginia. I guess I could call him."

"You're not thinking of sending him back to a *breeder*? Look at him. He's been a pet for who knows how long, and he's just lost a person who obviously loved him. Poor guy. He's probably been scared to death he'd have to go live with Brunhild and the sneezing Mercer."

The knock was loud, and the door opened immediately after it sounded. Harriet Spalding pushed her head in, Gatsby tucked up under her arm. "Give me that leash," she said, firmly. "You and I both know your mother needs a dog, Lawrie Elliot, and this one was sent here especially for her, I can feel it. I'll get him cleaned up and take him over to Margaret as soon as you trim Gatsby's toenails."

11

Margaret

Love lifted me,
Love lifted me.
When nothing else could help,
Love lifted me.

Like a Gordian knot of old Baptist words, the lyrics were fixed in her head. Margaret had tried to convince herself she'd not heard them, but she hadn't succeeded at all. The song remained wedged in her brain no matter how hard she tried to ignore it, and Margaret had tried since Saturday night.

All day the rain had poured from the skies above Wesleyan with an intensity that never ebbed a fraction. Unwilling to venture outside in the torrent, she had spent the better part of this dark Monday cleaning house, grateful for the mindless occupation, and playing Lawrence's old Beatles records as loud as she could to drown out the hymn that was stuck in her head, a hymn she hadn't even known she remembered.

She'd polished the hardwoods, stripped all the beds, and washed all the linens—going so far as to iron all the sheets—and finished off this overreach of domesticity with so many spritzes of Emlynn's lavender room spray that the whole house now smelled like a French garden, one in which the dinner she was cooking—roast chicken, green beans, and potatoes—mingled with woodsmoke from the fire she'd just built in the den. It was a comforting, slightly intoxicating aroma, and it cheered her a bit. She just wished the day could be a bit longer.

Margaret dreaded going to bed tonight and halfway wished she had some of those sleeping pills Sarah Lou Cobb had told her about. Sarah Lou had started taking them when her son, Bart, had come home from Georgia Southern with a fiancée he'd met on spring break, a divorcée twelve years his senior who'd insisted on calling Sarah Lou "Mother Cobb." She'd told Margaret the pills really helped, but her husband, Cecil, had flushed them all down the toilet after he found her sleepwalking down the middle of Pretty Branch Drive in the nightgown he'd given her for their twenty-fifth anniversary, a garment Sarah Lou had always been embarrassed to wear with the lights on. Still, Margaret thought she might risk taking one of Sarah Lou's pills if she had it tonight. She didn't want to dream again. She was too afraid of what she might see.

"Dear Prudence" was playing when Margaret heard a loud knock on the front door. Unable to imagine who it could be on such a stormy afternoon, she peered round the corner, the feather duster still in her hand, and jumped when she saw Harriet's face staring back at her, the old woman's nose pressed hard against the window, Gatsby held tight in her arms.

Duster still in her hand, Margaret hurried down the hallway, her slippers slapping against the clean floor. "What on earth are you doing out in this..." She opened the door and paused, her attention drawn immediately downward to where a large white dog with the face of a judge stood looking up at her as though trying to answer a difficult question. Margaret held the dog's gaze for a moment, then stepped aside to let them all in out of the rain.

The big dog dripped onto the entry hall rug as he looked around, assessing these new surroundings. "Don't worry," said Harriet, setting Gatsby down and bending toward the white dog. "I brought a towel to dry him off. And we've just left the groomer, so he's as clean as the day he was born." The spaniel lifted his fluffy paws one by one as she dried them, never taking his eyes off Margaret.

"His name's Jubal," said Harriet, standing up and rubbing the small of her back. "He's a great-looking boy, don't you think?" Margaret could've sworn Jubal returned Harriet's proud smile with one of his own.

Jubal then chose that moment to shake himself off with all the energy he could muster, and Margaret took a step back, sitting down hard on the stairs. When the shake had traveled from shoulders to tail, the dog walked over and placed his big head on her knees, his brown eyes looking up at her from beneath an unruly fringe of thick fur. This was a very successful move, and Margaret would've bet anything the dog knew it.

"Come on," said Harriet, picking up Jubal's leash and giving it a firm tug. "Let's take him to the den so you two can get a better look at each other." The dog lifted his head from Margaret's lap and followed Harriet and Gatsby, looking back over his shoulder as he was led off down the hall. Margaret tried to frown but discovered she couldn't.

Harriet took off her raincoat and hung it on the peg in the hall, turned to cross into the den, where she unleashed Jubal, then went to stand by the fire. "Perfect day for this," she said, backing up to the flames. "I may do the same thing when we get back home."

Margaret turned down the stereo and stared straight at Harriet, eyebrows raised in an unspoken question.

"Oh, okay," said Harriet, sighing heavily "His owner died. Her daughter-in-law tried to dump him at Lawrie's clinic like a sack of rotten potatoes. Gatsby and I were there. We saw the whole thing. Horrible woman. You couldn't imagine. So, Jubal here is much better off without *her*. Trust me, Margaret. This is meant to be. This dog needs you. And after what you told me at lunch on Saturday, you need him."

"So, you *do* think I'm crazy."

"Not in the least," said Harriet, brushing raindrops off her plaid skirt. "But I think things might be just starting to happen. It's a feeling I have. I'd bet you anything your aunt Edith hasn't told you all she wants you to know. Not yet."

Margaret's phone started to ring in the kitchen, and she crossed the hallway to get it. Lawrie's number stared up from the screen. "Well, hello there," she answered.

"Hey, Mama," said Lawrie. "I should've called you sooner, but it's been nonstop here today. Look, I need to tell you something. Miss Spalding's going to be coming by your place this afternoon and—"

"She's here now," said Margaret. "And she's not alone."

"Oh. Shoot. Well, did she explain about Jubal? I mean, he's really got nowhere else to go, and I *did* say I'd get you a dog for your birthday. Can we call him a present? Will you keep him?"

Margaret suddenly saw herself lying in bed awake tonight, waiting for Aunt Edith to appear in her room. She felt her stomach clench. Looking across into the den, she could see the big Clumber spaniel staring at her, his kind eyes shining in the firelight. "Yes, I'll keep him," she said, suddenly certain. She heard Harriet applaud loudly.

Margaret talked Harriet into staying for dinner, which wasn't hard, and as the two of them ate, she laid the newspaper clipping, the small, faded photograph of the four people, and the printout of the house on the beach between them on the kitchen table, anxious to hear just what her friend thought.

Squinting, Harriet stared down at the photo, then back up at Margaret, chewing thoughtfully. "Well, there's a resemblance, I can't deny it," she said. "Like you say, around the eyes. But at least you know for certain this is what Aunt Edith's been trying to give you. Didn't you tell me she's been holding a yellow envelope in her hands every time you've seen her?"

Margaret nodded.

"But as far as this house goes . . ." Harriet picked up the printout and studied the cottage. "I haven't a clue. But I wouldn't worry too much about it. Now that you've gotten your hands on what was in that yellow envelope, I'd bet your aunt Edith will see to it you find out the whole story. Like I say, she's not done with you."

"Oh no, she's not done," said Margaret. "Harriet, I heard *music* Saturday night. Right after I opened that envelope. An old hymn that was one of her favorites. That piano in there was playing it loud enough for the devil himself to hear. No, Aunt Edith's not done with me yet." Margaret slipped a piece of chicken to Jubal, who was leaning against her right leg.

"Don't you start feeding him from the table, or he'll expect it every day."

"I don't care," said Margaret. "He's had a rough day. You said so yourself. Pass me some more potatoes."

It was dark by the time Harriet picked up a snoring Gatsby and left. Kitchen cleared and bath taken, Margaret now lay under a quilt on the den's tapestry sofa in her pajamas, with her new dog curled up on her feet while sheets of rain beat against the dark windows. As she clicked her way through TV channels, she could see the wet poplar branches whirling around in the wind.

In anticipation of Halloween, the old movie channel had been showing films appropriate for the season, and Margaret was pleased to see that *Rebecca* was on. She turned up the sound and tossed the remote over onto the ottoman. "This is my favorite part," she said, wriggling her toes underneath Jubal, who sighed a deep sigh of contentment. "When they pull up to Manderley in the rain and she meets Mrs. Danvers for the first time. She should've fired the woman that very afternoon. Saved everybody a world of trouble."

As the flickering lights from the old black-and-white movie waltzed across the den, Margaret reached for the mug of hot chocolate she'd only just made, then realized with a curse she'd left it behind in the kitchen. The quilt fell to the floor as she got up. She padded across the shadowed hallway, her thick socks slipping a little on the just-polished hardwood, as a low rumble of thunder echoed off in the distance. In the dark kitchen, her fingers searched for the light switch on the wall.

She saw the little boy immediately. Briefly illuminated by a flash of lightning, he stood by the window at the end of the room, clad in overalls and a plaid shirt. He held the printout of the cottage tight in one hand, and Margaret looked toward the refrigerator door and saw, sure enough, it was no longer hanging there. She turned back to stare at the boy, and for a moment, she thought he was one of her sons, so alike were all three in appearance. But of course, he wasn't. He couldn't be. And besides, Margaret knew who he was.

She reached for the counter, swaying slightly in the darkness. And then the edges of the room started to melt, and Margaret Elliot faded away into another crystal-clear dream.

The men were outside in the pecan grove again. It was the last Saturday in October.

Sixteen-year-old Margaret could see them through her open bedroom window, spreading white tarps under the trees to catch the pecans that would rain down when they hit the limbs with those tall bamboo poles. The same men came back every fall; she recognized most of the faces and remembered most of the names. From her spot on the window seat, she heard Wink McCoy before she saw him; his laugh always sounded like hiccups. There was Sterling Bass, who had a face like a gingersnap, wore red socks, and slipped her Bit-O-Honeys when nobody was looking. And old Luther Winslett, who'd run over her cat years ago and still hung his head at the memory whenever he saw her. They'd all be at supper today, she supposed.

Margaret loved the fall harvest. It was that one time every year when the big white house shed its quiet serenity and was awash in activity and sound. Soon, pecans would start hitting the ground like thunderstorm rain. There'd be laughter and stories around the long dining room table. It was a magical month, and she had a front-row seat to it all.

The air outside smelled like freshly cut grass and the breeze blowing in through the window carried the men's voices inside it, each one threading through the others, creating a chorus Margaret knew well. High above the pecan trees, as thin as the pages of a Bible, clouds drifted and swung through the blue sky. They looked like white linen sheets on a line. Margaret felt perfectly happy. Wrapping her arms around her knees, she laid her head on the side of the window and watched.

Then something caught her eye, and looking down, she saw a tall, dark-haired young man standing at the edge of the hyacinth garden, staring off into the shade of the trees. He held his hands in front of his chest, fingers laced tight together as if in study or prayer, and when he took a small step backwards, she was sure he was getting ready to leave without anyone noticing. She wanted to tell him to wait. But then she saw Luther Winslett approach him. Old Luther put a gnarled hand on the young man's slim shoulder, and his voice rose up through Margaret's window, as present and clear as though she were standing beside him.

"Here, son. Take this." Luther handed the boy a long bamboo pole. "Start off with one of them smaller trees over there on the edges. Just stick this thing up and bang it against one of them limbs, and pecans will rain down on you like hailstones. You'll get the hang of it quick. Money's good, food's better, and the work don't last but a month or so. Most of us are here every year. I reckon anybody can do anything in the world for a month."

The young man dipped his head, looked up sideways at Luther, and gave him a dubious smile. "I didn't really come here to work. I was just looking for someone."

"Well, who you looking for?" Luther asked, cocking his head. But the young man stayed silent. Luther waited, a quizzical look on his face. He pointed back toward the house. "Okay then, the ladies are cooking inside there. You go knock on the back door and they'll help you."

Luther clapped the young man hard on the shoulder, then ambled off toward the other side of the grove. The young man stood where he was, watching him go, and once again, Margaret was sure he was going to leave. He took a few hesitant steps forward and then, almost as though he'd heard her call out his name, he wheeled around and looked straight up at her window.

Instinctively, she moved to pull back into shadow, but something made her stop and remain where she was. Facing the sun, holding her breath, Margaret sat as still as she could, her eyes locked on his, while the air in the room seemed to quicken like that second before the first flash of heat lightning that signals a storm. Could he see her from this far away? Margaret couldn't be sure. But his eyes stayed on her window till her own stung from not blinking, and then, without warning, he turned and headed out under the trees. As she watched, he disappeared into shade as dark and green as creek water.

"I see you," a voice rang out from below. Margaret's head bent sharply *downward, and there, right beneath her window, stood Lawrence, looking up from a circle of sunlight, with a grin on his face. Her heart leapt at the sight of him, something it had just started doing whenever she was around her old friend. "I'll be right down," she called. Lawrence nodded and grinned, pointing toward the huge oak tree that stood at the side of the yard, and she waved her agreement. That old live oak with its curtains of gray Spanish moss...*

Most humans are born with a deep desire to learn how to draw a straight line, one that stretches taut between cause and effect, action and consequence, sin and retribution. "I was there, now I'm here, and I know just how that happened." Everyone longs for that clarity. It's how we make sense of our lives. But when she came to, Margaret Elliot had no idea what had caused her to wake up on her kitchen floor, nose to nose with a dog.

She was lying on her back with a proprietary paw on her belly. It took her a second to remember her name. She tried to sit up, but Jubal was keeping his paw where it was. Having so recently lost his previous owner in worrisomely similar circumstances, he wasn't taking any chances with this one. Margaret reached up and placed her hand on the dog's head. "Seriously," she said, trying to sound calmer than she actually felt, "I'm fine."

Jubal took a cautious step back, allowing Margaret to sit up but keeping both eyes focused on her as she placed a hand on a chair and then slowly stood. She moved to the sink to pour herself a small glass of water and sipped it slowly, leaning against the counter, feeling Jubal's stare like a hand on her back. She glanced over to the refrigerator. The photo of the cottage was back on the door. Margaret reached out and removed it, holding it tight in her hands.

The dark-haired young man in her dream had been evaporating even as Margaret's eyelids fluttered open while she lay there on the floor, but in that liminal space, in that brief lucid moment, Margaret knew who she'd seen, what she'd remembered. Her hand shook as she refilled her glass. The movie forgotten, she suddenly felt tired right down to her bones. "Let's you and me go on up to bed," she said, and Jubal followed her out of the kitchen.

The dog paused briefly at the den door. Margaret had pulled Po'boy's old bed onto the hearthrug in front of the fire, but Jubal merely regarded it now with the coolness of an imperious tourist who'd been shown to a room lacking a view. The big spaniel turned on his paws without a backwards look and followed Margaret upstairs, where he leapt up onto her four-poster without effort or invitation as though he knew this was where he was needed. And the dog was certainly right. "Aunt Edith was one thing," Margaret said, climbing in beside him and pulling the blankets up to her chin, "but one ghost in my life is more than enough, don't you think?" Jubal snuggled up closer and laid his head on her thigh.

Then, just a few hours later, the dog gave Margaret Elliot what she'd needed since the night of Aunt Edith's first visit. He gave her confirmation.

She'd opened Lawrence's old copy of *And Then There Were None*, hoping to read until she got sleepy, but it was no use. She couldn't concentrate. So, she lay on her back in the darkness while the rain evaporated into mist and the fat, full face of the moon finally pushed its way out from behind the thick clouds. Water was still dripping loudly from the leaves of the trees, and this time Margaret sensed Aunt Edith long before she saw her. Diverging from her usual position at the foot of the bed, the old lady now stood outside on the wet balcony, raindrops on her black shoes.

No longer holding the yellow envelope, Aunt Edith's hands were spread wide on the balcony railing, and she gazed off through the darkness as though she were waiting for someone to come down the street. Margaret sat up in bed, and Jubal did the same. She noticed immediately the big dog was staring at Aunt Edith, too, his black nose twitching as though being tickled by the flowery fragrance of Arpège perfume. Margaret watched him for a long minute to make sure, following his unblinking stare straight out the window to where her aunt stood in the moonlight. Then she kissed Jubal on top of his head.

Margaret valued the opinions of dogs. She remembered the day she'd taken the kids on a summer picnic to Griffin Park when the boys had still just been toddlers. They'd brought Tinker, the dachshund, along with them as usual, and when a stranger approached to ask directions to Wesleyan Square (she'd had only a second to think that seemed strange; you couldn't drive into Wesleyan without passing the square), Tinker, whose adoration of all humanity had heretofore been as indiscriminate as a saint's, suddenly leapt to his paws and lunged at the man, teeth bared and growling. The stranger had scurried off out of the park and the very next week they saw in the paper that the same man had been arrested over in Sunnyvale for indecent exposure. Margaret had regarded the dachshund differently from then on. Dogs knew things humans did not.

So, both Margaret and Jubal watched as Aunt Edith stayed where she was for a minute or more, still looking off up Albemarle Way. Then they saw her slowly turn around, a hint of a smile on her face. As she faded away, car lights flashed, circling Margaret's bedroom. And two minutes later, she and Jubal heard a loud knock on the door.

12

Mouse

Two days of rain had washed the world clean, and if Mouse hadn't been so miserable, she might have liked sitting here beside the river in Seabrook. From her table in the restaurant's garden, the view was almost hypnotic, the water slowly rolling past, long ribbons of October sunlight alive on its surface. She could imagine herself on another day, in another year, gazing out at the bright river in total contentment. As it was, though, today her right leg kept bouncing up and down as though she were keeping time to a reel. Mouse uncrossed her legs, took a sip of water, and picked up the leather-bound menu, her eyes moving left to right without focus.

Why had she lied to Nick about having lunch with Kitty Goldsmith today? In the disorderly dance of the morning—one that had consisted of locating the menu for an upcoming retirement party that she'd mistakenly left in the trunk of her car but was, for a brief, desperate moment, certain she'd lost, as well as disposing of the skeletal remains of something Dinky the cat had left on the living room rug—when Nick had asked about her plans for the day, she'd lied. Stood right there in front of her husband and lied like a politician. Told him she was meeting with her team about the baby shower they were doing for Lucy-Jewel Adcock next weekend. "A working lunch," she'd said, without batting an eye. She never lied to Nicky.

Unable to focus on the menu, Mouse closed it with a loud snap. Lies are insidious, she thought. However casual and innocuous they seem when first uttered, the littlest one can begin to unravel that blanket of trust that covers a relationship, keeping it warm and protected. Starting small—just a tiny frazzle on the corner, a loose thread that nobody notices, nobody takes the time to repair, but one that's liable to catch on anything—annoyance, exhaustion, stress—until it eventually rends the whole cloth. She'd seen it happen with some of her friends.

Mouse shook her head sharply, a tiny cleansing spasm. She knew why she'd lied. It was because of what'd she said to Kitty at Paris's party last Saturday. She winced at the memory and recrossed her legs.

Why, oh *why*, had she said it? Had it been because Kitty was so free with her secrets it felt like permission for Mouse to be free with her own? No, it had been something else. Looking back over that moment, Mouse remembered that old woman she'd seen standing under the trees that day, the one who'd smiled at Mouse like she knew her, like she understood, like she was giving Mouse some sort of overt encouragement. The next thing Mouse knew she was blurting out something she'd not even yet managed to adequately articulate in her own mind.

An ugly image crept back into her head, and as if her thoughts were suddenly audible, Mouse looked around her, halfway expecting stares. She could see Nick as if through a dirty window, cozied up with someone who was much younger and prettier than she was. Someone who could make him laugh as she had once done. Someone without a care in the world. Nicky deserved nothing less. Her leg began bouncing again. Was she ever going to climb out of this hole she was in?

Mouse had yet to have a serious boyfriend when she met Nicholas Moretti. The pickings at Wesleyan High had been slim. When she'd arrived at Hyde Park after graduation, she'd been so focused on keeping up with her grueling schedule of classes, dating had been her lowest priority. Despite her parents' example, she'd never really believed in a soul mate. There were so many people on the planet, how was it possible there was only one perfect person for anyone? But then Nick had appeared, looking like a young Al Pacino, and all the colors in her world seemed to change to deeper, brighter hues, almost as though there'd been a film over her eyes until then.

Mouse had believed everything Nick ever told her, from that first time she'd spoken to the young doctor at a party in a grand old apartment just off Washington Square. She'd been hired at the last minute by one of her friends who'd just graduated, started a catering business, and was, on that weekend, sorely understaffed. Mouse and Nick had met in the kitchen when he'd stuck his head around the door to see if there was any ginger ale in the house. She'd rooted around in the refrigerator till she found some, and the two of them had ended up talking all night, Nick leaning against the sink and Mouse sitting on the counter. Nobody in Wesleyan looked like Nick Moretti. Her friend had fired Mouse the next day, and she and Nicky moved in together three short weeks later.

Optimistic and cheerful, Nick took things as they came, never borrowing trouble from a day so far out in the future it couldn't clearly be seen. It was, she figured, what made him such a good doctor. He just naturally made people feel better than they had any right to be. What a contrast they had lately become.

Mouse was ashamed to tell Nick how depressed she'd been, and then ashamed that she felt ashamed. She also worried that if she *did* tell him—or told anyone—then this... this *thing* might become visible, its edges growing sharper and harder for her to ignore. And ignoring these feelings until they got better was the only thing Mouse could think of to do.

But like rolls of fat escaping from a dress three sizes too tight, her dark emotions were finding new ways to make themselves seen. She was snappish and sleepless, and she'd lost too much weight. How could Nicky not notice? Those jeans he'd always said cupped her just right? Now they hung off her butt like a pair of old curtains. She'd stuffed the things in the back of the closet where she couldn't see them, planning to dig them out when she was back to herself. She knew she often seemed sullen and quiet, even as inside her head she was frantically searching for something positive and cheerful to say. It was only when she was sure Nicky had noticed, when he asked her what the matter was, that she managed to pull herself up into something resembling her usual self. It was like trying to keep the tip of her nose out of deep water.

But other things had recently started to happen as well. Things that were hard, even for Mouse, to explain. She squirmed a bit in her chair, picturing those five ugly fleece pullovers she'd ordered off QVC only last night. She'd taken to shopping on TV whenever Nick was on a late call at the hospital, so often the perky presenters sometimes recognized her name and put her on air. Chrissy Habersham. That was her alias. It sounded like a name off a soap opera. As Chrissy, Mouse had ordered items she'd never wear; the unopened boxes were hidden behind an old exercise bike in the basement. Two pairs of daisy-patterned capri pants. *Two*. A chunky gold-plated bracelet with a big letter "C" in the middle. A low-cut silk blouse the color of a honey-baked ham. And... Mouse lowered her chin... there was the incident with that young boy up at Davidson College, the one who'd helped Ben carry his cases into the dorm. She shuddered, glancing around once again. She could feel her face turning red. There was so much Nick didn't know.

If she couldn't snap out of this, Mouse was afraid Nicky was going to get tired of her and find someone else. It happened. She knew that it happened. And who'd blame him? Although it had been a ridiculous notion when she'd first thought it, increasingly, at night when she slipped out of bed and went to sit in the den by herself, it was becoming more and more of a worry. She was losing her grip on the reins.

Mouse had told no one her fears, and could think of no one to tell, until she'd stunned herself by blurting it out to Kitty Goldsmith, a woman she only halfway remembered, and one whose personality was diametrically opposed to her own. All because some old woman had smiled at her sympathetically from across the backyard. What was wrong with her? Mouse had to set Kitty straight before she told anyone else, and she had to do it today.

Hearing loud laughter, she turned just as the restaurant door opened and Kitty came through in a kaleidoscopic dress that made her look for all the world like some exotic bird. High heels clicking on the stone patio, she wove her way through the tables with an unstudied nonchalance, seemingly unaware of the stares her presence engendered, and waved expansively at Mouse when she saw her, an armful of gold bracelets jangling like cymbals in the crisp fall air.

Mouse looked down at her black pants and gray sweater. Sure, the sweater was cashmere, she thought, as she plucked one of Dinky's yellow hairs from her chest, and she was wearing that expensive gold locket Nicky had given her last Christmas, the one with her children's photos inside, but Mouse still wondered if she should have made more of an effort. She'd bet Kitty Goldsmith made every woman she met feel this way, and Mouse wondered if it might be intentional.

"One thing you may not remember about me, honey," Kitty said, as she bent to hug Mouse before sitting down in a cloud of musky fragrance, "I am *always* late." Kitty tossed a Prada bag onto the empty chair beside her, leaned back, and crossed her long legs. "I just can't seem to help it. I'm one of those people who needs a couple extra hours in every single day." She flashed a white-toothed smile at Mouse, one so artless and real that Mouse couldn't help but return it.

"That's a beautiful dress," said Mouse, curious where a person might find the guts to wear something so loud. These days she ordered most of her clothes from J.Crew.

Kitty held her arms out in front of her, staring at her billowing sleeves. "No kidding," she said. "I bought it straight outta the window of Bergdorf Goodman when I was up in the Big Apple with Vincent last spring. Dreese Van No-ten. Took me two months to learn how to pronounce that." She laughed. "What can I say, I like color. Cheers me up." She picked up the menu and opened it. "So, what you gettin'? I'd get the rib eye, but I'd just have to throw it up later."

Mouse stared, and Kitty laughed her yodeling laugh once again. "Just kiddin'! No, I'm gonna have the Cobb salad. I've had it before and it's good. Wanna split a bottle of Chardonnay?"

When their dishes were nearly empty and they were on their third glass of wine, Kitty reached into her bag, pulled out a black business card, and waved it around in the air. "Now," she said, "besides the fact that I think you and me have been given a second chance to finally be *real* good friends, here's the main reason I wanted to meet you today. See, I just felt so damn bad for you at Paris's shindig on Saturday that I wanted to do somethin'. Lord knows, there's a lot of things I'm not good at, but when it comes to findin' out if my husband is cheatin' or not, honey, I'm the best there is. One thing I got from my mama."

Mouse swallowed hard. "Listen," she said, "that's what I wanted to tell you today. Kitty, I should never have said that. I . . . I haven't been myself lately. It'll get better. I just need a little more time. But I never meant that Nick . . . my husband . . . would . . . you know . . . ever have . . . an *affair*." She whispered the last word as though it were profane.

"You're worried that he could, though, am I right?" Kitty flipped open her handbag and took out a small mirror, checking her teeth for wayward spinach. "I mean that's what you said at Paris's party, and I could tell by the way you said it, you weren't jokin'." She applied some fresh red lipstick and put the mirror back into her purse. "It's nothing to be ashamed of," she continued. "Honey, I have *been* there. More than a couple of times. And with Vincent, poor little bastard, sometimes he's been cheatin', and sometimes not. But I'll tell you this for damn sure, every time he has been, he's paid for it. Last time was two and a half years ago, and between you and me, that little romp cost him so much I don't think he'll *ever* try it again." As proof, Kitty pulled back the sleeve of her dress to reveal a bracelet with diamonds as big as her molars wrapped around her thin wrist. "Vinnie is *real* fond of his money. Got more than Croesus but still plays the lottery two times a week. Trust me, he hated to part with how much it took to buy this." She twirled the bracelet around, the diamonds catching the light.

"See, I've got me the best private detective in the whole Southeast, and whenever I get one of those little shimmies of doubt about Vincent... you know what that feels like, don't tell me you don't... well, I just pick up the phone and call Nathan. That's his name. Nathan Culpepper. Or at least that's what he *tells* me his name is. God only knows, really. The man looks different every time I see him. But he knows what he's doing. He's helped *loads* of my friends. Even managed to prove one's husband was the father of her best friend's baby. *I* helped her get the DNA that nailed him." Kitty said that last sentence with obvious pride.

Mouse felt like her legs were melting.

"Now, don't look so shocked," said Kitty. "He's discreet as hell."

The business card lay on the table. Mouse could see Nathan Culpepper's name written out in block letters, the color of blood. She picked it up. Private Detective. Good Lord Almighty. How had it come to this?

The laughter started somewhere in the vicinity of Mouse's belly button and rose up so suddenly, so unexpectedly, she didn't have time to temper it to something more appropriate for the well-heeled crowd. By the time it reached her throat, it was already too loud for the room. She laughed until tears rolled down her cheeks. The unholy absurdity of it all, she thought, then howled again, this time louder than ever.

Kitty looked around, returning all the quizzical stares with a tiny smile and a nod. Bending toward Mouse, she whispered, "Girl, I saw my own mama pick up a Gone with the Wind lamp and hurl it out the living room window the day she found out my third stepdaddy had a woman on the side. She almost hit the cat."

Mouse only laughed harder. "And I myself have taken a butcher knife to the tires of Vinnie's Cadillac, two times. But I swear to God, I've never seen a woman bust out laughin' before." She tipped more wine into Mouse's glass. "Here, honey, people are starin'. Take a big ol' sip of this. I know you haven't been feeling too good, but you need to get ahold of yourself."

Mama said there'd be days like this, there'd be days like this, Mama said . . . The old Shirelles song rang out from the depths of Mouse's handbag, the ringtone she'd assigned to her mother. The sound made her laugh all the harder. When it became clear she wasn't going to silence it, Kitty reached down and picked up the tote bag, rummaged around, and pulled out the phone. "Here," she said, sticking it in Mouse's face. "Answer this thing."

Still laughing, Mouse hit the button. "Hey, Mother," she said.

There was a pause. "Are you all right?" Margaret asked, as Mouse tried to stop laughing and hiccuped instead.

"I'm . . . Yes, I'm fine." Mouse wiped her eyes with the hem of her napkin.

"Well, I'm sorry to bother you, honey," said Margaret. "But I need you to swing by here if you can. Tommy came home last night, sick as a dog. He's still asleep, he didn't get here until three. I got Sam Peters to call something in to the drugstore for him, and I need to go pick it up. Do you think you could come by while I'm gone? I don't want Tom to wake up alone. He scared me last night. I've never seen anybody so sick."

13

Tom

Tom's forehead had been shining with sweat when he'd taken Gloria Hogan's advice yesterday morning and headed for home, packing a small suitcase, then driving out of his way to Jalisco, his favorite Mexican restaurant, to pick up the quart of chicken soup that was to be his only sustenance for the four-hour journey to Wesleyan. He'd lost most of that soup in a rest stop bathroom somewhere around Pea Ridge. Then he'd fallen asleep in his car.

When he woke around midnight—head pounding, teeth rattling—he'd known this was no ordinary cold, and at that moment, half-delirious and more alone than he'd ever been in his life, Tom prayed prayers he wouldn't remember, afraid he might die in this poorly lit parking lot on I-75, with no one to witness his passing. He'd shuddered at the thought, but the shudders had turned into chills that entered his bones and pushed him back onto the highway. Blinking, and gripping the wheel like a lifeline, Tom stayed in the slow lane the rest of the way.

It was a little past three when he finally stood swaying on Margaret's front porch, the now empty soup carton held in one hand, wishing that he'd brushed his teeth. They felt like they were wearing little sweaters. His mother had opened the door and pulled him inside. Tom didn't remember much after that.

He woke when the front door clicked shut downstairs. Curled up like a pill bug in his old bedroom, with the taste of vomit cellophaned to his tongue, for a half second Tom wondered whether he'd died. Maybe that's what happens, he thought. Maybe everybody just starts over in the same room where they started out the first time. Maybe we all get to tell a new story. Second chances being all that they are, Tom found this idea both exhilarating and exhausting. Then he heard Margaret's old Volvo start up in the driveway and he knew that the concept was moot.

Raising himself up on one elbow, he looked around. The morning light in this room was as familiar to Tom as his own face. All evidence of his shambolic arrival had been neatly disposed of by Margaret, his shirt, pants, and sport coat hung in the closet, his shoes side by side right beneath them. She'd obviously retrieved his suitcase from the backseat of his car as well. It sat, unopened, between the bay windows.

Head swimming, stomach roiling, Tom eased himself to the side of the bed and stood up. Then, with one hand on the dresser to steady himself, he went to the door and out onto the landing, where, still getting used to his vertical posture, he took the stairs slowly, one by one, holding on tight to the railing.

Wearing only his boxers, he now stood barefoot and unshaven in his mother's kitchen, squinting into a sharp October sun that streamed through the windows with irritating good humor, demanding a reciprocity Tom couldn't begin to conjure up in response. Looking around, he felt suddenly grateful this room had escaped all the modifications dictated by modern design. It looked nothing like his kitchen back in Atlanta. The deep yellow walls, the wood cabinets, and countertops. The old checkerboard floor and dark tiles. All were the same as they'd been when he was a child. He could be himself in this room.

On the counter before him sat the empty chicken soup carton, long grains of white rice, now hard as toenail clippings, clinging to its thin plastic walls. Just the sight made Tom queasy. He picked the thing up and threw it into the trash, almost audibly aware of censorious rebukes as he did so. "That's supposed to be *recycled!* What kind of world are you leaving the next generation?" What kind of world, indeed, he thought.

He opened the refrigerator and pulled out a Coke, the only thing he felt he could stomach right now. Throwing some ice into a glass, he poured it slowly, watching the caramel-colored foam rise to the rim, almost spill over, then suddenly slink back down. It felt like a small victory.

Turning toward the table, he avoided the chair that was nearest, the one that sat in front of the spot where a five-year-old Lawrie had carved his name into the wood. Tom could still hear Lawrence saying, "Well, Son, you've gone and done it now. This will have to be your place at this table for as long as you live. Don't even think of sitting in another chair now." Everybody had laughed at the time, but even now, Tom knew, nobody ever sat in that spot. He pulled out a chair on the other side of the table and plopped into it with a sigh. And that's when he saw the big oak limb lying atop the Hollifields' roof, way back at the end of the yard.

Slowly sipping his Coke, Tom stared out at the limb. Shriveled and dead, the thing hovered over his mother's hydrangeas like a gargantuan gargoyle, eating up the whole view. For some reason the sight made him mad. He stood up and walked back out of the room.

Tom found his father's old boots in the hall closet and sat down on the stairs to pull them on. Then, slightly dizzy, and not pausing to plan, he headed back through the kitchen and straight out the back door.

Over the decades, the pungent, yet oddly pleasing, smells of fertilizer, motor oil, and potting soil had joined forces, tunneling deep inside the plywood walls of the backyard shed to produce a distinctive aroma that slapped the half-naked Tom in the face the second he opened the door. He barely noticed. His eyes roamed over the shed's contents, past the lawnmower and rakes, the torn badminton net, the baseball bats, and the wheelbarrow, till they spotted what he had come for. Stepping over a large sack of birdseed, he reached behind a wooden ladder and pulled out the orange chain saw.

If anyone asked later what he'd been thinking, Tom could truthfully say that he didn't know. All he clearly remembered was how quiet it had been, how strange it seemed, that on such a beautiful morning, he was the only one out. He heard no voices, no laughter, no cars driving up Albemarle Way. Even the birds had stopped singing. Just an odd sound hitting the walls of his head, as though somewhere a bass note had been struck with such force it continued to thrum without stopping and would do so the rest of his life.

The hardest part of the whole thing was climbing the fence with the chain saw. It took him three tries, and he scratched his bare leg on the second. Fortunately, the Hollifields' roof was close enough to jump onto without too much trouble, and Tom reached it in one inelegant leap. He stood there for a long minute—swaying and taking in this new view of the neighborhood, reveling in his accomplishment—then, turning with purpose, he rested the chain saw on the dead limb and yanked as hard as he could on the cord.

The noise was concussive. It almost made him fall backwards, but Tom quickly recovered his balance, and with his legs wide apart to steady himself, he pointed the hideous blade at the huge tree limb, unsure what was about to happen next. The thing might as well have been made of sweet butter. The job was done in an instant.

Suddenly severed, the heaviest part of the limb dropped to the ground in the Hollifields' yard with a thud that thrilled Tom no end. The other half, made up as it was of skeletal branches, required him, moving awkwardly, to pull it to the side of the roof before it too started to fall. He tried to direct this half of the limb toward the Hollifields' yard like the other but didn't count on the thing being as heavy as it was. This was when Tom came face-to-face with his limited skill as a woodsman.

Sliding fast off the edge of the roof, the limb seemed to hang in the air for a second—or was it a lifetime—before falling faster than Lucifer, reaching out for Tom's foot as it went. He rode it down to the ground with his eyes closed and kept them closed for a good thirty seconds after he landed. When he finally opened them, he was surprised, then elated, to discover that, apart from a few minor scratches, he hadn't even been hurt.

Squeezed out by shock and relief, laughter suddenly burst from Tom with the force of a fire hose. Sitting there on the ground in his boxers, in that jagged gray cage of dead branches, he wheezed, giggled, and roared till he developed a stitch in his side. Every organ in his whole body seemed to want to participate, and by the time he settled back down, Tom felt like he'd run up a mountain. With the world spinning around him like an old 45 record, he stood up and dragged the heavy limb to the fence, then tilted it up, pushing it over into the Hollifields' yard. By the time he collapsed back inside Margaret's kitchen, Tom felt like a piece of warm cheese.

Ten minutes later, when he heard the soft knock on the front door, he jumped up from the table, looking right, then left, and then freezing. Nobody could see him from here. Could they? Tiptoeing to the door, Tom peeked around the corner, looking up the shadowy hallway with one eye. He could just see his sister, shielding her eyes from the sun as she stared through one of the long narrow windows that ran down each side of the door. Mouse knocked harder. "Tommy?" she called, and he snapped his head back into the kitchen.

Trapped as he was, Tom knew what Mouse would do next. He could almost see her, tipping back the third large pot of yellow chrysanthemums on the left side of the porch and retrieving the house key everyone knew hid beneath it. Then she'd let herself in. But Mouse was much quicker than Tom expected.

"Tommy?" The front door closed loudly behind her. Tom took several steps back, frantically looking around. "I can see your shadow from here, Tom. You're standing right there in the kitchen." He heard her brisk footfalls. "Mother asked me to check and make sure you're okay."

When Mouse reached the kitchen, Tom was sitting again at the table, hurriedly draping a dish towel across his bare lap. He saw his sister stifle a laugh, her hand to her mouth. "God," she said, "you look awful."

"I've been sick," said Tom, unable to think of any other response.

"Polish Frizzle," said Mouse, pointing at him and grinning.

"What?"

"One of those chickens Carly begged us to get during her sustainable living phase in high school. That's what you look like. A Polish Frizzle chicken. Something about the hair, I think."

"Gee, thanks," said Tom, glumly.

"Oh, Tommy, I'm sorry." Mouse pulled out a chair and sat down. "What happened? How are you?"

Tom rubbed his eyes with his fists, like a kid. "I don't know what I had, or what I *have*," he said, "but it knocked me out flat. I don't remember most of last night."

"Well, Mother said you scared her," said Mouse, setting her purse on the floor, "so you must've been really ill. Nothing scares *her*, normally. What on earth made you drive all the way down here in"—she waggled her fingers at Tom—"*this* state?"

Tom sipped his Coke, saying nothing. Then, his shoulders suddenly drooping, he said, "I didn't know where else to go."

He lifted his eyes toward his sister, and just as she started to speak, they heard another knock on the door.

"Crap," said Tom, stretching his dish towel out as far as it could go and looking at Mouse in alarm. "Who could *that* be?"

"I'll get rid of them," she said, standing up.

But before Mouse could take a step, they heard the front door open again, and Lawrie's voice in the hall.

"Hello?"

"We're in here, Lawrie," called Mouse, loudly.

"Oh, *God*," said Tom, putting his head in his hands.

Lawrie stopped at the doorway to the kitchen, his eyes lighting on his disheveled brother. "I thought that was your car in the driveway. What the hell are *you* doing here?" he asked.

"Tom just came home for a visit," said Mouse. "And he's sick. So, you be nice."

"Me?" said Lawrie, pulling out the chair in which he always sat. "I'm always nice." He stretched his legs out under the table. "You do look pretty rough, though, Tommy Boy. It's not catching, is it?"

When Tom didn't reply, Lawrie hopped up and went to the refrigerator. Removing a cold bottle of water, he looked out the window. "Hey," he said, pointing to the back of the yard. "They finally got rid of that eyesore. I swear, I was about ready to come over here myself and pull that limb down off that roof. It's been out there forever."

Tom smiled to himself as he sipped his Coke, saying nothing.

14

Margaret

The sedentary habits of his previous owner meant Jubal wasn't used to this much activity. Margaret could tell. Clearly surprised by her son's late-night arrival, the big dog had remained with her at his bedside until Tom's fever broke around dawn. Then came this trip to Walgreens. Not wanting to leave Jubal out in the car by himself, Margaret had confidently walked the dog inside the drugstore, her stern expression a dare to anyone considering an objection. Now the big spaniel sat as erect as a yardstick in the passenger seat of Margaret's old Volvo, looking straight ahead at the road like he knew just where they were going. He placed his right paw up on the dashboard whenever they caught a red light.

You could have blown Margaret over with a sigh when she opened the door at just after three this morning to find Tom on her porch, pale and subdued, with a dirty plastic container gripped in one hand. She'd been struck by how much smaller this son had looked standing there, something that could've easily been attributed to how sick he was but that seemed to her to have much more to do with spirit than with sinew. Her most dominant worry now, however, was that Aunt Edith might not consider Tom's presence to be any sort of impediment to her regular visits. Margaret didn't want to leave Tom alone for too long.

Pulling up to the house, Margaret was surprised to see all three of her children's cars in her driveway, and she hurriedly got out of the car. Picking up on her excitement, Jubal took off down the hallway as soon as she opened the door, his bark either greeting or warning, his position being so new, even Jubal himself didn't know. The dog skidded to a stop when he saw Tom, Lawrie, and Mouse looking back at him from the kitchen table.

"What on earth?" said Mouse, pulling her legs toward her and folding her arms across her chest. "Whose *dog* is that?"

"He's Mama's," said Lawrie, proudly, slapping his thighs with the palms of his hands. Jubal went straight to him, wagging his tail, and Lawrie ruffled his fur, grinning. "I came over here to see how y'all were doing. I'm so glad you're keeping him," he said, looking up at his mother. "He's a great dog."

"I *thought* I remembered a dog," said Tom, softly, staring at Jubal and nodding. "I'd nearly convinced myself that I'd dreamed it."

"No, you didn't dream it," said Margaret, throwing her purse onto the counter and opening the Walgreens sack. "This is Jubal. Best boy on Albemarle Way. He kept watch over you most of the night. You kept calling him Po'boy, and I don't think he appreciated that much. Here," she said, shaking a fat blue pill out of an orange plastic container. "Dr. Peters sent these over for you. He also made me promise to bring you in if you're not all better in twenty-four hours."

Tom swallowed the pill, then shuddered in distaste, while

Lawrie explained all about Jubal to Mouse. The dog was giving her a wide berth. "He knows you're a cat person," Lawrie said. "Dogs can tell."

"I remember now," said Tom, slowly sipping his Coke, and still nodding his head to himself. "Yeah. I do. I remember you sitting with him by my bed." He pointed at Jubal, who immediately left Lawrie and went to sit beside Tom. "But who was that other lady? The one who was sitting by my bed with y'all last night? I saw her standing out on your balcony when I drove up. I guess it was Harriet, right? Boy, she was wearing some strong perfume, wasn't she?"

Margaret gripped the side of the sink, staring out the window. The view seemed different, the sun shone brighter than it had a few hours earlier, and she suddenly realized the big tree on the Hollifields' roof was finally gone.

"Yeah, *right*," said Lawrie, laughing loudly. "Harriet *Spalding* was keeping vigil at *your* bedside, Tommy. Boy, you *must've* had a high fever."

Quietly, Margaret let out the breath she'd been holding and turned back around. "His fever *was* high, Lawrie. I could hardly believe it was 104 when I took it the first time. Did it twice to make sure. I must've told you, Tommy, Harriet was the one who brought Jubal over here yesterday. And you just got it all confused. That happens with high fevers sometimes. You need something to eat. I've got a good bit of roast chicken left over from yesterday. I'll make y'all some sandwiches. Now go upstairs and put some pants on, for God's sake."

"I've already eaten," said Mouse.

"But I haven't," said Lawrie.

"But . . . I could've sworn," said Tom, still staring down at Jubal and looking confused. "And I didn't dream *him*, did I?" He pointed at the dog and Jubal wagged his tail, soaking in everyone's stares. Tom shook his head slowly. "I swear I remember that old lady's perfume," he said. "It made me sneeze."

"Well of course you sneezed," said Margaret, briskly. "You were sick, and you still are. Go on, now. Go on up and get dressed. Look at you, sitting here half-naked. What are you thinking?" She went to the refrigerator and began taking out food, her back to her kids. Still holding his dish towel protectively over his lower half, Tom stood up slowly and walked out of the room, Jubal following close behind him.

"Man, he's kinda out of it, isn't he?" said Lawrie, when he heard Tom's bedroom door shut upstairs.

"You don't know the half of it," said Margaret, slicing the chicken. "He was nearly delirious when he got here last night. Talking out of his head. Kept mentioning Gloria."

"Who's *Gloria*?" asked Mouse.

"Well, the only Gloria that *I* know of is the lady who cleans at his office." Margaret hesitated. "I know I shouldn't have, you know, taken advantage of him being so sick, but I kept asking him questions and"—she lowered her voice and looked up at the ceiling—"from what I could gather, I think Tom and Meghan might've split up."

"Over *Gloria*?" said Mouse.

"No, of course not," said Margaret. "Gloria must have something to do with something else."

"Well, Meghan's not such a loss, is she?" asked Lawrie, looking at his sister, who frowned back at him. "Come on, Mouse," he said, defensively. "I've heard you say it yourself. I remember the very first day Tom brought that girl home, you said it seemed like he was just making some kind of point. And you were right. I can still hear him: 'The most *popular* University of Georgia sophomore, the girl *all* the guys wanted, the one with the *flawless* face and *perfect* figure.'" Lawrie leaned back in his chair, lacing his fingers behind his head. "I tried to shake off my doubts at the time, we all did. Didn't tell him what I really thought, that she was no deeper than a teaspoon. After all, when has Tom ever welcomed *my* opinion on anything? But I could see this day coming. Don't tell me *you* couldn't."

"None of that matters now, Lawrie," said Mouse. "It's still sad. Thank goodness they didn't have any kids."

"Yes, but that's not all," said Margaret, leaning toward the table and whispering. "I couldn't get the whole picture. Like I said, he was sort of babbling a lot of the time, but it's *possible* that Tom's lost his job. I think that's one of the reasons Meghan left him."

"Wow," said Lawrie, his eyes going back to the ceiling as though he could see through it to where his brother now was. "Lost his job, lost his wife. If he had a truck to wreck, he'd have the whole country song triumvirate sewed up."

"You know," said Mouse, frowning at Lawrie, "you can really be a little prick sometimes. Seriously. Never had a bad day in your life, did you? Don't you dare say anything like that to Tommy when he gets back down here. Maybe you could try and think how you'd feel if all that happened to you." Lawrie, looking wounded, sat up straighter and folded his arms over his chest.

The three of them looked from one to the other in silence till they heard Tom's bedroom door open and his footfalls on the stairs. "Don't you two utter a word about any of this," Margaret said, pointing at Lawrie and Mouse with a bread knife. "I doubt he remembers saying anything."

Lawrie pushed out a chair for Tom with his foot, and pausing briefly, Tom sat down as Margaret placed plates on the table in front of them both, then sat down herself. Picking up his fork, Lawrie paused, looking for something to say. When it became apparent he wasn't coming up with anything, Margaret looked at her children, her eyes pausing on each one in turn. "Now," she said, a bit tersely, "about last Saturday night."

Mouse was the first one to speak. "I'm sorry we made such a scene, Mother. It was unforgivable. And on your birthday. I've still got your present at home. You left it at the table."

Both Tom and Lawrie looked down at their plates, shamefaced. Margaret shook her head and sighed. She poured them all a glass of iced tea. "I know none of you act like you did at that restaurant with anyone else. And I'm not sure why it's so often easier to be kind to strangers. But you should remember, you three will be all that's left of this family after I'm gone. It might be good to think about that occasionally. Get some things worked out before then."

The silence was awkward, and after a minute Mouse broke it. "You're... you're not really thinking about moving, are you, Mother?"

"That's not what I meant, Mouse. And no, I'm not planning to move." She sighed again, heavily. "I was just trying to circumvent the argument between these two when I brought that up at dinner." She nodded toward her sons, frowning. "But it didn't work, did it? You both acted like little heathens anyway."

Lawrie and Tom remained quiet, color rising in their identical faces.

"So, is that it?" Mouse said. She pointed to the printout of the cottage hanging on the refrigerator door. "That's the place you were talking about Saturday night?"

"Yes. That's it. I don't even think it's for sale anymore. Maybe it never was. Frankly, I couldn't even tell you where it is." Margaret peeked around Lawrie to look at the photo. "But you have to admit," she said. "There's something about the place."

"Reminds me a little of that old dollhouse you gave Emlynn," said Mouse. "The one she keeps in the window. Both of them look like something out of a book."

"Hey," Lawrie said, snapping his fingers, "I know what I wanted to ask you. Emlynn's been dying to know what was in that envelope. You know, the one she found in the dollhouse? She thought it might be the plans used to build it. If it is, she'd love to see them when you're done."

Margaret sat still for a moment, looking at each of her children in turn. It was unusual, and she had to admit, oddly comforting, to have them all around this table in the middle of an ordinary day. Maybe there was a reason they were all here. Maybe she was supposed to tell them. Quietly, Margaret rose and went to her purse. Taking out the yellow envelope, she carried it back to the table and laid it down in front of her children. "No," she said, "what Emlynn found ... well, it wasn't the plans for the dollhouse. It ... it was something ... else. Something I think I need you three to see."

They each looked down at the envelope, then back up at their mother. "This is your father's handwriting," she said, pointing to the looping script. "Back from when we were teenagers. So, he must have known what was in here. But he never mentioned it once." Margaret shook her head. "And I don't know why. I've been trying to work that out since I saw what it was."

She took a sip of iced tea, feeling three pairs of eyes staring at her. "I waited until I got home Saturday night to open it. I ... I thought I recognized it, from ... a dream, or ... something.

But . . . well, what I found inside has spun me right around. I'd like to see what y'all think." She picked up the envelope, removed the old newspaper clipping, and placed it faceup on the table. "Take a look at that."

Their heads almost touching, the three of them did as their mother instructed, bending over the table, eyes moving left to right as they read. "So?" said Lawrie, sitting back up.

Margaret sighed. "*So*," she said. "You remember Aunt Edith told me my parents were killed in a motorcycle accident."

"Yes," said Mouse.

Without fanfare, Margaret slid the old photograph across the table. "This picture was inside that envelope, too. Take a good hard look at that woman."

Mouse picked up the photo and held it in front of her face. Margaret watched her daughter's expression slowly change over to the one she'd worn that spring she played softball and was constantly afraid the ball would be hit in her direction. Mouse then picked up the newspaper clipping again and reread it. "You're not saying . . . Who *are* these people, Mother?"

Lawrie reached for the photo the same time as Tom, and Tom let him have it.

"I've been asking myself that very same question," said Margaret. "And I think it's possible they might be my parents." Saying the words out loud to her children made them seem true, not just speculation, and Margaret felt suddenly cold. Rubbing her arms, she stood up and went to close the window. "I've never seen a picture of them," she said, turning back around. "Aunt Edith didn't have one. She didn't even know my mother's first name until she saw it written down on my birth certificate. But take another good look at that woman."

Lawrie had passed the photo over to Tom, who now looked at his mother, eyes wide.

"I know," said Margaret, looking at Tom. "I look just like her."

"Well . . . you do, a little," said Tom. "I mean, I *guess* you do."

"But this couldn't be *them*," said Lawrie. "You said it yourself. Your parents died in a motorcycle wreck." He picked up the clipping again. "And these poor people . . ."

"That's what Aunt Edith always *told* me," said Margaret. "It's what she told everybody. But if"—she pointed to the small bit of newsprint—"if this is really what happened? Who'd want a little girl to know that? It's awful. Who'd want *anybody* to know? And that *is* your father's handwriting on that envelope. I'd recognize it anywhere. Why did he never tell me? Why was it stuck inside that old dollhouse?"

Mouse's hand had risen to her face and was now covering her mouth as she continued to stare at the picture.

"But the most important question," said Margaret, pulling the photo toward her. "If that baby is *me*, then who on earth is that little boy? Did I have a *brother*? And if so, then what happened to him?"

Margaret rose and walked to the pantry, coming back with a bag of pecan sandies. "Here," she said, sitting down and pushing the cookies toward Tom. "Take one of these, Son. You look pale again." Tom did as he was told, then passed the bag toward Mouse.

"I've been all over the internet," Margaret continued, "but I can't find anything about my parents anywhere. It's like they never existed. I mean, it was so long ago when Aunt Edith and Ida Mae took me in. And God help me, I just accepted what they always told me. Maybe I wanted to, I don't know."

"Ida Mae," said Mouse, slowly. "Wasn't she that friend of your aunt's? The one who lived with y'all? Do you think *she* knew what had happened?"

Margaret suddenly saw Ida Mae in her mind. Barely five feet tall, with eyes the soft gray of wren feathers and hair like cotton candy, so thin and fine you could see her pink scalp in a stiff wind. "Well . . ." she said, drawing out the word to give her more time. "Ida Mae was . . . well, she was a bit more than Aunt Edith's *friend*." She raised her eyebrows at Mouse, and Mouse's rose in kind. Margaret grimaced, then smiled and shrugged her shoulders. "Oh, shoot," she said. "I should've told y'all this years ago. Of course, the topic never came up. Why would it?"

"Are you telling us . . ." said Lawrie, eyes wide.

"What?" said Tom, looking confused.

"Keep up," said Lawrie. "She's saying Great-Aunt Edith and Ida Mae were, you know, a couple. Did everybody know?"

"Now, that's a good question, isn't it?" said Margaret, reaching for the sack of pecan sandies and taking one out for herself. "I've thought a lot about that recently. You would think people would've had to've known. Aunt Edith and Ida Mae were together all the time, had been for years. Ida Mae lived at our house. Had her own bedroom. They sat by each other at Second Baptist every Sunday, drove to school together every morning. Ida Mae taught first grade at Tillman for years, you know. But it was different back then. Nobody talked about those kinds of things in polite conversations, and polite conversations were all people we knew ever had. You won't believe me, but I didn't know myself until Ida Mae got sick. It was your father who told me."

Lawrie laughed out loud. "Are you kidding?"

"Nope," said Margaret. "It just never occurred to me."

"Lord, what a secret to keep." Mouse bit into a cookie and chewed it as though it had all the flavor of paper. "How did they do it? I bet they were scared every day of their lives that someone would find out. I mean, the *principal* of the elementary school and the first-grade *teacher*? God."

Margaret shook her head at her daughter. "Maybe everybody knew, and nobody knew. Know what I mean? That's the way it was back then. When Ida Mae died, the whole town came to her funeral. Everybody treated Aunt Edith the way they'd have done if she'd been the widow, which she *was*, I guess. Now, if somebody had spoken the truth right out loud, the whole house of cards might've come down, but of course, nobody did. And isn't that the way we keep secrets? By acting like they just don't exist?"

Jubal had long ago fallen asleep under the table, and now he started snoring. Margaret slipped her foot underneath him and he let out a sigh, then quieted.

"What ever happened to Ida Mae?" asked Mouse, softly.

"Well, I guess it was Alzheimer's," said Margaret, with a small sigh, "but of course we didn't call it that. Back then, a lot of old people just went doolally without a real diagnosis. It seemed to come over Ida Mae quickly, though I'd bet Aunt Edith had been seeing the signs for a while. In the end, she completely forgot who I was. But she never forgot Aunt Edith. I can still hear them laughing together, right up until the night Ida Mae died. Ida Mae always had the best laugh. Way too big and throaty for her frame. Aunt Edith was never really the same after she died, though. She followed Ida Mae in less than two years."

The three Elliot children sat for a moment in silence, and Margaret, looking from one to another, saw the years reverse right on their faces. Each looked to her about six years old. "That's so sad, Mother," said Mouse. "I'm sorry. I never knew."

"Well, why would you?" asked Margaret. "It all happened a long time before you were born. I'm sorry I never told you about them, as a couple, I mean. Of course, like I said, I never realized they were a *couple-couple* until much later. Children rarely question their lives, and I certainly didn't. Now I wish that I had. They were both wonderful parents to me. Do you know, Ida Mae sewed tiny bells on the hems of my skirts when I was little? I made this tinkly sound wherever I went. Fairy song, Ida Mae called it. Aunt Edith made her snip them all off before my first day of school. *She's already the principal's niece,* she said. *People will be primed to think that she's going to be spoiled.* I guess I could see her point. And, I guess I was spoiled. But boy, how I missed that fairy song when I could no longer hear it." Margaret smiled, picking up the photo again. "Ida Mae and Aunt Edith never deserved to be secrets. And I don't think my parents—if that's who these people are—did either. No matter how they died. Or lived."

She held the photo in the palm of her hand, feeling the stares of her children. Margaret looked up. "You know, you all were sitting here at this table one afternoon years ago, doing homework while I cooked dinner. You won't remember. One of you, probably you, Mouse, was working on a paper on the Bloomsbury Group, I believe, and you'd pulled down this old copy of *Mrs. Dalloway,* and when you opened it up, a photo slid out from between the pages. Slid right across this table like the winning card in a poker game. You all stared down at it and you had the funniest looks on your faces. I'll never forget it. It was a picture of me, back when I was young, in a white strapless dress. You all stared at that thing, and then back up at me like you'd never seen me before. All because I looked so different from the way you'd always known me." She laughed. "Or was it because I was beautiful? I was, you know. Once you hit a certain age, you can say you were beautiful when you were young. It's like complimenting another person." Margaret turned the photo around to face them and pointed at it.

"But now I understand how you all felt that day. It's how I feel looking at this picture. I think there's a strong possibility this baby girl just might be me, a me I never even knew existed."

With one last look at the photo, she placed it carefully back inside the yellow envelope along with the newspaper clipping. "And I'm telling you," she said, "the very thought that I might have a brother I've never met, well, it's hard for me to take in. Exciting and scary at the same time, like being given a present from someone you don't even know. Y'all wouldn't understand, you've always had one another." Mouse, Lawrie, and Tom remained quiet. "But how on earth do I find him?" Margaret continued. "The police won't be interested. A lawyer wouldn't care unless there was some money at the other end, and there won't be. Who on earth do you get to *do* stuff like this?"

Bright color rose suddenly into Mouse's pale cheeks and her back went up straight as a broom handle. "I . . . uh, well . . . as it happens," she said, pulling her purse up from the floor. "I just had lunch with somebody who might know somebody." She opened her wallet and took out Nathan Culpepper's card.

15

Mouse

The water was getting chilly again. Mouse turned on the hot tap with her toe.

There were many things she'd loved about this house the day she and Nick first saw it. It was the seventh one they'd visited that sweltering weekend, and the only one that reminded her of the house in which she'd grown up. Of course, the fact that it sat only three streets away from that house hadn't hurt a bit either. She could easily walk there for lunch with her father, something she'd done frequently over the years.

Mouse had been so pregnant with Ben that day; her belly entered the front door a good three seconds before she did. From the kitchen windows she could see that the big backyard had just enough sun to grow gardenias and just enough shade to let you sit on the porch in the summer without passing out from the heat. The dark wood floors were shiny as glass beneath decades of polish, and those maple trees—Mouse didn't have to be told—would turn scarlet and gold in the fall. But it had been this bathtub on the second floor that really sealed the deal.

Claw-footed and deep as the grave, this tub was identical to the one that sat in that big blue boat of a house on Albemarle Way, but this time, Mouse didn't have to share it with a single soul. There were enough bathrooms here for both kids to have one of their own, and Nick only ever took showers. This tub was exclusively hers. Now, in a habit that had become almost ceremony, every night before bed Mouse filled the tub with hot water, threw in a handful of those freesia-scented bath salts Emlynn gave her every Christmas, and slipped in up to her chin. Usually, anything bad she'd experienced in the past twenty-four hours just dissolved and drained away, guaranteeing her a good night's sleep. But Mouse never took a bath at this time of day.

It was only four-thirty. She should've checked in with the office hours ago. Yet here she lay, her fingertips all pruney from being in hot water for over an hour. Every now and then, the wind would blow through the maple tree outside and one of those ruby-robed branches would scratch at the window as though trying to get her attention. But she stayed where she was, laid out like a trout in the water, staring straight up at the ceiling. It had been such a strange day. And this coming Saturday promised to be even stranger. She and her mother had an appointment with a private detective. Good Lord.

Nathan Culpepper had answered his phone on the first ring. Mouse was surprised that he sounded so normal, though really, she thought now, turning the tap back off with her toe, what exactly had she expected? Private detectives had heretofore existed only in her imagination. Holmes and Watson. Hercule Poirot. To think that someone like that could have an office on Wesleyan Square made her want to laugh. It seemed so completely absurd.

When she heard a key turn in the front door downstairs, Mouse felt her stomach flip so wildly she was surprised she didn't actually see it. "Mouse?" Nick called out. She could hear him taking the stairs two at a time. She pulled up the stopper and hauled herself out of the tub, wrapping up tight in her terry-cloth bathrobe before Nick opened the door. He was grinning.

"Why aren't you answering your phone?" he said, reaching out for Mouse, folding her into a hug, and twirling her around. "I've been calling you for the past hour. We've got reservations at Pirogue tonight! A gift from Bogey Crawford for me taking his calls on Saturday. Apparently, his daughter didn't do too well in her cheerleading competition, zigged when she should've zagged, or something—collapsed the whole pyramid—and they lost. He'd made this reservation thinking it would be celebratory, but Ellen told him nobody felt like celebrating now. So, he's given it to us. Between you and me, he looked pretty pissed." He bent to kiss Mouse's forehead. "Hurry up, we've got to be there at six. We don't want them to give our table away; it takes months to get into that place. I'm gonna take a quick shower. You think it's cold enough yet for my new tweed sport coat?"

Mouse stood in the middle of the bathroom floor, her robe wicking up the water still clinging to her bare flesh. Nick's enthusiasm hovered around her in the freesia-scented air and Mouse unexpectedly caught it. Suddenly it seemed like the best idea in the world to put on a pretty dress, sit in a fancy restaurant, and tell him everything she'd learned at her mother's not two hours before.

Pirogue was bubbling over with people, most of them young, and all of them looking like they were on their way to a football game. Glancing down at her elegant dress and high heels, Mouse realized this outfit marked her as part of a different, and older, generation, one that still dressed up to go out, but she didn't mind. Sitting here at this table by the window, she felt better than she had in six months.

On the way over, she'd told Nick everything Margaret had told her and her brothers, the words tumbling over one another like running water, and now Nick had run out of questions. "Well," he said, "if Margaret is up for it, I don't think it's a bad idea at all to go see this man—what'd you say his name was again?—just to see what he can find out."

"Nathan Culpepper," said Mouse. "I'm glad you think so, 'cause Mother and I have got an appointment with him this Saturday at noon. I still can't quite believe I called him. I wonder what he'll look like."

"You mean will he be wearing a deerstalker hat?"

Mouse shrugged, smiling. "No . . . it's just, well I didn't know private detectives even *existed* outside of books and TV. You didn't either, admit it."

"Never had much use to think about it," Nick said, buttering his bread.

"I don't really believe all that much can come from it," said Mouse. "I talked to Lawrie out in the driveway before I left, and he agrees. But still, it's sort of a mystery, don't you think? And Daddy obviously knew something about it. Mother swears up and down it's his handwriting on that envelope. Though frankly, it didn't look like it to me."

Nick leaned back in his chair, smiling broadly at her.

"What?" said Mouse, expertly twirling a forkful of linguine. "Why are you grinning at me like that?"

"I don't know, honey. Spending some time with your family today was obviously good for you. You all so rarely get together, and when you do, it seems to always disintegrate into some kind of argument, like it did last Saturday night. It's just good to see you get out of yourself for a change."

"Out of myself?" said Mouse, eyes widened. "What do you mean?"

Nick shook his head, sighing deeply. "I mean," he said, hesitating, "that it's good...good to see you...oh, I don't know... *brighter* again." He turned to look out the window, but it was now so dark outside all he could see was his own reflection. "Darlin', I don't know how to say this but just to say it. I've never seen anybody as depressed as you've been this past...Well, I guess it started with Lawrence's death. I've tried to talk to you about it so many times, but you just wave me off like it's nothing. You change the subject, then close up tighter than you'd been before."

Mouse felt like a fire ant under a magnifying glass. She lifted her chin. "That's...not true," she said.

"See," said Nick, leaning closer. "Right there. That's just what I mean. That's what you do. You won't *talk* to me, Mouse. And as far as I can tell, you don't talk to anyone. Not the girls at the office. Not your family. Do you remember last summer when I suggested you go on some kind of antidepressant? Just for a while, I said, just to see if it helped? You bit my fool head off. You've lost weight, you work all the time. I can't remember the last time you laughed. You haven't been getting better, and I haven't known what to do."

"I'm...sorry," Mouse said, taken aback, her face growing hot. "I mean, I don't...I'm not...Nicky, really, I'm *fine*." She looked him dead in the eyes, determined to erase the worry she saw there. "Haven't I been handling things just like I always do? The company is booked solid into next year. I got both Ben and Carly settled at school without even one hiccup. I'm *fine*!" Her smile was so wide even she could tell it looked fake. "If...well, if I'm still, occasionally, a little depressed since Daddy died, well, you're the doctor. Tell me that isn't a normal reaction. Seriously, Nicky, I'm *fine*."

"For God's sake, don't *apologize*, Mouse. I'm not accusing you of anything. But do you realize you've just said you're *fine* three times? Enough to make me not believe you." He ran his fingers through his dark hair. "I know you think you've kept it all hidden from me. From everyone, I suppose. That's what you do. But I also know *you*. You're not just depressed, Mouse. You're grieving. Do you realize you never cried during those awful days after Lawrence died? Not once. You just kept it all tamped down. If you don't give grief an outlet, it'll find one."

A waiter walked by just then carrying a hot apple tart right at nose level. It smelled like Halloween. Cinnamon and candy corn, her father dressed up like a pirate to take them all trick-or-treating. He'd made her costume every year. A princess, a ghost, and one year—her favorite—Julia Child. There were pictures somewhere, weren't there? Mouse in a sweater set, dark wig, and pearls.

"Well, you can't blame me for that," she said, raising her napkin to her mouth to settle her trembling lip. "I just . . . I still can't believe, even now, that he's really gone. And it seems sometimes like I'm the only one who misses him, the only one who wasn't ready to lose him. And nothing can change it. There's no pill I can take. No book I can read. I just have to wait till it passes." She took a deep, steadying breath. "And it will. That's what everyone says."

"I'm not sure it works that way," said Nick, slowly shaking his head and smiling gently. "Honey, I've stood on the edge of that chasm that can open up between what you know and what you feel, and not be able to close it." He paused for a second, running his forefinger around the rim of his wineglass, as though trying to decide whether to ask the next question. After a second, he looked up at her. "Do you remember that priest Dinky clawed in the face the day Carly made us take him to the Blessing of the Animals at St. Cyprian's? Must be, what? Seven years ago now."

Of course, Mouse remembered. It had been the only time they'd gone to church as a family, the implausibility of religion being one of the first things she and Nick had agreed on all those years ago. But twelve-year-old Carly had been impossible to shift once she got hold of an idea, and when she'd seen the sign out in front of that big Gothic church, off they'd all gone to get Dinky blessed. Mouse had known how much the imperious cat would hate it, but she'd kept quiet, and Reverend Allison Whipple had paid for that silence. When the first drop of holy water hit the top of Dinky's head, he'd unsheathed his claws, stretched out his paw, and raked the woman across the chin, drawing blood along with a host of horrified stares. "Well, Dinky is going to hell," Nick had singsonged to Mouse as they'd hurried back to the car, the unrepentant cat tucked under a tearful Carly's arm, and Nicky and Mouse trying hard not to laugh.

They had liked her. Reverend Whipple had taken Dinky's assault with a good-natured grin that appeared to absolve the whole family, even as blood poured from her chin, down onto her vestments. The unfortunate event had long ago become one of Mouse and Nick's favorite dinner party stories. It was part of Moretti family lore.

Mouse laughed now in spite of herself. "I remember Reverend Whipple," she said.

"Well, I went to talk to her recently to see if she had any idea what I could do to help you with what you've been going through, and that's when she told me what you were experiencing sounded like grief."

"Oh, *Nicky*," said Mouse, horrified. "You didn't."

He reached for her hand and held on to it tight. "When you don't talk to me, Minnie, I find it hard to talk to you. And I love you. I hate to see you so miserable, especially when I don't know what to do to fix it."

Mouse had started to protest but softened at the sound of his nickname for her.

"Do you think I don't know how you idolized your father?" Nick continued, still holding on to her hand. "Hell, he's the reason we moved back to Wesleyan, and I took the position at Elberta General instead of the one at New Haven. My dad had been gone a long time, and I knew how much you wanted to be close to yours. I just wanted to be with you. I didn't care where we lived. And I've never regretted that decision. Don't go and think that I have. But as long as Lawrence was around, that's where you went with your troubles. Now with him gone, I thought you'd turn to me, and when you didn't, I realized I didn't really know how to help you, and that scared me."

"So, you asked Reverend Whipple."

"So, I asked Reverend Whipple."

"Did she serve you crackers and wine?" asked Mouse, sardonically, pouring more wine into her glass. "Pour oil on your head? Make you confess all your sins?"

"Nope. Not once. She took me to some vegetarian restaurant called Flat Belly and neither one of us could find anything on the menu we wanted to eat. Then, she gave me the name of a grief counseling group that meets every Thursday at lunchtime. You'd like her, Mouse."

"I doubt it," said Mouse. Folding her hands on the table, she said, "I've been trying, Nicky, really, I have. To feel better, I mean. To act more like myself. I can't tell you how hard I've been trying. Don't give up on me."

"Like I ever would." Then, seeing the fear in her eyes, Nick leaned in and whispered, "What? You think I'm going to lock you up in the attic like poor Mrs. Rochester? Go off and find me somebody else? You underestimate me greatly, Minnie." He put both hands over hers.

Mouse grinned. "I didn't know you'd ever read *Jane Eyre*."

"See? Just like I said. Underestimated again."

Unnoticed by either of them, a group of waiters dressed all in black had circled the table behind them, and now, as they launched into "Happy Birthday" at a thunderous volume, both Mouse and Nick jumped. Mouse turned to see an oversize hot fudge sundae descending in front of a grinning girl who was wearing a hat with a big number sixteen written across it in glitter. She looked back at Nick, shrugged her shoulders, and started to sing along with everyone else.

Downstairs, Dinky was howling, as was the cat's habit when he wanted to go out for his nightly prowl. Angry and shrill, the sound rose an octave with each passing minute, yet Mouse remained where she was, curled up beside Nick, her head on his chest, staring into the corner at an overturned dead cricket Dinky had brought in as a gift during the previous night. She felt as though chains were falling off her body, allowing her to float far above the bed, far above the maple trees, far above Wesleyan, far above herself. As Nick bent to kiss her again, Mouse heard Dinky howl one more time, desperation added to fury. But the sound was like a siren on a faraway street; nothing to do with her.

16

Margaret

A Southern fall is notoriously fickle. The cold rains of Monday had been ushered out by weather that was much more suited for summer, and people who'd worn sweaters and scarves just a few days before were back in their short sleeves today. A line was already forming outside Rocky's Road Ice Cream Shop on the corner, even though Rocky Hunter wouldn't unlock the door until noon. Thermometers were supposed to hit eighty by then.

Margaret and Mouse were early. Margaret had parked the car in front of Epiphanies Bookshop, and now they were both looking up through the windshield in confusion. "This can't be it," said Margaret. She picked up Mouse's phone and squinted at the screen. "It says we're sitting right in front of the place, but Epiphanies is 1555 and the florist is 1559. There just isn't any 1557. Not unless it's that old green door right there, but that's got to be some kind of delivery access, don't you think? There's no room for anything else." She turned the phone toward Mouse, who frowned. Margaret sat back in her seat. "I told you there wasn't any sort of *detective* on the square. I'd've known if there was."

"Let's just give it a minute," said Mouse. "He doesn't expect us till noon. Maybe we'll see him coming." She looked up and down the sidewalk, already starting to fill with shoppers. "Even though we don't have any idea what he looks like." She said this last sentence almost to herself, then bit her bottom lip.

Margaret sighed, swallowing her nervousness. A private detective. Good Lord. Should they really be doing this? She stole a tense glance at Mouse, who returned it with one of her own.

"So, how was Tommy this morning?" asked Mouse, changing the subject. She unbuckled her seatbelt and crossed her legs, getting comfortable.

The mention of Tom sent adrenaline whisking through Margaret's body. Uncontrolled and unbidden, it rushed down her arms, making the tips of her fingers tingle. Since the appearance at Tom's bedside the night he'd come home so sick, she'd prayed that Aunt Edith, somehow cognizant of her wishes, would choose to remain in whichever part of the hereafter she now called home for the duration of his stay. But apparently her son's presence hadn't been the impediment she'd hoped for. Just this morning, as darkness was melting from the corners of her bedroom, she'd once again been awakened by the faint, lyrical notes of "Love Lifted Me." This time, she didn't bother going downstairs. Even as the music swirled round her, as soft and finespun as an audible mist, she knew no one sat at Aunt Edith's piano, no one was touching the keys.

Margaret had left Jubal snuggled down in her bed and tiptoed out into the hall, the music never receding as she padded to Tom's bedroom to listen at his door. His snores had continued unabated, thank God.

But later, as she'd been doing the breakfast dishes, she'd heard Tom in the hallway, humming as he leashed Jubal for a walk. At first, the tune had seemed random, as improvised as a mockingbird's song, but soon Margaret found herself humming along, unconsciously following notes she herself had once forgotten but now knew only too well. She'd frozen right where she was. It couldn't be "Love Lifted Me."

"What's that you're humming?" she'd called out, trying to keep her voice casual.

"Huh?" Tom looked into the kitchen, Jubal by his side. "I don't know. Is it anything?"

Margaret had kept her face turned away from her son. "I thought it sounded familiar," she said. "Where'd you hear it?"

His voice muted by the T-shirt he was pulling over his head, Tom said, "Couldn't tell you. It was just swinging through my brain when I woke up. Probably some jingle I heard on TV before I went to bed."

Margaret had managed to convince Tom the old woman he'd seen by his bed that first night was nothing more than a dream conjured up by his fever, but what would she say if he saw Aunt Edith again?

"So, are you ready to kick him out, or what?" said Mouse, and Margaret looked at her, barely registering the question.

"Tommy?" said Mouse, raising her eyebrows.

"Oh. Right," said Margaret. "He's . . . he's much better. He slept most all of Tuesday and Wednesday." She rolled down the car window to let in a breeze. "But he's made breakfast the past two days," she said. "French toast, if you can believe it. I've never eaten so well in my life. Apparently, he does all the cooking at home."

"Not surprising," said Mouse, wryly. "Meghan never looked like much of a cook. Or much of an eater, for that matter."

"*And*, he's growing a beard," said Margaret. "It must be coming in pretty fast. Just two days ago it looked like one of those fake ones you get at Eddie's Trick Shop down the street, all patchy and straggly, but it looks a lot better today. It kinda suits him, I think. One good thing, too, Jubal loves him. Tommy took him for another long walk after breakfast, and then he showed me some plans he drew up last night for those old flower beds in the front yard. Said he's going to dig them all up and plant new stuff. I've never thought of Tom as much of a gardener, have you?"

"Nope. And I can't imagine Meghan letting him loose on her gardens at that big place of theirs, can you? Not in one million years. That's always been much more her house than Tommy's."

"Her *mother's* house, you mean," said Margaret.

Five years ago, she and Lawrence had driven up to Atlanta for Tom's housewarming party and been shocked at the size of the place, and more so by the décor. It was clearly a woman's house, even Lawrence had said so. Those anemic pastel florals in every single room were clearly the handiwork of Tom's mother-in-law, a woman who still back-combed her hair as high as a sixties country star and who could never quite manage to keep her coral-colored lipstick off her slightly protuberant front teeth. Armed with swatches of fabric and samples of paint, Marilyn DuBose had descended on her baby daughter's new place even before Meghan and Tom moved in, and Tom had obviously been powerless to stop her. That night Margaret had thought, without reservation or guilt, that the rooms this woman had "designed" looked like those gift shops at Cracker Barrel, and sitting here now, it occurred to her that, if Tommy and Meghan really did get divorced, she'd never again have to pretend to be comfortable on one of those ruffled pink sofas. She couldn't help smiling to herself, and this time the guilt, although present, was too flimsy to cause her much pain.

"Well, he sure seems to know what he's doing," she said, looking up and down the sidewalk. "He made two trips to Bloomin' Nursery before ten o'clock this morning. Brought home a ton of black dirt and a bucketload of pink tulip bulbs. Then went back out for flats of white pansies. It's going to look like it's snowed at my house. I heard him whistling through the window. Actually whistling. I don't think I've ever heard Tom whistle in his life. I hope he's really all right. He was pretty sick, you know."

Mouse let out a laugh. "What does it say about a person when they start doing nice things and people think there's something wrong with them?"

Margaret, who'd been asking herself the same question, didn't reply. "And I was right about him and Meghan," she said, the topic causing her to lower her voice. "And about his job. He told me last night. No details, of course, but apparently, he lost some big account or something and he's pretty sure he's going to be fired. Meghan's hightailed it up to her parents, and Tom hasn't heard one word from her in nearly two weeks." Margaret raised her voice back to a normal level. "He doesn't seem all that upset about it, to tell you the truth."

The clock on the courthouse began to chime out the noon hour, those large circles of sound that had wrapped themselves around Wesleyan for so many years nobody noticed them much at all anymore. "Maybe I should text him," said Mouse, looking down at her phone. "Make sure we're at the right place."

She had just started typing when the green door flew open and a stiletto-heeled woman walked out, a phone clamped hard to her ear. Her corn-colored hair was pulled back so tight Margaret doubted she could blink her eyes, though she had to admit it was a hairstyle well suited for a face so rigid with fury. She didn't think she'd seen an expression like that since the day Mouse's fourth-grade teacher, old Miss Mauldin, had been run down by that hell-bent goose on the class field trip to Buttner's Family Farm down in New Hope. Margaret had been one of the mothers who'd helped pull that goose off Miss Mauldin, and she'd received a bite on her wrist for the effort. You could still see the razor-thin scar. The resemblance between that goose and this woman was distinct.

Every word the woman was yelling into her phone had obviously been searching for a satisfying outlet through which to seethe for a very long time. Both Margaret and Mouse heard it all as she passed in front of their car. "I just want you to tell your wife that she can *have* Harold. She's fucking welcome to him. But if she thinks for one minute that she'll get the houses, or the children, or the *money*, she's got another think coming. I'm going to take that bastard for every red cent he has. I know things, Marty. I've kept records. You tell your backstabbing little wife to take a good hard look at ol' Harold and imagine that little runt poor. I bet she'll see he's not such a prize without his wallet in the picture. But he's hers now. All hers. You tell her that for me."

"Huh," said Mouse, as the woman's voice ebbed away down the sidewalk. "Apparently, it *is* that green door." She looked over at Margaret, who raised her eyebrows again and repeated the question she'd already asked several times since picking Mouse up twenty minutes before. "Honey, are you sure about this?"

"Mother," Mouse sighed, "I've told you. I've been all over the internet, and like you, I can't find one single sentence about your parents. Not one. We'll never know who the people in that photograph are without some professional help. If you want to know...and you do, don't you?" Margaret nodded, ruefully.

"Well, then," said Mouse, "that's what this man does. He may not find out much, it's been such a long time, and we don't have much to go on, but I think he's the best chance we've got."

Mother and daughter stared at each other for a short moment, each gathering courage from the other, then got out of the car and crossed the sidewalk to the door. The paint was peeling in places right down to the wood, but what color remained was as green as a pickle. How many times had Margaret passed by here without ever noticing it? It was, she supposed, easy to overlook. There was no number plate, no sign, nothing to hint at anything whatsoever inside. Mouse didn't bother to knock, and after glancing around to make sure no one they knew saw them enter, both women stepped quickly inside.

The stairs began at the door. They rose up in shadow, at least twenty of them, an unseen lamp from the hallway above throwing down a thin carpet of light. Mouse stared up, swallowed hard, then took hold of the handrail and started to climb, Margaret two steps behind her.

Whatever they'd expected wasn't what they found when they reached the top of the stairs. A long hallway stretched out in front of them, sunlight pouring from open doors on each side. The ceilings were so high they disappeared into complete darkness, and sisal rugs lay over floors that looked as unpolished and raw as the day they were laid. Having long ago succumbed to the abuses of time, the plaster walls had peeled and cracked through the years and now wore a patina of gold and green that looked almost intentionally done. Just to their left, a taxidermied black swan, with a red satin bow tied around its neck, stared down at them from the top of a tall wooden display cabinet full of snakeskins and seashells, and they could see more of its kind on the walls up ahead: a pheasant, a mallard, an owl. A Jacques Brel song, its words cryptic and strange, played in the background, out of place, yet somehow fitting.

Mouse and Margaret stood still, looking up and around in fascinated silence, until a voice drawled out from the room down the hall to their right, making both of them jump.

"Y'all coming in, or what?"

Mouse reached back for Margaret's elbow, and together they walked down the hallway and in through the tall open door.

Though bisected by a huge colorful tapestry that hung from the ceiling like theater curtains, the room felt as big as the football field down the road at Wesleyan High. Long horizontal windows of beveled glass hugged the high ceilings on two of the walls, throwing rainbows across the old floors, and the walls were hung with the sort of art that Margaret could only call modern. Directly in front of them, behind a large burl-wood desk, sat Nathan Culpepper, his appearance more than worthy of his eccentric surroundings.

His blue flannel shirtsleeves were rolled up just far enough to see the anchor tattoo on his forearm, and his Levi's were cuffed at the ankle. Though more fashionable in an earlier decade, his buzz cut seemed to suit him somehow; it was so short it was nearly impossible to tell what color hair he actually had, though his eyebrows were as red as a fox. When he stood up and motioned to the two empty chairs, his grin was so disarming, both Margaret and Mouse couldn't help but return it with smiles of their own, prompting him to step out from behind the desk and issue a more direct invitation.

"You ladies sit on down now," he said, and when they'd obeyed, Nathan Culpepper went back around his desk and did the same.

He had one of those Adam's apples that jumped up and down when he talked. Margaret tried not to stare.

"Don't feel bad," he said. "Just about everybody's struck dumb by this place. Partly because, as you probably see, I'm a man of eclectic tastes. But mostly because they never had a clue it was even here. You know, I've been up in this office for twenty years, but I'd bet you could go out there and pull one hundred people off that sidewalk and not a one of them would know it."

"Well, I certainly didn't," said Margaret, her eyes stuck to a large painting of what she assumed was a cow. "I can't believe you've been here that long."

"That's just a sign I'm good at what I do, ma'am. You're not supposed to know I'm around." He grinned again and nodded toward Margaret. "I take it you're Mrs. Elliot."

"Oh, yes. Yes, I'm sorry." Mouse, her own eyes still wandering the room, turned back to Nathan Culpepper with difficulty. "I'm Agatha Moretti. We spoke on the phone Tuesday, and this is my mother, Margaret Elliot. We . . . Uh, if you don't mind me asking, what *is* this place? I mean, what was it, you know, originally?"

"This whole block used to be an old cotton warehouse," said Culpepper. "A hundred and fifty years ago, I guess. My place here runs along the top of it all. Believe it or not, I only use about a third of it. But it's all I need. Kitchen and living room's back across the hall. You can take a peek later if you want." He folded his hands on top of his desk. "So now, tell me, ladies. What is it you want to talk to me about?"

Mouse gave a nervous little laugh so unlike her that Margaret stared. "Well, okay . . . right," she continued. "Like I said when we spoke on the phone, Kitty Goldsmith told me how good you were, how quick and efficient, and . . . You see, my mother, she's been trying to find out, well, she has this photo . . ." Mouse looked over at Margaret, and Margaret, clearing her throat, took over the conversation.

"I'm trying to find out anything I can about my parents," she said, relieved to hear her voice was much steadier than she would've predicted a minute before. "But I'm sure everybody who ever knew them is long gone." She opened her purse and took out the long yellow envelope, placing it faceup on Nathan Culpepper's desk. "See, last week my daughter-in-law found this... Well, she's not really my daughter-in-law, but she might as well..." Mouse coughed, and Margaret started again. "It was in an old dollhouse that once belonged to my great-aunt. That's my husband's writing on the front there. So, I'm assuming he knew what was in there, but he never mentioned it once. Go ahead, open it."

The detective picked up the envelope, removing the items inside. His brow wrinkled as he read the small slice of newsprint, and when his eyes fell on the photograph, he looked up sharply at Margaret. She wondered if he'd noticed the resemblance.

"I was always told my parents were killed in a motorcycle accident. Somewhere outside Bentonia, Mississippi, before I was a year old," Margaret said. "I couldn't even tell you what they looked like. I was raised here in Wesleyan by my great-aunt Edith Lowry, she used to be the principal of Tillman Elementary. She's been dead for ages, of course. And I have no other family. At least, well, not that I know of. But now, after seeing this... Could that article be about them?" She pointed to the photograph. "Could this *be* them? Why else would it have been hidden away? In an envelope with my name on it?"

Culpepper picked up the newspaper clipping and silently read it again. "Well, if these were your parents, I can certainly see why your aunt never told you about this. It would be a hard thing to tell a little girl."

"Well, yes," said Margaret. "I imagine it would've been. But you can see why I'd want to know, now that I've found this?"

"'Course I can," he said, thoughtfully.

Nathan Culpepper's equable expression told Margaret this was hardly the worst thing that he'd ever encountered. He held the photo up to the light, then picked up the newspaper clipping, looking from one to the other for a long minute. The music of Jacques Brel continued playing in the background. The words sounded exotic to Margaret, so indecipherable they were open to any interpretation.

"I've been to the library, twice this week, and it feels like I've combed the whole internet," Margaret said. "But haven't come up with a thing."

"Well, I'd be surprised if you had," said Culpepper. "A lot of things that happened back then never made it online. Lots of folks fell through the cracks. People didn't feel the need to document their every burp and hiccup like they do today. Even births and deaths were ignored in some places." He turned the photograph over, squinting down. "Sometimes they wrote on the back of these old pictures in pencil, and of course that soon faded to nothing. But it doesn't look like anybody ever did that to this one." He turned the photo back over, staring at the faces. "The only one you can see clearly is the woman. That little boy looks to be about two, three at the most. And you think that baby she's holding might be you?"

"That's what I've been wondering," said Margaret. The three of them sat silent for a minute or two. "This is probably just a big waste of your time." She sat farther back in her chair.

Nathan grinned and looked up at Margaret. "Not at all, Mrs. Elliot. Not at all." He held up a finger and cocked his head. "Listen to that song," he said, closing his eyes for a second. "Y'all know what he's saying right there?"

Margaret and Mouse shook their heads, dumbly. "We don't speak French, I'm afraid," said Mouse.

"*It appears that the scorched fields can give more corn than the best of springs.*"

He waved the photo around in the air. "Kind of prophetic, I'd say."

Both Mouse and Margaret wore expressions of total confusion that the detective disregarded completely. He leaned back, lacing his fingers behind his head. "I like a challenge, ladies, and Lord knows, something like this beats tailing hound dog husbands and weedy kids, which is most of what I do these days. I haven't had something like this to chew on in . . . well, I can't tell you how long."

Smiling, he reached down beside him and opened the bottom drawer of his desk, pulling out a shiny blue notebook still wrapped in the cellophane it had worn at the store. He tore a corner off with his teeth, ripped the clear covering away, and tossed it aside. Then he opened the desk's center drawer, took out a new fine-point Sharpie, and pulled off the cap, again with his teeth. Margaret wanted to look over at Mouse, but her eyes were glued to the detective.

The notebook made a crackling sound as it opened for the first time, and with new pen poised over clean paper, Nathan Culpepper looked up at Margaret and smiled. "Now, Mrs. Elliot, tell me everything you remember about your childhood."

And maybe it was the way the man looked at her over that burl-wood desk, his gaze as open and interested as that of a child. Or maybe it was the room itself, so curious and strange, it seemed to welcome her secrets. It could've been that song Tom had been humming not three hours before, or the one the Frenchman was singing right now. Whatever it was, the words Margaret spoke next were unexpected, even to her. Hesitating only briefly, she reached back into her purse, pulled out the picture of the house on the beach, slid it across the desk, and then said...

"Tell me, Mr. Culpepper. Do you believe in ghosts?"

PART THREE

17

Mouse

Mouse had followed her mother down the steep stairs and out onto the sidewalk of Wesleyan Square like Anne Boleyn on her way to the chopping block. Neither woman said a word, both climbing into the Volvo and closing the doors in silence. After a minute or two in which Mouse stared straight ahead, Margaret, beads of sweat forming on her upper lip, switched on the car and rolled down the windows. A soft breeze swept past them, carrying snippets of conversation from people passing by on the sidewalk, like indecipherable sounds from a faraway planet.

"Well," Margaret said, resting her head on the back of her seat. "It's out now. And don't worry, Mouse. I know that man won't say a word to anybody. I could just tell." Mouse sat as still as a rock.

"I'm really sorry you had to find out that way, honey," said Margaret, looking over at her daughter. "But . . . well, I don't know, it just no longer made any sense to me not to tell it, even if it means you'll think I've totally popped my balloon. Mouse, I've been seeing Aunt Edith since the week your father died, and I've been quiet about it because, well, let's face it ... that's not something you just run out and tell, is it?" Margaret giggled, and when Mouse didn't respond, she went on. "See, at first, I didn't know if she was just some sort of figment I managed to conjure up out of thin air. And then, *naturally*, I worried that I might be ... you know ... turning funny. Well, you would, wouldn't you? But then Harriet told me something that once happened with her own father—he saw the ghost of *his* father and it turned out to be a wonderful thing for him—and so then, when Emlynn found that envelope—the *same* envelope I'd seen in Aunt Edith's hands for *so* many nights—well, it was as though Aunt Edith had just reached out from wherever she is, and handed the thing right to me. And then, of course, Monday night, when I saw that little *boy*—the *same* little boy in that photo I showed you all, wearing the same *clothes* and everything? Well, after all that, telling this man was just a risk I was willing to take. Aunt Edith wants me to find out the truth, I know she does, and if Nathan Culpepper can help me do that, then he deserves to hear the whole story. As do you, I suppose."

Mouse couldn't tell if her heart had slowed down or sped up. She sat with her hands folded in her lap like a child posing for a school photo, trying to imagine the look on her two brothers' faces when she told them their mother has been seeing ghosts.

"You okay?" Margaret asked, and Mouse gave a small twitch that might have been read as a nod. "It's nothing to be afraid of, darlin'," said Margaret. "Aunt Edith, I mean. I figure she's just another of life's mysteries we're not meant to solve."

Her mother put the old Volvo into reverse, and Mouse, too tired, too bewildered, to think up a response, sat in silence all the way home.

Now she stood in her kitchen, the counters crowded with cookies and cupcakes, waiting on the timer to signal another batch of gingersnaps was ready to come out of the oven. It was almost time for Nick to come home. He'd said he wanted her to talk to him. Well, wait till he heard what she had to tell him tonight. This was one of those times Mouse was glad she'd married a doctor. There had to be something wrong with her mother. Surely Nicky would know what it was. The knock on the back door caused her to jump as she stirred another bowlful of batter. She went to answer it with chocolate all over her chin.

Kitty Goldsmith stood in the garage, a bottle of Jack Daniel's in one hand, and three large bouquets of sunflowers in the other. She raised the bottle up over her head. "Lord, I could smell sugar from the driveway!" she said, pushing past Mouse and into the kitchen. "And it makes sense now. Looks like Willy Wonka lives here."

She handed the sunflowers to a dumbfounded Mouse and sat the Jack Daniel's on the counter between two racks of freshly iced chocolate cupcakes. "I've come to apologize," she said, pulling up a kitchen stool, sitting down, and kicking off her silver sandals. "I was talkin' to some friends at lunch this afternoon and your name came up. I had told them your catering company was the best in the whole city, and that's not a lie. But then somebody mentioned your husband—don't *worry*, I didn't tell them about what you've been worryin' about—and *everybody* started sayin' how he worships the very ground you walk on in those little black loafers of yours. And not only *him*, apparently. You, Aggie honey, are beloved in this town. Hell, from what I heard today, if Dr. Nick Moretti ever *did* do what you were afraid he *might* do, why, a whole squadron of Wesleyanites would ride at dawn to tar and feather that man's tight little ass right out of this city. So, I'm *sorry* if I made it a bigger deal than it needed to be. Giving you Nathan Culpepper's card and all. I hope I didn't go and make things worse. I can do that sometimes." Kitty reached for a chocolate chip cookie. "You don't mind, do you?" she said, waving the cookie over the crowded counter. "I mean, it looks like you got plenty."

"I bake when I'm upset," said Mouse, wishing the woman would stop calling her Aggie. The oven buzzer sounded and she went to retrieve a tray of hot gingersnaps, while Dinky the cat strode purposefully into the kitchen, signaling that it was now six on the dot, one minute more and his dinner would officially be late. "I appreciate you coming by, Kitty," Mouse said, taking the cookies off the sheet pan one by one and placing them on a cooling rack. "But you really didn't have to. I told you at lunch, it was all just a big misunderstanding. I know Nick would never cheat on me."

Dinky let out a yowl just then, and Mouse hurried back across the room and took a can of Fancy Feast from a cabinet. After she'd set a full bowl of food down in front of the impatient cat, she plopped onto the stool beside Kitty and picked up a cupcake, running her forefinger through the thick chocolate icing and sticking it into her mouth.

"You're a right funny color, you know that?" said Kitty, staring over at Mouse and rocking her hand in the air. "Somewhere between storm gray and pea green. You about to throw up?"

Mouse let out a tiny, weak laugh. "No, Kitty," she said. "I'm not about to throw up." Taking a deep breath to make sure that was true, she rested her head on the palm of her hand and sighed.

"Look," said Kitty, pushing the plate of cupcakes away and leaning in closer to Mouse. "You and me go way back, Aggie.

We've known each other since we were just kids, even if we *were* in two different groups way back then. I know we haven't seen each other for years, and if you went out shoppin' for a new friend, you'd most likely pass me right by. I know what some people think. That I'm a little too much. Too much talk, too much drama. Hell, too much *trouble*. But history has to count for *something* when it comes to friendship. Right? You know, I can still see you sittin' across that room in Miss Hester's class, with a skint knee. You'd fallen down at recess, I remember. And what was that ... third *grade*? So, you might say I'm really a *very* old friend. And if you can't talk to an old friend, well, who can you talk to? I'm not somebody you have to impress, Aggie. If you want to talk, honey, you can talk to me. Anytime."

Mouse sat still for a minute, then surprised herself once again. "Kitty," she said, looking into the woman's eyes and noticing for the first time how green they were, "my father died last March. I was close to him and ... and since then I guess I've slid into some kind of dark hole. I've started doing these crazy things, like ordering stuff off TV in the middle of the night. Things I don't want and wouldn't wear if you paid me. And I don't sleep, not hardly at all anymore. I say critical things about people inside of my head, *awful* things, sometimes. Things I used to not even *think*. And I ... I flirted with a *college* student when I took my son up to school in September. Made a complete *fool* of myself. I mean nothing *happened*. Obviously. The poor boy probably didn't even know I was flirting with him, now that I think about it. I bet he just thought I was some crazy old woman with some kind of hormonal imbalance, which might be true, for all I know. But all that's neither here nor there now, because just a few *hours* ago I learned—"

"Well, at least you've had a *reason*," interrupted Kitty, laughing loudly as she reached back for the bottle of Jack Daniel's. "Shit,

Aggs, I do worse stuff than all that *all the time*. And why? I couldn't even begin to tell you *why*! I never even *met* my daddy, but if I'd had a good one, I can only imagine how hard it'd be to lose him. No wonder you've run off the rails. You got cause."

"But you didn't let me finish," said Mouse, watching as Kitty poured Jack Daniel's into a measuring cup and handed it over to her. She could see a thin layer of flour floating on top. She took a large sip, ignoring the flour and feeling only the burn. Closing her eyes, she said, "Kitty, now I'm afraid something's wrong with my *mother*. I . . . I found out today that . . . she's been seeing *ghosts*. She said so, right out loud. She's seen her great-aunt, and some little boy she thinks might be her brother." Mouse took another sip of bourbon and shuddered. "I haven't told Nick this yet, he's on call today and still at the hospital. Like I said, I just found out myself. And I don't have a clue what to do."

Whatever reaction Mouse was expecting did not materialize. Kitty just threw back her head and again laughed her yodeling laugh. "Your mama's seen a ghost? Good *Lord*, is that *all*?" she said.

"Isn't that *enough*?"

"Aggie." Kitty slowly shook her blond head, looking at Mouse with something like pity. "This cannot be the first time you've heard of people poppin' through the veil. Hell, it's a Southern tradition! Listen, I sat with Grandma Calhoun while she was dying. My mother's mother—we all called her Birdie—she lived with us when she got too old to cook for herself. Now, that woman had a passel of long-dead sisters, and I swear she saw every one of 'em sittin' across the room from her every single day. Picked right up with whatever argument they'd been having last time she saw 'em. And for two weeks or more—right up until she finally threw off the quilts and joined 'em for good—they'd talk about all the people they'd known, the boys they'd dated, the men they'd married. I swear, I learned things my own *mama* didn't know. All one-sided conversations, of course, at least to my ears. But I'll swear on a saint's Bible, Birdie heard it all. To tell you the God's honest truth, I'll be kinda disappointed if the same thing doesn't happen to me when I take my leave of this earth."

"My mother's not on her deathbed, Kitty. She pulled out of my driveway less than two hours ago, on her way to buy pumpkins for the front porch."

"Oh, you don't have to be *dyin'* to see a ghost," said Kitty, matter-of-factly. "I had this cousin, Bonnie. Used to live down in Mobile and visit us in the summer. Well, her husband, Bertram, died young, and when their son, Bubber, got married—I remember this like it was yesterday—Bonnie sat right there in that Church of God reception hall with a little plastic glass of pineapple punch in her hand and told a whole table full of Calhouns she still sees Bertram sittin' in the laundry room every time she goes in there to wash a load of clothes. Now I tell you what, this is the straightest little white woman God ever made—a tax accountant for over twenty years—hell, she does the preacher's taxes—and she told that story like she was tellin' you what she planned to fix for dinner." Kitty patted Mouse on the arm, her diamond bracelet jangling. "No, ma'am, I don't ever judge somebody's sanity by standards as flimsy as whether or not they see ghosts. You shouldn't either, Aggie."

"*Please* call me Mouse." Mouse took a large bite of chocolate cupcake and washed it down with another sip of Jack Daniel's. This was now the third time that talking with Kitty Goldsmith seemed to be making her feel better. "So," she said, her mouth full, "*you* don't think I have anything to worry about."

"I didn't say *that*," said Kitty, picking up a warm gingersnap.

"From where I sit, you've got a few things to worry about. First off, you can't have your mama telling people her dead kinfolk are droppin' by willy-nilly. You gotta stop her from doin' that. You know how people are, and you don't want her to get a reputation. But I can tell you this from experience: don't run headlong into thinking your mama's losin' her mind, or you might just start to lose yours. Now, can I wrap up a few of these cupcakes to take with me?"

18

Emlynn

Every Sunday morning at eleven o'clock, an impressive chunk of the citizenry of Wesleyan, those who generally tend to mix and mingle without giving voice to the differences they all know exist, peel off into tribes of like minds and assemble inside the six old churches that sit within walking distance of the town square. Presbyterians, Baptists, Episcopalians. Catholics, Methodists, Lutherans. Separated thusly, they sit in familiar pews, sing familiar songs, hear familiar words, and for that one blessed hour each week, they find comfort in the assurance of accord and congruity, which is no small thing in a small Southern town. But when the clock strikes noon, all are united again as they race one another to Mama's Way Cafe for Sunday lunch, each of them hoping for a booth by the window. It is a point of commonality, and not being churchgoers themselves, this morning, the Elliot children had a head start.

After her last time with the family, Emlynn wasn't looking forward to this brunch. She wasn't feeling herself today, was afraid she might be coming down with something, and had no desire for a repeat performance of Lawrie and Tom's contentious relationship. She could still see herself sitting at that table in the Yamacraw Room, her risotto going cold as her eyes pinged between the two brothers like a pinball just before tilt. When she got up and left the table that night, she fled to the bathroom, where she'd sat on a closed toilet and cried like a baby, recalling those days when her parents' arguments had spilled out from their tight circle of three, into restaurants and shopping malls where others could hear them, leaving her, the only child, standing off to the side feeling somehow responsible for their bad behavior. She'd felt like she should apologize for Lawrie that night at Jessamine, and she didn't want to feel like that ever again.

Over her tall menu, Emlynn stole another glance at Tom. He looked like a different person with the new beard; only his eyes were still Lawrie's. Now, instead of being seen as identical from fifty paces away, the twins only appeared to share a strong resemblance, rather like first cousins, or royalty.

"I was early, so I've already ordered some coffee for us all," said Mouse. "But feel free to get something else to drink if you want. The waitress should be back in a minute."

"Coffee's fine," said Lawrie, looking around the room. "Being heathens obviously has its advantages," he said. "Y'all scored the best table. Well done."

Emlynn laughed, a fraction too loudly, then she felt tears prick her eyes. She blinked them back furiously. What was wrong with her?

"I'm sorry Nicky couldn't be here," said Mouse. "He was getting dressed to come with me when he got a call. But I've told him all about this. He's not too concerned, but he agrees that you all should know."

Four cups of coffee in Mama's Way mugs were placed on the table and each person reached for their own. Lawrie ripped open two packets of sugar, and Tom opened two containers of cream. Spoons clanked as they all stirred, then expectantly turned back toward Mouse.

"I'm ... Okay ... Well, I'm sorry to be so dramatic," said Mouse, "I mean, having you meet me here while Mother's at church. You didn't tell her where you were going, did you, Tommy?"

"I told you I didn't," said Tom. "I was still in bed when she left."

"Oh, right. It's just, well, I found out something kind of ... I don't know ... disturbing, yesterday. And I don't want her to know that I've told you. Not yet anyway." Mouse was fiddling with her paper napkin, tearing off little pieces of white and slowly constructing a small snowy mountain.

"Well, what *is* it?" said Lawrie, impatiently.

Mouse took a deep breath, then a long sip of coffee. When she finally began, Emlynn noticed a tremor in her voice. "Okay, here it is. You know we went to see that investigator yesterday, Nathan Culpepper, and ..."

"Does he think there's anything to that stuff she found?" asked Lawrie, flipping his napkin onto his lap.

"There might be," said Mouse. "I mean, I don't know, he's going to check into it. But that's not the thing ... Listen, Mother told him she's been ... well, she's been *seeing* things. Like ... ghosts."

Everyone froze, staring at Mouse. Emlynn saw Lawrie start to grin. "I'm not kidding," said Mouse, firmly, her eyes darting warningly to her brother. She leaned across the table toward him. Speaking faster and more forcefully, she said, "Mother told that investigator yesterday that she's been seeing the ghost of Aunt

Edith. She said she sees her at night, in her bedroom, and ... *apparently*, it's been going on since the week Daddy died. Seven months ago. And *then*, she said ... just last week—the very night you came home, Tommy—she said she saw the ... the ghost of that little boy we all saw in that old photo Emlynn found. I didn't know *what* to say when she told him that. I just sat there like an idiot and let her talk. I swear, she acted like it was the most normal thing in the world. Told me later not to worry, said she could never be afraid of Aunt Edith. Like that was the worrisome part."

The waitress approached the table just then, and Emlynn shook her head. "Could you give us a few more minutes?" she said. "We haven't taken time to look at the menu yet, I'm afraid. Sorry."

Frowning slightly, the waitress moved away to the next table, and Lawrie stared hard at Mouse. "Are you sure you heard her right?" he asked, still looking a little amused. Emlynn could tell that Mouse had expected this response.

"God, *yes*, Lawrie." Mouse's shoulders sagged, as if an invisible string that was holding them up had just been suddenly cut. "Why else do you think I called you two? I wanted to ask you, face-to-face, have either of you noticed anything, you know, *unusual* about her lately? Something she might have said that seemed odd, something you might've just explained away at the time? You've been with her since Monday night, Tom. Has she done anything out of the ordinary?"

"Well, no," said Tom, rubbing the bridge of his nose between his forefinger and thumb in a gesture of worry Emlynn could read. Lawrie was, at this moment, doing the very same thing.

"Seriously, Mouse, don't you think she was kidding?" said Lawrie. "Maybe just pulling that man's leg or something like that?"

"She was *not* pulling his leg." Mouse pushed aside her coffee, folded her arms on the green Formica table, and plopped her head down, a curtain of dark hair covering her face. Her voice muffled, she said, "Lawrie, she told him all this so matter-of-factly, I swear I thought *I* was the one who was nuts." She raised her head back up. "Not that I'm saying Mother is nuts," she said, quickly, then let out a long breath. "I stayed up half the night, talking this all over with Nicky, because I was worried it might be small strokes or something like that. I remember what happened to Bethann Bixby's mother. Bethann told me. The woman could act completely normal, and then just ... I don't know ... go all funny. Bethann said one afternoon her mother was completely convinced there was a spider monkey out in her rose garden. She actually called some wild animal park over in Albany. 'Course it turned out Bethann's mother had just got ahold of some Xanax and was taking too much. And anyway, Nick said small strokes don't work that way. People don't hallucinate with those."

"Well, what does Nick think we should do?" asked Lawrie.

"He says to just keep an eye on her. See if she does anything strange. I mean, she told us herself she'd had a checkup with Dr. Peters not two months ago. Personally, I think it's that picture and that old newspaper clipping that's got her all wrought up," said Mouse. "But I thought y'all should know about it. So, we can *all* keep an eye on her."

The waitress came back and stood by the table, her pencil pointedly raised. Her appetite nonexistent, Emlynn ordered dry toast, then listened as everyone else ordered breakfast. As they slid their menus to the end of the table, she said quietly, "Of course, there's always the possibility Margaret's telling the truth." Everyone looked at her with varying degrees of incredulity. "Well, you know," she continued, blinking, "it *was* strange that I happened to find that old envelope stuffed inside the dollhouse when I did. With her name written on it. In your father's handwriting. On her *birthday*. Don't y'all think that's a bit odd? Maybe, well, I could've been led to it, somehow." Emlynn absorbed their stares, reevaluating the wisdom of speaking her thoughts out loud. She could feel her cheeks getting warm. "I mean, *I* don't know how to explain it, but I just had the oddest feeling when I pulled that envelope out of the dollhouse. Like I was *meant* to find it, or something." Emlynn took a sip of cold water, then held the glass to her now burning cheek.

"So, what? You're saying Mama's right?" said Lawrie. "The ghost of her aunt Edith was ... what? Pointing it *out* to you or something?"

"Nooo," said Emlynn, slowly. "I mean, I didn't *see* anything. Or anybody. But it's always ... possible, that your mother did. Isn't it? You hear of stuff like this happening to people. Why shouldn't it happen to us?"

"That's what this friend of mine said yesterday," said Mouse, wryly. "The same woman who gave me that investigator's card. Lord, if I'd known I was going to hear what I heard at his office, I would've torn that card up into little pieces the minute she handed it to me."

"Look," said Lawrie, sitting up straighter and taking command. "Let's face it. None of us believe in ghosts, for God's sake. So that's not even a consideration. But if Mama truly thinks she's seen something, or someone—and personally, I'm still not discounting the possibility that she might've just been playing with you a bit, Mouse—but, if she really thinks she has, well, y'all consider this: she's never lived alone before. I'm sure that can play with somebody's mind. Make them hear all those house noises they've never heard, maybe even cause them to see things, I don't know. And let's face it, finding that newspaper clipping and that old photo ... well, Mama said it herself, didn't she? 'It's spun me right around.' Didn't she say that?"

Mouse and Tom nodded, both with their eyes on their brother, the hope for a reasonable explanation written all over their faces.

"Frankly," Lawrie continued, his confidence rising, "I don't think much will come of all that. If the investigator finds out anything, it'll just be that the people in that old picture were some folks her aunt used to know, something simple like that. And let's all admit, up till now, Mama's not shown any signs of unusual behavior. I mean, look at her last Saturday night. She seemed more than fine. Even told us all to shut up, which was, according to Emlynn, perfectly reasonable considering the way we were acting. I'm with Nick. Let's just all calm down and keep an eye on her. Tom's home at the moment, he can watch her. And we'll all check in with her this week."

It was reasonable. It made sense. So, they all picked up their forks and began eating breakfast in silence, each of them trying to convince themselves Lawrie was right.

19

Tom

It had been optimistic for Tom to order bacon and eggs. He realized this now. He was sweating; the skin on his face felt slimy underneath his new beard. The few bites of toast and sips of hot coffee he'd managed to swallow had slid down into his stomach like a load of soft concrete that now felt like it was rapidly hardening. He said goodbye to the others with as few words as he could, then watched as they disappeared down the sidewalk on the way to their cars. Now, stepping back to let people pass, he leaned against the outer brick wall of Mama's Way and took a few deep cleansing breaths.

After five minutes, during which it occurred to him that he might feel better sitting down, Tom stood up straight and headed for the square, not bothering to cross at the light. Strangely, not one person stopped him. This was unusual. Whenever he was back home here in Wesleyan, at least a handful of people always came up to him, thinking he was Lawrie. As he walked, it took Tom several minutes to work out the reason this wasn't happening now. When he figured it out, he wondered why on earth he hadn't started growing a beard the first day he'd sprouted hair on his face.

It was a beautiful afternoon, clear and cool. Sunlight lay like a chrome blanket on the water in the fountain, so bright it hurt his tired eyes, and Tom was reminded of that old shiny metal slide that used to sit in the playground over at Tillman Elementary. The bigger boys used to save the wax paper from their sandwiches and rub it all over the thing to make it as slick as it could possibly be, then they'd hide behind the trees to watch as the little ones climbed up the ladder and sat at the top, their short legs sticking out in front of them, trying to work up the nerve to slide down. When they finally did, their descent was so fast on that well-waxed surface, they were never able to stop themselves from shooting out the bottom and landing hard in the dirt. Tom remembered this well. He had been one of those little kids. Shaken, his head spinning, he felt now like he'd once again fallen fast and hit the ground hard. Passing the dazzling fountain, he turned his head away from the glare.

He'd stayed quiet as he listened to Mouse relate what Margaret had said yesterday. Though the humor escaped him, like Lawrie, Tom thought at first that it had to be some kind of joke. But then, like a curtain being jerked back, the image of the old lady he'd seen in his office last Monday flashed into his mind and left him with nothing to say. That memory was so clear. But it wasn't possible, was it? Even now, Tom couldn't explain why he'd felt such an overwhelming desire to come home the moment he'd seen that old woman smile at him from the end of the hallway. The idea had blown into his head like a decision he'd already made. He hadn't even paused to consider. Sick as he'd been, he'd just packed a bag and pointed his car toward the highway. It was the last thing he would've expected of himself.

Who *was* that old lady he'd seen? Gloria hadn't seen her, and she'd been standing right there. Had she even existed? By the time Tom reached his car and climbed in, his heart was beating as fast as a rabbit's.

That first night home, he'd been so certain an old lady had been by his bed. He'd seen her sitting right there with his mother. Hadn't he? But Margaret had sworn that she'd been alone. Tom put both hands on the steering wheel and rested his head. It was true that he'd had a high fever that night. But what if that wasn't what caused him to see her? What if she'd really been there? As hard as he was trying not to, Tom knew, if he wasn't careful, he could picture that old lady right now. She'd been wearing pearls. They'd shone white in the moonlight. And hadn't he smelled her perfume? Hadn't the smell made him sneeze?

What if Margaret wasn't the only one in the Elliot family Aunt Edith was visiting? Or were both he and his mother losing their minds simultaneously? Tom's arms felt a bit numb as he raised his head and started the car. He didn't need this on top of everything else.

He'd spent most of yesterday afternoon on the phone, finally facing up to what he'd left behind in Atlanta. As he'd expected, Chuck Warren believed Tom would be much better off finding another position, one where he could start over with a clean slate. Though even he said that would probably be hard in Atlanta. Since the Public Land Trust had purchased Pinckney Woods, Tom had apparently gotten a reputation that wasn't exactly development friendly.

And he'd finally been able to get hold of Meghan. They'd admitted to each other that their marriage wasn't working out as they'd planned, a realization that had come long ago to them both but was only now made inescapable, especially for Meghan, by the imminent change in their finances. She told him she wanted the divorce to be easy and quick, an idea with which Tom readily agreed, though he was certain when she, and especially her father, found out how many mortgages he now had on the house, her equanimity was likely to change. No doubt due to how comfortable he'd gotten with dread, Tom felt no discernible emotion about this, and that was the thing that troubled him most. He saw it as just one more of his failures. He hadn't even loved Meghan enough to be sad.

Turning left at Griffin Park, Tom took the long way home without planning to. The streets were so familiar he knew every bend, every curve. He passed by houses of people he knew, or had once known, taking note of each change of paint color, remembering the cars that used to sit in each driveway. Tom could almost see himself as a kid, still walking these sidewalks, schoolbooks in his backpack. Maybe we're all just ghosts, he thought. Maybe a part of me is still here, will always be here. Just because we can't see them doesn't mean these sidewalks aren't crowded with people who've already gone on. He gripped the steering wheel a little bit tighter.

Turning up Dornoch Lane, Tom slowed when he noticed Harriet Spalding's window boxes full of plastic flowers, their Technicolor perfection just slightly disturbing. The memory came back to Tom fully formed, that day he'd hurled those eggs at Miss Spalding's front porch in response to a gauntlet thrown down by the Hulsey brothers to test his bravery, and one he'd picked up with more bravado than he'd actually felt. Thick-necked and fearsome, the Hulseys were given a wide berth by most kids in Wesleyan, who'd cross the street to avoid them. But they'd caught

Tom out on his way home from school, Lawrie having gone to Mama's Way Cafe with some of his friends, just as he usually did. Tom could still remember how he'd felt when he did what the Hulseys told him to do, the shame so much worse than the fear. And when he'd seen Miss Spalding out in her yard the next morning, with a brush and a bucket of soapy water, scrubbing hard at the mess, something—he still couldn't say what—had pushed Tom up her driveway to confess to the crime. She'd stared down at him, hard, suds dripping from the brush in her hand, and then said she didn't believe him. "You wouldn't do something like that, Tom Elliot," she'd said. "Not you. You're not that type of boy." He'd stayed to help her wash off the brick until it was cleaner than it had been before, earning two demerits for being late getting to school.

Now, without pausing to think, Tom turned in to Harriet's driveway, got out of the car, and went to the door. One knock was all it took to set off a chorus of unwelcoming barks. From somewhere in the back of the house, Tom heard a familiar voice call out, "Shut up, Gatsby!" and when Harriet Spalding opened the door, he was relieved to see she was holding the indignant Chihuahua tight under one arm. It took her a second to see past the beard.

"Tommy Elliot!" said Harriet. "Right here on my porch. Your mama told me you were home for a few days. Said you'd been sick; did I get that right? Come on in, son. You still look a bit peaked to me."

"No, Miss Spalding, I'm all right. And I don't have time to come in right now, thanks. I was just passing and I . . . well, I saw your window boxes. I thought I might like to . . . if you wouldn't mind, that is . . . I'd like to redo them for you."

Tom backed up as Harriet stuck her head out the door and

stared at the indestructible flowers. "Has somebody complained?" she asked, eyes narrowed.

"No. I mean, not that I know of. It's just that, I'm going to be home for another week or so, at least, and I just thought . . . Well, I'd just like to do it. If you don't mind, that is."

"Well, of course I don't mind, Tom," said Harriet, eyeing him curiously. It was a look Tom remembered. "I saw you, you know," she said, hoisting the Chihuahua up a bit higher. "Last Tuesday morning, when Gatsby and I were out for our morning walk. Saw you over your mother's fence. I thought for a minute I was seeing things, but no, it was you, standing up there on the Hollifields' roof in your underpants, holding a chain saw. We watched the whole thing, Gatsby and me. That was quite a performance, son. I'd already pulled my phone out of my pocket, ready to call 911. I knew you were bound to fall, and of course, I was right. But then I heard you laughing like a hyena, and I figured you must be okay. You know, the Hollifields think the wind blew that limb off their roof. Idiots. Haven't even noticed the clean cut."

"Well, I'd appreciate it if you didn't tell anyone it was me that did it," said Tom, a smile now playing around his lips.

"Did what?" said Harriet, winking.

Tom turned to go. "I'll be by tomorrow to fix those boxes," he called back over his shoulder as Harriet and Gatsby stood watching him go.

The old Volvo was in the driveway when he pulled in. Getting out, Tom could hear Margaret in the backyard, Jubal's barks punctuating the sound of a tennis ball bouncing on the lawn. He leaned against the car door, rubbing his forehead, trying to decide what to do next. He was just supposed to keep an eye on his mother, that was it. Mouse had made them all promise not to mention any of this business about Aunt Edith to her. He hoped he could manage to keep his end of that promise.

Tom trudged up to the front porch and let himself in. Turning left at the stairs, he entered the dining room, which was always the coolest, quietest room in the house. With its casement windows and carved crown moldings, it could also be judged the best room in the house, but the Elliot family rarely, if ever, used it for its intended purpose, preferring to eat in the kitchen on the rare occasions they were all together for a meal. Though undeniably elegant, the large round mahogany table had mostly been used as a place for the kids to do homework. Tom could still see them, textbooks spread open on that well-polished surface, he and Lawrie silently racing each other to see which one would finish first, Tom pretending not to care when Lawrie inevitably did. These days Margaret used the table only to wrap presents or address Christmas cards. Standing here now, he was surprised to see it almost completely covered in photos.

A fancy old hatbox sat in the midst of them, its once sharply delineated pink and white stripes now faded and blurred to a sickly, uniform beige. Its lid was askew, and from its satin-lined interior came a faint scent of jasmine and lilies, an antique perfume that Tom immediately recognized as the same one he'd experienced in his bedroom last Monday night when he'd been so sick. Shakily, he walked to the table, pulled out one of the Hepplewhite chairs, and sneezed. Sitting down heavily, he stared at the black-and-white photos scattered around him, as from down in the kitchen he heard the back door open and close, then the sound of Jubal skidding around the corners on his way up the hall, Margaret's footsteps close behind him.

"There you are," she said, coming into the room, her arms full of hydrangeas. "Just look at these things!" She lifted the bouquet of chartreuse blooms in the air. "Have you ever seen such glorious color? I swear, unlike you, I've never considered myself any sort of gardener. But the year *Southern Living* put these Limelight hydrangeas on their cover and said any fool could grow them, I had your father plant thirty-four bushes. And lo and behold, they were right!" Bending down, she opened the sideboard and took out a cut crystal vase. "I've just been out there in the backyard cutting enough to fill every room in this house, and I still have tons more to go. I'm going to walk these down to Harriet."

Turning back, she looked Tom full in the face for the first time, then sat the vase on the table and stuck the hydrangeas inside it. "Son, you look awful. Why don't you go up and take a nap. You can finish planting all those pansies later."

"Maybe in a minute," said Tom, weakly. "What's all this?"

Margaret pulled a chair over beside him and sat down. "Oh well, I got all these out this morning before you got up," she said, wiping her hands on her shirt and reaching for a small stack of photos. "I've kept this old hatbox of Aunt Edith's under my bed for years. Thought I'd look again and just make sure there weren't any pictures of my parents, you know. But of course, there weren't. I mean, I knew there wouldn't be. Still, I love looking at these." She picked up a photo and held it out to Tom.

He turned his head. Looking down, he saw it was torn at the corner. The scar had been carefully taped over, and the name "Gulliver" was written in an elegant, spidery script along its sawtooth-edged border. A little girl stared up at Tom out of the black-and-white past. She held a dark kitten in her chubby arms, delight clearly visible on her small face.

"I've looked at this picture so many times," said Margaret, leaning over. "I swear I can fully remember that cat, right down to the way his fur felt warm under my hands that day when we took this. But..." she sighed, "poor Gulliver was transported to glory beneath the wheels of old Luther Winslett's pickup truck before he reached his third birthday." She shook her head slowly and shrugged. "So, I can never be sure if it's the cat I remember, or this picture of him."

Reaching across Tom, Margaret picked up another photo. "See now," she said, handing it to him. "I think I can remember that dress. You can't tell in this picture, of course, but it was red. With a white grosgrain ribbon that tied in the back. Ida Mae always did it up for me. She could tie the perfect bow."

Looking down, Tom saw the same little girl, smiling again. This time she was standing knee-deep in hyacinths, wearing a full-skirted dress with white piping. Her dark curls were held back from her face with little lamb barrettes, and plastic grass spilled over the rim of an Easter basket held in her hand. A tall gray-haired woman was standing beside her. Tom stared, and then felt his stomach flip like a fish.

"Who..." he began. "Is that... Aunt Edith?" His voice sounded higher than normal.

"Well, of course." Margaret took the old photo out of his hand. "See there," she said, "you'd think she was just dressed up for Easter, but like I said the other night, this was the sort of thing Aunt Edith always wore. I swear, I've seen her plant those flowers we're standing in—she planted more every fall—wearing that very same outfit. And always that same string of pearls."

"I... I think I need to go lie down," said Tom, rising slowly, both hands flat on the table.

"You shouldn't have gone out," said Margaret, frowning up at him. "You should've just stayed in bed. I bet you went to Bloomin' Nursery again, didn't you?" She stood up and placed the back of her hand to his forehead. "I thought you were doing so much better; Lord knows we don't want you to relapse or anything. That can happen with the flu."

"Is any of Dad's bourbon still here?" asked Tom.

"Well, yes," said Margaret. "But I didn't think you were a drinker."

"I'm not. Not usually. But I think I'd like a little bit right now."

Tom followed Margaret into the kitchen, where she opened a cabinet and took out a half-full bottle of Four Roses. She poured an inch of the amber liquid into a juice glass and handed it to him. "Well, it *was* your father's remedy for whatever ails you," she said. "And you know what mine is."

"Open my window. I remember," said Tom.

"Nobody gets enough fresh air anymore."

"In this house they do." Tom grabbed the bottle of bourbon and filled the glass up to the brim. "Thanks, Mom," he said.

Margaret's eyes widened at the sound of the name. "Careful, Son," she said, as he turned to head upstairs to his room, the glass in his hand. "You're not used to spirits."

It was true, Tom wasn't a drinker, had never liked the taste of the stuff, but he downed the full glass in two eye-watering gulps the second he closed his bedroom door. It would burn his insides with satisfying cruelty and, having made landfall in the empty stomach of a teetotaler, soon set about pulling him into a sleep both dreamless and dizzy. The last thing he would remember was the sound of his mother playing the piano downstairs and he would sleep until long after dark.

20

Margaret

Harriet's old plastic flowers, still unnaturally bright, were now blooming somewhere in a landfill. Tom had spent the whole of yesterday redoing all her window boxes, filling them with cinnamon ferns, purple cabbages, and ivy, and last night, while Margaret and Jubal had been curled up on the sofa watching *Wuthering Heights*, he'd drawn up plans to yank out the row of hoary boxwoods that had been struggling to survive in Harriet's side yard since the Clinton administration. He intended to replace them with gardenia bushes as soon as he could, and if Harriet was agreeable, he was going to plant three tulip trees by her sidewalk and two Lady Banks roses, one on either side of her porch. Amidst all this industry, Tom had continued to pop back into Margaret's, sweaty and dirt-covered, every couple of hours just to "see how she was doing." Margaret was finding this rather intrusive, yet hardly surprising.

Yesterday had been tedious. It was now perfectly clear to her that all three of her children were concerned she was losing the thread. Though none of them had mentioned Aunt Edith outright, Emlynn had come by for a visit in the afternoon, and Lawrie had phoned twice last night. Even Nick had stopped in around noon, still wearing his stethoscope around his neck, and bearing a tray of freshly baked muffins from Mouse. Margaret had caught him looking at her with a decidedly professional stare. Margaret figured Mouse must have told them all Sunday while she'd been at church.

Last night as she sat in bed, a copy of *Dumb Witness* open in her lap and Jubal asleep with his big head on her ankles, Margaret wondered whether she might have made a mistake in telling Nathan Culpepper she'd been seeing Aunt Edith, especially with Mouse present to hear it. Surely, she'd known Mouse would feel compelled to tell her brothers. This is precisely the type of information for which grown children are always on the alert, worrisome evidence that their roles in the family might be about to change due to a mother or father who's slid headfirst round the bend.

But the news had obviously brought them together, all three of them, and God knows when that had last happened without an official occasion to prompt it. Despite the reason, this pleased Margaret. And Tom, of all people, was asleep in his room down the hall. That pleased her, too. Margaret couldn't shake the notion that Aunt Edith had a hand in all this, though she felt a bit silly for feeling that way. Looking up from the pages of her book, she let her eyes roam the empty room. Aunt Edith, having gotten her into all this, had apparently decided to just let it play out as it would. It had been almost a week since she'd appeared.

Margaret was surprised to discover she missed Aunt Edith's ephemeral presence more than she'd like to admit, and apparently, she wasn't alone. Jubal, she was sure, had been waiting for the old lady, too, occasionally raising his head and staring into the corners of the bedroom as though wondering when she was coming. But the bedroom had felt so devoid of Aunt Edith, it was difficult to imagine either one of them had ever actually seen her.

There were moments when she distrusted her own faculties, her own memory of events... Margaret had read the sentence on page 42 of this, her favorite Agatha Christie, at least four times already. She closed the book with a snap, causing Jubal to raise his head and look at her quizzically. "Well, I for one trust my own faculties," Margaret said, scratching Jubal behind the ear, "*and* my own memory of events. You know as well as I do that Aunt Edith has been here. You've seen her yourself. Haven't you, boy?" The dog wagged his tail in what Margaret chose to interpret as unqualified agreement. She placed the book on the night table, turned off the bedside lamp, and scooted down under the covers. It was already going on one. And Margaret needed some sleep.

It happened the second the room went dark. Suddenly, the scent of Arpège blew in through the window, sweetening the air with the fragrance of jasmine and lilies. And there she was. Bathed in a shaft of white moonlight, Aunt Edith sat in the chair by the window, legs crossed at the ankles, with one of those satisfied smiles on her face, looking for all the world like she was waiting on a bus to take her to town. If she'd been wearing a watch, Margaret would've bet she'd been just about to check the time before complaining the thing was again running late.

"I'm doing what you want. I've got somebody looking." This time, Margaret sat up and spoke directly to her great-aunt, one arm around Jubal, who himself stared over to where Aunt Edith sat, his tail tentatively wagging. "If my brother is out there, I'm going to find him." Aunt Edith sat still and quiet, her eyes on Margaret, smiling. "So, is there anything *else* you want me to know?" Margaret asked in a loud whisper. Aunt Edith slowly nodded, but then, true to her habit, a mere three seconds later, she faded away to a monochrome mist. Jubal had had no trouble falling right back to sleep, but Margaret stayed awake most of the night.

The room was just beginning to turn pink with the new morning when her phone rang, the sound piercing the quiet like a bugle. Raising herself up on one elbow to answer it, plumping her pillows behind her back as she did so, Margaret barely said the first syllable of "hello" when she heard a voice say, "Mrs. Elliot?"

"Yes."

"Nathan Culpepper here. I know I'm calling too early. You're probably still asleep."

Margaret's heart seemed to stop for a second, then flutter to an unnatural speed. "No, Mr. Culpepper. I'm awake."

"Well, good. I just couldn't make myself wait any longer. I tell you, this is a new one on me. Not sure what to say exactly. First off, remind me again how you found the photo of that house. The one by the beach?"

Instinctively, Margaret scooted over closer to Jubal. "Well... like I said when I saw you, I came across it on the internet, one night last summer when I couldn't sleep. I could never find it again."

"And you're absolutely sure you'd never seen it before?"

"Positive. Why?"

"Well..." Margaret heard the man sigh. "I don't know how to tell you this, but I'm standing right in front of the place. And if I have all my ducks lined up right, this just might be where your brother lives."

For a minute, Margaret wasn't sure she'd heard Nathan Culpepper correctly. His words seemed as insubstantial as soap bubbles, hanging there in the air for a moment, then popping as soon as he spoke them. How could they possibly be true? She tried to verbalize something coherent but wasn't surprised when nothing came out. Fortunately, the detective wasn't waiting for a response.

"See, I got on the phone after we met Saturday and found out who the police officers were in Bentonia, Mississippi, you know, back when that article came out. This lady in the station over there looked it up in the old records for me. I reckon things are slow over there, 'cause it only took her a few hours to turn up the name of the fellow who found that poor couple that day. Sheriff Hutch Dilbeck. Had a wife named Martine. But no kids. And it turns out Dilbeck left the state just two months after it happened. Took a job as the police chief out on Enoree Island, off the coast of South Carolina. You ever heard of it?"

"N . . . no."

"Hmmm. Well, it's a quiet little place. And Dilbeck must've liked it. Lived here till the day he died. He wasn't difficult to trace. But here's the thing. Like I said, the Dilbecks didn't have any kids when they left Mississippi. But they sure had one when they showed up here. Little boy. So yesterday afternoon, I decided to take me a drive to the coast. Spent the night here on Enoree Island. Just looking around, talking to folks. Turns out that son still lives here. I found his address. And I just pulled up in front of his house, not five minutes ago. I . . . I swear to you, I can't quite believe what I'm seeing. That picture you gave me? Mrs. Elliot, it's the same place."

Margaret had gone cold as an ice cube. "It can't be," she whispered.

"Yeah, that's what I told myself, right out loud standing here in the sand. But I'm holding that picture in front of my face, and there's no doubt about it. Same red roof, same wraparound porch, same crooked palm trees. Here, I'm going to text you a photo. Hold on a minute."

Her lips pressed tight together, Margaret pulled the phone from her ear and cradled it in the palm of her hand. The text came through with a tiny pinging sound, and she clicked on the photo immediately, suddenly grateful she wasn't standing up.

She noticed the palm trees first. One crossed in front of the other. Nathan Culpepper was right. It was the same house.

"D'you get it?" Margaret heard the detective's voice and put the phone back up to her ear.

"Yes," she said, softly.

"So, what do you want me to do? I won't knock on his door unless you say so."

"What's his name?" Margaret asked.

"John. John Dilbeck."

Margaret realized now that she'd never really expected this. It had all been like some sort of fancy, like a story from out of a book. She hadn't thought it through. Those few months of her life before she came to live with Aunt Edith? There were reasons her aunt had kept all that from her. Probably the very same reasons Lawrence had done the same thing. Did she really want to know everything now that both of them were gone? Wouldn't it be simpler just to leave it all tucked up in the past?

But then she remembered Aunt Edith. If her aunt had known Margaret had a brother, she would have taken him in to live with her, too. Margaret had no doubt about that. And no matter what anyone said, what anyone thought, Margaret knew in her heart that her aunt now wanted Margaret to know what Lawrence obviously hadn't. Why else had she shown up the very week Lawrence died? Margaret also knew, like she knew the sun would rise every morning, that Aunt Edith meant all this for her good.

"Yes, Mr. Culpepper. I want you to talk to him. Find out for sure if he is who we think he might be. And if he is, see if he'd like to meet me, because I sure would like to meet him."

PART FOUR

21

Margaret

Nathan Culpepper was playing zydeco music this evening, the jaunty rhythm a stark contrast to the anxiety bubbling up in his office. The Elliot children sat in a row in front of his burlwood desk, lined up in their order of birth, with Nick beside Mouse, and Margaret and Emlynn side by side at one end. Emlynn had just returned from her second trip to the bathroom, and in the early evening light, Margaret thought she looked rather green around the gills. Nick was tapping his foot as he stared up at a painting, his head cocked so far toward his shoulder, his ear almost touched it.

"I think it's supposed to be a cow," whispered Margaret, and Nick laughed, but he was the only one who did.

"Look," Margaret said, finally breaking the tension that was radiating in the high-ceilinged room like a blue flame. "I'm well aware of your skepticism about this meeting tonight, but you've all been very polite about it, and I want to thank you for that." Margaret saw Nicky reach over and squeeze Mouse's knee. Lawrie and Tom sat still as statues, neither one looking at the other. "Now, I know none of you believe that I've been seeing the ghost of my aunt Edith, or the one of this man who's on his way here right now." Everyone stole a glance at everyone else, and Margaret continued, pretending she didn't see. "And frankly, I don't blame you at all. That's something no one expects to hear about their mother, or about anybody, I guess. I know you've all been watching me since Mouse told you, and yes, I know that she must've told you on Sunday. Tommy came home that afternoon white as a sheet and downed a whole glass of bourbon." Everybody looked over at Tom, who was keeping his eyes on the floor.

"I don't blame Mouse for telling you," Margaret continued. "I'd have done the same thing." She smiled, shaking her head. "You're all pretty obvious, you know. Tom's been like a microscope trained right on me. Mouse and Lawrie have called so much I've been tempted to turn off my phone. And I can never remember Nicky leaving work to come visit me in the middle of an afternoon. I've known you've all been waiting for me to forget to turn off the stove, or leave the water running in the bathtub, or—oh, I don't know—maybe start clucking like a chicken."

Emlynn giggled, and Mouse winced.

"But I doubt any of you can adequately explain why I found this man's house on the internet. Why I printed out the photo and kept it on my refrigerator for months. You must admit that falls outside the realm of coincidence. Now, you don't have to believe my aunt Edith had anything whatsoever to do with all this. But I want you to know *I* believe it. So please, just listen to what this man has to tell me. Don't be defensive. Don't make jokes. Remember, I'm almost certain this is *your* family he's talking about, too. Not just mine. I'm pretty sure y'all are about to meet an uncle you've never even known about. That's why I wanted you here. This is about you, too."

From across the long hallway outside the room they could hear the rattling of glasses and cutlery. Then Nathan Culpepper entered, carrying a large tray in his hands. No longer clad in blue jeans and flannel with his eyebrows bright red, coming toward them was a rather handsome man in chinos and a soft suede blazer. His hair, though still achingly short, was dark, and on his feet, he wore Docksides and no socks, like most Southern males who wish they lived a bit closer to water. His eyes swept the room, stopping briefly at each of them, and somehow Margaret felt that, without hardly trying, Nathan Culpepper now knew all their secrets.

"Here we go," he said, placing the tray on his desk. "Iced tea for everybody. Got some sweet and unsweet, so take your pick. There's some of those macaroons from McEntyre's Bakery, too. Y'all help yourself."

"I'm sorry," Margaret said, reaching for a glass. "I don't mean to keep staring, but I swear, I can still hardly recognize you."

"Yes, ma'am, that happens. I'd just finished the Oliver case when we saw each other on Saturday. I hated that red hair." Nathan Culpepper laughed. "I change up my appearance for each job. To be honest with you, Mrs. Elliot, I don't think any of my clients can say for certain just what I look like." Sitting down, he took a macaroon, broke off a piece, and put it in his mouth. Reaching for the folder in front of him, he opened it, chewing thoughtfully. "Now, let's see. We've got a few minutes. I think we've gone over most everything. Anything y'all want to ask me before he gets here?"

Mouse spoke up almost immediately. "Well, I just want to know how you can, how *we* can, be *sure* this is really my mother's brother. I mean, is there a birth certificate or something? Shouldn't they take some sort of DNA test? Couldn't this guy just be *anybody*?"

"We won't need to take a DNA test, for God's sake," said Margaret. "I'll know if it's him."

"Mother," Mouse sighed, "I'm sorry, but you're basing all this on visions and dreams. We all know that now. This man could be trying to take advantage of you. I just think we need some kind of proof."

"Oh, Mouse," Margaret said, "I could never *prove* the most important things I *know*. And, you know what? You wouldn't be able to either. How did I know your father loved me? Because he said so? Because of our marriage certificate? Or because he remembered I'd worn daisies in my hair for our wedding, and brought me some every year for our anniversary? It was so much more than all that. It was something carved somewhere inside me, on my bones or ... no, even deeper. On my soul." She rearranged herself in her chair, her irritation at Mouse clearly evident. "Believe me, I'll know if this man is my brother."

"And, if I may," said Culpepper, holding up a finger, and looking at Mouse, who was about to say something else that might not have been helpful. "Let's not let our imaginations run away with us, Mrs. Moretti. Remember, Mr. Dilbeck didn't go looking for your mother. She came looking for him."

"Yes, because she thinks a *ghost* told her to," muttered Mouse. "Everyone in this room is aware of that. I'd just like some more proof, if you have it."

"Well, we've got a little bit more to go on than a couple of pale apparitions. Though, you're right, there isn't exactly a paper trail as such," said Culpepper. "From talking to John, I gather his parents—your parents, too, if I'm right, Mrs. Elliot—were just some of those unfortunate people who fell through the cracks back then. Nobody knows where they came from when they showed up in Bentonia, and from what John told me, his father—Sheriff Dilbeck, that is—told him that there'd been some serious alcohol problems long before the tragedy happened that day. Apparently, he'd visited the house a good many times before then, though he had no idea there were any kids living there. Seems he never went inside the place till that day. All Dilbeck knew about them was what the hospital found written on your birth certificate, nothing more than their names and that old address of your aunt's, that house out on Boundary Road. They were able to trace her with that. But they never found a birth certificate for John. Frankly, the Dilbecks wanted kids of their own so bad, I don't think they looked very hard. They wanted to keep him, so that's what they did. But you can ask him all about that when he gets here." Culpepper looked at his watch. "Which should be about now."

The silence was thick in the room. From somewhere outside, a dog barked. Emlynn crossed and uncrossed her legs. "It feels like we're waiting for Max von Sydow," she said, nervously. Culpepper was the only one who laughed.

Just then they heard a door open and close on the street. A pause. Footfalls on the steep stairs, and then quiet.

"Down here on the right, John," Culpepper called out, and the Elliot family stood up as one, all of them nervous, save Margaret. She'd been waiting for this moment, certain of a positive outcome. The footsteps started again.

He was tall and his hair was still dark. The glasses that perched on his nose accentuated the shape of his face, which was a bit angular, like hers. His smile was hesitant; it managed to be both sincere and slightly anxious, but his gaze was totally focused on her. As she knew it would be, the recognition was instant, and although he resembled her sons, it had nothing to do with appearance. Margaret felt that old familiar quickening from somewhere in the center of her chest, the same blood-to-blood current she'd always felt in that moment just before seeing one of her children, the same feeling she'd had when she'd been sixteen and seen that tall dark-haired young man from her window. She gripped the back of her chair with one hand and reached out toward John Dilbeck with the other. When he took it, they both smiled an identical smile.

His face was a canvas on which time had painted a story and Margaret knew without asking that he remembered her, too. Her hand remained warm when he released it. She started to speak, but John Dilbeck stopped her, holding up his right palm, his crooked little finger clearly visible in the light of the lamp on Nathan Culpepper's desk.

"Mouse, Lawrie, and Tom," said John Dilbeck, turning to face them, his eyes stopping a moment to rest on each face. "Emlynn and Nick. I've known you all for such a long time."

"Here, you need someplace to sit," said Culpepper, reaching through the gap in the old tapestry that divided the room and pulling out a ladder-back chair. He sat it beside Margaret and motioned for John to sit down.

Nobody seemed to be able to think of anything to say that didn't sound trivial or slightly ridiculous. Finally, it was Emlynn who spoke.

"So, Mr. Dilbeck, did you have a nice drive down?" Lawrie looked at Emlynn, and Margaret could feel how much he wanted to roll his eyes at such a perfunctory question.

"Well, Mr. Culpepper here drove me," said John Dilbeck, smiling over at Emlynn. "But please do call me John. I always feel like

I'm in some kind of trouble when 'Mister' takes the place of my first name."

"Mr. Culpepper told us you were a shrimp fisher?" asked Lawrie.

John laughed. "We call them shrimpers back home. But yes, that's what I always wanted to be. I think my folks hoped college would change that, but it didn't. Loved being out on the water. Still do. And shrimping was one way I could make money doing it."

"Margaret said you're retired now. Is that right?" Nick asked.

"Yes. Retired at sixty, a few years ago. Glad I did, too. Gave Carrie and me, that was my wife, Carrie, well, it gave us some time to travel before she died. I've been a bit at loose ends since she passed. Even thought about selling up and moving over to the mainland earlier this year, but only for a half second. Listed my house on one of those For Sale by Owner sites on the internet one night last June, then took it down the very next day. I couldn't live anywhere else."

Mouse sat up a bit straighter, crossing her arms over her chest. "You said you *knew* us all? How is that possible?" There was an edge in her voice that everyone noticed, including John.

"Well, Mouse," he began, smiling at her. "Or would you rather I call you Agatha? I know you only let a select few call you Mouse."

Mouse looked at Nathan Culpepper accusatorially, and he shook his head. "I didn't tell him that," he said. "I didn't even know that."

"No, your father told me," John said, picking up a glass of sweet tea and looking Mouse in the eye. "You see, I've known Lawrence Elliot since I was eighteen years old. I knew when you graduated from that culinary school up in New York. Knew when you married Nick here. Knew when Carly and Ben were born."

"And, Tom," he said, turning from Mouse, "I heard about what happened up in Atlanta last month. How you saved that piece of beautiful land. Caused quite a stir, I believe. News made the *Charleston Post*; bet you didn't know that. A lot of investors were pretty mad over there, I can tell you. I imagine you've taken a good bit of heat for what you did. That took guts, especially in your line of work. But I can tell you this for certain, your dad would've been so proud of you for taking a stand like that. Not even thinking about what it would cost you. That's a rare thing these days."

Everyone looked over at Tom, who was staring at John, open-mouthed.

"See, I've been keeping up with all three of you over the years," said John, smiling again.

"What's he talking about?" said Lawrie, looking at Tom.

"Oh," said Tom, shifting in his seat. "Nothing."

"You mean y'all don't know?" asked John. "Why, some guys were going to buy up these woods that run behind a bunch of old houses in the middle of the city, and they came to Tom to handle the development plans. Would've been a big project, am I right?" Tom nodded, his cheeks flushing pink. "But instead of helping them do it, Tom here got in touch with a lot of conservation groups and blew the thing right out of the water. Now the Public Land Trust has stepped up to buy it. They're turning it into a nature preserve."

"Tom," said Margaret. "Why didn't you tell us this?"

Tom remained silent, his face now a glorious red.

Everyone looked at everyone else, then back to John Dilbeck. "Well, if all that's true, and you know so much about us, then why haven't you ever let Mother even know you *existed*?" said Mouse. "If you expect us to believe you're her brother, then why are you just telling us *now*? Why did you never, in all these many years, get in touch with her? Why did she have to find out about you by . . . by some sort of accident?"

The tapestry moved as though a breath had gone through the room. Margaret turned in her seat toward John. "I would have preferred to wait for this a bit," she said, sighing. "At least till we'd gotten through some general pleasantries. But maybe you should tell us the whole story. I can't imagine what we'll talk about now if you don't."

John pushed back his chair and crossed his long legs. He remained still and quiet for a full minute, as though feeling the weight of the words he was getting ready to say.

"You know, Agatha," he began, looking over at Mouse, "I've heard it said that none of us really remembers anything before the age of three, maybe four. Like there's a fog in our heads up until then. That's probably true about facts, but I don't think it's true about feelings. Those seep through your skin early on." He took off his glasses, pulled a folded white handkerchief from his shirt pocket. "Growing up on the island when I was a kid," he said, slowly polishing his lenses, "I'd hear a snippet of song from a car bouncing down a dirt road, and all of a sudden, I'd get scared. My mother would drop a plate in the kitchen, or a limb might fall outside my window during a storm, and the sound would just slap terrify me. And I had no idea why. Other people didn't react like that. Why did I?

"If it'd been up to my mother, I'd never have known what happened that day to my parents. Well, to *our* parents, I guess." He nodded at Margaret and smiled. "But it had always weighed on my daddy. That day he found me there at that house. I don't think he ever got those images out of his head. He said he'd seen worse things in the war, but those were in context, you know? Expected, somehow, maybe easier to just put away." John bent his head and replaced his glasses. "Dad told me I'd had these dreams that first year. Said I'd wake up screaming my head off in the middle of an ordinary night. 'Course I didn't remember any of that. Still don't. Like I said, I was too little to remember the facts, but it sure seemed like I remembered the feelings.

"I know now that my parents—the Dilbecks, I mean—weren't even sure how old I actually was. They'd found out from the midwife that you'd been born the year before, Margaret, so they figured I had to be around two and a half, and since Mother's Day fell on May twelfth the next year, that was the birthday they gave me. I turned three that day. Since finding that out, I've woken up every morning, wondering if this might be the real day I was born."

"That's awful," whispered Emlynn, who immediately blushed after saying it.

"Depends on how you look at it," said John, smiling. "It's not such a bad thing to think every day might be your birthday. Carrie used to accuse me of using that as an excuse to eat cake every night."

"So how did you find out what happened?" asked Lawrie.

"Dad finally told me when I was eighteen. The night before I left for college. Made me promise never to tell Mama he had. He said he felt I deserved to know the whole truth. That I was old enough now. Said it might help answer some questions I didn't even know I had. And I guess it did.

"I remember he handed me a newspaper article. And this old picture he'd found clutched in my hand that day he found me. He'd kept them both in his billfold for years. He told me to never forget how lucky I was. Lucky I'd wandered out into the woods that day. Lucky he'd found me when he did. But luck was always a hard one for me. Too easy for it to turn bad, I suppose." John smiled over at Margaret again. "Besides, from where I sat, I knew you were the lucky one. You'd been too little to remember anything at all. You weren't ever bothered by those shadows that used to come for me in the night, were you?" He looked at Margaret expectantly, and she shook her head. No.

"Of course," he said, "it didn't take two months before I wanted to see you. That's only natural, I guess. All Dad had was that old address of your aunt's, but I figured it was worth a try. So, one fall weekend, I slipped off from school and drove down here to Wesleyan. Stood in the weeds on the other side of the road from that big white house, just staring up at it all. I swear, that place looked like a palace to me. I went around out back, and I could hear women laughing through the kitchen window. I saw all these trees, hundreds of them, it looked like a big green church. A bunch of men were spreading white blankets underneath them, like some ceremony or something." He paused and looked over at Margaret again. "I guess that old place is gone now."

"No, it's still there," she said. "Just barely. I've heard it's for sale. Tommy and I can take you out there tomorrow."

"I'd like that. I'd like that a lot." John Dilbeck folded his hands in his lap, his crooked little finger sticking out like a quotation mark. "Well, that afternoon, I just stood there in front of all those trees, and that's when I saw you. Just felt you behind me. It was the strangest thing. I turned around, looked up, and there you were, sitting in an upstairs window. I couldn't tell whether you could see me or not, but I knew it was you right away. Just knew it down deep in my bones, felt it like some kind of electrical shock. I went out under those trees to hide, hoping you'd come outside so I could get a better look at you, and maybe work up the nerve to introduce myself.

"And sure enough, after a minute or two, I heard that back door slam and there you were, running out to meet this young man who was standing there waiting for you. You were laughing. Lord, I can still see you." The zydeco songs had stopped, leaving an echoing silence in their wake. All eyes were turned toward John. "Well," he continued, "of course that was Lawrence, and one look at the two of you together? Anybody would've known what you meant to each other. And it was like... I don't know if I can properly explain it... but, suddenly I could see everything, from right there where I stood under those trees. I could see your whole life unfolding before me, like a vision in front of my eyes. The wedding, the kids, all the happy days that were coming.

"And I could tell, in that moment, that you'd never been told what had happened all those years ago to our parents. That big old house you were living in? It seemed to radiate happiness. And looking at you, I could tell it was all you'd ever known. I just knew, right then, that *I'd* never tell you. Why would I bring that darkness into your life? I knew what it felt like. Like something awful just out of your reach. Real, because it happened—unreal, because you couldn't remember it all. What good would that serve? Standing there inside that cathedral of trees, I swear it felt like some kind of atonement for me not to tell you. Like I had the power to erase a stain from both of our lives, and from our parents' lives, too.

"But I wanted to lay the story down somewhere. Lay it down and just walk away. It felt too heavy to carry alone. So, when you went back inside, I walked over to that young man, to Lawrence, and I told him who I was. Gave him the newspaper article and the photograph. Told him never to tell you unless the day came when he felt like you needed to know. I made him promise, just like my daddy made me. And I think Lawrence understood. The last thing he wanted to do was to hurt you in any way. Of course, at the time I'm not even completely sure he believed me, but he told me he'd put it someplace safe, someplace you'd never find it. And then, before I walked away, he asked for my address at school, and that's how it started, I guess. We began writing each other. And we kept it up all these years. Last March, when I saw in the paper he'd died, it felt like I'd lost a best friend. His last letter was sitting in my mailbox the day I came home from his funeral."

"You were at Lawrence's *funeral?*" said Margaret, eyes wide.

"I was."

Everyone stared at John Dilbeck as a whole minute passed by in silence.

"I'll . . . I'll bet you anything the reason Daddy never told her was because he didn't believe it was true himself. He wouldn't have kept something like that a secret," said Mouse, her words thick with emotion. "Not from *me*, we told each other everything. And Mother showed us that old picture. Those people could be anybody. We're just supposed to accept you're her brother because you *say* so?"

"I made Lawrence promise not to tell any of you," said John. "Margaret's life was about to change that day I met him. Her aunt's friend, Ida Mae? She was already getting sick, and she died not too long after. And then Edith got sick herself and was gone just a couple years later. Your parents got married two months after that. When would've been a good time to tell her? Besides," he said, shifting a bit in his seat, "I didn't want her to know, Lawrence knew that. Like you say, Agatha, there wasn't really any proof. I could've easily denied everything if he'd told her. But over the years, I think he became convinced I was right not to tell. Lawrence was always big on cause and effect; how one little ripple can change the whole course of history. Your mother, if I'm not wrong"—he glanced over at Margaret—"has had a real happy life. No ugliness at all in her past. And I don't know, I liked feeling I had a small part in that."

"Then why tell her now?" said Mouse. "Why suddenly show up now that Daddy's gone? Because, I have to tell you, Mother thinks the *ghost* of her aunt Edith orchestrated all this. Apparently, Aunt Edith's been visiting her a lot since our father died. Bet you didn't know that." Mouse waved her hand in front of her face like she was trying to disperse a bad smell.

"Mouse," said Lawrie, and Mouse waved him away, too.

Some of the color had drained from John Dilbeck's face. He turned from Mouse and swiveled toward Margaret, looking her full in the face. "That was Aunt Edith?" he whispered.

"She's been to see *you*?" said Margaret.

"Four times since last Easter," said John, shaking his head.

22

Mouse

She could feel the hot tears in her eyes, but still they refused to fall. Mouse slammed the car door as hard as she could, pulled the seatbelt over her chest with a jerk. Nick got in beside her and quietly closed his own door.

"Now, Mouse," he began, but she cut him off.

"How I wish Daddy was here!" she exclaimed. "He would've contradicted everything that man said, I just know it." Nick's silence conveyed a traitorous lack of accord, and Mouse turned to him, her eyes flashing. "Don't tell me you buy all that horseshit. That man's just looking to take advantage of Mother. You heard him. *I've been at loose ends since my wife passed.* Please. You hear about these kinds of people. They show up after somebody famous dies and they claim some sort of family rights or something. He could so easily have found out about Daddy. It was in the paper. Hell, *all* our names were in the paper."

"But, Minnie," said Nick, "take a breath and think about this. It's like Culpepper said. John didn't come looking for *Margaret*. She went looking for him."

"Yes, and they both think a *ghost* told her to. For God's sake, Nicky. You don't believe any of this. You can't possibly."

Nick rested his arm on the steering wheel and looked out the car window, frowning. They were parked in front of Epiphanies Bookshop, its windows already decorated for Halloween with copies of classic mysteries and ghost stories strategically displayed alongside the Cinderella pumpkins and limp cheesecloth ghosts. "Well, I don't believe in *ghosts*, if that's what you mean," he said, measuring his words. "But I don't think I *have* to believe in them to understand why your mother might feel like this man is who he says he is. You heard what Culpepper told us, and it all seems pretty plausible to me. Yes, I'll admit some of this other business is a bit . . . well, strange. I mean, that house your mother found, turning out to be the same house that he's lived in for years. I can see where that's hard for your mother to categorize as a mere coincidence. But weird things happen, I guess. Even if they've never happened to us. Mouse, some of the stuff my patients have told me would stretch your imagination till it snapped. More than a few of them have sworn they've seen ghosts, too, you know. Especially right before somebody dies. But, Minnie, you need to calm down. This'll all work itself out."

Mouse sighed theatrically and closed her eyes. "Nicky, when, in all the years you've been alive, has anybody ever calmed down just because you told them to?"

Nick laughed, which only made Mouse a bit madder. "I'm telling you," she said, "something's wrong with Mother, and that man is going to be trouble for her. For all of us. You notice, he didn't mention a ghost until I brought it up."

"Well, frankly, I don't blame him for that."

"He's some kind of charlatan," said Mouse, twisting in her seat. "I just know it." She pointed her finger at Nick. "But if this . . . this

John Dilbeck, or whoever he is, thinks he's going to just waltz into Mother's life and try to take Daddy's place in our family... or, or get his hands on her house, or something like that, he's got another think coming. I will *not* let that happen."

"I don't think that's what he's planning to do at all, Mouse," said Nick, shaking his head. "From what I could tell of the man, he has no intention of taking your father's *place* in anything, and you yourself heard him say he'd never live anywhere but on that little island, so why would he be interested in Margaret's *house*?"

"But she's invited him to *stay* there! With her! Sleeping in the guest room right down the hall," said Mouse, glaring at Nick. "A perfect stranger! It's not safe. And Daddy would never have allowed *that*, don't tell me he would have."

"Mouse, Tom is at the house with them. Believe me, I got a good look at John Dilbeck. Even if Tom's lost a few pounds since having the flu, I still believe he could take him."

"Don't joke about this, Nick Moretti. Don't you dare joke about this."

"I wouldn't," said Nick, sighing, "I'm not." He put the key in the ignition. After starting the car, he paused, then turned to look over at Mouse. "Honey, do me a favor," he said. "Hold out your right hand."

"What? Why?"

"Just do it. For me. Hold your right hand out in front of you, palm facing the dashboard." Mouse did as she was told, and they both looked at her hand. Her little finger sticking out like her mother's. Mouse made a fist and pulled it back into her lap.

"His was pretty obvious, too," said Nick. "You might want to think about that."

Mouse swallowed hard. "Just take me home," she said.

The shops on the square were dark now. Most closed early this time of the year. But as their car rolled slowly past Verbena Apothecary, Mouse saw Emlynn had left all the fairy lights on in the window. They lit up her mother's old dollhouse like memory itself. Mouse closed her eyes as they passed. She didn't need Nick to tell her she wasn't handling this well, and most infuriatingly, she seemed to be the only one who wasn't. Even the normally disdainful Tom had been quietly pliant tonight. Of course, Tommy had been acting out of character for days now.

Why was the prospect of her mother's lost brother such a threat to her? Mouse had no idea. Her emotions had been strangers to her for months, and now a heavy dose of unfocused anger had been thrown into the mix. It was settling on top of everything else she'd been trying her best to tamp down. If she could've jumped out of the car at the next light, Mouse didn't think she'd ever be able to stop running.

She slipped out of bed as soon as she knew Nick was asleep. Kitty Goldsmith answered on the first ring.

"What's up?" Kitty said, and Mouse heard the tinkle of ice against glass.

"You're not asleep yet, are you?"

"Oh, hell no. *Pit Bulls and Parolees* is on. It's my new favorite show."

"Well, good. I won't keep you but a minute. Listen, Kitty. I seem to remember you told me about having to get somebody's DNA once. Have I got that right?"

"Oh, yeah. Layla Calloway's husband. She was a cousin of mine from Pooler. Her best friend had a baby that was the spittin' image of Layla's husband, Todd, but he denied it up and down like the asshole he is. I mean, the kid was born with a full head of red hair, just like Todd's. Dead giveaway. But Todd wouldn't own up. 'Course DNA don't lie, and we nailed him that way."

"How'd you do it? I mean, how'd you get what you needed?"

"Oh, easy peasy. Layla left a house key for me under the dog bowl on the back porch one night when she and Todd had gone out to dinner. So, I just let myself in and stole his toothbrush right out of his bathroom. Then Layla took a present over for that baby one day and snipped a bit of that red hair off the kid's head while her friend wasn't lookin'. We sent it all up to some lab and got the results back in two days. Layla's living in Malibu now."

"Thanks, Kitty," whispered Mouse. "I owe you one. Talk to you later."

Kitty's voice was still crackling from inside the phone as Mouse pressed the off button and made her way quietly back down the hallway to bed.

23

Lawrie

Bright autumn sunlight sliced through a gap in the curtains, a vertical line of white that remained vivid on the undersides of Lawrie's eyelids even after he'd turned over, away from the window. Beside him, Emlynn's breathing was soft and slow, and he couldn't stretch out his right leg, which told him the dogs were all up on the bed. Raising his head, he saw Eric, Ginger, and Jack snuggled tight against Emlynn, reminding Lawrie immediately of Cerberus himself. Their snores were deep and steady, a sound that on any other morning would have been comforting for Lawrie to hear and would have, no doubt, lulled him right back to sleep. But not today. He let his head drop back down on the pillow. Why, he wondered, was it such a lonely feeling to be the only one awake?

Emlynn sighed in her sleep. It was a delicate little sound, like a child's, and it only made Lawrie feel worse. He'd snapped at her last night when she switched off the television without asking him if he'd mind. "I might have been watching that, you know," he said, even though he couldn't have told her what was on if she'd asked him. "I thought you were reading," she'd replied, the hurt in her voice clearly perceptible, right below the annoyance. "You're sitting there with a book open in your lap. Even if you haven't turned the page in thirty minutes."

That was the downside of a close relationship, he thought, watching Emlynn as she slept. The other person knows you so well you can't hide anything. Even lying gets you nowhere. Last night had scrambled several of Lawrie's assumptions about his family, and this had unsettled him more than he'd like to admit.

Pulling himself up into a sitting position, he looked around at the barely organized chaos that signified a blessed normality. Emlynn's polka-dot dress draped across a chair, his Nikes kicked under the dresser, soft balls of fur settled into the corners waiting to be vacuumed away, all evidence that nothing of significance had changed. So why did he feel that it had?

Slipping out of bed quietly so as not to wake anyone, he crossed the room, went into the bathroom, and closed the door. He turned on the tap in the sink, splashed two handfuls of cold water onto his face, then stared at himself in the mirror. For the first time in his life, his brother didn't stare back. Tom's beard now obscured their resemblance.

Tom had remained strangely silent all through last night's meeting with John Dilbeck, the man Lawrie supposed he should now refer to as his uncle. Lawrie noticed how quiet Tom had been only later. Of course, Lawrie had been preoccupied with concern for their sister. Sitting right next to Mouse as he'd been, he'd felt anger and doubt radiating off her like gamma rays. It was a wonder the whole left side of his body hadn't been burned. He'd sat there, anticipating her impending explosion, as tense as a stretched rubber band.

But Lawrie had had no doubt John Dilbeck was who he said

he was from the moment the man walked into the room. For one thing, the physical resemblance between him and Margaret was more than distinct, their profiles were exactly the same. And there was something in their voices, as well. He'd heard it clearly, that shared cadence and tone, those similar inflections, qualities you hear only in the voices of people who've crawled out of the same gene pool. Couldn't Mouse hear it? Couldn't she see?

But he had to hand it to his sister. She'd kept it together most of the evening, right up until the moment Margaret invited John to stay at the house.

"There's no reason in the world for you to get a *hotel*," his mother had said. "We have plenty of room, and so much to talk about, right?" Lawrie had recognized the look on her face, the one that would brook no refusals, the one Mouse should've seen. He could've told his sister her objection would be overruled.

"Mother," Mouse had said, standing up. "I'm sure Mr. Dilbeck would be *much* more comfortable in a hotel. The Mimosa Inn is just down the street and it's lovely. Besides, nobody likes to stay with *strangers*."

Lawrie had then been reminded of a porcupine he'd once observed in a class back in college, that fascinating, slightly scary half second before the creature raises its quills. Most animals know this is the time to back off, but apparently, Mouse wasn't as adept at reading the signals as he was.

"Mouse," Margaret had said, standing up too, and leveling a steely gaze at her daughter. "Why are you being so rude?"

Her question had been tantamount to sticking a needle into a balloon. As they watched, all the air seemed to go out of Mouse while at the same time she whirled and spun off out of the room, leaving Nick to pick up her purse and apologize. "I'm sorry," he said. "She's not been herself. I better go take her home."

Lawrie knew he should be happy for his mother. He should take his cues from the look on her face as she'd sat by John Dilbeck, listening raptly to his story. How could he help but feel happy for her? When she'd invited them all to dinner this coming Saturday, she'd squeezed Lawrie's arm tight, whispering, "I'll make pot roast. I know that's your favorite." But as he'd watched her walk off with both John and Tom by her side, something had gnawed at his insides, something he couldn't quite name. He'd chosen not to tell Margaret she was mistaken. Pot roast was Tom's favorite, not his.

Misjudging the cleft in his chin, Lawrie nicked himself and hissed out a curse to the mirror. Peeved, he placed a tiny bit of Kleenex over the cut and watched the white tissue turn red.

He wondered now if anybody else had taken the time to look John Dilbeck up online, as he had last night after getting back home. Lawrie had not been entirely surprised to learn the man was no mere shrimper, as he'd allowed them all to believe. By the time he retired six years ago, John had owned a fleet of fishing boats that sailed the deep waters of both the Gulf and the Atlantic, all the way from South Carolina to the shores of Galveston Bay. Their unassuming new relative could buy and sell the whole Elliot family a good five times over, at least.

After this discovery, Lawrie had, rather reluctantly, looked up what John Dilbeck had said about Tom. He'd thought at the time that the man must be mistaken—this was Tom, after all—but lo and behold, it was all there if you knew where to look. Lord, Tom had gotten some serious bad press in the industry weeklies. Apparently, it was equivalent to high treason for a commercial developer to take conservation's side in a real estate deal the way he'd done. From the comments Lawrie had read on the internet, some in Tom's business believed he'd made a journey to the dark side from which he might never return. This news had kept Lawrie awake most of the night, wondering if he'd ever really known his brother at all.

24

Margaret

The morning sky was beginning to darken, and an insistent cool wind had whipped up out of nowhere, threatening to pierce the old corduroy jacket she wore. Margaret stopped for a moment and buttoned it up. Tom and John were already paces ahead, and she'd lost sight of Jubal not five minutes after he bounded out of the Volvo. She could hear the dog barking excitedly now, somewhere out under the pecan trees. Margaret paused, hesitant to go any farther. Looking around her, she wondered now if she should've stayed home.

The paint on the For Sale sign out by the road had already started to peel, broadcasting the fact that qualified buyers were not lining up. She wasn't surprised. She could see that both the house and the orchard had been relinquished to the vagaries of time long ago. This was no mere fixer-upper. Picking her way through the overgrown grass, she stopped at the bottom of the front porch stairs, squinting up at the once welcoming farmhouse, now rendered mute by the absence of people. The second-floor windows stared down at her like a row of unblinking eyes.

The first floor was dressed for a hurricane that wasn't forecast. Windows boarded up tight, wood nailed across the front door. Margaret went around the side yard, holding back vines and pushing through branches, making mental notes of all the missing shutters and broken windows, till she reached the back of the house. Here the pecan trees still stood, their wide trunks now crowded with weeds and encircled by tangles of vines.

She could clearly remember how they'd looked on her wedding day, this steadfast army in green and brown, forever posted outside her bedroom window, marching off from the hyacinth garden, all the long way down to that sagging chain-link fence that had been the only barrier between this place and the Elliots'. The old trees still stood in ramrod-straight rows, their glory, though faded, abiding.

To her right, she could see Tom and John up on the back porch, both men standing on tiptoes trying in vain to see past the boards that covered the tall kitchen windows. Margaret didn't need to see inside. As if they were whispers that only got louder as she acknowledged their presence, it was easy for her to hear those long-ago voices, see right past those boarded-up windows. She closed her eyes to picture it all.

Yes, there was the large metal box fan whirring in the center of the room, its breeze ruffling the aprons Aunt Edith and Ida Mae wore tied around their dresses. It was October, and a layer of hot, salty air had blown in from the coast. It hovered over Wesleyan with no apparent intention of moving. It was hot as July in the kitchen.

A bright blue bandanna was twisted around Aunt Edith's gray hair, and her face was beet red from the steam rising from pots of boiling corn and pans of fried okra. Margaret saw her take a handkerchief from inside her sleeve and press it against her damp upper lip.

But those old rooms are all empty now, Margaret thought, opening her eyes. And the people she'd loved had all gone. That's the thing about traveling back into the past. When you arrive, there's nobody there. Looking over, she saw Tom jumping up and down, still trying to see in the windows. Turning, she walked out underneath the tall trees by herself, down the same row she'd walked on the day that she married, staring up into nothing but green.

Just as it had done on her wedding day, shade fell over her shoulders like water, leaves rippling and twirling in a quickening wind. Family trees, she thought now to herself. Each leaf allied with the others, on branches akin to one another and connected to something deep-rooted and strong. With her head held back, she watched one leaf break away, sailing out on an invisible current, up into the breeze all alone. It seesawed and swayed like a feather, floating and falling in slow motion, till it landed, right into her palm. She heard John's laughter coming from the back porch, and she smiled.

Last night, Tom had gone to bed not long after carrying John's suitcase up to the guest room, but Margaret had sat in the den with John till early this morning, telling him all about her life with Ida Mae and Aunt Edith, listening to the story of how he'd grown up on Enoree Island. Most of her stories, John already knew. Lawrence's letters had apparently been regular.

Sometime around midnight, she'd gone upstairs and retrieved the old hatbox from under her bed. Placing it between them on the sofa, Margaret had opened it up, releasing its flowery fragrance, those signature notes of Arpège. She reached inside and pulled out a photo of Aunt Edith, the one of her standing by the piano at Christmas. John took it, stared down, and began slowly shaking his head.

"Is that who you saw?" asked Margaret.

"It sure is," said John, his hand on his glasses. "Like I said, four times. The first couple of times I was sure I'd just dreamed her up. By the third, well, I figured not. But I'd never seen a picture of her. I had no idea who she was."

Margaret then handed him the old studio photo of Maynard Lowry. "That's our grandfather," she said. "In his uniform." Leaning over, she looked at the upside-down face. "I don't think Aunt Edith ever knew why he left," she said. "She told me he had a hard war, and sometimes that happens, I guess. I've got a friend whose son hasn't darkened her door since he came back from Afghanistan." Sitting back up, she picked up a photo of Ida Mae.

"Well, it's certainly true that the man who goes to war is often not the same one who comes home," said John, still staring at Maynard Lowry's young face. "But you know the real reason, don't you?"

"The real reason?"

"The real reason he left. I guess there's no use not telling you now. Lawrence wrote me about it years ago. Said his sister told him. She said their parents remembered hearing the shouting that night, Maynard calling Ida Mae and Edith some pretty awful things. They heard him tell Edith that she had to choose. Said he wouldn't live in that house with them if she and Ida Mae remained like they were. You know, together. Next thing Lawrence's parents knew, Maynard was gone."

"What do you mean, he made Aunt Edith choose?" said Margaret, dumbfounded. "You mean choose between him and Ida Mae?"

"Apparently so," said John.

"Why on earth didn't Lawrence ever tell me all this?" said Margaret, shaking her head. "He told me about Ida Mae and Aunt Edith. About their relationship, I mean. I remember him laughing when he realized that I didn't know. So why didn't he tell me about Maynard?"

John handed her back the photo of their grandfather. "I guess for the same reason I didn't want you to know about me, about what happened when our real parents died. He wanted to protect you. Didn't want you to feel bad about your grandfather. You know, Lawrence told me Aunt Edith made him promise, way back when y'all were little, to watch out for you. She said, 'Never let anything trouble her soul.' Those were her exact words. And he took that to heart."

"But that wasn't their decision to make!" said Margaret, her eyes flashing. "To think all these people around me—Aunt Edith, Ida Mae, *you*—were carrying such burdens while I walked around with bells on my skirts. It makes me feel, I don't know... ashamed. Like I've lived my whole life under glass."

"I'm sorry, Margaret," said John, softly. "Maybe we all did the wrong thing. I might have done differently if I'd been a bit older. But like I said, I didn't want the tragedy of our beginning to color your life, and it was out of love for you that I made Lawrence promise never to tell you. It was out of love for you that he didn't."

He picked up another photo of Aunt Edith, holding it under the lamp. "Maybe that's why she came back after Lawrence passed on," he said, his glasses down on his nose. "Don't get me wrong, I'm not somebody who would normally say something like this. I've always thought, well, people die and get sorted to heaven or hell. They don't pop back up on this side whenever they feel like it. That's what I was taught. But when Nathan Culpepper showed up on my porch this morning, telling me you were trying to find me, well, something inside of me shifted, I guess. I thought right then about that old woman I'd seen, wondered if this was why I had seen her. That's why I agreed to come right on down here to meet you tonight. I never dreamed you'd seen her, too." He looked up at Margaret. "And now," he said, waving the photo in the air between them, "now I'm wondering if Edith just never got over losing her brother. She chose Ida Mae because she probably couldn't imagine living without her. But I'd bet losing Maynard haunted her for the rest of her life. So as soon as she had the chance, as soon as Lawrence was no longer held to the promise I'd talked him into, she showed up to get us back together. I don't know, one brother and sister reunited to make up for the brother and sister who got ripped apart." He took off his glasses and rubbed the small spot between his dark eyebrows. "I guess that sounds nuts."

"It's as good an explanation as any," Margaret said, sighing, as the clock chimed two in the morning. "Did you ever know anything about our parents? Anything at all?"

"Just the little bit Daddy told me," John said. "And most of that I sort of read in his silences. I was too little to remember the details, like I said, just the feelings seeped in. But from what he did say, that place they were living in? I don't think anybody even knew who owned it. Just a shack, I guess you could say. We've all seen places like that."

Margaret certainly had. Gray and forgotten, some of them still crouched along the old roads, rotten, barely upright, splintered reminders of a past nobody wanted to claim or remember. She'd passed by them all her life. Now to think she herself had come from such a place, had once lived in that sort of hopelessness. And she'd never even known. Margaret felt like she should apologize to someone, but for the life of her, she couldn't think of who that might be.

She'd lain awake long after she and John said good night, thinking how sheltered she'd been. First by Aunt Edith and Ida Mae, then by Lawrence, and of course, by John himself. What had she done to deserve it? Nothing, except to be born. Nothing, except to be loved. She didn't know whether to be grateful, or angry. For a historian, Lawrence had certainly been willing to play a big part in the rewriting of *her* history. So much for him saying life was nothing more than a coin toss. So many people had helped guarantee that hers came up heads.

But how might those hard truths have changed her if she'd known them? Perhaps that knowledge would've been harmful, just like John and Aunt Edith had feared. She might have turned anxious, or bitter, who knows? But then again, maybe it would have carved a deep groove of empathy inside her, one that comes only from experience, one that might've deepened her understanding, pushed her closer to her children, her friends, by giving her questions that she'd never had.

"And this old orchard could be restored." John's voice drifted around the trees, reaching her. Looking back, she could see him and Tom a few rows over, and now moved behind a wide tree to listen. "It's not impossible. You'd have to thin some of these out, of course. And irrigate the whole thing, which wouldn't be cheap. But with some work and some money, these old beauties could be producing in, oh, about three years or so, I guess."

"But then, what about the house?" said Tom, his hands on his hips, looking back. "That'd take a fortune."

"Maybe less than you think," said John. "You couldn't know till you got inside. Hopefully, it hasn't been bastardized by folks knocking down walls and pulling off molding. Maybe all you'd have to do is tend to some brightwork." He leaned against a tree, folding his arms across his chest. "Doesn't surprise me you'd want to see the old place saved. Not after what you managed to pull off up in Atlanta. How'd you do that exactly?"

Tom sighed heavily. "I don't really know," he said. "It wasn't something I meant to do, I can tell you that. But there's this lady, Gloria Hogan, who's worked at my office for years. She's lived there next to that land all her life, and I guess she helped put a face to the thing. Listening to those guys talking about their plans to tear it all up, plow it all under. For some reason, it just flew all over me. And I just... well, I just got mad, to tell you the truth. Like I say, nobody was more surprised than I was at what I did."

"Well, it's what we do on pure instinct that shows what we're made of." John laughed, bending over to pick up a newly fallen pecan and pitching it from palm to palm. He smiled. "You might be a better man than you realize."

Tom laughed and Margaret realized it was the first laugh she'd heard out of him since the night he came home. "It's like these gardens here, I guess," he said, looking back toward the house. "It'd be a shame to see them ripped up. They're a mess now, but you can still see the lines of all the old beds. Look at that big buckeye bush over there by the porch. That thing must be something in springtime."

"So, you're a gardener, too?" asked John, grinning. "That's something your dad never told me."

Margaret heard Tom laugh again. "I doubt Dad ever knew. If I'm being honest, that's the only part of my place up in Atlanta that I actually like. You can keep the house. I guess that's because I did all those gardens myself." He put his hands deep in his pockets, rocking up on his toes and back down again. "See, I didn't want to tell my wife... my soon to be *ex*-wife, that is... that the real reason I decided to let our gardeners go was because they were as expensive as hell, and we were pretty much hanging off a financial cliff every month. I didn't want Meghan to know *that*. So, I just told her I'd always wanted to try my hand at gardening. Said I thought it might help me relax." Margaret saw Tom's familiar sardonic grin, saw him shake his head. "I figured I'd have to rehire the same guys after a month or two. Between you and me, I have this . . . this tendency to abandon any activity at which I don't exactly excel." He paused, listening to Jubal snuffling through the weeds just behind them. "But damn, if I didn't like it. Gardening, I mean. Again, nobody was more surprised about that than I was. There was just something about having a spade in my hands and dirt on my knees. I forgot every trouble I had. The real ones *and* the imaginary ones. Soon I had these big sheets of white paper spread out on the dining room table and I was drawing up plans for pathways and peony beds. The dadgum botanical garden wants us on their tour next May. Can you believe that?" Tom scuffed the ground with the toe of his shoe. "'Course, I most likely won't be living there then."

John let the pecan in his hand fall back to the ground. "Seems to me you surprise yourself a lot, Tommy. Could be you've gotten too used to selling yourself short. Might be possible you've been measuring yourself against somebody else's yardstick for years."

Tom stared at John quizzically, as color rose in his face. From close by came the bass notes of thunder, and the wind answered by shaking the tops of the trees. Pecans rained down all around them. "What are you two discussing over there?" Margaret called out, weaving her way through the undergrowth. John and Tom turned.

"There you are," said John. "I thought you were still around front. We were wondering what it'd take to get this old place looking like it once did," said John. "Tom here was just saying how he'd love to see all these gardens restored."

Looking back toward the house, Margaret could see the old gardens alive in her mind—the lavender hyacinths, the roses, the trees, a picture she could call up whenever she wanted. Somehow, she knew these memories were more vivid than any re-creation could ever manage to be. And even if that were possible, it didn't seem necessary now. Standing here beside John, Margaret knew this old house of memories wasn't something she needed. The gap in Margaret's circle had closed. Aunt Edith had seen to that by giving her a future as well as a past.

Here and there, saucer-size raindrops began to hit the ground one by one, a lazy prelude to the torrent that was gathering steam just behind them. Tom called out for Jubal, and all four of them ran for the car.

25

Mouse

All those candy-colored houses clinging tight to the mountains high above the Amalfi coast looked too much like Legos to be real. Mouse pulled another brochure from the stack Kitty Goldsmith had dropped off for her yesterday, smoothing the accordion of glossy photos out on her desk, each one more spectacular than the last. A medieval stone balcony hanging out over a glassy blue sea, skeins of hot pink bougainvillea weaving their way through the balustrades. Two white-cushioned chaises sitting on a tiled floor beneath a cloudless, cerulean sky. Two tall glasses sweating ever so slightly in the warmth of a sun so mild Mouse doubted she'd even need sunscreen. Closing her eyes, she could almost feel the lemon-scented breeze waft toward her, blowing her hair from her forehead.

"How many lemon squares did you say were ordered for the Goldsmiths' wedding? We've grated forty-eight lemons this morning, but I'm thinking we'll need at least a few dozen more. And did I get this right? Are they really having an Elvis impersonator marry them? Is that even legal in Georgia?"

Mouse blinked up to see Marcy Weller standing on an idyllic Italian porch that immediately pixelated back into the dark wood of her office. One hand on the doorknob, Marcy peered into the room, waiting patiently for an answer.

"Oh," said Mouse. "Right. Kitty's due here any minute, isn't she? Uh, let me see." She raked the brochures toward her, stacked them up neatly, then pulled out a bright green notebook and flipped through it. "Here it is," she said. "Two hundred and forty lemon squares. Good Lord, twenty dozen." Mouse rubbed a spot on the top of her head where the last images of Italy seemed to have settled. "Personally, I think that's way too many, especially with all the cakes that we're doing. But I wasn't going to argue with Kitty. And yes, Elvis will be doing the honors." Sighing, Mouse handed Marcy a picture of a pudgy man trussed up in a tight rhinestone jumpsuit, his hair the shade of black only found in a bottle of dye. He was holding a microphone in one hand and a Bible in the other.

"Huh," said Marcy, her eyebrows up near her hairline. "So, they're going with fat Elvis, are they? Brave choice."

"I agree," said Mouse, trying hard not to grin. She took back the photo and returned it to the green folder. Then as Marcy turned to go, she said, "You're sweet to help us out on all this, Marcy. I know how busy you are during the week."

"School's out for fall break. It was this or sit home with the cats," said Marcy, turning to go. "Besides, I wouldn't miss this particular wedding for anything." She closed the office door, and Mouse heard her giggling all the way back down the hall.

Mouse didn't feel like laughing. She placed her palms on her desk, took a deep breath, held it for four seconds, then let it out slowly. She was sweating like it was August, even though this was the coolest day Wesleyan had seen in a week. She picked up a brochure from the Hotel Villa Cimbrone and fanned herself vigorously with it, still shaken by what she'd just seen, not to mention what she'd just done.

It hadn't been all that hard, to be honest. Last night, when she'd heard her mother promise to take John Dilbeck out to the old place on Boundary Road this morning, she'd guessed that Tom would go with them. So, after giving them all enough time to get away, she'd driven over to the house and found the old Volvo gone, just as she'd hoped. Her heart racing, she'd whipped into the driveway, found the key under the third pot from the door, and let herself inside.

Not indulging in the time it might take to reconsider, Mouse ran up the stairs two at a time and upon reaching the landing, paused only briefly at Tom's closed bedroom door to make certain she didn't hear him inside. When everything stayed quiet, she hurried down the hall to the guest room.

The bed was neatly made, the apple-green duvet pulled up under the fluffy white pillows. An aged leather satchel sat by the window seat and Mouse could see an indentation in the down cushion where someone had recently sat looking out at the front yard. Mouse leaned in and peered out. For the first time, she noticed all the white pansies Tom had planted since coming home. Margaret had been right. It did look like it had snowed.

Then remembering her mission, she rushed into the bathroom and stood for a brief second, looking around. And there it was. In a glass by the sink, just as she'd figured. Pulling a small plastic bag out of her pocket, Mouse had taken a Kleenex from the box on the back of the toilet and carefully picked up John Dilbeck's toothbrush. She'd placed it into the bag, then sealed the bag between her forefinger and thumb. Then she reached into her purse and took out a dozen new toothbrushes, choosing the one that most resembled the one she'd removed and dropping it into the glass where the old one had been.

Going through the same process in her mother's bathroom had felt more like the deception it was. Mouse avoided her reflection in Margaret's mirror, trying, without success, to adequately justify what she was doing, and finally deciding to just not think about it. She'd hurried out of the room as soon as she finished her task.

She'd picked up the old floral scent the minute she reached the last stair, surprised not to have noticed it upon coming in. Hardly subtle, it stopped her right where she stood. Looking around her, Mouse could see vases of hydrangeas in the living room to her left, a large arrangement of the same on the hall table, but she knew these flowers, no matter how lush and lovely they were, had no fragrance at all. Besides, this smell was more like one of those perfumes old ladies wear, a feeble facsimile of the real flowers it mimics, one designed to make up in heaviness what it lacks in authenticity. Without any warning, Mouse sneezed.

Standing on the stairs, one hand on the newel cap, she swiveled slowly around to peer down the hall toward the kitchen. It was against her better judgment to investigate further—she had no desire to still be here when her mother got back. But curiosity doesn't always kill cats, she thought, turning around. Sometimes it just answers questions.

She crept down the hallway and stopped still between the kitchen and den. To her right, the kitchen sat dimly quiet in the shade of the poplars outside, the sun splashing bits of gold on the walls in response to the occasional breeze that ruffled the leaves, while to her left, it pierced the tall windows of the den like a klieg light, muting the room's colors like bleach. Mouse followed the light and stepped into the den.

The scent of old flowers was much stronger in here. It hung in the air, thick and sweet, like something you should be able to touch. An old hatbox sat in a puddle of sun on the table in front of the sofa, right in her sight line. Feeling almost as though she'd been pushed, Mouse walked over, sat down, and pulled the hatbox into her lap. The image of Pandora popped into her head as she rocked the lid back and forth till it opened.

The hatbox was full of old photos and right there on top was one of Aunt Edith, standing with Margaret at Easter. Mouse lifted the picture out of the box and held it out in her hand. The bright sunlight made the two figures shine and Mouse suddenly recognized someone she had forgotten. Fear and confusion entered her veins like venom, fuel to her now racing heart. She stood up and the hatbox slid to the floor. Backing away, Mouse turned and ran from the room, not stopping till she reached the driveway outside.

She sped back across Wesleyan like she was driving a stolen car, slowing only when she reached her own house. She ran inside and put the toothbrushes into the packages she'd already prepared, along with the forms she'd filled out. Dinky watched her with narrowed green eyes. Sealing up the packages, she pushed past the cat, ran back to the car, drove straight to the post office, and mailed them express.

It was only when she got back to Elegant Agatha's that the door in her mind behind which she'd stuffed the old woman she saw in that picture began to crack open wide. Try as she might, Mouse couldn't keep it shut any longer. She sat down heavily in her desk chair, putting her head in her hands, then took out the travel brochures Kitty had brought over, to try to distract herself from what she was thinking. That had worked for a minute or two, but Marcy Weller had now broken the spell. Mouse could no longer stop the images unspooling inside her head.

There was a hand-tinted portrait of Principal Edith Lowry that hung outside the lunchroom at Tillman Elementary. It had been there for decades, and no doubt was hanging there still. If she tried, Mouse could still see the face clearly, sternly handsome, old-fashioned in both style and expression. Mouse picked up her hair and fanned the back of her neck, her thoughts chasing one another round and round in her mind. There was also that framed photo of Aunt Edith on the wall of the landing in her mother's house. It had hung there since before she was born. Mouse must have passed by the thing hundreds, no, thousands, of times.

So why hadn't she realized? Why hadn't she recognized Aunt Edith as the old woman she'd seen that day in Kitty Goldsmith's backyard? The one who'd stood in the shade smiling at her the second before she'd blurted out that she was afraid Nicky might be tempted by her odd behavior to go off and have an affair. Mouse had never been able to figure out why she'd said that to Kitty, somebody she barely knew. That one stupid admission had caused Kitty to give her Nathan Culpepper's card, which she in turn had given to Margaret. And Nathan Culpepper had found John Dilbeck only days later. Mouse started sweating again.

Was this why she was so angry at Margaret? So determined to convince everyone that this John Dilbeck was nothing more than a fraud? God, she'd acted like such a witch last night. Had she not understood her own anger? Just like she hadn't understood her own grief. Could it be she was afraid to admit she might've seen Aunt Edith herself? Had she unknowingly played a part in the old woman's plan to make everything right between Margaret and

John? To get them together again? Even as she dabbed the sweat on her forehead, Mouse shivered.

She got up quickly and strode to the window, opening it as wide as she could. Her office faced the woods, and far beyond the long, crooked arms of the live oaks and pines lay the river, as fecund and black as worm-wriggled dirt. Sometimes when the air was weightless and cool like today, Mouse thought she could hear it licking the banks as it passed. Now what she heard was thunder, stomping in from the west. She leaned in closer to the window, breathing in the iron scent of approaching rain. Already she could see it coming in through the trees. A thin white curtain.

But despite its herald of thunder, when the rain reached her, it was a soft one. It slipped gently down through the leaves, taking its time, before dripping onto the pine-needled ground like warm melted butter. "Sleeping weather," her father had called it, and as she stood looking out of her office window, Mouse remembered how good it had felt curling up in her bedroom on Albemarle Way on those long-ago fall afternoons. Being lulled to sleep by the sound of a steady rain falling outside: that sweet safety had stayed with her most of her life. She missed it now.

Despite her promise to Nicky last week, the one about her being more forthcoming and open with him, Mouse knew she wouldn't tell him about seeing Aunt Edith herself. If that was really who that old lady at the Goldsmiths' party had been... and already Mouse was desperately trying to convince herself otherwise. Nick had been right; grief had probably done things to her equilibrium. She just needed something solid to hold on to. She'd wait until she got those DNA results back, in a couple of days, and then she'd decide what to do. Yes, that was the best plan. One thing was for certain, she was not letting John Dilbeck into her family without making damn sure who he was. Until then, she vowed to herself not to think about Aunt Edith at all.

Mouse could see Kitty Goldsmith's baby-blue BMW turn in to the lot, its windshield wipers swatting away at the rain with more force than was needed. From her window, Mouse watched Kitty stick a long toile-patterned umbrella out the car door, pop it open, and position herself underneath it. Tiptoeing gingerly across the gravel, Kitty disappeared around the front of the building and Mouse returned to her desk and folded her hands, ready to pretend everything was as normal as could be.

26

Emlynn

From the outside, Elegant Agatha's looked exactly like what it had once been. Never lain for aesthetics, the bricks that covered the imposing old structure were sun-bleached and rough, the mortar squished between them like cake icing spread on while still hot and left to harden through decades. Though a curved stone sidewalk now led up to the entrance, flanked by thick borders of lavender, there were no fancy signs on the side of the building, no beveled glass in the windows. It was only when you pushed open the tall wooden doors, which still swelled on hot, humid days, that the old Stieglitz Icehouse melted away and the bright, bustling catering company owned by Mouse Moretti took form.

Emlynn pulled into an empty parking space, turned off the car, and sat staring up at the windowless side of the building. Closing her eyes to steady herself, her hands still gripping the steering wheel, she took a deep breath. She could feel the beads of sweat on her upper lip, her forehead was as clammy as fish skin. Reaching for the door handle, she barely had time to get herself out of the car before she was throwing up in a thick cluster of overgrown laurel. It was the second time today. At first, she'd thought it was all the excitement of last night. But now, she wasn't so sure.

Elegant Agatha's had free delivery, but Emlynn felt like she needed fresh air, so she'd driven over herself to pick up the Halloween cookies they made for the shop every year. Elaborately decorated in shapes of witches and ghosts, these cookies were a staple at Verbena Apothecary during the month of October. People loved them, and more important, they expected them. Now, the mere thought of those cookies made Emlynn's stomach roll over. Leaning heavily against the side of her car, she wiped her mouth with the back of her hand. She always felt a bit skimpy and young around Mouse and didn't fancy the idea of throwing up in her beautiful office this afternoon.

Closing her eyes again, Emlynn went over her symptoms in preparation for the doctor's visit she now felt might be coming. She hadn't slept all that well last night, Lawrie had stayed on his laptop till well after one. But she'd felt pretty good when she woke up. Skipping breakfast completely, she'd gone to the shop early to do the accounts, then unpacked and tagged an order of cashmere pajamas she hoped would be a big seller at Christmas. Then she went to the window and stared at the dollhouse, reliving the moment she found the old envelope under its front stairs. That was when a wave of nausea had hit her like a slap, sending her running for the bathroom at the back of the store. She'd even thought about going home and crawling into bed, but after a few minutes she'd felt fine again.

And she'd felt fine on the drive over here, felt fine when she turned in and parked. Once again, this nausea had been like a bolt from the blue. Emlynn opened her handbag and took out a mirror. God, she was pale. Refreshing her lipstick, she stood up tall and straightened her shoulders, then practiced a smile. Feeling just a bit better, she headed for the front door.

The lavender bushes lining the walk were wearing a late autumn bloom, and though sparse, the tiny blue flowers filled the rain-dampened air with a fragrance that was both sweet and strong. Emlynn held her breath as she passed. She put her hip into the heavy wooden door, pushing it open with difficulty and letting it close with a slow, soft thump behind her.

At over a foot thick, the walls of the old icehouse had been built to keep in the cold, and today they simply shut out the world. No traffic could be heard from outside, no slamming doors, no voices. The soothing sound of James Taylor floated out from an unseen source, coming from everywhere and nowhere at once. He was singing about the secret of life. Emlynn wondered if you could hear a tornado siren in here.

There was nobody at the reception desk, but scores of pink-lidded boxes with green cursive lettering were stacked on wooden shelves all around her, ready for people to pick up, and through the glass windows that lined the large airy office, she could see people in beige linen aprons working at stainless steel tables, icing sheet cakes and rolling out cookies. Emlynn waved until someone looked up and saw her. A stout older woman then burst through the side door on her right.

"Oh, I'm so sorry," the woman said, dabbing a paper towel at the corner of her mouth. "I was just grabbing a bite of lunch. I don't like to eat at my desk, but that'd be better than leaving it empty, wouldn't it?" She laughed, and Emlynn laughed back. "You must be Emlynn! Mouse told me you were coming by. I'm Miriam. Let's see now... your order is over here somewhere." She ran her finger down a long shelf. "S...T...U," she mur-

mured before stopping at the end of the row right in front of six boxes tied together with a green velvet ribbon. "Here it is," she said, happily. "Verbena Apothecary. Six dozen witches and six dozen ghosts. I gotta tell you, I just love that store. All my friends do, too. It's yours, isn't it?"

Emlynn nodded.

"I thought so. You look just like somebody who would own a pretty shop like that. We're all so tickled to have it here in Wesleyan. I remember the days when you'd have to go all the way up to Atlanta to find such pretty things. And now we have you!" Miriam picked up the stack of boxes and turned around to set them down on the counter. Looking up, she exclaimed, "Lord, honey, what's the matter?"

The spontaneous compliment had caused Emlynn to burst into tears. She shook her head, embarrassed, then said, "No, I... I'm fine. Really. Not... not sure why..."

Looking frightened, Miriam hurriedly said, "You just stay right there, sweetheart. I'll get Mouse." Then she rushed back through the side door and disappeared.

Tears streaming uncontrollably now, Emlynn thought about leaving. She could easily pick up the boxes—they were right there before her—and run to the car before Mouse could be found. But just as she took a step forward, Mouse burst into the room, came around the counter, and put her hands onto Emlynn's shoulders. Emlynn wished the floor would just open and swallow her whole.

"What on earth?" Mouse asked, staring at Emlynn. "What's happened, Em? Are you all right?"

"I... I don't know," blubbered Emlynn. "I think I'm fine. She... she was so nice..." Emlynn looked over at Miriam and smiled weakly, "and for some reason . . . I just . . . just started to cry."

Mouse turned toward Miriam, who shrugged, then put her arms around Emlynn and began to steer her toward the side door. "Come with me," she said. "I was just down in my office, a lunch meeting with a client. There's a big, comfy chair in there, and you can just sit as long as it takes for you to get your sea legs back."

Obediently, Emlynn let Mouse lead her down a window-lined corridor and into a cozy, low-ceilinged room that looked more like a den than an office. At a round table in the corner sat a blond woman in black leggings and a canary-yellow sweater, a half-eaten plate of crab salad before her. Emlynn's stomach quivered again.

"Emlynn, this is Kitty Goldsmith," said Mouse. "I'm doing her daughter's wedding on Friday, and we were just going over a few last-minute details. And Kitty, this is my friend Emlynn. She's also my brother Lawrie's . . . Well, what are you exactly? You're much more than a girlfriend, certainly." Mouse put her arm on Emlynn's shoulder and steered her toward a fat leather armchair.

Kitty flashed a fulgent smile at Emlynn, who tried to return it, but failed. "Whoa, darlin'," said Kitty. "You better sit down 'fore you fall down. You're as pale as a ghost." Emlynn sank like a rock into the chair, her hands shaky and limp in her lap.

Mouse opened a tiny red refrigerator beside her desk and handed Emlynn a cold can of Coke. "Here," she said, "take a few sips of this. Now, what's going on?"

"I . . . I didn't mean to interrupt your meeting," said Emlynn, holding the can of Coke to her forehead and rolling it back and forth. "This isn't like me. I think I must be coming down with something. I was sick at the shop . . . earlier, and now . . ." She shook her head. Tears were threatening again. "Now, I don't know."

"You're not interruptin' anything," said Kitty. "I should've left here twenty minutes ago. I just dropped by to make sure Mouse found these travel ideas I left for her, and to make sure we've got Elvis lined up." She pointed to a collection of shiny brochures that were fanned out like cards atop Mouse's desk. "I've been telling her; she and Nick need to take a vacation. She told me they haven't been anywhere, just the two of them, in over five years! Don't you think that's outrageous?" Kitty pushed up the arm of her sweater and looked at the large diamond watch on her wrist. "Shoot! I'm gonna be so late. Paris'll be spittin' nails. Who knew picking out the perfect bridal nail polish was such a big deal?"

"You want to call her?" asked Mouse, placing the back of her hand on Emlynn's forehead.

"Nope. It'll be good for her. Girl's never been on time in her life. Time she learned how it feels." Kitty stood up and fluffed out her hair. "Oh," she said, snapping her fingers, "I knew there was something else I wanted to tell you." She rolled her green eyes at Mouse. "Paris told me last night she and Donnie are writin' their own vows. Lord, we shoulda sold tickets! This thing is gonna be downright Shakespearean."

Kitty drew out that last word as far as she could and still keep it halfway recognizable, and Emlynn laughed, weakly. "See? There you go," said Kitty, happily turning to face her. "You're comin' around." Bending over, Kitty placed her hands on the arms of Emlynn's chair and stared into her face for a long moment. Then she stood up, put her hands on her hips, and grinned. "Why, honey," she said, winking impishly over at Mouse. "There's not a thing wrong with you. Not one thing. 'Cept that you're pregnant, of course."

Mouse stared at Emlynn, who stared back at Kitty in shock. "No," Emlynn said, firmly. "No, I'm not."

"Oh, honey. I beg to differ," said Kitty, slinging a Mulberry tote bag over her shoulder. "I can always tell. It's a gift I have. Had it for as long as I can remember. Just ask my daughter."

And as sudden as a clap of thunder, Emlynn started to cry again, this time not caring who heard her. Raising both hands in mock surrender, Kitty said, "And that's my cue." She patted Emlynn's head. "Everything's going to be okay, honey. I'll bet you anything." Over Emlynn's sobs, Kitty turned back to Mouse, pointing to the brochures stacked up on the desk. "Like I said. Italy. For two long, glorious weeks. Maybe three." Kitty waved over her shoulder, opened the office door, and was gone in a cloud of Acqua di Parma perfume.

Mouse waited a moment, listening to the sound of Kitty's stilettos recede down the hall, then she pulled up a chair before Emlynn, handed her a paper towel, and watched as her sobs ebbed into sighs. "Isn't this . . . good news?" she asked, softly.

"I don't know," said Emlynn, miserably. She'd never cried in front of Mouse before, was embarrassed to be doing so now, but found she wasn't able to stop. "I've . . . I've wanted to have a baby more than anything, for as long as I can remember . . . but Lawrie's always said he doesn't want to unless . . . unless we get married first and I've . . . I've always been afraid of marriage. My parents didn't exactly have the best one, you know, and I was in the front row for that show."

"But you know, well, you do know Lawrie's . . . the one, don't you?"

"Yes," said Emlynn, quickly. "Without a doubt. And to be honest, I was almost ready to tell him that I would . . . we should . . . go ahead and . . . that night of your mother's birthday dinner. But then that turned ugly between him and Tom. It ruined the whole thing."

Mouse shook her head and leaned back in her chair, sighing. "I know," she said. "Tom and Lawrie ... well, they've never ... I mean, they've always had trouble getting along. I don't know if that's supposed to be easier or harder as you get older."

Emlynn blew her nose on the white paper towel. "I think it should get easier, don't you?"

Mouse shrugged. "Between you and me, sometimes I think they sort of enjoy playing these roles. You know, Lawrie the affable one, the one everyone likes, and Tom the imperious businessman, the one everybody's a little afraid of. Definitions they can't break away from. Lawrie goads Tom into acting like an ass, then gets to enjoy being the good one again when Tom takes the bait."

"Well, that night they both acted like asses," said Emlynn, sniffing and twisting her paper towel in her hands. "Personally, I think brothers should be closer. Especially twins, for Pete's sake. Just look at how thrilled your mother is to have found a brother she never even knew she had." Mouse crossed her arms in silent communication that Emlynn was too upset to pick up on. "I know you were shocked last night, and I don't really blame you for leaving like you did. It was an emotional meeting. I guess we all felt it. I stayed awake till early this morning thinking about it. I couldn't get over how thrilled Margaret was. I mean, I've never had any siblings myself, but Lord knows I always wanted some." She looked over at Mouse and sniffed loudly. "Frankly," she said, "I've always thought the three of you take one another for granted."

Mouse stiffened, then stood up abruptly and walked to the window, her back toward Emlynn, who blithely continued on. "Just imagine," she said, "if that Kitty woman really knows what she's talking about—and between you and me, the jury's still out on that, she seemed like some kind of nut—but if she does, and I ... I really *am* pregnant ... then our baby now has a great-*uncle*! That's wonderful, isn't it? Somebody older to take the place of the grandfather it won't have." Feeling suddenly better, Emlynn blew her nose again, then popped open the cold can of Coke. "I can barely believe this all started with that envelope I found in the old dollhouse. I mean, what are the odds? I can still see myself, squatting there in the window and seeing the thing poking out from under those little stairs, never once dreaming what it would unleash. And here we are."

Mouse wheeled around. "I think you're jumping the gun a bit, don't you? You can't possibly know for certain this man is who he says he is. Can you? I mean, really. Can *any* of us?"

"I ... I don't," Emlynn sputtered, her receding tears whipping around and popping back into her eyes.

"Look, Emlynn," said Mouse, briskly. "You seem to be feeling a bit better. If you don't mind, I really need to get back to work. This wedding Friday night is one of our biggest this year, and I just don't have time to talk anymore." She walked to the door and opened it, and Emlynn, shocked into silence, picked up her purse and walked quickly out of the office, down the hall, and out the front door, leaving her six boxes of cookies still sitting atop the front counter.

It took her longer than usual to nudge the last customers out of Verbena Apothecary. At closing time, Susie Blanchard was still nosing around in the new fall shipment of scarves and shawls from Drake Island Woolens before finally deciding—another ten minutes later, and after trying each one of them on in front of the old floor-length mirror, then throwing them, unfolded, back onto the shelf—that Wesleyan probably didn't really get cold enough anymore to justify such a dear purchase. Emlynn was, for her, a bit terse in saying goodbye, but if the woman noticed, Emlynn couldn't honestly say that she cared. The bell clanged loudly when she shut the door behind Susie, and Emlynn flipped the sign over from Open to Closed with such force the thing took a whole minute to stop swinging.

Her emotions had been on a fair ride all afternoon. Leaving Elegant Agatha's, Emlynn had bawled her way up Old Chimney Brick Road, slammed her fist on the steering wheel as she turned onto Pierce Avenue, and then, wondering again if it could be possibly true she was pregnant, grinned all the way down Meridian Street. Had she been caught by traffic cameras, one look at the footage and she would've been shipped straight off to the psych ward at Elberta General.

By the time she pulled into the narrow gravel lot that ran behind the stores on the square, Emlynn had worn herself down to a dull depression that would last the rest of the day. Now, finally alone, she felt exhausted and weepy as she walked to the shelf and began to refold all the Drake Island Woolens that Susie Blanchard had left in a pile.

As she folded a gray tartan shawl, Emlynn thought again how quickly Mouse had ushered her from her office this afternoon, and she grimaced once more with embarrassment. It should've been obvious to her that Mouse wouldn't want to talk about the sudden appearance of John Dilbeck. That boundary had been made perfectly clear by Mouse's behavior last night. And yet, Emlynn had jumped right over it anyway. She now rested her head against the tall wooden shelf and closed her tired eyes, her mind trying to sidestep recrimination. In the eight years she and Lawrie had been together, she'd never once had a cross word with his sister.

But she'd really thought, hadn't she, that Mouse would've come around since last night, that she might've already called Margaret to apologize for doubting the man. It was so clear he was who he said he was. Like Lawrie had said as they'd driven away from Nathan Culpepper's last night, anybody could see it, even before they noticed that catawampus little finger sticking out from Margaret's and John's—and *Mouse's*—right hands. These people were family. It was there in the way they cocked their heads when they listened, the way they both crossed their left leg over their right. And for goodness' sake, their voices were almost the same.

Placing the neat stack of soft woolens back in their place, Emlynn wondered now if Mouse blamed her for all this. After all, she'd been the one who'd pulled that old yellow envelope out from under the stairs of the dollhouse. She'd been the one to give it to Margaret. And as far as Emlynn could tell, she was the only one who agreed with Margaret that something bigger was obviously at work here. A little practical magic was all right with her. She didn't doubt for a minute that Margaret had seen the ghost of her aunt. And if the old lady wanted to use Emlynn in some small way to help facilitate the reunion of her great-niece and great-nephew, then she was happy to be placed into service.

Emlynn wandered through the shop, turning out all the lamps. A gentle rain had begun falling again, the sound like fingertips softly tapping on the awning outside. She placed a hand on her tummy. The baby was smaller than a sunflower seed, but somehow, she knew it was there. Almost like magic.

From where Emlynn stood in the shadows, she saw Enid Harper hurrying by, her two-year-old son, Sergio, frequently darting out from under the umbrella Enid was trying to keep steady above them. They were halfway past Verbena Apothecary's window when little Sergio skidded to a stop, pointing. With one exasperated look to the heavens, Enid bent down beside him, listening and nodding as Sergio commented on the Halloween décor. Every colored light, every tiny pumpkin, and finally, the magical dollhouse. Emlynn's eyes followed theirs and she suddenly gasped. Why hadn't she thought of this earlier?

She could see the tiny screws lined up along the edge of the roofline, each one about the size of the head of a pin. They shone silver in the white glow of the streetlight outside. Only slightly aware of a high-pitched whine in her ears, Emlynn turned and walked quickly to the back of the shop, returning with the smallest screwdriver she could find.

It took her a good thirty minutes to loosen each one, the tiny screws pinging against one another as she dropped them into a small jar. When they were all out, she placed both hands wide on the roof of the dollhouse, took a deep breath, and lifted it off. She placed it down in the window beside her, then, with both hands crossed under her chin, she peered over the rim.

So many letters. There must have been a hundred of them. All addressed to Lawrence Elliot. All postmarked from Enoree Island.

27

Mouse

Nick Moretti lay sprawled on the sofa, watching the news with the sound off. From where Mouse stood in the kitchen, stirring a chicken perloo, she could see he was losing the battle to stay awake. Well, he'd been up since four-thirty this morning. Over at the end of the counter, Mouse saw her phone flash again. It was the third time in the past five minutes.

Her conversation with her mother hadn't gone well and Mouse knew it. She'd taken the call in the laundry room so as not to disturb Nick, and stood straight-backed by the dryer, one hand gripping a bottle of Mrs. Meyer's detergent, while Margaret told her all about going back to Aunt Edith's old house this morning. Then there'd been the visit she and John made to Lawrie's clinic, and the lunch with Harriet Spalding they had scheduled for tomorrow. "Would you like to go with us?" Margaret asked. Mouse would not.

Faced with her daughter's unresponsiveness, Margaret had continued to talk, no doubt hoping a flood of innocuous conversation would break down Mouse's defenses. "And Tom thinks I should let him put in a pond over in the corner out back. Fill it with cattails and water lilies, you know, that sort of thing. He says there's plenty of room, but I told him Jubal would probably just lay in it all day." A long quiet pause. "What do you think, Mouse?"

What did Mouse think? She thought her whole family had lost their minds. Why was nobody listening to her? Why had they all just taken this stranger into their lives like crazy people? Those DNA results couldn't come fast enough. She'd gotten off the phone with her mother with the always reliable excuse that she had something cooking on the stove, which she had, and then immediately silenced the thing. But it had flashed just three minutes later. And now it was flashing again.

Throwing her damp dish towel over her shoulder, Mouse crept up to the phone as though afraid the caller might see her. It wasn't Margaret, after all. It was Emlynn. Mouse backed away, looking up to the ceiling and closing her eyes.

She had been perfectly horrible to Emlynn, and she knew it. The one person in the whole family who was always sweet and uncomplicated, who came without a sheaf of operating instructions you had to decipher to get through an evening unscathed. And Mouse had treated Emlynn like a mere annoyance, shown her out of the office in the rudest way possible. After Emlynn had come to her crying. Mouse took the dish towel and whipped it down on the counter, the loud wet smack waking Nick.

"What the hell?" Mouse heard the TV remote hit the floor.

"Sorry! Sorry. I just . . . dropped something."

"Oh, okay. Right." Nick sat up a bit straighter. "Ah, heck," he said, staring at the TV screen. "I bet I missed Bogey's interview, didn't I? They were supposed to talk to him about the new flu vaccine tonight. I told him I'd watch. Shoot." Nick turned up the sound. "You didn't happen to see any of it, did you? Maybe just what he was wearing? I could comment on his tie, or something. Make him think I saw the thing."

"Nope. Sorry," said Mouse, giving the chicken perloo another stir before putting the lid back on the pot with a clatter.

Nick rose from the sofa and went around to stand behind her, fastening his hands on her hips. "Boy, that smells good," he said. "But you didn't have to do all this tonight. We could've gone out. I know you're covered up this week with that wedding."

His kindness was genuine, but Mouse was sure she could hear implicit questions burrowed inside it. She could tell how much he wanted to ask her about John Dilbeck. Had she talked to her mother? Had she changed her mind? Had she come to the realization that Margaret was probably right to believe John was her brother? Didn't she see now how great this all was? An equivocal resentment made Mouse stiffen her spine when she felt Nick brush back her hair to kiss her neck, but before it registered with him, the doorbell rang, and he suddenly released her.

"Who on earth could that be?" he asked, not expecting an answer as he moved toward the hallway.

Mouse cocked her head, listening, but couldn't hear anything over the sound of the television. Glancing back into the den, she saw the doughy, red face of Bogey Crawford staring at her from the large screen, the words "coming up next" crawling slowly beneath him.

She had just started to call out to Nick when he walked back into the kitchen holding a large cardboard box in his arms. He set it down on the table and switched on the lamp that sat on the sideboard. "Well, that was weird," he said, stepping back and turning to Mouse.

"What was weird?" she asked, looking over at the box. "Who was it?"

"It was Emlynn," said Nick, drying his hands on his trousers. "She just kinda pushed this into my arms and took off. Said she was late for dinner or something. Told me to give you this note." He handed Mouse a folded piece of paper, her name written in pencil on top.

Mouse took the note and stared at the box for a moment. "Uh . . . Bogey," she said, without looking at Nick. "He's about to come on. You know, the news." She pointed over her shoulder. "I mean, he'll be on next."

"Oh, great," said Nick, loping off into the den.

Unfolding the small piece of white paper, Mouse read the short sentence written in Emlynn's hand. "I just found these in the dollhouse."

The box was slightly damp from the rain. Drake Island Woolens was printed in black on the side, but for some reason, Mouse knew it wouldn't contain anything like that. She walked slowly over to the table. Bogey Crawford's wide drawl suddenly got louder as Nick turned the sound up on the TV. "Nobody likes to do it, exactly," Bogey was saying, "but it's just part of life these days if you want to stay well. Believe me, if you put it off, and you get the flu, you'll wish like the dickens you'd gotten the shot."

Mouse lifted the lid off the box.

PART FIVE

28

Mouse

Though the sun had yet to crack the horizon, Mouse could tell it was going to be a beautiful day. The sky had that satiny look, the last of the stars still stubbornly glowing.

She was glad to be the first person here, glad to have a few minutes of quiet before the commotion began. The Goldsmith wedding was a big one; she wouldn't get to bed until midnight, at least. As she pulled into her usual place at the side of the long brick building, her headlights caught a family of deer gathered at the edge of the woods. The doe hesitated a moment, staring boldly at Mouse, almost in recognition, then bolted away into the darkness, her two spotted young ones close on her heels. Smiling, Mouse felt tears prick her tired eyes. Now that the tears had finally started, she didn't seem to be able to stop them.

There'd been too many letters to read in one sitting, so Mouse had taken out only a few at a time, she and Nicky sitting cross-legged on the sofa till late in the night. Some were so thin and flimsy with age, only the ink on their pages seemed to hold them together. At first, she'd tried to tell herself none of them constituted any proof that John Dilbeck was really her uncle, but the more she read, the less that seemed to matter. Each sentence written in his hand had been in response to something her father had written, and as she read through John's letters to Lawrence, she heard her father's voice in her head as clearly as though the two of them were having a conversation beside her.

Sometime around ten that first night, she and Nick each reading a letter, he'd suddenly gone quiet, staring over at her. "What?" she'd said, reaching for the one he held in his hand. Nicky snatched it away.

"What does that one say?" Mouse demanded.

"I'm not sure you should read this, Minnie. In fact, maybe we shouldn't be looking at these things at all."

"Give it here, Nicky," said Mouse, firmly. And Nick handed it over to her.

August 21, 2001

Dear Lawrence,

Heard you on the radio last night. I swear, if I didn't know better, I would've thought you knew what you were talking about. Ha, Ha. Personally, I've always felt there was more to be mined from Disraeli's story myself. You're just the fellow to do it. Sounds like that interviewer agrees. Carrie and I wish you great success with this new book.

Thanks so much for the picture of Ben. A handsome baby if ever I saw one. And I think you may be right; he does look a bit like his grandfather. Ha, Ha, again. Boy, that Mouse doesn't let the grass grow under her feet, does she? Two babies in less than two years. I wouldn't worry, though. You've always said she could do anything

*she put her mind to. And by the way, I'm not going to say this
again, Lawrence, but don't even think about paying me back that
money. I told you at the time it was a gift. I like being able to think I
had a small hand in her success. And that catering company of hers
is going to be a success. I just know it . . .*

Mouse had read the letter three times, turning it over to see if anything else was written on the backs of the pages, something that might make more sense. "You mean . . ." she began, looking up at Nick. "You mean, he loaned Daddy the money? The money I used to start Elegant Agatha's?"

"Doesn't sound like a loan. Sounds more like a gift."

Mouse remembered how empathetic her father had been about not telling Margaret what he had done. It had given Mouse the uncomfortable notion that, deep down, her mother might not have approved. That thought had festered inside her, unacknowledged, yet constant, for years. And it had never been true. It had been John that gave her the money. And of course, Margaret hadn't even known. She hadn't known John even existed.

Mouse had wept on and off for two days.

Closing the car door, she headed now toward the building, pea gravel crunching under her shoes. The choir of crickets and tree frogs was singing their one last song before dawn, a wall of sound so familiar, so Southern, Mouse normally gave it no mind. But she paused to listen today. Then, pushing open the tall, heavy door, Mouse heard her phone ring, the tone strangely intrusive here in the darkness. The door thudded shut behind her, and she flipped on the lights.

Throwing her bag on the counter, Mouse opened it up and the ring of the phone got much louder. Kitty's number was shining up from the screen. No surprise, Mouse thought. Mothers always had a few meltdowns the day of their daughters' weddings, and Lord knows, she'd never expected Kitty Goldsmith would be an exception. She was probably worried there wouldn't be enough lemon squares. "Hey, Kitty," Mouse said, pulling off her jacket.

The sound that hit Mouse's ears was strangely reminiscent of the one Dinky emitted when someone stepped on his tail. Reflexively, Mouse pulled the phone three inches away from her ear. "Slow *down*, Kitty," she said. "I can't understand a word you're saying. What? *Who's* gone?"

"PARIS!" wailed Kitty. "*Paris* is gone. The ungrateful little DEVIL! I just went in her bedroom to wake her up and the place was emptier than the tomb. At first, I thought, Well now, look at her, her wedding day and she's finally cleaned the place up. I'm such a *fool*! Such an IDIOT! It only took me half a minute to realize she hadn't cleaned up; she'd stripped the place bare! Closet empty. Drawers, too! God, she even took the *sheets*! You know the only thing she left? Her wedding dress! Wadded up on the floor in the corner. I swear I almost grabbed the thing and ripped it to shreds till I remembered it was a Vera Wang that cost me fifteen thousand *dollars*!"

"Well, maybe she . . ."

"*Maybe*, nothin'! I'll tell you *exactly* what's she's gone and done. She's *skated*!"

"No! No, now, Kitty. I'm *sure* she wouldn't do that. Not today, the very morning of her wedding. Not after all we've . . . all *you've* done . . . she wouldn't . . ."

"Oh, yes she would," yelled Kitty. "She *has*! And you know how I know for double dog sure? I called my mama, that's how. She told me the whole story. Hell, I'd be willin' to bet you this Vera Wang dress I'm holdin' in my hand that this was all Mama's *idea*! You remember that boy Paris was crazy about before she had to come home with the chicken pox? The one from up at college? Well, Mama told me he's been comin' down here to see her for the past three weeks. They've been meetin' over at Mama's condo. I mean, of COURSE they have!" Mouse heard something break that sounded heavier than glass.

"And Mama said the two of them were really in *love*—like *she* could tell—and the boy wants to help raise this baby Paris is gonna have in six months—like he'll still be around by then. But *this* is the kicker... Mama said Donnie—you remember him, don't you? The one with his *name* on the *wedding* invitations—well, she said Donnie doesn't mind! He *doesn't* mind! Like they're just switching seats at the movies! Good God, Mouse! What am I gonna *do*? The florist is gonna be pullin' in here in a few hours. People are going to be showin' up this evening in their fancy clothes to watch my pregnant daughter get *married*! Lord, if I could find me a high enough ledge, I swear I'd jump off, I really would."

Mouse didn't remember going into the workroom and sitting down with her head on a long wooden table, but here she was. The Goldsmith wedding cake sat across from her, regal, expectant, three tiers of buttercream roses and white sugar pearls.

"Mouse?" Kitty wailed. "Are you still there?"

"Yes, Kitty. I'm here. I'm just thinking."

"Well, you better think fast. Like I said, Fletcher McClatchey's supposed to be pulling up here at one with a truckload of roses and seventy-five chairs. And then there's that dumbass string quartet Vinnie insisted we get. Wonder if they can play "What Kind of Fool Am I?" Oh, and all that stuff *you've* been cooking all week! That *cake*! What on earth are we gonna do with it all? Oh, God!"

"Hush," said Mouse, sharply, her head spinning. "Just be quiet a minute and let me think."

Kitty continued to breathe so heavily into the phone it sounded as though she were running, and for a second Mouse wondered if she might be. Mouse ignored her, a plan taking shape in her head. She couldn't be sure if it was just another idea she'd regret a few hours later or if it might, just might, be the solution to more than one problem. Mouse was weary of thinking. But she was also weary of being so sad.

"Listen, Kitty. There's probably no way you're going to get your money back for all this, right?"

Kitty let out a groan. "The whole thing was paid for weeks ago, so no, I can't imagine we will. But I don't give a tinker's damn about the *money*! Vinnie'll find some way to write it all off our taxes anyway. What I'm worried about are all those *people* showing up here at seven tonight." Kitty's rage was tempering down to an impotent simmer. In a much calmer voice, she said, sighing loudly, "You know anybody who wants a free wedding?"

"See that's the thing," said Mouse, her thoughts racing ahead of her. "I . . . I just might." She had no idea if they'd even consider the idea, but if she went ahead and set the plans in motion, wouldn't it be harder for them to say no? Mouse decided not to weigh the pros and cons. She was just going on instinct.

"Okay, Kitty. If you want a way out of this, I think I have one. Just do what I tell you. Call Fletcher and tell him to take all those flowers across town to 2156 Albemarle Way. Do the same thing with that quartet. Then draw up some sort of sign and put it at the end of your driveway. Just say the wedding's been moved, and direct everybody to that same address. That way they'll still get a party, and we'll make it a good one. And . . . Kitty? What size is that Vera Wang dress?"

29

Margaret

The workmen had shown up at noon. They now filled the backyard like a swarm of uniformed bees, and as she stood watching from Tom's bedroom window, Margaret could see him helping to string little white lights through the tree limbs. Mouse's crew was already down in the kitchen; she could hear them all setting up. The rattle of cutlery, the tinkling of glass. Ten minutes ago, almost certain of imminent disaster, she'd stood with one hand holding Jubal tight by the scruff of his neck as two girls from Elegant Agatha's carried the tall wedding cake in through the front door. The magnificent cake now rested safely on her dining room table, waiting for the celebration to begin.

Margaret had been sound asleep this morning when Mouse called her with the news, and it had taken her a few seconds to realize it wasn't a joke. Lawrie and Emlynn would be getting married in her backyard tonight at seven o'clock. Hearing this, Margaret had sat up in bed, her eyes shooting immediately to the old wooden chair in the corner, almost sure Aunt Edith would be sitting there smiling at her. But the chair had been empty. Aunt

Edith hadn't been seen since the morning John Dilbeck was found.

From her place at the window, Margaret could see John now, setting up chairs with Jubal following along right behind him. The dog had liked Tommy, but he obviously adored John, another canine confirmation she welcomed. Margaret knew she'd never be able to explain all that had happened since that first night Aunt Edith appeared, but she'd thought often of Ida Mae's words. *What if all I believe doesn't turn out to be the whole story?* There was still so much she'd never know about her parents, but somehow Aunt Edith had managed to lead her to the one salvageable part of her story. She'd led her back to her brother. That gap in her circle was closed.

"Yoo-hoo!"

Margaret heard Harriet's voice ring out from downstairs. She stepped onto the landing. "Up here," she called back, and stood by the railing as Harriet climbed the stairs, Gatsby held fast in her arms.

"What in the world is going on over here?" Harriet plopped the Chihuahua down unceremoniously and joined Margaret at the window. "I've never seen so many people."

"Oh, Harriet," said Margaret, grabbing the old woman's arm. "Lawrie and Emlynn are getting married. Here! Tonight."

"Why didn't you tell me?"

"Because I didn't *know* till this morning," said Margaret. "And since then, I haven't had time. This is all happening so fast." She steered Harriet back down the stairs by the elbow. "See, Mouse had this client whose daughter was getting married tonight, and the girl skedaddled this morning. Leaving her mother with a whole wedding ready to go. From what I've been able to find out, Mouse jumped in the car, went over to Lawrie and Emlynn's, offered the wedding to them, and lo and behold, they said yes. Only trouble is, we might have a whole slew of people showing up here for the ceremony at seven and we're not going to know a one of them. Apparently, this tickles Lawrie and Emlynn no end. So, I'm just going with it."

Harriet threw back her head and laughed. "Didn't I say your aunt Edith wasn't done with you yet?"

"You know, I haven't seen Aunt Edith for a whole week," said Margaret, as they reached the bottom stair. Harriet opened her mouth to reply, but just then the front door flew open and Emlynn rushed in with Lawrie behind her. "There you are!" called Margaret. "Don't you two know I'm too old for this kind of excitement?"

"Oh, I hope it's all right," said Emlynn. Her cheeks were flushed, and she was out of breath. "Mouse said it would be, said she'd talked to you, but to be honest, we didn't really stop to think what all this might mean for you. We've been too rattled to think about anybody but ourselves!" She threw her arms around Margaret, and Margaret returned her hug. "There's so many people here already."

"It's fine, fine," said Margaret, reaching one hand around Emlynn to take Lawrie's. "Just a bit unexpected, is all."

"Tell me about it," said Lawrie. "We were both still in bed when Mouse started banging on the door. She had us talked into this before we'd had our coffee. It's a hoot, isn't it?" He grinned. "We've just been to get a license. Only had to wait an hour. So, it's all going to be legal and everything." Lawrie pulled a sheet of white paper out of his pocket and waved it around in the air. "Where's Tommy Boy?" he asked, looking upstairs.

"He's out back with John. They're helping set everything up," said Margaret. "Go on out there, you'll see him."

The three women watched Lawrie go, and when they heard the back door slam, Emlynn bent toward Margaret and whispered, "He wants Tom to be his best man."

Margaret stepped back. "Really?"

"Yes," said Emlynn, grinning. "I was a little surprised, too. But I'm so happy. Who better to be best man than his brother?"

30

Mouse

The Goldsmiths' street was quiet when Mouse rolled to a stop in front of their house. Denied the lavish preparations expected just hours before, the place looked strangely diminished, almost sullen, as though it had absorbed its owners' shocked disappointment right into its white-stuccoed walls. The sign Kitty had made was stuck in the ground by the mailbox. Black Magic Marker on pink poster board. It looked hurriedly done, but the scrawled words got straight to the point and looked to Mouse, somehow, strangely familiar.

I'm so sorry for the inconvenience, but there's been a slight hitch in the proceedings. I've made a terrible fool of myself, which isn't unusual, and my fiancé—my fiancé that was, that is—he thinks we'd better call it a day, and I quite agree with him.

But doing you out of a wedding in this house is very bad manners, so I want to make it up to you by going through with the ceremony as originally planned, with only a couple of changes:

> *The wedding is now being held at 2156 Albemarle Way, and the bride and groom will be Emlynn Cates and Dr. Lawrie Elliot.*
>
> *If any of you still want to attend, I'm sure you will be welcome.*
>
> *Signed,*
> *Paris Vivienlee Goldsmith*

The motor running, Mouse sat in the car trying to figure out where she'd read those words before, when out of the corner of her eye she caught a flash of color moving toward her. Looking to her right, she saw Kitty running down the driveway in a hot pink nightgown, a short leopard-print robe flying out behind her like a cape. Mouse unlocked the car door, and Kitty jumped in.

"You can pull on up to the house," Kitty said, breathlessly. "It's okay. Vinnie flew out of here fifteen minutes ago, so mad he couldn't verbalize a whole sentence. This is a man who can pinch a penny so tight Lincoln squeals, and my God, we spent so much money on this wedding. Paris has cooked her goose with him this time, I can tell you. He swears he won't ever give her and Wally a red cent. That's that boy's name, did I tell you?" Kitty's laugh was more like a yodel than ever. "Wally Plunkett. Sounds just like the hillbilly he probably is." Kitty paused, swallowed hard, and then widened her eyes. "God, she'll be Paris *Plunkett*, won't she? I just realized that." She stared straight out the windshield and bit the side of her thumbnail.

Pulling into the driveway, Mouse nodded toward the handwritten sign. "Did you write that?"

"'Course I did," said Kitty. "Thank God I'd watched that old movie just a couple of weeks ago. You know the one with Cary Grant? And Audrey...no, Katharine...Hepburn. She had to cancel her wedding, remember? And the guests were already there! I figured what she says in that movie is more eloquent than anything I could come up with on my own, so I found it on TV and copied down her words. Not that it matters."

Mouse stopped the car at the Goldsmiths' front door. Two tall cedar topiaries underplanted with white roses and dahlias stood sentry, one on either side of the porch. Kitty followed Mouse's eyes and sighed, loudly.

"If I could pick those things up and throw them in your car, I'd do it," she said. "But they weigh a ton. Took four big ol' men to get 'em in place."

Probably because she was wearing no makeup or eyelashes, in addition to appearing paler than usual, Kitty also looked younger, and Mouse could suddenly see the little girl who'd once sat in the same classroom as she had. She put her hand on Kitty's bare knee and squeezed.

"Don't be too nice to me, or I'll start bawling right here in this car," said Kitty, reaching for the door handle and pushing Mouse's hand away. "I'm savin' it all up. I figure I'll wait until sometime Tuesday to lose it, and when I do, believe you me, it's gonna be epic." She reached into the pocket of her leopard-print robe and took out a card. "Here now," she said. "Take this." She stuck the card into Mouse's large tote bag. "I don't want you to open it till after all this is over. Wait till you get home tonight. Promise me?" Mouse nodded. "And don't worry," said Kitty, "it's not a bill. It's kind of a . . . a thank-you note. She smiled almost wistfully over at Mouse. "Okay, that's done," she said, slapping her palms on her thighs. "Come on now, let's get that damn wedding dress out of this house."

By the time Mouse got back to Albemarle Way, a line of white delivery vans stretched all the way around the curve, the last one parked in front of the Scogginses' house. She could see Penny Scoggins standing on tiptoe, looking up to Margaret's, where the front door stood open wide. Mouse pulled in behind Marcy Weller's gray Volkswagen, and as she got out, she saw a gargantuan vase full of white roses moving slowly down the sidewalk toward her, Fletcher McClatchey's bald head just visible behind the flowers. She threw her tote over her shoulder, opened the back door, and carefully draped the black garment bag over her arms.

"That you, Agatha?" asked Fletcher, leaning around the roses. "I'd hug your neck, but as you can see . . ."

"Yeah, you kinda got your hands full today, don't you?" Mouse stepped down off the curb to let Fletcher pass.

"You don't know the half of it," Fletcher said, stopping to carefully hoist the large vase a few inches higher. "This is the fifth one of these, and I've got three more to go. We've never done so many flowers, not even for my own mother's funeral, and everybody in town ordered something for that."

"Well, I hope moving the location at the last minute didn't mess you up any," said Mouse, falling in step behind him.

"Not a bit. Hell, this is closer to the shop anyway. And you know me, I don't ask any questions." After a few heavy seconds came the contradictory words. "Hey, did I get this right . . . we got us a runaway bride and now your brother's the one getting married? The vet? To that girl from the gift shop?"

"Yep," said Mouse, as they both turned in to the driveway. "You and Carolyn should come back for the ceremony. I'm sure Emlynn and Lawrie would've invited you if they'd had the time. They'd love to have you here; I know they would."

"Well, we just might do that," said Fletcher, climbing the porch stairs carefully. "I always love me a good wedding."

Fletcher and Mouse entered the house, and as Fletcher went straight through to the backyard, Mouse stopped by the kitchen door and listened. Above the low drone of the voices outside, she could hear Emlynn. It sounded like her voice was coming from Margaret's bedroom. Mouse doubled back and went up the stairs.

"Do you think I should wear my hair up?" Emlynn was asking as Mouse came across the landing and down the hall.

"Why don't we wait till we see the dress?" said Margaret.

"Oh, God! What if it's some gaudy polyester explosion? All bright white and cheap lace? Or some vulgar micromini? I look awful in white, and didn't Mouse say that this girl was only eighteen years old? You know how girls that age dress! Why did I agree to wear it?"

"You haven't signed a contract, Em. If the dress is horrendous, then you don't even have to try it on. We'll run over and get something you like from your own closet. There's plenty of time. But just wait till you see it, and then decide. Who knows, it might turn out to be stunning."

"Maybe," said Emlynn, sounding unconvinced.

"Sounds like I'm just in time," said Mouse, coming into the room and holding the black garment bag out before her, draped across both of her arms. Mouse waited for a dramatic second before reaching down and unzipping the bag. She pulled out the dress and hung it up on the closet door with a flourish, standing back to take in the expressions she knew would be coming.

No one who'd ever met her would have expected Paris Goldsmith to choose such an exquisite dress. The cloud of candlelight tulle that fell from the small, fitted waist was overlain with a layer of goldenrod yellow that billowed out onto the floor. It was all held in place by a mauve velvet bow, so pale it was almost the color of Emlynn's complexion. The dress could have been made just for her.

"It's like something an angel would wear," whispered Margaret.

"I'll wear my hair down," said Emlynn.

"And it's got pockets," said Mouse, triumphantly.

"I've got to go get my phone and text a picture of this to Harriet," said Margaret, her hands on each side of her face. "That woman told me, not an hour ago, she could see you in something yellow, and I swear I still don't know how she seems to know these things before they happen." She left the room, closing the door behind her.

"It's amazing, isn't it?" said Mouse, turning back to the dress. "To tell you the truth, I was prepared for some sort of monstrosity, but when Kitty said it was a Vera Wang, I thought I'd give it a try."

"And she doesn't want anything for it?" asked Emlynn. She was running the soft velvet bow through her fingers. "I mean, there's no way we could afford something like this."

"No worries there," said Mouse, lifting a handful of tulle in the air and watching it float back down to the floor, so light it fell in slow motion. "This is pocket change for the Goldsmiths. Besides, Paris had it altered several times, so Kitty couldn't take it back if she wanted to. I think it'll make her feel better if somebody wears it today like she planned. And that somebody is you." She sat down on Margaret's bed. "Let's see now," she said, crossing her legs and taking a large green folder out of her tote bag. "I still feel like there's something I've forgotten to do." She counted things off on her fingers. "My girls are here setting up in the kitchen, and I know they have everything under control. The flowers and chairs are here. Kitty said the string quartet would arrive around four. I'll need to talk to them about their set list. Make sure they know something appropriate, some old hymns or Vivaldi, something like that. Knowing Paris, she'll have told them to play Lil Nas X and DaBaby."

Emlynn burst out laughing. Mouse looked up, completely nonplussed. "I've got college-age kids, don't forget," she said, peering at Emlynn from over the top of her reading glasses. She tapped a pencil against the Goldsmiths' green folder, her finger traveling down the list of things still left to be sorted.

"Lawrie has asked Tom to be his best man," said Emlynn, sitting down on the other side of the bed. Mouse looked up in surprise. "And . . ." Emlynn hesitated, then said, shyly, "and I'd like you to be my matron of honor. If that's all right."

Mouse looked back at the list in her lap, her eyes suddenly filling with tears. Trying hard to compose herself, she reached over and squeezed Emlynn's hand. After a long moment, she swallowed hard and whispered, "I'd love to be your matron of honor, Em." She looked toward the door, then back at Emlynn, her voice low. "Was Kitty right? Did you find out if you're—"

"Pregnant?" Emlynn interjected immediately, grinning. "Oh yeah, your friend must be some kind of witch, I guess. I've taken about a dozen tests since she told me, and that pink line just keeps coming up pinker and pinker. This morning it looked like somebody drew it in neon. If that's any indication, I might be having quadruplets."

"What did Lawrie say?"

Emlynn blushed. "I still haven't told him."

"What? Why not?"

"There's just been . . . been too much going on. I want the moment to be special, you know? Between John, and—" Emlynn stopped suddenly, looking down at her hands. "Look, I'm sorry I brought all those letters over to your house the way I did. With no warning, or anything. Especially after how we left each other at your office the other day. I shouldn't have just laid those on you, but I thought somebody should have them, and I wondered if maybe they'd help. But I shouldn't have assumed like that..."

Mouse took a deep breath, shaking her head. "No, Emlynn. It's me that needs to apologize. For the way I treated you at the office. There's no excuse. All I can say is... Well, I don't know what to say except that I haven't been myself. Not since... well, not since Daddy died. I didn't really think anyone had noticed, thought I was hiding it all so well, but last week Nicky told me I'd been dead wrong about that. Apparently, grief can mess you up if you don't know how to deal with it. And I'm finding out that I don't." She shook her head slowly back and forth. "I never believed there was going to be anything to that picture you found in the dollhouse, you know? That old newspaper clipping? I didn't dream somebody would turn up claiming to be part of the family because of those. But then I sat in Nathan Culpepper's office and listened to my own mother tell him that she'd been seeing Aunt Edith's ghost, and I have to tell you, that scared me half to death. It still does, if I'm honest. It... it made me feel so alone. Made me miss Daddy more than ever. When you came over on Wednesday, I'd just realized, well... to be honest, I think... and if you tell anybody this, I swear I'll deny it... but, I might have seen Aunt Edith myself."

Emlynn's eyes were round, a tiny smile on her face. "I know," said Mouse, holding her hand out as though pushing something away. "I'm not saying it makes any sense, and I'm still not sure I believe it. But Mother's convinced Aunt Edith led her to John, she told us all that. And then when he showed up in the flesh Tuesday night, saying Daddy had known all about him, that they'd corresponded for years... well... I can't explain it, but I felt... not only afraid, but... I don't know, almost jealous, I guess. Like, how dare there be someone who had something of him that I didn't." Mouse looked out to Margaret's balcony, its pale blue wooden floor an inch deep in leaves. A minute passed, during which both women stayed silent.

"You know, I haven't been able to cry for my father? Not once, since the morning he died. But those letters you brought over..." Mouse sighed, closing her eyes. "Reading those just cracked me in two. It was like I could hear Daddy's voice. I've learned so much more about my father from reading them. And about John, too. I mean, I've had this person who loved me, loved us all, just standing off in the shadows all my life. And I never even knew he was there." Mouse reached up and wiped her eyes with her shirtsleeve. "No, you were right to bring them to me, and kind, too, after the haughty way I treated you Wednesday. These letters really are such a gift, and if Aunt Edith had something to do with you finding them..." Mouse smiled at the way Emlynn's face lit up at this thought. "Well, I guess we'll just never know. Of course, I tell myself there's still no real concrete *proof* that John Dilbeck is my mother's brother. But I know now that he believes he is, and Daddy did, too. That's going to have to be good enough for me, I suppose."

"Thanks for saying all that, Mouse," said Emlynn, softly. "I'm glad you're going to give John a chance. So much good has been happening since he came here."

The idea came to Mouse like something meant to be; still, she waited for a moment before she said, "Have you... have you thought about who's going to give you away? I mean, it's up to you, of course, and originally, I was going to offer up Nicky. He'd be the most logical choice, I suppose. But now . . ." She rose and walked to the balcony door, opening it wider. She could smell the fragrance of roses wafting up from the yard. "I was wondering whether John should do it. I know Mother would like that. I mean, it's totally up to you whether you want to ask him. It's just an idea." She looked over her shoulder at Emlynn, who beamed back at her.

"I think that would be great," said Emlynn. "Standing there in front of a preacher, getting married in that beautiful dress? With Lawrie, you, Tommy, and John, right beside us? Right now, that sounds like the most perfect thing in the world."

Mouse whirled around. "A *preacher!*" she said. "Oh no. *That's* what I forgot! There's no way in hell Fat Elvis is doing this wedding!"

"What?" said Emlynn, sensing Mouse's panic and looking confused. Mouse reached across her and grabbed up the Goldsmiths' green folder. "Don't worry," she said, turning to leave the room. "I'll take care of this. You just put your feet up and rest for a while." She pointed toward Margaret's bathroom door. "Take a hot bath. She's got plenty of your bath salts in there and you know how great those are." Mouse smiled reassuringly and rushed from the room, already punching the Elvis impersonator's number into her phone.

Once he knew no one expected him to return the fee he'd already been paid, the man seemed only too happy to hear that the wedding was canceled. Mouse pictured him hanging that rhinestone white jumpsuit back up in his closet, then cracking open a beer, and she almost laughed right out loud. She stood at the landing window, staring down into the bustling backyard. The beige wooden chairs were now all in place, a white silk bow tied on the back of each one. A center aisle sliced between them, pointing straight toward a half circle of lawn at the end of the yard bordered by large floppy hydrangeas. In a few hours, Lawrie and Emlynn would stand right there, sheltered beneath the yellow-leafed branches of poplar trees. Mouse could almost see them. And the idea came to her then. She dialed Nick's number.

"Honey," she said, when he answered. "Do you think your friend Allison Whipple might be up for a wedding tonight?"

31

Margaret

The string quartet were on their second song, a lyrical rendition of Pachelbel's Canon in D, the same song Forrest Elliot had played on Aunt Edith's piano as Margaret walked down that row of pecan trees on her own wedding day years ago. Forrest had pulled the piano right up to a wide-open window and played it as loud as he could so it could be heard clearly over the birdsong outside.

They'd gotten married in August, two months after Aunt Edith died. Standing here in the dim light, looking out the den window at the lights twinkling in the low limbs of the poplars, Margaret remembered how small she'd felt that morning walking out under the pecan trees toward Lawrence in the white dress his sister, Prudie, had made for her from a Vogue pattern she'd found at Trudy Magill's fabric shop down on the square. Prudie had worked on that dress for weeks. She'd helped weave daisies all through Margaret's dark hair.

Nothing could ever take those memories from her. If she'd been asked what she would change if she could, Margaret would have easily labeled that a useless, ridiculous question. No one possesses the power to change what's already happened. All you can do is move forward. She'd had no choice in the life she'd been given, and to those people who'd kept her away from the hard truths of her past, well, she supposed she should only be grateful. Like John said, it had all been done out of love.

People were assembling in the yard, but no one could see her here in the dark. Apparently, very few of the Goldsmiths' guests had decided to drive across town for the wedding of two people they'd never met, and the seats were now being filled by neighbors and friends of the various Elliots, most of whom had happily canceled more ordinary Friday night plans. Following the express wishes of Emlynn and Lawrie, none of these people were dressed for a wedding, something that broadcast how delighted both bride and groom were by the impromptu nature of this happy event.

Margaret could see Nick escorting Lawrie's receptionist, Rosie—the girl in a white pair of pants and a wooly black sweater—to her seat on the groom's side of the aisle. Next to Rosie sat Ray Kuckleburg and his wife, both looking around as though neither was quite sure why they were here. She knew some of her friends would be livid, but when asked if there was anyone she wanted to invite on such short notice, Margaret had been so flustered, the mailman was the only name she'd come up with. Well, that was fine, she thought now. He'd known the family for years. Without really meaning to, Margaret couldn't help but scan the crowd for Aunt Edith, but she was nowhere to be seen.

Behind her, she heard the door open, and turning, she saw Harriet enter the room, her wrinkled face stippled with white from the lights outside in the trees, Gatsby in the large black purse on her arm. The Chihuahua was wearing a tiny bow tie.

Margaret laughed out loud as Harriet closed the door and went over to stand beside her.

"Beautiful dress," said Harriet. "You've always looked good in green. By the way, I put in a special song request with that quartet, one just for you," she said, grinning and draping one arm around Margaret's shoulders. "You'll know it when you hear it." Harriet craned her neck to take in the whole of the backyard. "Well, this is something now, isn't it?" she said, as both she and Gatsby looked out over the scene. "Like something straight out of a fairy tale. All those lights up there in the trees."

"Yes, and I'm so glad the Hollifields finally got that ugly old limb taken down from their roof. That thing would've been hideous. It was huge. Can you imagine? Would've ruined the whole picture."

Harriet snickered. "You still don't know?" she said.

"Know what?"

"Tom pulled that thing down. First morning he was here. Gatsby and I saw him when we were coming back from our walk. Up there in his undershorts with a chain saw."

"What? No. That's the morning he was so sick. That couldn't have been him."

"Well, it was. We watched the whole thing. Saw him ride that limb down to the ground like a cowboy. Thought for sure he'd injured himself, but he popped back up before I could pull out my phone to call 911. I could hear him laughing from out in the street."

Margaret stood still, looking out the window. The string quartet had switched from classical to religious, the notes of "Be Thou My Vision" drifting into the room. "Have you seen the kids?" asked Margaret. "Or Jubal? I've been down here for the past hour and haven't seen any of them. I guess they're all getting ready."

"Well, let's see," said Harriet. "The last time I saw Jubal he was heading upstairs with John. Mouse just left the kitchen, so she's probably with Emlynn."

"I better go on up. Just wait till you see Emlynn in that dream of a dress. You wait here if you want, I'll send Tommy to escort you to your seat." Turning to leave, Margaret heard the familiar song and felt her knees buckle. She sat down heavily on the arm of the sofa as the quartet outside began to play "Love Lifted Me."

"That's the song you requested?" Margaret said, her eyes searching Harriet's face.

"No," said Harriet, still gazing out the window. "I never heard that song in my life. What is it?" She turned to face Margaret. "What's the matter with you? You've gone all white."

"That's . . . that's the song Aunt Edith's been playing on the piano at night," said Margaret, slowly. "'Love Lifted Me.' This old hymn that she used to play all the time when I was little. Are you *sure* you didn't ask them to play it?"

Harriet smiled. "Of course not," she said, walking over to place her hand onto Margaret's shoulder. "It's just Aunt Edith's way of letting you know that she's here."

"I don't understand any of this," said Margaret, softly.

Harriet sat down beside her. "Do you have to? Understand it, I mean? I don't think my father ever understood why his own father appeared to him that night I told you about. But like my mother said, Dad's whole life changed afterward. What was there to understand but that? If it's any comfort, I don't think you'll see Aunt Edith again. She's done what she came to do. Just rest in the mystery of that if you can."

The old hymn had finished, and the musicians had moved on to Elvis. "Can't Help Falling in Love." Margaret rose to leave, patting Harriet gratefully on the arm as she did so. "I need to go up and check on Emlynn and Mouse," she said, just as the den door opened.

Tommy stood there in one of Lawrie's best suits. "Perfect fit," he said, grinning and turning around in a circle. "That's the good thing about being a twin, I suppose. Come on, Miss Spalding. Don't you look pretty. I'll escort you and Gatsby down the aisle to your seat."

32

Mouse

Emlynn and Mouse stood in front of the mirror in Margaret's bedroom, wearing identical expressions of awe. Blinking, Mouse reached over for the glass of sparkling water she'd snitched from downstairs and held it up in the air. "Emily Lynn Cates, soon to be Elliot, you are, without a doubt, the most beautiful bride I've ever seen. And don't forget, I do a whole lot of weddings. I've seen a whole lot of brides." Emlynn's eyes grew bright with tears and Mouse immediately changed tack. "Oh no, you don't," she said, pushing her glass toward Emlynn. "Don't you dare cry and ruin that makeup. Here, take a swig of this."

Emlynn did as she was told, looking over at Margaret's bedside clock. Mouse squeezed her shoulder. "I'll go get him," she said.

Closing the door behind her, Mouse stood for a second in the dimly lit hallway, then took a deep breath and turned toward the guest room.

John Dilbeck was standing over his suitcase, one hand on his chin. Mouse stayed where she was in the doorway, saying nothing, watching as he lifted out one shirt after the other, laying them on the bed, and frowning. Finally, she cleared her throat softly, and John turned quickly around.

"It's almost time," said Mouse.

John stood up a little bit straighter. "You sure this is okay with you, Agatha?"

"It was my idea," Mouse replied.

John nodded toward the closet, where a gray suit hung on the doorframe. "Lawrie brought over a gray one for me and a brown one for Tom. We're going to look a little mismatched, I'm afraid, but neither of us brought a suit with us. Only trouble is, I was just looking, and I don't seem to have a shirt that'll go. All I packed was plaid. I should've said something before now."

Mouse took a step closer and looked at the three shirts John had laid out on the bed. "Give me a minute," she said. She left the room and returned three minutes later with a white shirt and a tie that had belonged to her father. "This might be a bit big, but under that coat, I don't think anybody will notice." She held the shirt out to John, and he took it from her.

She turned away and walked to the window, looking down on all the white pansies Tom had planted a few days before. "It's almost like Tommy knew we were going to have a wedding here," she said, quietly. "All those flowers he's been planting. The yard looks like a magazine cover. But he couldn't have known, could he?"

"Most of our best impulses come without us knowing why," said John. "We just trust there's a reason, I guess."

Mouse laughed. "I've been doing and thinking nonsensical things for months now, and only recently figured out why," she said. "See, I haven't known how to let Daddy go out of my life."

"But you don't have to. Lawrence will always be with you, Agatha. You know that."

Mouse turned to him, her eyes bright. "That's what people always say, isn't it? But I don't really feel him anywhere anymore. He's just disappeared. I keep waiting, too. Waiting to sense him somewhere around me. Waiting to hear his voice in my head. But I've felt nothing for months now. I guess that's why I was so rude to you the other night. I mean, your relationship with Daddy was . . . It felt like you had something of him that I didn't. There was a whole part of his life I knew nothing about. You were just another reminder he was gone, and as crazy as it sounds, right then, I almost hated you for that. I'd missed out on the day he might have told me all about you, and I didn't want to hear it from you."

John sat down on the edge of the bed and looked up at Mouse. "If you don't feel Lawrence with you right now, maybe he's just stepped aside for a bit to let you see other things, other people, a bit clearer," he said, gently. "And I hope you can forgive him for doing what he thought was right for your mother. Forgive me for doing the same thing. So much is way beyond our control in this life, but if we're granted the power, I guess we always want to protect the people we love if we can. At least for as long as we can. I know that's what we were trying to do, both of us."

"Until Aunt Edith stepped in."

John laughed, rubbing his chin. "Like I tried to tell your mother the other night, I wouldn't have believed it if the woman hadn't shown up right in front of my eyes. And if you give me a month, I bet you a nickel I'll have managed to convince myself I never saw any such thing as the ghost of my long-dead aunt Edith."

"But you did," Mouse said, her eyes searching his face.

"Like I said, get back with me in a month," said John, winking over at her. "Your mother showed me her picture, you know. Aunt Edith. And all I can tell you is, yes, that's the lady I saw. Saw her four times. The first time was the very week your father died. Middle of the night, she was standing right there in my bedroom." He shook his head. "I don't have the words to explain it. But, I've been thinking, it's like in one of those old fairy tales my mother used to read to me when I was little. You know, how the hero gets released from a promise when somebody dies? I think that's what Aunt Edith was coming to tell me. I'd made Lawrence promise to keep my story a secret from Margaret, but his death broke those bonds right in two. That's all I can say, Agatha."

Mouse sat down heavily onto the window seat, looking at her hands. "You should really call me Mouse," she said. "You know, Mother's very happy to have you back in her life, I can see that. And whatever brought you to her, well, we don't have to worry about that now, I don't guess. As long as Aunt Edith has done what she set out to do, maybe she'll just drift back off somewhere else, back to where she came from." She looked up at John with hope on her face.

"That'll be just fine with me," said John, smiling.

"Me, too," replied Mouse. "Now hurry up and get dressed. We've got a wedding to go to."

Mouse went out of the guest room, closing the door softly behind her.

33

Margaret

The upstairs hallway lay in darkness now. Climbing the stairs, Margaret could just make out Mouse, standing alone at the landing window, elegant as ever in a long maroon dress, gazing down at the small, smiling crowd below. Mouse had opened the window, and soft music and murmurings floated up through the trees into the hallway. Margaret paused at the top of the stairs for a second, took a deep breath, then walked over to stand beside Mouse.

"You've done an amazing job," she whispered. "And you got Reverend Whipple to do the service. I didn't even know you knew her." Mouse kept her eyes straight ahead.

"Nicky knows her," she said, softly. "And besides, it was either her or a fat Elvis impersonator that the original bride had lined up. Somehow, I didn't think Lawrie and Emlynn would've seen the humor in that."

Margaret laughed. "Well, I don't know about Lawrie, but I'd bet Elvis wasn't in Emlynn's picture of the perfect wedding." Down below, the string quartet began to play "When I'm Sixty-

Four." Knowing at once that this had to be Harriet's song request for her, Margaret inwardly grinned.

"I'm sorry, Mother," Mouse suddenly said, turning toward Margaret, a tear making its way down her cheek. "I really am."

"Sorry for what, honey?" asked Margaret.

"Sorry I gave you such a hard time the other night about John, of course," said Mouse. "I acted like a jerk. I know I did. I knew it even as I was doing it. I wasn't even sure why at the time, but . . . but now I think it had something to do with me missing Daddy so much."

Margaret put her arm around Mouse's shoulders. The lights from outside lit the brimming tears in her eyes, making them shine. "You don't have anything to apologize for," she said, taking her daughter's hand in her own and squeezing it. "I've always known how close you were to your father, Mouse. It only makes sense you should be having a hard time losing him."

"Aren't you having a hard time?" asked Mouse. There was a faint accusatory note in the question, which Margaret chose not to notice.

"Of course I am," she said. "But I was expecting it, Mouse. I'd been expecting it for years. That first heart attack of his? The doctor told us, that very day, that from then on, he'd be living on borrowed time." Margaret's voice caught in her throat. "I . . . guess I did the biggest part of my grieving back then. Every day after that day was a gift. You kids never knew how sick he actually was. I made Lawrence promise to keep that a secret. And then, of course, there were two other attacks before that last one. But I didn't want you to carry that around with you all the time, always expecting the worst. You couldn't have done anything to change it, after all."

Mouse made a little sound, something akin to a laugh. "That's just what John said about you, isn't it? That he didn't want you to carry the knowledge of what your parents did around with you for the rest of your life, like he had. No offense to either of you, Mother, but I'm not sure that was the best decision. Sometimes people might need to face the hard things, even if they don't have the power to change what's been or what's coming."

Margaret sighed. "You may be right," she said. The two of them watched as down below in the yard Tom led Harriet Spalding to a chair in the first row, Harriet holding tight to his arm. "You know, honey," Margaret said, "since before you could walk, you always seemed so sure of yourself. I felt like, of all of my children, you were the one who could weather any storm God got a notion to hurl down. I'm sorry if I didn't prepare you for them well enough." She tightened her grip on her daughter's shoulders. "Honestly, Mouse, I think most of what we learn from our parents are things they never meant to teach us." Turning her head slightly, she looked at the framed photo of Aunt Edith hanging on the wall just behind them.

Mouse, following Margaret's eyes, paused for a moment before softly saying, "You really think she's real, don't you? I mean, you think you, and John, really saw her." Mouse looked back at Margaret, who was now smiling.

"You know, Mouse," she said, "I do. I really do. But if it makes you feel any better, I don't think I'll be seeing her anymore. She's done what she set out to do." Speaking this out loud made Margaret feel suddenly sad. "I'll tell you, Mouse, whatever faith I have, I got from Aunt Edith. But the faith I've needed these past months, the faith that let me believe that Aunt Edith's appearances have been real? Well, I think I got that from Ida Mae. She once asked me, *What if all I believe doesn't turn out to be the whole story?* Who knows what all we miss out on by having our minds made up about things."

Behind them, they heard Nick's footfalls on the stairs. "There you two are," he said, offering his arm to Margaret. "I need to get you seated. Everything's about to start, and we can't get going without the mother of the groom, now, can we?"

34

Tom

The old widow's walk encircled the roof like a crown. It was no small feat to get up here. Access required pulling down the stairs to the attic, then placing a chair underneath a small door in the ceiling and hoisting yourself up. If, in your struggle, you managed to kick over that chair (or your brother moved it away without meaning to, as he always claimed), well, you could be up on this roof for hours. Despite the risk, the widow's walk had, at one time or another, been claimed by each Elliot kid as their personal kingdom, its ownership causing more than its share of proprietarial fights. Margaret had finally settled the matter by drawing up a schedule. Mouse could have it on Mondays and Thursdays, Lawrie on Wednesdays and Saturdays. It was Tom's on Tuesdays and Fridays, and they all had to share it on Sundays. It had never escaped Tom's notice that Lawrie had been given an entire whole day, whereas he and Mouse could only use the place after school. Now, as he sat on the floor with his back against the brick chimney, it occurred to Tom that this was Friday. His appointed night. Old habits, he thought.

The laughter coming from the backyard was nearly as loud as the music. There must be something about sartorial casualness that freed people up on occasions like this, Tom thought. The dancing had started almost as soon as the I Dos had been said, and the music had only gotten louder as the night wore on, the string quartet having long ago been replaced by a DJ friend of Lawrie's who'd arrived late but well prepared. It helped that nearly all of Margaret's neighbors were here. There was nobody to phone the police and complain.

Tom had to admit he'd been caught off guard when Lawrie asked him to be his best man. It would've been the expected thing, he supposed, them being brothers, but still it surprised him a little. It had felt right, though, standing there beside Lawrie. And it was a good thing he'd been there, Tom thought, shaking his head. Just before Reverend Whipple pronounced them man and wife, Emlynn had leaned over to whisper something in Lawrie's ear, and he'd swayed like he was trying to stand up on water. Tom had caught him and pushed him upright, and everybody had laughed.

From where he now sat, Tom could see large perfect circles of white lying beneath all the streetlights lining Albemarle Way, and bats, so tiny, so fast, darting and whizzing through the front yard like Chinese kanji written in ink, only to be quickly erased by the soft evening breeze. He pulled his knees up to his chest, his bottom damp from the remnants of the week's rain still clinging to the wood floor.

Reaching inside his coat pocket, Tom pulled out the sheet of notepaper John had given him right after the ceremony, telling him not to open it until he was alone. Later, Tom had gone to his bedroom to see what John had written, and what he'd read had sent him straight up here to the roof. Now he unfolded the notepaper once again to make sure he hadn't been dreaming. He knew he had to go back down and talk this all over with John. Tom had just started to work his way into a standing position when he heard voices and plopped back down where he'd been.

"You're going to have to give me a leg up," said Mouse. "And don't let me fall."

"Pull your dress up a little more. I can't see. I won't let you fall, but don't dig your heel in my thigh like that. God, when did you get so tall?"

"I'm the same size I was in ninth grade. Just be careful..."

"O*kay*. Ready? One, two, three..." Tom heard a thud as Mouse clambered out from the attic, holding up the hem of her dress.

"Here, give me your hand," she said.

"No, just let me climb out on my own. I don't want you pitching over backwards. God, this is a lot smaller than it used to be, right?"

Another scramble, another thud, and then silence. "Well, you said you saw him, so where is he?" said Lawrie. "It's so dark up here."

Tom could hear his brother going around the back of the chimney. "I'm right behind you," he said. "On the other side."

Mouse and Lawrie looked around the tall chimney, then came slowly toward him, Mouse keeping close to the brick. "I don't remember this being so high." She sat down heavily beside Tom. "Ew, it's wet."

"Oh, it's not that bad. You'll dry off on the climb back down," said Lawrie, easing himself down on Tom's other side. "What you hiding up here for, Tommy?"

"I'm not hiding," said Tom. "You forget, Brother. It's Friday. *My* night. You two aren't even supposed to be up here."

"Oh, I'd forgotten about that," said Mouse with a sigh.

"Yeah, I had too, till I sat down," said Tom.

"What were my days?" asked Lawrie. "I don't remember."

"You had Saturdays," said Tom. "Of course. Got to stay up here *all* day if you wanted to. Mouse and I had to wait till after school."

"And you just hated me for that, didn't you?"

"I swear to God," said Mouse. "If you two start up again, I'm going to push the both of you right off this roof."

Tom started to laugh. "Then it's probably lucky we have a doctor in the house. Nick bring his bag with him?" He looked over at Lawrie. "I thought we were going to need smelling salts back there during the ceremony. What happened to you?"

Lawrie shrugged, looking sheepish.

"I bet I know," said Mouse, leaning up to look past Tom. "Emlynn told you, didn't she?"

"Told him what?" asked Tom, head turning from one sibling to the other.

Mouse tilted her head toward Lawrie, who took a deep breath and then said, "I'm going to be a dad."

"What?"

"Yep. You heard me. She's known for a couple of days. Said she was waiting for the right time to tell me. And that seemed like the perfect moment to her." He laughed. "God, Tommy, if you hadn't caught me, I'd have pitched headfirst into Mama's hydrangeas."

"Well, congratulations twice over," said Tom. "Wow. You. A husband, *and* a father. All in one day."

"Yeah. Me, a father." Lawrie's voice went up a bit higher on that last word, but Tom noticed he was grinning. "Pretty weird week, huh? By the way, I saw you dancing with Rosie. Don't get any ideas. I don't want to lose her."

"I like Rosie," said Mouse, sleepily.

"Everybody likes Rosie," said Lawrie. "Including Tom, I could tell." Tom remained silent. "By the way," said Lawrie, "John's invited us all to his place for the rest of the weekend. I mean, we're not going to have time for a honeymoon, obviously. We've both got to be back at work on Monday. But apparently, that cottage John lives in is bigger than it looks in that photo, so Emlynn suggested we all come, and John was thrilled with the idea. It's right on the beach. I mean, Mama was going to do a big dinner here tomorrow night, but, well, after all this"—he waved his arm in the general direction of the music now lifting out over the street—"I think we all could use a bit of a break, don't you? Em and I'll take a proper honeymoon later. Maybe Disney World or something."

"You're not taking my new sister-in-law to Disney World for her honeymoon," said Mouse, with an eye roll. "I'll lie down in front of your car before I let that happen. I've got some great brochures for Italy. I'll give them to you."

Lawrie feigned disappointment. "Shoot. No Haunted Mansion for me, then." Looking over at Tom, he said, "I meant to ask . . . speaking of haunted houses, Mama been acting all right? No more talk about ghosts?"

Mouse suddenly stiffened beside him, and Tom cut his eyes over her way. Even in the darkness he could see how pale his sister had suddenly gone. And he didn't know how, but he knew. "Oh my God. You saw her, too, didn't you? Aunt Edith's ghost."

Mouse laid her head back on the brick, closed her eyes, and silently nodded.

"When?" asked Tom.

"What?" asked Lawrie.

"I think . . . I saw her a couple of weeks ago," said Mouse. "At a party I was doing for the girl who was supposed to get married tonight. She was standing under some trees, out in the yard. And she . . . she smiled at me . . . and I suddenly blurted out something I never intended to say to Paris's mother. Kitty. And that led to Kitty giving me Nathan Culpepper's name, led him to find John. I've spent the last few days trying to convince myself I didn't actually see her, but then I found these photos Mother had left out, and there was one of Aunt Edith." Mouse let out a soul-cleansing sigh. "And that was the lady I'd seen at the party. I'm certain it was." She raised her head and looked over at Tom. "How did you know?"

"Because," Tom said, wearily, "When Lawrie mentioned ghosts, you turned into my mirror image. That same freaked-out look I've had on my face since last Sunday, right there on yours. I saw her in my office the morning I got sick, I know I did. Aunt Edith's the reason I came home."

Mouse stared at Tom, shaking her head slowly back and forth, and Lawrie leaned up to look at them both. "*I* haven't seen anybody," he said.

"Be glad for that," said Mouse, wearily. "It kind of ruins your whole week."

"Yeah, but, think about it," said Lawrie. "You, and Tommy. Mama and John. You all swear you've seen Aunt Edith now. And she hasn't said it out loud, but I know Emlynn totally believes Aunt Edith led her to find all that stuff in the dollhouse." Lawrie stared at the others, a tiny frown on his face.

"Oh, my God," said Tom, grinning over at Mouse. "He actually feels left out, doesn't he?"

"Well, of course I don't," said Lawrie, emphatically. "That'd be nuts."

"You're right. It sure would be," said Tom, sitting up a bit straighter. "Look, I drank a half bottle of bourbon last Sunday afternoon when I realized I'd seen Aunt Edith myself, that *she* was the old woman who'd been in my office hallway. Where do you put that kind of thing in your head? If you believe it's true, it kinda rejiggers your whole world." Hesitating a moment, he pulled out John's note and handed it over to Lawrie. "And my world has changed, there's no doubt about that."

Looking puzzled, Lawrie took the note and opened it, his eyes getting rounder with each word he read. "My God," he said. "He bought it?" Tom merely nodded. Lawrie stretched his arm across Tom and gave the paper to Mouse. "What are you going to do? *Live* there?"

"He's bought Aunt Edith's old house!" said Mouse. "And the pecan grove. And he wants you to restore them. Oh, Tom. That's . . . that's wonderful."

"I can't take it, of course," said Tom. "It's too much."

"Well, don't worry that John can't afford it," said Lawrie, taking back the letter from Mouse. "That little shrimp boat we all thought he had? Turns out it was a fleet. I've looked it all up online. The man's worth a fortune."

"Do you *want* to do it?" asked Mouse. "Restore the farm, I mean."

"More than anything I've ever wanted to do in my whole life." Speaking the words out loud, Tom realized they were true.

"Then you have to," said Mouse. "You could look on it as a gift from Aunt Edith. Mother thinks she's orchestrated all this anyway. Maybe she has. If so, I would think you refuse a ghost at your peril."

The three of them sat in companionable silence, looking down into the shadowed front yard. Tom felt grateful for the unchanged landscape of his childhood. The moon still knew where to look, he thought. Its light fell to the ground in all the same places, illuminating the circular lawn, leaving the corners in darkness. And the trees had grown with him, it seemed. They still appeared to be the same size they'd been when he was a boy.

It was then that Tom saw her, standing in a puddle of darkness, her navy-blue dress the same shade as the shadows that pooled on the ground at her feet. He said nothing but felt Mouse's breath stop beside him, the slight push of her elbow into his ribs. Tom wondered whether he should wave, or nod, but he just kept sitting there, looking down, staring at something or someone, he still wasn't sure which. He glanced over at Lawrie, who was picking a wet leaf off the sleeve of his suit. He could tell his brother saw nothing, and suddenly Tom started to laugh.

"What?" said Lawrie, looking up and frowning at Tom.

"You've always been one happy bastard, haven't you?" said Tom, scooting over and putting his arm around Lawrie.

Lawrie twisted away, looking confused. "What are you talking about?" he said.

"Only, that . . . Oh, I don't know. Maybe Aunt Edith only shows up when people need her. And you, you lucky dog, you don't need a thing, do you?"

Lawrie frowned. "For God's sake, Tom. I just told you I'm going to be a father. You think I've got that all figured out? Geez."

"Well, then, you better keep an eye out. Check the corners of your bedroom before you fall asleep at night. Aunt Edith might be coming to see you before long."

Lawrie pushed Tom hard on the shoulder, then folded his arms over his chest. Tom grinned at Mouse, who grinned back. The two of them met Aunt Edith's gaze one last time, watching in silence as she stood there under the trees for just one second more, before vanishing completely away, erased like a letter once written in ink.

35

Mouse

In 2009, Ray Kuckleburg had been given a certificate from the Wesleyan post office. He had it framed in his den. Twenty years on the job, without missing a day. He'd hit another ten in December, and there'd been talk of a party this time. Someone had even mentioned a watch, though Ray had told Mouse he wasn't getting his hopes up about that. So, she wasn't surprised to see him coming up her driveway this morning, even though she'd bet money he was every bit as tired as she was herself. It wasn't yet seven o'clock. Ray and his wife had still been dancing at midnight.

Mouse waited, her second cup of coffee hot in her hands, for the familiar squeak and clatter of the mailbox outside but was surprised to hear a soft knock on the front door instead. Barefooted and still in an old pair of Nick's flannel pajamas, she rose from the kitchen table and went into the foyer.

"Oh, hey, Agatha," said Ray, stepping back as she opened the door. "Happy to see you're awake. I saw you sitting there through the window. Gosh, I hate to bother you at this hour. Today of all days. You couldn't have gotten to bed till early this morning." He spoke in a whisper, in deference to the hour.

"Not that long after you did yourself, I'd imagine," said Mouse. "You and Maisie were there when the party broke up."

"Yeah, I swear, I don't know what got into us," he said, laughing. "Can't remember when we've had a better time. We didn't even dance like that when our daughter got married. Trina, you know? Well, that wedding and reception were in a church, and they kinda frowned on all that. This one was a whole lot more fun. But don't you tell Trina I said that." Grinning, he held out a large white envelope to Mouse. "You need to sign for this," he said. "Or I'd'a just stuck it in the mailbox with the other stuff. Glad I didn't wake you."

Mouse paused for a half second, then reached out for the envelope, dutifully signing the small computer Ray held steady for her in his hands. "Thanks, Ray," she said. "I'm glad you could come last night. Mother really enjoyed having you there."

"Well, we sure appreciated being invited," said Ray, handing her the rest of the mail, then turning to leave. "And we both wish the new couple all the best." He trotted back down the driveway, on his way to the sidewalk, and Mouse stood for a second, her hand on the doorknob, watching him go.

She knew what she'd just been given. What else would be arriving today, express mail? Mouse put the envelope on the bottom of the small stack of catalogs and bills and laid it all on the long table that sat across from the stairs. A large vase of sunflowers sat on one end, and she placed it on top of the mail, trapping the envelope there. Then, turning away, she walked back to the kitchen, lowering herself into the same chair she'd occupied for hours already. One thing at a time, Mouse said to herself. She felt like a blown-up balloon, stretched thin and ready to pop.

She'd done as Kitty Goldsmith asked her to do. She'd not opened the card Kitty gave her until she got home from the wedding. Truth be told, Mouse had forgotten all about the card. It had only been when she'd gone looking through her purse for an aspirin, just before bed, that she'd seen it, and even then, she'd been in no hurry to open the thing. A "thank-you" card from Kitty? Surely that could wait until morning.

But something had told her to open it, and open it when she was alone. Mouse had swallowed her aspirin and gone on to bed, lying there awake until she heard Nick's breathing become steady and soft. Then she'd slipped out and gone into the bathroom, taking Kitty's card with her. She'd sat down on the side of the claw-footed tub and sliced the envelope open with a nail file, her reading glasses balanced on her nose to better see in the moonlight.

It wasn't a thank-you card, although it featured Snoopy on the front, his paws awhirl in movement, his head held back in glee. Where "Thank You" should've been written, "Congratulations" was printed instead, along with Snoopy's effusive declaration, "This Calls for a Happy Dance!" Mouse opened the card. Inside, Kitty had written only four words, words that still, even now, rang like a gong through Mouse's tired head.

You're pregnant, you know.

Sitting there in the dark on the side of her tub, Mouse had turned the card over, reading the publisher's name on the back. She had studied the drawing of Snoopy, wondered just how long that beagle had been a fixture in everyone's mind. Then she'd peeked inside the card once again, forcing herself to reread Kitty's fanciful scrawl. This time she noticed that Kitty had dotted the "i" in her name with a heart.

Mouse had been down here in the kitchen since then, without one wink of sleep, alternately laughing and crying. But mostly—the fact surprised her—laughing. It was, of course, always possible that Kitty was wrong. She wasn't a sorceress, after all. But something made Mouse hesitant to doubt Kitty's powers of maternal deduction. First Paris, then Emlynn. Her success rate was, so far, pretty good.

The ceiling creaked overhead, the precursor to Nicky's imminent arrival downstairs. Sure enough, she heard him taking the steps two at a time. "You shouldn't have let me sleep so late," he said, sliding into the kitchen in jeans and a T-shirt, his dark hair standing on end. "We gotta be at your mother's by eight. And I'm supposed to make deviled eggs." Nick had grabbed a pot off the wall and was filling it with water. "Margaret wants to have a picnic on the beach when we get there," he said, over his shoulder. "I told her we'd meet them all over at her house and follow them there in our car. There's no way I'm going to ride all the way out to that island in that smelly old Volvo of hers. Not with three other people and a big dog. What? Why are you grinning at me like that?"

Mouse blinked, trying her best to imagine where a baby would fit into this scene, trying to hear the words she would use when she told Nicky they were going to be parents again. Trying to imagine telling her nearly grown children. She could feel inappropriate laughter starting again and quickly stood up, finishing the last of her coffee in one large swallow. "I . . . I'm just punchy, I guess," she said, smiling. "Didn't get a whole lot of sleep. I better go up and get ready."

When she glanced at the stack of letters pinned beneath the tall vase of sunflowers on the foyer table, the large envelope on the bottom looked bigger than it had when Ray first handed it to her, not eight minutes before. But of course, Mouse thought, that was impossible. Turning away, she flew up the stairs to her bedroom and straight into Nick's shower, stripping off his old flannel pajamas as she went. She stood underneath the hot water, her eyes closed tight, her face taking the full force of the spray.

Just three days ago, Mouse been so certain what the DNA results would reveal, so sure they would hand her the proof she needed to send John Dilbeck back where he'd come from, confident he was an impostor. It hadn't mattered to her how much her mother wanted to believe everything he told her was true. She hadn't cared about that. Not then. And she still needed to know, didn't she?

As she began brushing her teeth, Mouse suddenly stopped, staring into the mirror. There, on the hand holding her toothbrush, she saw her crooked little finger, sticking out into the air. Nick had been right, of course. It was the same quirk of genetics she shared with her mother and John.

So, she must have been wrong, right? John Dilbeck was truly her uncle. All those letters he'd shared with her father. Lawrence certainly trusted he was telling the truth. Surely, that definitive news was now printed inside the envelope lying on the table downstairs. Proof that he was exactly who her own father believed him to be.

Mouse dressed with more care than she normally would've done on an ordinary Saturday in October, even going so far as to rub a bit of pink blush onto her pale cheeks.

"You ready, Minnie?" she heard Nicky call from the back door. "I've already put food out for Dinky and set the lights on the timer. I'm going to go ahead and back the car out. I'll meet you in the driveway. Let's go!"

Mouse could see the white envelope from where she stood at

the top of the stairs. There on the bottom of that stack of ordinary mail, it seemed almost to glow. Holding on to the railing, she took the stairs slowly, one by one, her legs leaden, her heart galloping.

Reaching the foyer, she heard the garage door closing, felt Dinky threading through her legs as she stood stock-still at the base of the stairs.

Her eyes on the envelope, Mouse walked toward the table. She set the vase of sunflowers aside and slid the white envelope from beneath the small stack of mail. After opening the long center drawer in the table, she pulled out an old letter opener, the brass one with the owl's head, and in one quick motion, she sliced the white envelope open.

"Mouse!" called Nick from the driveway. "We're going to be late!"

Mouse stood frozen to the shiny hardwood floor, a sheet of white paper held in her hand, her eyes moving from left to right. When she'd read what was there, she took a deep breath to steady herself. And it was then that she saw her, standing where Mouse had just stood, at the top of the stairs. That navy-blue dress, that string of old pearls, that little half smile on her face. The fragrance of jasmine and lilies filling the air. That hint of Ivory soap.

But this time, Aunt Edith wasn't alone. Beside her in the shadows stood three other figures, their outlines indistinct, like chalk paintings in the rain. All pastels and soft light, Ida Mae stood closest to Aunt Edith; Mouse recognized her from Margaret's description. Helms and Lorena stood off to the right. Margaret's parents, drawn in shades of charcoal and gray, but clearer than they'd been in that old photo. Even through tear-filled eyes, Mouse could tell that all four were smiling at her.

Staring up at them, she placed the sheet of paper over her

heart, the confirmation she no longer needed, and just as they all faded away, she saw, standing tall behind them, in watery shades of bright blue, her father. Lawrence lifted a hand toward her, a benediction, a blessing, a sign. It was all Mouse needed.

As she watched, his image evaporated before her eyes, leaving no trace of his presence up there at the top of the stairs. But as she turned to go out the door, Mouse felt the calm assurance that had eluded her for months. It was like she had her eyes on something level. Whatever happened from here on out, everything would be all right.

ACKNOWLEDGMENTS

By now, I suppose I should've given up trying to decipher how stories are born. Some spring from snippets of memory, some from traveling to a place you've never been before, while others emerge from chance conversations with strangers. But then there are the stories that are simply determined to be told. This was one of those. It began as something entirely different, but as soon as Aunt Edith showed up at the foot of Margaret Elliot's bed, it walked off in its own direction, ignoring any foot-stomping or handwringing from its author. One more illustration of the importance in keeping an open mind, just like Ida Mae said.

My sincere thanks to my editor, Shauna Summers, who kept assuring me that stories emerge in their own time. She always knows best. To Karen Fink, Taylor Noel, Mae Martinez, Susan Brown, Megan Whalen, Cindy Berman, and the entire wonderful team at Penguin Random House/Ballantine, I'm very grateful for you all.

To my smart, kind, indefatigable agent, Kimberly Whalen, who has the best laugh, and who always has my back.

To Professor Lenny Wells, from whom I learned all I know about growing pecans, which isn't a fraction of what he knows.

To my early readers: Allison Adams, Janet Harvey, and Vickie Mabry. I so appreciate your insight and friendship.

To the Smyrna Public Library for always having a desk free for me.

To the circle of faithful heretics: Stan Anderson, Reese and Ella Gray, Bruce McKelvy, David Moake, Frances MacIver, Jayne Parker, Beckie Yon, Jennifer Isbell, Sandee O, Peggy Green, Jennifer Bennett, Gary and Vickie Mabry, Claire Winskill, Iain Roden, Greg Gray, Sam and Janet Harvey, Allison Adams, Johnny Pierce, Rick Bragg, Thea Beasley, Bill and Jaime Adcock, Butch and Judi Adkins, Tim and Tracy Alderson, Phil Madeira, R. J. and Kim Kuckleburg, Carole Ford, Fritz and Wanda Dostall, Gray and Pam Norsworthy, and the cabdriver in Edinburgh who told me that the pendulum always swings back.

And last, but always first, to my sweet, supportive pack: Pat, Andrew, and George. You are my home.

A lifelong Southerner, PAMELA TERRY learned the power of storytelling at a very early age. Terry is the author of *When the Moon Turns Blue*, *The Sweet Taste of Muscadines*, and the internationally popular blog From the House of Edward, which was named one of the top ten home blogs of the year by London's *Telegraph*. She lives in Georgia with her songwriter husband, Pat, and their two dogs, Andrew and George. She travels to the Scottish Highlands as frequently as possible.

@pamelaandedward

ABOUT THE TYPE

This book was set in Albertina, a typeface created by Dutch calligrapher and designer Chris Brand (1921–98). Brand's original drawings, based on calligraphic principles, were modified considerably to conform to the technological limitations of typesetting in the early 1960s. The development of digital technology later allowed Frank E. Blokland (b. 1959) of the Dutch Type Library to restore the typeface to its creator's original intentions.